The Law of
Tall Girls

JOANNE MACGREGOR

D1372210

OTHER YOUNG ADULT BOOKS BY THIS AUTHOR

Hushed

Scarred

Recoil

Refuse

Rebel

VIP Readers' Group: If you would like to receive my author's newsletter, with tips on great books, a behind-the-scenes look at my writing and publishing processes, and notice of new books, giveaways and special offers, then sign up at my website, www.joannemacgregor.com.

First published in 2017 by KDP

ISBN: 978-0-9947230-0-0 (print)

ISBN: 978-0-9947230-1-7 (eBook)

Copyright 2017 Joanne Macgregor

The right of Joanne Macgregor to be identified as the author of this work has been asserted by her in accordance with sections 77 and 78 of the Copyright, Designs and Patents Act, 1988.

All rights reserved. No parts of this book may be reproduced or transmitted in any form of by any means, mechanical or electronic, including photocopying and recording, or be stored in any information storage or retrieval system, without the prior written permission from the author.

Disclaimer: This is a work of fiction. All the characters, institutions and events described in it are fictional and the products of the author's imagination.

Cover design by Jenny Zemanek at Seedlings Design Studio

Formatting by Polgarus Studio

"Your playing small does not serve the world."
— *Marianne Williamson*

~ 1 ~

"When I am queen of the world, the second thing I'll do is to pass the Law of Tall Girls," I said.

"The law of what, now?" Steve asked.

"I'll bite," said Tori. "What's the first thing?"

"I'll outlaw ketchup and mustard bottles."

I wiped the gummed-up nozzle of another sticky ketchup bottle. So gross. Why did I always get stuck with this disgusting job?

It was a slow Friday night at Jumping Jim's Diner, and we three servers were clustered at the back, waiting for the last few tables to leave. Steve was polishing glasses, Tori was wrapping paper napkins around flatware, and I was stuck on condiments clean-up.

"So, Peyton, tell us: what's the law of tall girls?" Steve said.

"The Law of Tall Girls," I said, "states that no male over the height of six feet shall be permitted to date any female under the height of five foot eight inches."

Tori raised a critical eyebrow at me. "Heterocentric much?"

"Sorry. No *person* over six feet shall be permitted to date any

1

person under the height of five foot eight. Though," I added, "I don't think it matters for male couples. They probably wouldn't want to wear heels, and would female couples really care if one of them was taller?"

"Probably not. We're less into ego issues like that," Tori replied.

She always wore super-glossy black lipstick, and a piercing of a silver skeleton hand cuffed her bottom lip, so that even when she smiled smugly, like now, she still looked threatening.

"Yeah, well, some of us girls are not so evolved. We like our partners to be taller." I glanced over at the table in the far corner and scowled.

Steve shoved the polished beer mugs across the counter toward me. "Put these back on the top shelf for me? I can't reach."

"You could just use the step stool," I said.

"Don't need to. I've got you — the human stepladder."

Smartass. I began packing the glasses away.

"Why, though?" Tori asked.

"Why what?"

"Why do tall girls need — if I understand the purpose of this proposed legislation correctly — legal protection for dating?"

"Because there are so few tall guys. Too few to go around — even if we limit them to tall girls. And definitely too few to waste on short girls, who do not *need* tall guys. They have a massive pool of average-height guys to choose from."

A sudden burst of laughter drew my gaze back to the corner booth. A bunch of kids from my high school sat there, but the one face that kept attracting my gaze belonged to someone I'd never met. I'd have remembered.

"Case in point: look at your table over there, Tori." I jerked my chin in the direction of the rowdy crowd. "That girl in the blue dress — she can't be over five-three. And she's putting the moves on *him* — green shirt, in the far corner." I ran an expert eye over his length. Six-two, I estimated. And hot. "Now if they hook up, there's one less tall guy available for tall girls like me."

"You're assuming that — even if he was available — he'd be interested in you," Tori said.

"Slice!" Steve cackled.

Tori gave a sexy wiggle to draw attention to her own pint-sized figure. Even in her super-high, peep-toe stilettos, she didn't top five-five, and she couldn't weigh more than one hundred and twenty pounds – at least five of which were from her multiple piercings, many rings, and heavy eyeliner.

"Maybe," she continued, "he *prefers* petite girls."

That wouldn't surprise me — the whole world did.

"Many men do, I believe," she continued. "It bolsters their fragile egos."

I lifted my chin and gave a sniff. "If he does prefer them, it can only be because he's never experienced the superior species that is the tall girl. Once you go tall, you never go small."

Steve hooted with laughter. Perhaps he could hear the lack of conviction beneath my confident words.

"Pul-lease. You *know* guys don't find treetops-tall attractive — that's why you always hunch, and wear flat shoes, and try to make yourself look smaller," Tori said.

I wished Chloe was here with me — she'd have a snappy comeback to put Tori in her place. Chloe had been my best friend since we both made ourselves sick eating blue, yellow and pink wax crayons in kindergarten because Billy Beaumont told us it would make us poop rainbows. She was a regular-sized package of dynamism and sass, but she never insulted me. Well, not about things I couldn't change — like my height. Though she did nag me all the time to stop slouching.

I stood up straighter and told Tori, "Guys can be attracted to more than a girl's appearance, you know. They are capable of being attracted to her personality, or her brains."

Tori seemed skeptical — she didn't have a very high opinion of the male of the species.

"Not true," said Steve. "Zombies are the only dudes that want a girl for her brains and not her body."

"What's going on here?" Jim, wider than he was tall, and probably not capable of jumping at all, had slipped out of the kitchen to check on the tables and his wait staff. "What we need is less talking, and more action," he said and treated us to the chorus of Elvis's *A Little Less Conversation*.

Jim *loved* Elvis, probably even more than he loved bacon-and-egg burgers with deep-fried pickles. Which was a lot.

"Yes, boss," Steve said. Pulling a revolted face, he grabbed a cloth and began wiping the crusted yellow goo off a mustard bottle.

Tori sighed loudly. "Managers cracking the whip over the workers again. When *I* am queen of the world, I'll abolish the class structure and redress the inequities of capitalism."

"Then you wouldn't be a queen anymore. Communists and socialists aren't big on royalty," I pointed out.

"Now you quit riling folks up, Tori," said Jim. "Isn't that table ready for their check yet?"

"Already done. And I wasn't riling anyone. I just said that tall guy in the corner might not actually *want* to date Peyton, even if the law forbade him to date the pretty petite girl beside him."

"Now that is nonsense. Why, Peyton is a beautiful young lady." Jim defended me loyally. "*Anyone* would want to date her."

Sadly, experience had taught me that this was not true. I wasn't unattractive — I had big brown eyes, shoulder-length hair with a slight curl, and a slim body, but other people only ever saw my height.

"Heck, *I'd* want to date her, if I was forty years younger!" Jim added.

Tori and Steve chortled like this was the funniest thing they'd ever heard. I stared down at my feet. My very large feet.

"Pay them no mind, Peyton. Steve here knows less of the world than a June-bug."

That shut Steve up.

"And Tori — well, Tori might know all about capitalism and such, but she would agree that she doesn't know the first thing about what men want."

"Thank the goddess!" Tori said.

"And that big fella? I reckon he'd love to kiss on someone his own size rather than putting a crick in his neck just to get to a girl's lips. Why, I bet he'd want to kiss our Peyton just as soon as he met her."

"Thank you, Jim." I gave him a side-hug.

"You're on!" Tori said, an evil glint in her eyes. "I'll take you up on that challenge. You talk a good game, Peyton, let's see if you can walk your talk. Jim, I'll bet you a hundred bucks that you couldn't get the Jolly Green Giant over there to kiss our Amazon."

"Our what?" Jim asked.

"Peyton."

"No," I said.

"I'll sweeten the deal," Tori said. "One-fifty."

"*No.*"

"Two hundred. That's *two hundred dollars*, Peyton."

"Deal!" Jim stuck out his meaty paw and shook Tori's hand.

"Hang on a sec, don't I have a say in this?" I protested.

"You think he's hot, don't you?" said Steve. "I've seen you checking him out all evening."

"Yeah, don't you *want* to kiss him?" Tori challenged.

"Well, yeah, maybe — if I actually *knew* him. But I don't. And I can't just go kiss a strange man."

"Girl, they're *all* strange."

"And why are you making a bet with Jim about something I'd have to pull off?"

"Good point. It's only fair you get something out of it," Tori said. "Steve — you want in on this?"

"You bet. He isn't going to kiss her, no way, man. He'll 401 her for sure."

"401?" I said.

"Error 401: access denied," Steve sniggered.

"Steve and I will *each* give you" — Tori indicated Jim and me with a finger — "two hundred bucks if Peyton can get that guy to kiss her, within five minutes of introducing herself."

I ignored her ridiculous suggestion and turned instead to

Steve, still stinging from his comment and not willing to let it go unchallenged. "Why not?" I asked him. "Why wouldn't he want to kiss me?"

"Because you're enormous, man. You're not even, like, a girl."

"You are such a jerk, Steve!"

He just smirked back at me. "Time to put your money where your mouth is, Gigantor."

~ 2 ~

I hesitated. This was crazy. I wasn't the sort of girl who could confidently march up to a guy and demand kisses. Heck, I wasn't the sort of girl who could march confidently. And I wasn't sure I could succeed in getting the hot guy to kiss me. Scratch that — I was sure. That I *couldn't* succeed.

But just maybe I was irritated enough to try.

"I'll give you my two hundred if you win, Peyton. *When* you win," said Jim.

I stood to win four hundred bucks, and I could seriously use that kind of money.

Of course, if I lost … I shuddered.

"Too scared to try? Chicken?" Steve flapped his elbows and made clucking noises.

"Huh, more like ostrich," Tori goaded.

She was so sure I'd bomb out. It might be worth the embarrassment to wipe that self-satisfied smile off her face.

"Or like Big Bird," Steve said.

"Fine, I'll do it." Had those words just come out of my mouth? Oh, jeez.

"Atta girl!" Jim said. "But better do it quickly — they're leaving."

Sure enough, the group was getting to their feet, the three girls grabbing their bags, and the tall guy unfurling himself from the corner seat. Oh, man, six-three. Short hair, pretty much the same light brown as mine, light eyes — I couldn't tell the color from where I stood — and broad shoulders. I couldn't decide if he was really hot, really *really* hot, or really freaking hot.

"It's got to be a real kiss, not just a peck," Tori said.

"Yeah, there's got to be tongue," Steve added.

Panic skittered up my spine. Maybe it showed on my face, because Jim gave me an encouraging smile and a pat on the shoulder, and said, "Relax, kiddo — you look like you're about to be fried in the electric chair."

I fixed a smile onto my lips. "Better?"

"Uh, can you do something with your hair and maybe put some color in your cheeks?"

I yanked my hair free of its ponytail and fluffed it up, pinched my cheeks, and undid another button on my shirt for good measure. Then, to the accompaniment of Jim's rendition of *It's Now or Never*, I turned to face the corner booth, and started walking.

I am a queen. I *am* a queen.

I repeated the words silently to myself with each reluctant step, but it did no good. I was no regal creature, just a seriously tall girl. And right now I'd rather be doing anything — even writing a calculus test or cleaning up the kitchen at home — than this.

"Hey, Micayla, Greg," I said, when I drew up to the table.

I recognized all of the faces — except *his* — from school. Four of them, including the predatory girl in the blue dress, were a year below me, but Greg and Micayla would be seniors with me when the new school year started in ten days' time.

Greg Baker was vice-captain of the school's varsity basketball team, and forever trying to get me to try out for the girls' team. I estimated his height at a respectable six-one, but he looked short beside the tall guy who stood beside him, filling my peripheral vision with green. Every cell in my body was already attuned to him, like sunflowers rotating to face the light.

"Hey," I said. My voice came out embarrassingly high. Instantly my cheeks grew hot. "I need to speak to …"

My gaze slid up to the tall guy's. Oh, boy. Six-four — six-four if he was an inch. And his eyes were an unusual olive green.

"Oh, this is my cousin Jay Young, he's from DC," Greg said. "Jay, this is Peyton Lane. She's also a senior at Longford High."

"Hi," Jay said. *His* voice was deep and steady.

"Hey, Big P," said one of the junior boys. "What's the weather like up there?"

I blushed harder. I hated that nickname — it made me sound like giant genitals or something. If I ever found out who at school had started it …

Jay gave me a puzzled grin and said, "Sooo, what's up?"

"Um …" Now what? I had no idea how to say this. I wished the rest of the group would go away and leave us alone, but they were all staring at me as if I was the bearded lady at a freak show. "Look, is there any way I could persuade you to kiss me?" I finally blurted out.

"Say what?" said one of the girls.

Blue Dress rolled her eyes and made a disgusted sound, and Greg burst out laughing.

"Come again?" Jay said.

"Three minutes!" Tori called from the other side of the restaurant.

"They," I said, indicating Steve and Tori, "bet me that I couldn't get you to kiss me. And … I took them up on it."

He still appeared bewildered. Probably thinking, *And this is my problem, how?*

"Dumb, I know, but I did. It's just that I could really use the money."

I looked away from him. I could feel heat radiating out from my face — my cheeks must be the color of the cherry-red leather seats, the crimson checkered suit of Jumping Jim on the window decals, the ketchup-scarlet of pure humiliation.

"Hey, I'm flattered. But I don't generally go around kissing strange girls."

"Strange, man, you said it," Junior quipped, and Blue Dress and her friend giggled.

"Sure, no problem," I stammered. "It was always going to be a long shot. Sorry I bothered you."

I'd never been so mortified in my entire life. My eyes were prickling with shame and anger at myself, and my chest felt like it was clenched in the crushing grip of a giant. A real one, twenty feet tall at least. Why in the name of all that's holy had I ever taken the freaking bet? What had made me think, even for one crazy moment, that a tall, hot guy would want to kiss me? I turned to go and was halfway back to where Steve and Tori stood gloating at how fast and how entirely I'd struck out, when I heard the deep voice again.

"Hey, Peyton?"

"Yeah?" I turned to face him. He still stood beside the girl in the blue dress. The rest of the group were at the door, ready to go.

"What was the bet?"

"Four hundred dollars."

He gave a low whistle. "That's a lot of money."

"Yeah — go big or go home, right?" I said, trying to force a note of humor into my voice and a carefree smile onto my face. But none of this was amusing. I didn't have four hundred bucks to burn. "Like I said, dumb."

I shrugged and turned back. Tori and Steve high-fived each other, then both held out their hands as if I was going to hand over the money right there and then.

A warm hand grabbed mine from behind and tugged, spinning me around. Jay stood there, his head tilted to one side, a grin on his lips, and a challenge in his eyes.

"Let's disappoint them, yeah?"

~ 3 ~

Jay pulled me toward him, twirling his arm above my head so that I pirouetted like an old-timey ballroom dancer before thudding into his chest. I had to tilt my head back to look up into his amused eyes. It felt extraordinary to be the shorter person — rare and amazing. And a little unnerving.

One of his hands wound around my waist, pulling me close. His other hand cupped my cheek, and then he was kissing me. He. Was kissing. *Me*. I tasted the smoky sweetness of chocolate milkshake and, for just a moment, I was acutely aware of the snickering, of wolf-whistles, cheers and jeers, but then a roaring in my head drove it all away.

Once, when I was about nine years old, a tornado raged a path of destruction through Baltimore. My mother and I were safely down in the basement by the time it passed over us, but we could still hear it — a terrifying, roaring rush of power that thundered over and around us. The sound and sensation overwhelmed me, reached into my chest and sucked out my breath, drove like a freight train through my brain, and swept all my thoughts away.

That's how I felt now.

No chance for breath. No time for thought. No impulse to do anything but hang on tight, and *be*.

And then, almost before it began, or maybe after a few hours, it was over. My lips, which had been his, were my own again. Pulsing, as if calling out for the lost warmth.

"You okay?" He chuckled down at me as he let go. He had crinkles at the corners of his eyes which curved upwards like tiny stacked smiles.

"Huh?"

I could feel a dopey smile on my face. Couldn't begin to figure out how to replace it with anything approaching nonchalance. My brain still felt empty, light, dizzy. Perhaps I swayed a little, because he put out a hand to steady me.

"Are you okay?"

"Uh-huh." I had to get it together. "Yeah. Thanks."

"C'mon, Jay, let's go already," Blue Dress whined from the door, giving me some serious stink-eye.

"Okay, then." He stepped back a few paces. "See you around."

"Yeah." Sense was beginning to creep back, and, with it, embarrassment. I must look and sound like a complete idiot. "Hey, Jay?" I said as he turned to join his friends. "Thank you. That might have been the nicest thing anyone's ever done for me."

A look of surprise flickered across his face, but then the girl was tugging at his arm, and his cousin was teasing him, and the other two girls were shooting me incredulous looks as they left. Then he was gone. And the spot where he had stood was just an empty space.

From behind me I heard Jim's rich voice singing, "I'm all shook up."

My lips still tingled as I floated across the restaurant, light-hearted and brimming with satisfaction, to where Jim, Steve and Tori stood. A huge smile lit up Jim's round face, but Steve wore a sour look — losing a couple hundred bucks will do that to you, little guy. Tori's expression was less easy to read. More speculative than disappointed.

"There you go," I said, puffing out a relieved breath.

"Knew you could do it, kiddo," Jim said, patting my back before disappearing into the kitchen.

"So," I said, "it looks like tall boys *are* attracted to tall girls."

"Are you so sure of that?" Tori asked.

"He kissed me, didn't he?"

"I'm guessing you told him it was a wager, right?"

"Yeah, so?"

"So, it was probably just a pity-kiss."

Ouch.

Steve snickered. "Want some ice for that burn?"

What I *wanted* was to wipe the smiles off their mean faces. A dozen clever comebacks would no doubt occur to me later — sharp, funny replies to all the insults sent my way this evening. But right now, I couldn't think of anything.

"It doesn't prove anything about whether tall guys do, in fact, want to date tall girls," Tori needled.

I shrugged. I could fault her manners, but not her logic.

"How about we ramp this up?" Tori said. "I'll bet you couldn't get a tall guy — any tall guy — to date you. If you win, you get eight hundred beautiful smackeroos."

"Do you even *have* eight hundred smackeroos?"

"Of course."

It was possible that she did, but it was more likely that she was just entirely sure she couldn't lose the bet. I packed more polished glasses onto the high shelf while I considered.

"And if *you* win?" I asked Tori.

"You pay us eight hundred dollars."

I winced.

"I guess it depends how confident you are that tall girls are attractive," said Tori, a truly evil smile curving her shining black lips.

"Yeah, feeling pretty, Stretch?" Steve taunted.

Pretty? No. I'd never felt pretty in my life. Almost by definition, very tall girls couldn't be pretty, or cute. Striking, yes. Attractive, maybe. Eye-catching — always, unfortunately. But pretty? No, *pretty* was for petite and dainty girls. Girls whose knees didn't touch the back of the seats in front of them in the cinema. Girls who didn't have to bend their knees to ensure their faces weren't cut off in group photos.

And how confident was I that I could get any guy to date me, let alone a tall guy? Not confident at all.

But still, eight hundred bucks.

"He must be really tall, though. At least a couple of inches taller than you," Tori said. "How tall are you anyway?"

"Six feet and three-quarters of an inch," I mumbled. Every time I stated my height, it felt like I was making a confession.

"Let's call it six foot one," Tori said.

"Let's not," I said.

"He needs to be at least six-two."

"Six-four," Steve chipped in.

I glared at him. "Guys of that height are rarer than unicorns."

"Fine, let's meet in the middle — six-three," said Tori. "And you need to have at least three dates with him."

"Four," said Steve. "Four dates with the same guy."

"And because this is a social experiment in the willingness of males to date tall females, the dates need to be public," Tori said, pointing a fork at me. "No staying at home to watch videos in the basement, or having a picnic in some deserted field."

"And, and," said Steve, his eyes bright with excitement, "the last date needs to be the ultimate in public dates — he has to take you to the prom."

"Ooh, nice one!" Tori bumped fists with her collaborator.

I picked up my rag and wiped gunk off the nozzle of a ketchup bottle.

"So, four public dates with one guy six-three or over, the last of which is the prom, and I win eight hundred dollars? And if I lose, I pay you that?" I clarified.

Tori nodded. "That's about the sum of it."

It was hugely tempting. I wanted to prove that tall girls could be attractive. Plus, more than anything, I wanted to leave home and go to college somewhere exciting — California perhaps, or New York. True, I hadn't yet decided *what* I wanted to study, but whatever I signed up for, eight hundred dollars would add a nice chunk of change to my college fund.

"What'll it be, Peyton?" Tori asked. "A bird in the hand or two in the bush?"

Oh, what the heck. "You've got yourself a deal."

I stuck out my hand and shook hers, feeling like I might just have done a deal with the devil herself.

~ *4* ~

Three days later, I still hadn't wrapped my head around the craziness of that Friday night. And neither, apparently, had Chloe.

"And he just kissed you?" she asked again, although she already knew the answer.

I'd described what had happened at least three times, but clearly we weren't through dissecting every last detail.

"No, he didn't just kiss me. He tugged my hand, spun me around, clutched me against his chest, and cupped my face. And *then* he kissed me."

She sighed in satisfaction. I rotated on my towel, wriggling hollows into the sand so that I could lie comfortably on my stomach. It was time to roast the back of my body. The first semester of our senior year started in one week's time, and Chloe and I were working hard on our tans, spending most of our days on Blue Crab Bay's small beach.

I was six years old when my parents divorced, and as I grew older, I'd had less and less to do with Dad, especially since he moved out of Baltimore to this tiny spot on the Chesapeake

Bay, where he ran a not very profitable sailing school. I was now down to visiting him once a year in the summer vacation. I looked forward to my visits, but more because they gave me a break from my mother, and her issues, than because I wanted to spend time with Dad.

He was a nice enough person, as was his second wife, Lucy, but I had little in common with either of them. This year he'd warned me that he wouldn't be able to take off work to spend time with me (not too devastated about that, Pops), and suggested that I bring a friend for company. Chloe's bubbling small talk, her questions about Dad's business, and her extravagant compliments on Lucy's cooking had helped fill the awkward silences that normally characterized our "family" suppers.

"And it was good?" Chloe asked now, still focused on that kiss.

"No, it wasn't good. It was fireworks and angel choirs good."

"Huh. And now you've got to get him to date you?"

"It doesn't have to be him — I think he lives over in D.C. anyway. It just has to be a really tall guy."

"The lifeguard is cute," Chloe said. Generous of her considering she'd been eyeing him all morning.

I gave the guy on the high chair a quick assessing glance. Five-nine, tops. One inch shorter than the official average height of the adult American male. Five-nine males, even cute ones, didn't raise a blip on my guy radar. I had no desire to date someone whose hands and feet were smaller than my own — nothing made me feel as freakishly big as that.

"He's too short," I said.

"He's not short!" Chloe protested.

From her height of five foot four — the exact average height for American females — I guess most guys looked tall.

"Too short *for me*," I conceded. "But he'd be perfect for you. You could wear four-inch heels and still be shorter than him. And, more importantly, you wouldn't be breaking The Law."

Chloe knew all about The Law of Tall Girls.

"Well," she said, pulling a T-shirt and shorts over her bikini, "if I'm going to razzle-dazzle him, I'll need a new bikini and maybe a cute sundress. Let's go shopping."

Blue Crab Bay was a tourist trap of a beachside town with souvenir stores standing shoulder to shoulder along the main road. At Chloe's insistence, we stopped in at every tacky one of them. She was fascinated by the racks stacked with plush toys in the shape of sharks ("Do they even have sharks here?" she demanded); T-shirts reading *Talk Nauti to me* and *Keep calm and dock your boat in **my** port!*; glass bottles filled with sand ("What fool would buy a bottle of sand?"); bags of hushpuppy ready-mix; and an endless variety of objects made from shells — cockle shell necklaces and tiny whelk earrings, shell-encrusted cellphone covers, ashtrays and soap dishes made from clams, and even pet shells — which came complete with names, miniature birth certificates, and stuck-on googly eyes that reminded me of the girl in the blue dress at the diner.

Worst of all were the mobiles with their trails of shells, coral and sand dollars which hung from the roof beams and door frames of every store we entered. I couldn't take five steps without braining myself on a dangling conch or a chunk of driftwood.

"Ooh, this one looks nice," said Chloe, gazing into the window of a tiny store called *She Sells Sea-Shells*.

"Haven't you seen enough? They're all the same."

"Not so. See that?" She pointed at something in the jam-packed window display. "It's a sand-globe! You know, like a snow-globe, but filled with sand. How awesome is that?"

I sighed and trailed after her into the store. The interior was crammed from floor to ceiling with all kinds of novelties and trinkets — my worst kind of place. Standing still so as not to bump anything off the brimming shelves, I tried to ignore the sense that everything was closing in on me. I took a deep, steadying breath and instantly regretted it. Dust. Dust with undertones of mildew and mold. Automatically, I switched to breathing through my mouth.

"Hah! This is great — come see what's written on it," Chloe said.

Resisting the urge to flee the claustrophobic collection of crap, I eased carefully toward her. As I leaned forward to read the inscription on the sand-globe, something snagged in my hair, pulling me up short. I gave my head a sharp jerk, and heard tinkling and jangling from just above me. Great, another mobile.

"Careful there!" said a sharp-featured man wearing an *I heart NautiGirls* T-shirt and a badge which identified him as the store owner.

I reached up my hand and felt rough bulges and a bumpy pitted surface snared in my hair. Working blindly, I tried to work the mysterious object free, but only got myself more thoroughly entangled. At the continued tinkling, other shoppers turned to stare. My face grew hot, my heart was beating unpleasantly hard, and the dust and mildew made it hard for me to catch my breath. I needed to get out of here — now. I tugged away from the grasp of the thing like a wild animal fighting a snare. I could feel tears rising.

Then Chloe was in front of me, holding my hands tightly, and forcing me to meet her eye.

"Just breathe. Just breathe with me, Peyton. In, 2, 3, 4… and slowly out, 2, 3, 4…"

By now, everyone in the store was gaping at me. A few were sniggering in amusement. A woman in a neon-yellow sundress said, "You should cut it out, that's what I do when my girl gets gum stuck in her hair."

"Nobody is cutting my friend's hair," Chloe said firmly.

I yanked again at the trap.

"Watch it! You'll break it!" said the man. He shoved aside my hands and stood on tiptoe to reach up to the matted snarl. "Starfish are very fragile, you know."

"Get me free, Chloe," I whispered through clenched teeth.

"You're too tall. I can't see what I'm doing," the store owner said.

"Here, let me help you," a tall man volunteered, stepping around the back of me. "Wow, it's a regular bird's nest up here." He chuckled.

"Chloe!" I pleaded.

"Just a few more seconds," she promised.

There was a sharp tug of hair at the crown of my head, and then I was free. I bolted for the door, and once outside, sat on my haunches and dropped my head between my knees.

From inside I heard the sound of laughter and the owner saying, "Honestly! You'd think some people would be more careful where they put their heads, so they don't destroy property."

"And maybe *some people* should be more careful where they hang their mobiles, so they don't injure customers," Chloe snapped as she stomped out of the store.

She gripped my arm and pulled me to my feet.

"You okay?"

"Yeah." I nodded. My breathing was already slowing down. "It was just all that stuff all around me, you know? And getting stuck in my hair."

"I'm sorry, I should have thought. Well, no more of those tacky tourist stores. Let's go grab a cup of coffee somewhere, or maybe," she said, casting me a still-worried glance, "some calming chamomile tea. Then we'll get our fashion on."

"No, I'm fine now, really. I can handle a nice clean, spacious clothing store."

"Okay, if you're sure? Where do we start?"

I led her into the swimwear boutique with the best variety and steered her to the full rack of bikinis in her size. She immediately picked out one in a hideous leopard print, held it against her chest and studied her appearance in a full-length mirror.

"What do you think?"

"Fabulous!" gushed the young assistant. Clearly, she was on commission.

I knew the style would make her legs look shorter, and the burnt-orange color would make her already fair skin look paler than the pink inside of an abalone shell.

"No." I tugged the bikini out of Chloe's grasp, replaced it on the rail, flicked through the hangers, and handed her a baby-blue two-piece with a high-leg cut, and another in a flattering soft coral. "These will work better with your body and your coloring."

"Yes, of course. I see it now," said the assistant.

Chloe tried on first one and then the other, declared herself gorgeous in both, and instructed me to choose for her.

"The blue one, no question."

I snagged a large, floppy sunhat in natural straw off a nearby hat stand, tied a long, floaty scarf of palest turquoise around its brim, and popped the hat on top of her blond hair, leaving a flirty tail to hang down between her shoulders.

"Hot or what?" I asked, stepping aside so she could admire herself in the mirror.

"T*ssss!*" She burned a fingertip on the imaginary heat of her sexy shoulder.

"Perfect!" The shop assistant clapped her hands in an ecstasy of anticipated commissions. "I'll just ring those up for you."

It had taken us all of ten minutes. For normal-sized girls, clothes-shopping was a piece of cake.

"Aren't *you* going to look at the bikinis?" Chloe asked, slipping back into her shorts.

"No."

"Why not? That one you're wearing is looking a little worn. Just saying."

"Sure, but it has the advantage of fitting."

"There'll be plenty of new ones here that fit you."

"Wanna bet?"

~ *5* ~

"So, my shoulders and ribcage are wide," I told Chloe, leading her to a rail at the back of the store. "Which means I always need tops in a bigger size. These swimsuits over here would fit my top, but I wouldn't be seen dead in them."

"No, I see what you mean," said Chloe, crinkling her nose at the few items on the rail — ugly one-pieces in muted colors, fitted with tummy- and thigh-disguising frills, and obviously intended for weighty women. "They're grannytastic."

"With my long torso, they'd give me a serious camel-toe. And with these" — I pointed to a more fully stocked rail of smaller-sized bikinis — "the ones which would fit my butt, won't fit my top."

"Now, I'm sure that's not true," the assistant said.

She freed a bikini top from a hanger and hung the halter strap around my neck, then frowned at the cups which rested just south of my collar bones, nowhere near my boobs.

I directed an I-told-you-so look at Chloe.

"How about a boob-tube style top?" The assistant offered

me the top half of a gorgeous bikini in a shimmering cobalt blue. "That way we wouldn't have to worry about the ..." She gestured vaguely to the distance between my neck and my nipples.

"True, but we would have to worry about the ..." I gestured to the circumference of my ribcage.

"Let's see, shall we?" The assistant gave it her best shot, but no amount of pulling or stretching could get the two ends of the back strap to meet.

"Perhaps you should just go topless?" Chloe suggested.

"Can we go now?"

The assistant didn't try to stop me leaving.

"On the subject of clothing," said Chloe, admiring the effect of her new hat in a store window as we strolled down the street, "for someone with such obvious good taste and fashion fundiship, you wear kinda boring stuff."

"Thank you, Chloe, that makes me feel fabulous."

"It's true! You always wear the same old jeans and T-shirts. You could dress a whole lot better."

"No, I couldn't."

"Why not?"

"Several excellent reasons."

"Such as?"

"Well, firstly, real style costs plenty. And as you know, my mother and I aren't exactly swimming in dollars."

"Fair point," she conceded.

"Secondly, I keep my look kind of neutral because —"

"Is 'neutral' another word for bland and boring?"

"Because" — I elbowed her — "more dramatic clothes

would only draw more attention to my height, and I get enough of that already, thank you very much."

"That's a big, steaming pile of nonsense. You've got to own your height, stand tall and proud."

"Easy for you to say, Frodo."

"Ru-ude!" This time it was her turn to elbow me.

"And fourthly —"

"Thirdly," she corrected.

"Whatever. The main reason is that even if I wanted to wear something more stylish, it's sure as pigs are made of bacon that I wouldn't be able to find it in my size."

"More BS."

"That last store didn't convince you?"

"Swimsuits are hard for everyone," she said. "But I reckon we could totally find something to fit your hot bod."

Although Chloe had been my friend forever, I only ever went clothes shopping alone so as to minimize the embarrassment. Maybe it was time to let her see for herself.

"Come on, let's start here." She grabbed me by the arm and dragged me inside the largest fashion store in town.

"They won't have anything that fits," I said in a singsong voice.

"I don't buy that."

"Oh yeah? Where did you shop when you were tall?"

Chloe led me to a rack of extra-long tops in a variety of bold patterns.

"These are great. You can wear it as a shirt over leggings, or" — she pointed to a nearby mannequin rocking the garment worn with only a pair of kick-ass boots — "you can wear it as a dress."

"*You* could. *I* can't."

"I don't want to hear any more no's from you, Peyton. Your negativity is starting to give me irritable scowl syndrome."

"Fine, I'll prove it." I took one of the long tops and went into the fitting room.

"So," Chloe said from the other side of the stall door while I stripped. "How is your mom doing?"

"Next question."

"That bad?"

"Yes," I said, and changed the subject. "Have you decided on your college major yet?"

"I'm still leaning toward Economics. You?" Chloe said.

"All I know is that I want to get away from home."

What I didn't know was whether I'd ever be able to.

I tried to wrestle myself into the shirt-dress, but couldn't get it over my head. I searched for a zip at the neck, but found nothing.

I flung it over the top of the fitting room door. "It's too small."

"Are you sure? It's an extra-large."

"I can't even get it over my head."

"Here, try the extra-extra-large." An orange garment patterned with yellow cubes came sailing over the door. "That's the only color they have it in."

I yanked the top over my head to the sound of ripping stitches.

"Ta-da!" I opened the door so she could see how the waist hung out way too wide from my sides.

Chloe blinked at the enormous block of sunshine colors that was me.

"Told you so," I couldn't resist saying. "When you get them extra-large, they always fit like a potato sack."

A pimply shop assistant, who'd come over to check the fit, said, "You're too slim, that's the problem."

"No, the problem is it's too wide – the proportions are all wrong. You can't just upsize a garment and expect it to fit tall people. And this one is *still* not long enough."

Chloe eyed the hem, which came to just below my lady parts, with wide eyes. "*Oh.* With tights, then." She scurried off and returned with a pair.

Not bothering to return to the fitting room, I wriggled into the tights in front of her, grunting as I squirmed and tugged them up as far as they would go.

"Oh," she said again, this time more faintly, staring at the crotch which reached only midway up my thighs. "I see."

"Seeing *is* believing."

"I'm not giving up. You get back in there. I'll bring you more to try on."

Under her direction, I tried on shirts, jeans and dresses. Hems were too short; tops were either so tight that I battled to breathe in them, or large as circus tents; waists were at my boobs, hips were at my waists, long sleeves weren't, and one-size-fits-all didn't. They never did.

"For goodness' sake," said Chloe, sweating with the effort of running around the crowded store in an increasingly desperate attempt to find something — anything — that would fit, "let's just take a hat!"

I knew how this would end, too, but said nothing. Chloe pushed me down onto a stool and perched a succession of hats and caps on my head. The only one that came even close to fitting was a purple cloche hat in knitted cotton, and then only because she pulled and tugged it down with all her might.

"There!" she said triumphantly.

"It's so tight, it's going to squeeze my brains out of my ears," I complained, tugging the hat off.

"Don't you have any hats in larger sizes?" Chloe asked the assistant.

"Sure," said the girl, smirking and pointing to the opposite side of the store. "In the men's department."

Story of my life.

"She's not going to wear a man's hat!" said Chloe hotly.

Wearing men's clothes was nothing new. The T-shirt I was wearing that very day hadn't been purchased from the ladies' section of Walmart.

Hands on hips, Chloe rotated on the spot, searching for some type of garment we had not yet tried. Her eyes lighted on the display racks of shoes.

"Huh?" she said, smiling in anticipation. "*Huh?*"

"Stop right there." I held up a hand to stem her enthusiasm. No type of shopping was more disappointing and frustrating, more freaking impossible for me than shoe-shopping. I needed to nip this in the bud. "Excuse me, miss?" I called across to the assistant. "What's the biggest size you have in women's shoes?"

"The biggest?"

"Yes, the biggest."

"A ten."

I turned back to Chloe. "There you go — at least three sizes too small."

"You don't have any size thirteens then?" Chloe asked.

"*Size thirteen?*"

Was there an echo in here?

"You want ladies' shoes in a size *thirteen?*" the assistant exclaimed loudly.

Several heads turned to see the giant female with the clown feet. I groaned.

"No, I don't think they even *make* women's shoes that big. You might want to try in the men's department."

"Believe me now?" I asked Chloe, marching her out the store.

"I'll admit I am feeling a *little* of your pain. Everybody wants to be tall and slim — you'd think it would be easier to find clothes that fit."

"The struggle is real."

"But surely there are places where you can shop online? Or go to a big-and-tall outfitters? And I'm sure I've seen tall clothing sections in some of the department stores back home."

"Those in-store tall ranges are made for women who're five-ten, not six foot plus. The super-size outfitters are for big *and* tall, not big or tall. Their stuff is made for wider people. And online? It's extra expensive, and that's *before* shipping costs."

"Well, you're not the only ones who have it hard. It's got to be the same for super-short girls, right?"

"Chloe, they can just take up a hem — I can't grow extra fabric on the ends of my clothes. Besides, there's a much wider range for petites. Extra-sized clothing is almost always old-fashioned and fugly, it's never stylish or cute or trendy." I frowned, made a circle with my hand, and said, "One does not merely walk into Topshop and demand a thirty-seven-inch inseam."

Chloe burst out laughing at my Boromir impersonation. "Okay, I believe you. Let's check out this street. No clothing and no curio stores."

Antique Alley was a quiet side street lined with stores selling vintage and secondhand goods. Fearing another freak-out, I refused to go into any of the stores crammed with junk, but we enjoyed window-shopping and checking out the wares set out on tables on the sidewalk.

Chloe bought herself an art nouveau teapot, and when she saw me admiring a pair of delicate silver earrings, she insisted on buying them for me.

"They're an apology gift, for dragging you into stupid souvenir stores and not believing you about the clothes," she said. "I mean, you've complained before about getting jeans and shoes to fit, but I never realized it was that bad. Is it always like that?"

"Yes. Yes, it is *always* like that. Frustrating and futile and embarrassing. Every. Single. Time." I put the earrings on and tossed my head happily. Finally — something that fit me. "One day, when I'm queen of the world, I'll assemble a royal fashion team of designers and dressmakers and the shoe-people. What do you call them?"

"Cobblers?"

"Yeah, cobblers! I reckon the only way I'll ever get great-looking stuff that actually fits me properly is if someone makes it especially for me."

"Or if you make it yourself."

Chloe was laughing, but I wasn't. I was staring at an object on a trestle table outside *Forget Me Not Collectibles.* If she'd said the exact same words while I'd been looking at the table of brooches and beaded handbags, or if I'd seen the shiny old object while she'd been talking about souvenirs or careers or lifeguards, I wouldn't have made the connection. But those words coming at the exact moment when my eyes fell on this object made neurons fire wildly in my brain.

Unless I make it myself.

I tugged at the object, pulling it to the front of the table.

"What *is* that?" Chloe asked.

It was heavy and black, with the word *Singer* lettered in gold along the side, and an electric cord, complete with an old-fashioned plug, coming out of the back. At one end was a metal wheel, and at the other was a complicated arrangement of steel clamps, notched wheels, and a needle. Threaded through the needle was a strand of white cotton which led to a spool perched on an upright pin at the very top of the whole contraption.

My mind was filling with so many possibilities that my head must surely be swelling beyond the fit of any hat on the planet.

"This" — I stroked the curved lines of the beautiful old object — "is a sewing machine."

~ *6* ~

The school bus on the first day of the new semester was always crazy — yelled greetings and insults, flipped birds, paper missiles, spilled coffee, a cacophony of music played on cellphones, and a scramble for territorial dominance over the best seats.

The bus driver eyed us all as though we were a bully-bomb ready to explode, and directed so many nervous glances back at the tumult via her rearview mirror, that I wanted to remind her to keep her eyes on the road.

Chloe and I would've bypassed the first-day bus blues by walking to school as we often did, but it was raining, and the wind had a chilly edge. Fall was on the way.

As usual, Chloe took the window seat while I sat on the aisle so I could stretch my legs out. She rummaged in her bag and brought out a packet of wrapped candies.

"Want some?" she offered.

"Thanks, but it's a little early in the morning for me to start mainlining sugar."

She shrugged, unwrapped one of the treats, popped it in her

mouth and closed her eyes in ecstasy.

"Hey, so I've set up the sewing machine on the desk in my bedroom. I even fitted a new plug on it."

"How'd you know how to do that?"

"Professor Google."

"Better keep an eye on it so you don't burn down the house," said Chloe. "I'm with your father when it comes to the safety of that ancient artifact."

My father had grumbled about transporting the heavy machine on the drive back to Baltimore, and repeatedly warned me against actually trying to use it, insisting, "The thing's a damn fire hazard."

"Are you going to keep the mannequin?" Chloe asked.

The antiques store had thrown in a dressmaker's dummy for free. I'd hesitated before accepting, because not only would Chloe and I have to make the journey home with the heavy thing resting across our laps, but also because I didn't like too many things messing up the streamlined neatness of my bedroom.

"Yeah, I reckon I'll need it if I'm going to give the sewing a serious go."

Chloe nodded, then half-turned in her bus seat to direct a withering glance at the boy behind us.

"Hey, keep your fingers out of my hair, okay?" she said.

"Sorry." The boy had all the hallmarks of a freshman: too-neat clothes, a nervously bobbing Adam's apple, a hand clenched tight on the back of our seat, and an overstuffed backpack — he'd brought *all* the books.

"Don't worry," I tried to reassure him. "It's not a bad school — you'll be okay."

"Thanks," he said, looking pathetically grateful.

"I'm Peyton, by the way. Senior."

"I'm Will, freshman."

"No kidding," said Chloe.

"And this friendly person is Chloe."

"Hi," he said to the back of Chloe's head.

She was facing front again, working her way through the bag of candies.

"Well, good luck," I told Will.

"You're very tall," was his reply.

"Really? She had no idea," Chloe muttered beside me.

"Do you play basketball? Or volleyball?"

"No," I snapped, turning my back on him, and slumping down in the seat.

"And does it work?" Chloe asked me. "The antique sewing machine?"

"Yeah! I tried it out on an old dishcloth, and it only got jammed twice. And that might have been my fault because I'm still learning how to use it. The instruction booklet that came with it is missing a few pages."

It was a little worse than that — the aged yellow paper was crumbling to pieces, and pages 11b to 15c were stuck together with a gross brown substance — but I was determined to figure the thing out.

"Are those dress patterns that the storekeeper threw in any good?"

"Maybe," I hedged. The truth was, they could be the best patterns on the planet and I wouldn't know it. To me, they were a mystifying collection of shapes cut from what looked like baking parchment, printed with baffling dots, dashes, arrows, numbers and a bunch of other enigmatic symbols. It was like trying to decode hieroglyphics. "But they're a little old fashioned. I think I'll start with something newer, something of my own, even."

From the book bag on my lap, I hauled out a sketchbook which I'd discovered in an overflowing stationery drawer at home, and showed Chloe my first attempts at fashion design.

"Those don't look half bad. You might have some skills at this," she said, then peered into the almost empty bag of candies. "Last one — sure you don't want it?"

"Really, no."

"Ah, a caramel crème. Your loss."

My eyes fell on the indigo square of foil and the silver-striped cellophane Chloe had unwrapped from the last candy.

"But can I have the wrappers?"

"You want my candy wrappers?" Her tone was disbelieving, her eyebrows arched.

"Yep."

I took the foil and cellophane squares from her hand, smoothed them out carefully and, as the bus lurched to a stop outside Longford High, tucked them into the back of my sketchbook for safekeeping.

A sharp pain in my left ankle made me gasp. I'd forgotten how quickly I needed to move my legs out of the aisle once the bus stopped.

"Excuse me," Brooke, the girl who'd kicked my ankle, said. "Could you get your feet out of my way, if it's not too much trouble. They're completely blocking the aisle."

"Yeah, how're we supposed to exit with Bigfoot blocking the way?" her friend added.

I pulled my legs out of the way, banging a knee on the seat in front of me in my rush.

"Thank you so much," Brooke said in a falsely sweet voice.

"Hey, we should call *Monster Hunters*," her friend said loudly as they walked down the aisle, "and tell them we've found Sasquatch."

"Yeah, you call them, Brooke, so I can tell them how I found a two-legged talking cow!" Chloe yelled after them. Then she sighed at me. "You need to stand up to them, Peyton. Just ignoring it doesn't help."

"Yeah, yeah."

It wasn't the first, or even the fifty-first, time that Chloe had urged me to give as good as I got, but I always thought of the perfect putdown only after the offender had moved off and my blushes had faded.

I followed Chloe off the bus and ran beside her through the pelting rain toward the staired entrance of the school, wishing my fleece jacket had a hood.

As we reached the bottom stair, I glimpsed a figure in a black leather jacket disappearing through the glass doors at the top. For a moment, it looked like … But no, it couldn't be.

Inside, we pushed through the throng of students, sidestepping lost-looking newbies and greeting classmates we hadn't seen in months, until we reached the senior lockers at the end of the main hallway. Chloe and I began transferring the contents of our bags into the lockers. For once, I'd been assigned a top locker and didn't have to crouch down on my haunches to reach it.

"Here." Chloe handed me a fistful of candy wrappers scraped from the bowels of her bag. "Now you can start a collection."

"You're so tall, you really ought to play basketball," someone said from the other side of my open locker door.

I recognized the voice. It was Greg Baker, nagging me about trying out for the girls' team again. Why did everyone think that height was coded on the same genes as hand-eye coordination?

I shouldered my locker door shut, trying to work up the nerve to tell Greg, *What part of 'no' don't you understand?*

But Greg wasn't looking at me. He was talking to the figure in the black jacket. The tall figure. The familiar, very tall figure with the green eyes and smiley eye crinkles. The one I'd had to lift my face up to when we'd kissed.

I stood gaping, wet hair hanging in rat-tails, brightly colored foil and cellophane squares clutched in my hands.

Jay must have felt my stare, because he sent a quick look in my direction, then did a double-take, dropping puzzled eyes to the candy wrappers, before meeting my gaze. I could tell that, despite my drowned appearance and the look of idiocy which must be on my face, he recognized me. My face and neck grew so hot, I figured steam must be rising off the top of my head. I probably resembled Chloe's favorite red china teapot.

"Hey," he said. "It's you — Tiger Eyes."

"Huh?" I said, brushing a soggy lock of hair out of my face with my forearm.

"We met in the diner that night when —"

"I remember." More blushing.

"Me, too." He grinned.

Oh, my... I wanted to just stand and stare at the beauty of

that grin, but I forced myself to speak. "So, you're at Longford High now?"

"Yeah, I transferred. I'm officially the new kid."

"I'm trying to get him to try out for the basketball team. That height shouldn't go to waste," said Greg. "Tryouts are on Friday. Will you come?"

"Sorry, man, I have an ankle injury," Jay said.

Greg groaned in disappointment and then pinned me with a pleading look. "Peyton? It's your final year, your last chance."

"Er, no, sorry." At his hangdog expression, I added, "Really, Greg, you don't want me. I couldn't catch a ball if it was handed to me in slow motion. Honest."

"Okay, okay." He sighed and gave my long legs a regretful look, then asked his cousin, "Got what you need?"

Jay nodded. He was still looking at me.

I met his gaze, but couldn't think of anything to say other than, *You've got freckles!* I managed to restrain myself from actually saying the words, and settled for silently admiring the sprinkle across his nose and cheeks.

Someone jostled me, and I glanced down to see Chloe standing at my side.

"Introduce me maybe?"

"Oh, right. This is Jay Young. He's from DC."

I admired Jay Young and his freckles for a little while longer, though I could feel Chloe looking up at me expectantly. What did she want?

Someone pushed in between Jay and Greg and gave an annoyed cough. My eyes slid down sideways and took in a pair of big blue eyes. No, not big, *googly*. It was her, the girl in the blue dress from the diner. Today, she was wearing a pink shirt dress which fit her perfectly.

"Hi," I said, with zero enthusiasm.

"Sure," she said.

She looked me up one side and down the other, from the tip of my dripping head to the bottom of my toes in their unflattering men's sneakers, lingering a moment to frown at my handful of candy wrappers.

"Seems I'll have to introduce *myself*," Chloe said. "Hi Jay, I'm Chloe DiCaprio — no relation to Leonardo — and I'm Peyton's friend."

Googly Eyes slipped her arm through the crook of Jay's elbow, even though it was a good ten inches higher than her own and she looked absurd doing it, and said, "I'm Faye Fenton. And I'm Jay's girlfriend."

~ 7 ~

At four-thirty that afternoon, my phone buzzed an alert from Chloe. She was outside my house, below my bedroom window, waiting to be let in so we could have our usual first-day-of-school dissection ritual — herb tea with a spicy side of hot gossip.

I set aside the fabric I'd been attempting to sew on the old Singer, walked over to my sash window, pushed it all the way open, lifted the heavy roll of rope ladder — which was Chloe's and my preferred way of accessing my second-story bedroom — and tossed it out of the window, yelling, "Beware below!"

"Hey," said Chloe as she climbed over the window sill.

"Hi. What'll it be? Tea or chocolate milk?"

"Tea. I've brought 'Orange Orgasm' today. And" — she rummaged in her small backpack and brought out two packages — "Berger cookies!"

Good. Buttery shortbread topped with chocolate fudge would help sweeten my mood. I was still bummed out that although there was a hot new guy at the school — one big and tall enough to make even *me* feel dainty, and one who was an amazing kisser, too — he had already been snapped up. This rare and precious tall boy was close enough to touch, but still out of my reach. Figured.

In one corner of my bedroom — on top of a mini fridge stocked with essentials in the way of food and drinks — was a tray with an electric kettle, cups, tea, coffee, sugar, teaspoons, and even a red china teapot and strainer for when we made Chloe's exotic loose-leaf varieties.

While she boiled the kettle and made the tea, we gossiped about the day — who'd obviously spent their vacation in sunnier spots than Maryland ("Did you see Brooke? She's the exact orange of a kumquat,"); which teachers we'd been assigned for our classes ("I've still got Dumas for French, so that's good. But Watkins for Calculus? Kill me now."), and who'd hooked up with whom over the summer ("Neither of us, friend. Another summer has passed, and we remain single.")

Which brought my thoughts around to where they'd been tethered all day.

"And I would never have figured Gabe and Liu for a couple," said Chloe, blowing on her tea. "They don't seem to fit together, you know?"

"Yeah. Just like Jay and Faye. *Jay and Faye?* It even sounds ridiculous. Faye — what kind of name is that anyway? I'll tell you what sort of girls are called Faye — felons, that's who," I grumbled.

"Uh, felons?" Chloe took a sip of her tea and nodded at the amber liquid approvingly. "This is pretty good. I mean, not orgasmic-good, but nice. Kinda perfumy on top, with earthy ginger notes below."

"Yeah, felons," I said darkly. "People who break the law."

Chloe rolled her eyes. "Are we talking about the law of tall girls? Again?"

"She is in flagrant violation of it, Chloe. Jay and Faye — they look as dumb as they sound."

"They do look hilarious together — I'll give you that. She'll have to stand on a stool when they kiss. Or he'll have to lift her up."

The image of that pinched at me. Some girls had a list of qualities they wanted in a guy: good looks, intelligence, sense of humor, a cool car. (I'd just bet Faye ranked the cool car on her priority list.) But my boy bucket list included a very different set of attributes. I wanted a guy to have bigger feet than me. Bigger hands. A guy who could scoop me up without having a hernia. Who had to bend his head — or lift me up — to kiss me. Freaking Faye probably got these things all the time.

"It's just such a waste," I moaned, downing my non-orgasmic tea as if it was a shot of bourbon handed to me by a sympathetic barman. "He's tall *and* he's gorgeous — well, you saw him."

"Yeah, but he wouldn't ping 'sizzling' on my hot-o-meter."

I shook my head like a spaniel with water in its ears. "I'm sorry, can you repeat that? I thought I just heard you say Jay Young is not hot."

"No, I mean I can see that he's good-looking, he's just not my kind of hot."

"But how can that even be?"

"Beauty — beholder?" said Chloe, flipping first one hand and then the other in the air. "He's too big, too tall."

"There's no such thing!"

"He's just too … much. Anyway, a guy that size? He's probably a jock. And you know how much I love them. Not. Or maybe he's a cowboy — did you see his bowlegs?"

I hadn't. But the idea of Jay in a Stetson and chaps, calling me ma'am or *purrty*, brought a dreamy smile to my lips.

"There was a flyer on the main notice board from the drama club, did you see it?" Chloe asked, pouring herself another cup of tea. "They're doing something called *Romero and Juliet*."

"Romero? Not Romeo?"

"Maybe it was a typo. Auditions are on September twenty-second. Going to try out?"

"Maybe." Probably. I enjoyed the experience of disappearing into someone else's skin for a while, and an extracurricular activity would look good on a college application. "Even though they'll probably make me play the butler again, or the narrator."

My height limited my role options. More often than not, I was given male roles.

"They're doing two performances in December, right at the end of the semester. And senior prom has been scheduled for the end of April."

"That gives me loads of time to find tall guys and date them," I said, relieved.

"Have you begun making a list of potential candidates yet?"

"Nope. I was waiting for you to come and help me."

"Peyton, *I* can't tell at a glance who's over — How tall does he have to be again?"

"Six-three, minimum."

"Well, I can't calculate heights at a glance. That's your spidey-sense."

I grabbed a legal pad, wrote *The Tall Boys List* at the top, and underlined it twice. I doubted I would need such a big piece of paper. I figured there would be only a handful of qualifying candidates.

"Right, number one, Jay Young." I wrote his name down.

"He's taken," Chloe pointed out. Unnecessarily.

Sad, but true. I drew a line through his name.

"Tim Anderson," I said, adding his name. "He must be six-six or -seven." Tiny Tim was the tallest boy in the school. "How come he gets called Tiny Tim and I get called Big P?"

"It's a mystery of the universe." Chloe collected our dirty cups, carefully wiped crumbs into the trash can, and headed into the bathroom that led directly off my room to wash the cups in the basin. She knew how much I hated a mess.

"How about Dylan Jones?" I chewed the end of my pen, considering. "He might just scrape in. If he stands straight."

Like me, Dylan was a sloucher. I wrote his name down, grabbed a dishcloth and followed Chloe.

"What I need," I said, drying a cup, "is a rack to stretch boys, like those ones they had in medieval times."

"I think that was more for torture than posture."

"Either way, they'd be elongated."

When we'd put away the dishes and were back on my bed, I asked, "Can you think of anyone else?"

"This is boring," Chloe complained.

"Yeah, I know. But it must be done, friend. I've *got* to win that bet. I need the money."

I did. But I was also more than a little enchanted by the idea of dating a tall guy, of dancing with someone so tall that my head would rest on his chest or shoulder, rather than having his face mashed up against my chest.

In the Venn diagram of dating, the intersection of what boys find attractive in a girl, and what I find attractive in a boy, is tiny, so my dating experience has been majorly limited. I'd only ever been out with four boys, and not a single sorry one of them was as tall as me.

I had my first kiss when I was a sophomore. The top of Carlos's head reached about to my collarbone — so we had to sit down in order to kiss comfortably. And even then, I had to hunch over. Slow-dancing with him was excruciating, and when he nestled his face between my boobs and began motorboating noisily, any attraction I might have imagined I felt for him died instantly.

My longest-lasting and most recent relationship — if it could even be called that — was with Wayne, who was *almost* tall enough to look me directly in the eye. We lasted a total of five dates, three of which were spent playing World of Warcraft in his basement. The other two were at house parties, where he spent most of the night dancing with other (shorter) girls.

I haven't dated anyone since, and I've never dated anyone taller than myself. So if I could get over my insecurities, this bet might just be fun.

A knock at the door jarred me out of my fantasies.

"Hi, girls," my mother said from the other side of the door. "Is that you, Chloe?"

"Yes, Mrs. Lane," Chloe called back.

There was another, softer knock. "May I come in?"

I sighed and walked over to unlock the door. My mother

came in, clutching a turquoise plush toy to her chest.

Seeing her there in my room, I felt the usual spasm of annoyance. Her hair, self-cut and already graying at the temples, needed a wash. And her lipstick, probably hastily applied in honor of Chloe's presence, was already bleeding into the lines around her mouth. My mother was only in her early forties — a good decade younger than Chloe's mom — but she looked much older.

"Yes?" I asked. "What do you want?"

Chloe gave me a look that clearly said she thought I was being rude.

"I wanted to say hi to Chloe, Peyton. Is that allowed?"

"How are you, Mrs. Lane?"

"Very well. Very, very well, thank you for asking. Look what I found today." She waved the stuffed toy at me. "Remember this? It was that sweet monster who didn't like scaring kids, from that movie. What was his name again?"

"It's Sully, from *Monster's Inc.*," Chloe said. "I loved that movie."

"That's right!" my mother said happily, perching the toy on top of a chest of drawers. "Peyton used to call him Solly-monster. He used to be hers before —"

"I don't want it," I said quickly.

"You don't want it?" my mother said, like I'd just turned down the first prize in the state lottery. "Why not?"

"Mom, just look at it." The monster had only one eye, its blue fur was faded and mangy-looking, and one of its arms hung limply, empty of stuffing. "Besides, I'm seventeen, not a baby."

I hadn't meant to hurt her, but my words were enough to make her press her lips together and tear up. Enough to make me feel guilty and say, in a gentler tone, "But thanks for thinking of me."

"I've kept it safe all these years. I thought you might like it back — for sentimental reasons."

"I'm not sentimental. You know that."

"It would look lovely here." She pushed the stuffed toy to the center of the chest of drawers. "It brings a bit of life, see? Your room is so bare, so sterile."

"It's not bare. Or sterile. It's tidy."

I loved my room. It was my very own space where I could relax and be myself. I kept it clean and neat — compulsively so according to Chloe, who had a theory that I might be mildly OCD. I loved the simplicity of the furnishings: pale, dove-gray bedding and drapes, and one huge purple velvet cushion perched at the head of the bed. The walls were free of posters and pictures, and I tried to keep the surfaces clear. It wasn't the typical messy environment of your average feral teen, and I guess to my mother it seemed pretty spartan. But it was my refuge and retreat.

"What are you sewing?" my mother asked, eyeing the small puddle of sky-blue chiffon beside the Singer.

"I'm trying to make a scarf." Trying was the operative word. The presser foot and needle plate kept jamming, snarling great knots of thread in the sheer fabric.

"I used to sew when I was a young girl, you know. I could help you out."

"No thanks, I'll figure it out."

"I could buy you some fabric," my mother continued, while Chloe glanced anxiously from one to the other of us.

"No, thanks." My mother already spent more than we could afford shopping online.

"I found a great site called Sew Happy — like S-E-W — clever, isn't it? And they're got a massive sale on, so —"

"*No.*"

Instantly she looked hurt again.

"I'd like to choose my own patterns and colors, and there's a great little store downtown that sells fabric scraps and offcuts."

She wrinkled her nose. "Remnants and offcuts — not very nice."

"They're fine. And cheap."

"Well, I'll let you girls get back to whatever you were doing before I interrupted. Goodbye, Chloe." My mother pulled the door shut behind her.

"You left the flipping monster," I called after her, but she didn't return. "Every time!" I snatched the toy and flung it into the trashcan before I turned the key in the lock.

"She was just trying to be kind," Chloe chided me. "Maybe you could be a bit more patient with her?"

"You try living here and see how patient *you* feel." I puffed out a breath. "Now can we get back to the tall-boy list?"

"I'll leave it to you, I need to get going — Dad's grilling chicken for supper."

Once she'd disappeared over the window sill, I rolled the rope ladder back up and stowed it in its spot behind the drapes, then went back to staring glumly at the list. I doodled in the margin while racking my brain for more names, but could only come up with one other.

My eye fell on my sketchbook, and soon I was cutting one of Chloe's candy wrappers into the shape of a skirt and sticking it on a sketch, all the while mulling about tall boys and trying not to dwell on one tall boy in particular.

I twisted a square of indigo foil into a scarf and positioned it on my sketched figure, so that it billowed out behind her, as if she was walking into a stiff headwind. By this time tomorrow, if all went well, I might have my first tall-boy date all set up.

I'd start with Tiny Tim. He was in my World History class, and I sometimes let him copy my homework, so at least we knew each other's names. I didn't know much else about him except that he had a reputation as a stoner and a slacker. He never volunteered anything in class, and when a teacher called on him to answer a question, he gave the dumbest answers.

But perhaps he was being ironic — what did I know about being cool?

~ 8 ~

The Tall Boys List:
1. ~~Jay Young~~
2. *Tim Anderson*
3. *Mark Rodriguez*
4. *Dylan Jones*

I ate nothing at lunch the next day, provoking a disbelieving look from Chloe. It wasn't often I went without food. But at that moment, the thought of eating made me feel queasy.

Last year, on a dare, one of the lunch ladies had smooshed together about twenty meatballs into one giant lump of protein, plonked it on a bed of spaghetti and sauce, and served it to the captain of the football team. That's what my stomach felt like in the period after lunch — a heavy meatball of dread.

I glanced over at Tim Anderson, whose long legs were wound around the legs of his desk, and wondered how on earth boys did this? How did they find the courage and confidence to ask a girl out when she might laugh, or sneer, "No way!"?

The end-of-period bell rang — time to put on my big-girl panties and pop the question. I reminded myself that I was the fearless girl who'd asked Jay Young for a kiss. And gotten it. By comparison, asking Tim for a date should be as easy as tripping over my own feet, which I tried not to do as I headed over to his desk.

He was yawning and blinking sleepily. Had he been napping through Hitler's invasion of Poland?

"Hey, Tim."

"Hey …" Judging by his blank stare and the sickly sweet smell still clinging to his clothes and hair, Tim had spent his lunch period getting blazed.

"Peyton," I supplied.

"Yeah, Peyton. That's right. That's your name."

"Can I ask you something?"

"Sure." He dropped his blank pad of paper into his book bag, unwound his legs and stood up, stretching. He *was* tall — at least five inches taller than me.

"Um …" Just say it already, Peyton. "I just wondered if — if you'd like to go out sometime?"

It took a few moments for this to percolate down through his brain. Then he blinked in surprise and said, "With you?"

"It's okay if you don't want to. I just thought that maybe —"

"S'cool," he said, interrupting my embarrassing gabble. "When? Where?"

"Jumping Jim's Diner?" I got a staff discount there. "Friday night, at seven?"

"I'll be there." With another bone-cracking stretch, he ambled out of the room.

Asking Tim out had been so easy that I figured the date would be, too. If he was as ultra-laid-back as he seemed — kind of stop-the-world-I-want-to-get-*on* — then maybe four dates with him would be doable. Fifteen minutes into our first date on Friday evening, though, I knew I'd been wrong.

Finding something to talk about with Tim was harder than tracking down a pair of elegant shoes in a size thirteen medium.

"What kind of movies do you like?" I'd asked for openers.

"Action ones. Like the *Fast and Furious* series — those cars, dude!" For a moment a tender, dopey look softened his features. He looked like a man in love. "Too bad about Paul Walker."

"Who?"

"The lead actor — he took a one-way ticket to the great street race in the sky. He was the finest, man."

"Right."

Jim arrived with our drinks then — coke for Tim and my favorite double-thick chocolate milkshake for me. "On the house!" Jim told us happily.

As soon as he walked off, humming Elvis's *Hound Dog*, Tim pulled a miniature bottle of rum out of his jacket pocket and poured a slug into his Coke, before offering me a shot. When I shook my head, he emptied the bottle into his soda and took a long drink. His bloodshot eyes told me it wasn't his first use of mind-altering substances that day.

"Those are my best movies — I've got the full collection at home. The first was the best of course, though the sixth wasn't bad. 'Ride or die, remember?'"

"Huh?"

"It's a line, from the sixth movie. Which one was your favorite?"

"I've never seen them," I admitted.

"Never seen them?" Tim said it like it was the most unbelievable thing he'd ever heard.

I shook my head.

He took another long pull on his Coke. "Like, any of them?"

"I prefer old movies."

"Yeah, there were some cool movies in the 90's. *The Matrix*, *The Crow*. All the *Die Hards*."

"No, I mean I like *old* movies. You know, like *Ninotchka*, *Breakfast at Tiffany's*, *Vertigo* and *Rear Window* — well, all the Hitchcocks, really."

Tim stared at me blankly. "Huh," he said finally.

There was a silence. Not a comfortable one. Tim finished his drink, slumped back in the seat and stretched out his legs. I had to move mine to one side — there wasn't a lot of room under tables when you had two sets of long limbs.

It had been a novelty walking into the diner beside such a tall guy, and I'd seriously enjoyed giving Tori an I-told-you-so look, but once we were seated, it didn't seem to make much difference that Tim was a Tall Boy. He was just like any other guy, except that his legs took up more room.

"So-ooo," Tim said next, puffing out his cheeks on the word, "you into sports?"

"Not unless you count reading as a sport."

"Yeah. Not so much."

"Music?" We must have *something* we had in common.

"Rap?"

"Indie Rock."

More silence.

Tori arrived with our burgers. I would have been grateful for the interruption, but she winked broadly at me and said loudly, "Caught yourself a tall one, then, Peyton? A bacon and cheese burger with fries for you" — she plonked a plate down in front of Tim — "and a bacon and cheese burger with fries for *you*. Wow, you two sure do have a lot in common."

"Bring me another coke?" Tim said. "You want something, Peyton?"

"Nah, I'm good."

"I'll bring just the one," Tori said. "But I'll bring two straws so you can share."

Tim grabbed the ketchup bottle and squirted zigzag stripes over his pile of fries. When his hand hovered over my plate, offering to do the same for me, I squeaked, "No!" and took the bottle, squeezing a neat blob to the side of — but not touching — my fries.

We ate in silence for a while, with me wondering whether this was the most awkward I had ever felt in my entire life and him, no doubt, wondering if I was the most uptight, boring girl he'd ever met in his.

"Peyton," he finally said when he'd hoovered up his burger, "tell me something interesting about you. Surprise me, quick."

"Interesting?"

"Yeah, something that might actually interest me. What is *the* most amazing thing about Peyton Lane?"

He slid even lower in his seat and yawned widely. He obviously wasn't expecting anything too fascinating, which was a good thing, because the most interesting thing about me was not something I wanted to tell anyone, let alone Tim.

"Well?"

"Um, well, I work here — at the diner — and I make a mean double-thick shake." It came out sounding like a question.

"Man, if that's the most interesting thing about you, then your life is sad."

More than he even knew.

"Tell me something interesting about your life, then," I challenged.

"Fine. I have a job, too, and it's way cooler than yours. I'm a spy. A spy for hire."

He was right — this was more interesting.

"Who do you spy on?"

"Anyone in Longford High."

"No way!" I laughed.

"Yes, way. Tell me something you wanna know about the people at our school."

"Okay." There *was* something I needed researched. "I want to know the names of all the males in our school who are six foot three or taller."

"Too easy!" he scoffed.

He extracted a tablet from one of his pockets and started tapping away enthusiastically. For the first time that night, he looked animated — I'd been upstaged by a device.

"I can just run an extract on height. Sort the results from

tallest to shortest, like so. And ... there you go!"

I stared down at the tablet's screen, amazed. There were six names, including that of Longford High's newest tall boy, and one I hadn't thought of when I'd made my list — Robert Scott.

"Mr. Washington is a teacher," I complained.

Tim shrugged. "You said males. Didn't specify age or occupation." He deleted the name. And then there were five. "Want me to send a screenshot to your phone?"

"Sure."

His thumbs tapped a few more keys. "Done."

"Wait — how did you know my number?"

He canted his head and gave me a smug smile.

"I'm impressed," I said. I was also a bit worried — what other information might he have on me?

"Anything or anyone else you're curious about?" he asked.

Oh, yes.

He leaned forward and lowered his voice. "For a very reasonable price, I can, for example, get you the full lowdown on your worst enemy. Or your latest crush — his class schedule, extracurricular activities, relationship status, GPA, when and where he eats lunch, and what his most frequent cafeteria purchase is, the make and model of his car, and plenty more besides."

"You can do that?" I asked, shocked.

"Sure."

"Where do you get all the information?"

"I have connections, informants, access to databases." He made it sound like he was CIA or NSA. "So, is there someone you want me to research?"

"There is this guy …"

I might only share a couple of classes with Jay, but I was forever bumping into him in the hallways, and whenever I went to my locker, he seemed to be there at his. It wouldn't surprise me if he thought I was stalking him in the hopes of wangling another kiss. It was so embarrassing. Every time I saw his head above the throng of approaching students, I fought the urge to duck into the restroom. It would be great to have his schedule so I knew where *not* to be.

"He's not a crush or anything," I said hastily, because Tim's lips were twisted in a knowing smirk. "He's someone I'm trying to *avoid*. I just want his class schedule. It's not like I'm interested in all that other stuff." My ears burned at that last statement, as they always did when I lied.

"Sure, whatever. The full profile comes as a package deal."

"How much?"

"Two crisp C-notes."

"*Two hundred dollars?*"

"Making more bets you won't win and can't afford to pay, Peyton?" Tori was back to collect our plates, even though neither of us had finished our fries.

"Tim's still waiting for his soda," I snapped.

"I didn't want to interrupt the lovebirds. Not when it looks like the date is going so well."

"What bet?" Tim asked. He asked casually, as if he had no real interest in hearing the answer, but now I knew he was an information-collector — and dealer — I had no desire for him to know my secrets.

"Nothing," I said quickly. "Shut up, Tori."

"Yeah, get lost. We're doing business here," Tim said.

"I'm not surprised Ms. Man Hands here has to pay for it," Tori retorted, but at least she left.

I tucked my hands under the table.

Tim asked, "Pay for what?"

"Nothing. And forget about the report — there's no way I can pay two hundred dollars for some information."

He ate some ketchup-covered fries. "I'd like to have your business, Peyton. I'd like to assist you in your boy-avoidance."

"I can't afford your services," I said glumly.

"I prefer hard cash, but I'm open to payment in kind."

In kind — just what did that mean? I squinted at him suspiciously. "I'm not going to sleep with you, Tim."

"Jeez, man! Who asked you to?"

Tori had finally arrived with the soda, just in time to overhear this last exchange. She laughed loudly and said, "No one, that's who. I rest my case."

She thumped the glass down so hard on the table that some coke splashed over the side and onto my plate. My last three fries — the most perfectly brown and crispy ones that I had been saving for last — were now drowned.

Tori gave me an evil smile and sauntered off.

I moved my gaze from the sad, soggy mess on my plate, to the last fry on Tim's. If we were destined for happily-ever-after — or even just for three dates plus the prom — he'd offer me that piece of potato.

He picked up the fry and paused. I leaned forward expectantly, mouth slightly open. "You," he said, pointing the fry at me, "are a cynical so-and-so." He popped the fry into his

61

own mouth, and I slumped back in my seat. "I don't trade information for sex." He paused, frowned, and seemed to rethink what he'd just said. "I mean, I *could*, if you want."

"I don't. No offense."

He nodded. "What I meant was that I'd be happy to trade for a couple of history papers. You write that one on the causes of the second world war for me, plus whatever paper Perez gives us next semester, and in exchange I'll give you a report on your guy."

"I'm hardly a gifted student. I'm happy to get a B- in history." It seemed only fair to warn him.

"'S'cool. Perez'd get suspicious if I suddenly did too well, given that I usually get a C. So, have we got a deal?"

"Yes." We clinked our glasses. "When can I expect the report on your sleazy dealings?"

"Give me a week. No, wait a sec —" Suddenly all business, he checked a planner on his tablet. "I've got a big order due on Friday. Three girls on the cheerleading squad. Let's meet Wednesday after next, before school, in those trees behind the parking lot. You bring the history paper, and I'll bring my report."

"Fine. I'll be the one in the trench coat and fedora, whistling *As Time Goes By*."

"Huh?" he said, clearly mystified.

"It's from *Casablanca*. Because, you know, spies and secret meetings?" He still looked bewildered. "Forget it," I said.

I gave him the name of the subject to be researched, and after that, we lapsed back into a silence which was broken only by Tim ordering a double-chocolate brownie and ice cream, and me calling for the bill before he added any more munchies to my tab.

I was poorer than I had been at the start of the evening, and the tall-boy list now had one less name, but I felt strangely happy as I watched Tim all but lick his plate while I mused on the possible extracurricular activities of Jay Young.

~ 9 ~

The Tall Boys List:
1. ~~Jay Young~~
2. ~~Tim Anderson~~
3. Mark Rodriguez
4. Dylan Jones
5. Robert Scott

J stared down morosely at my list. There were exactly five guys within striking distance that were six foot three or taller. One of them was already a bust, and another had been taken. Feloniously.

I slanted my eyes sideways to glance at the tall boy in question. Jay sat two desks to the left and one row ahead of me in our Psychology class, and on the other side of the classroom in English. Two weeks into the semester, I knew these were the only two classes we shared.

"For this assignment, you need to pick one of the depression or anxiety mood disorders and answer the questions on symptoms, etiology and treatment coherently and thoughtfully. Show me some insight, people!" said Mrs. Evans. "You'll be working in pairs. Let's see, there are twenty-two of you in this class, so that's exactly eleven pairs. Liu, you're number one, Chad, you're two."

Mrs. Evans tapped the shoulder of each student as she assigned them a number and after number eleven, began again at one. If my life was a teen romance, I would've been paired with Jay. But no, Chad and Jay were partners. I got Brooke. She looked about as delighted at being paired up with Sasquatch the Big-Footed as I was at the prospect of working with Brooke the Bronzed.

"Well?" she said as I moved a chair to the opposite side of her desk and sat down. "Depression or anxiety?"

"Anxiety."

"Why anxiety? Why not something more cool, like bipolar depression?"

I crossed my legs. Big mistake. My legs were too long and my knees too high to fit under those desks if I crossed them. My movement briefly lifted the table into the air, tilting the surface and sending Brooke's assortment of colored pens skittering to the floor.

"Oh, crap! Now look what you've done."

"Sorry, sorry," I said, bending over to retrieve the pens.

"They're my special collector's edition of *One Direction* gel pens. And, FYI, they're super-valuable now that the band has broken up."

"Here you go." I handed her the few I'd rounded up.

"Zayn is missing!"

From her panicky tone of voice, I could tell this was a big deal. I searched the floor around us, moved our bags to see if Zayn had holed up there, and bent double to check under the desk. I tried to keep my head well clear of the lumps of gum stuck to the underside of its surface — some of them looked disgustingly fresh and sticky. I was in this awkward position when Jay's face suddenly appeared opposite mine. Startled, I banged my head on the table and judging by the shriek above me, sent the 1D boys scattering in all directions again.

"Hi," said Jay.

"Um, hi."

This close, I could see there were honey-colored flecks in the green of his eyes.

He held up a pen. "Looking for this?"

"Zayn!" I said in relief.

"It's yours?"

"No!" I shuddered. "Definitely not mine." I pointed upwards to where Brooke was doing a head-count of her boys.

"Better reunite the band, then." He offered me the pen. As I took it, our fingers touched, and a soft echo of the kiss-wind passed through me. It was enough to make me jerk and bang my head again.

"Peyton, I swear to God, if you do that again!" Brooke's livid face was at the other side of the table now. "Get out from under there already."

I wanted out, I did — I was getting a crick in my neck from my cramped position — but I couldn't be the first to withdraw because I suspected that my hair was stuck to one of the gum tumors.

"So, bye," I said to Jay.

"Bye." There was a brief flash of that grin before he disappeared.

When I saw his feet retreat, I yanked my head down and out from under the desk. Sure enough, the sharp pinch on the back of my scalp told me I'd left some of my DNA behind in the gum growth.

I handed Brooke her pen and, keeping my gaze from straying to the back of Jay's head, forced myself to concentrate on the psych assignment. A part of my brain, though, was still focused on the list. With numbers one and two struck off, it was time to move on to number three.

Mark Rodriguez, I discovered that Friday afternoon, wasn't into rap music or action movies. Nor was he a sports-mad jock, even though he played football.

He was six feet three inches of sweet and considerate — holding doors open for me, insisting on paying for the first date, and listening when I spoke. He was even kind of cute-looking with his straight black hair and basset-hound eyes.

Our first date at the local Starbucks was ... not bad. We spoke about ethically sourced coffee beans, the effect of caffeine on sleeping patterns, and how he felt about calculus. (He liked it, and that pleased his father.) He knew exactly what he wanted to study when we graduated, because it had always been his life's ambition to be a certified public accountant.

Okay, so our date wasn't a laugh a minute — Mark was kind of serious — but at least we could have a conversation about the same subject. He even seemed interested in my new hobby and complimented me on my first ever home-sewn garment — a blue blouse with super-long sleeves.

"See," I said, holding out my arms, "The cuffs actually reach my wrists, that's a first for me. 'Long sleeves' are always only three-quarters for me."

"I see," he said, nodding thoughtfully. "And you designed and sewed this yourself?"

"I used an existing pattern, but I changed it so that the sleeve was longer, and then sewed it up. What do you think?"

He sipped his decaf vanilla latte. "I don't know much about women's fashion. Or, to be precise, about any fashion. But I think it's commendable that you made this yourself."

"I was getting desperate," I confessed. "One more unsuccessful clothes-shopping expedition, and I'd go certifiably crazy. Maybe give up clothes altogether, and run naked through the streets tearing out my hair."

"That wouldn't solve the problem of too-short sleeves, though, would it?" he said, straight-faced.

I checked his eyes to see whether he was kidding me, but saw no teasing glint there.

I downed the rest of my chocolate iced coffee. "No, I guess not."

"My father says necessity is the mother of invention, and it seems you proved the proverb true." He gave me a satisfied smile.

I could tell Mark was the kind of guy who got a kick from proverbs being proved true.

"Right," I said.

After coffee, despite my protests that it wasn't necessary, he insisted on walking me back to my house. At the front step, he politely thanked me for the date.

"Would you come to the movies with me next Wednesday?" he said.

Wednesday was the day I was getting Tim's report on Jay. The report whose contents were perfectly irrelevant and completely uninteresting to me, except insofar as it would help me avoid him. Today, I'd bumped into him outside the drama room and then again at the lockers. When I'd seen him heading toward his locker, I'd quickly opened the door of my own and hidden my face behind it. I had to bend my knees to do this, and was still half-crouched and gnawing on a knuckle when he peered over the top and grinned down at me.

Insta-blush. Why was he always catching me in embarrassing situations?

"You alright there, Peyton?"

"Yeah?" It sounded like a question.

"You look hungry and ready to pounce. Should I be worried?"

Was he implying that I was planning to jump his bones and devour him?

"Look, I won't ask you for another kiss, if that's what you're worried about," I said hotly.

"Oh, I wasn't worried."

What did that mean? Before I could find the words or the courage to ask, he'd taken a book from his locker and walked off. A soon as I had Tim's report, I could steer clear of encounters like that.

"… a romance or a crime thriller or the latest Batman?" Oh, Mark was asking me something. "Should I fetch you here, from home?"

"No, I'd rather meet you there." I preferred to keep people away from my home, and my mother.

"Of course. Well, goodnight, Peyton."

I was relieved when he made no move to kiss me, but he gazed at me expectantly. Guessing that he wanted to see me safe inside, I searched for an excuse to avoid that.

"Um, I just want to pick a flower for my mother from the back yard, but you go on, Mark. I'll be fine. See you later."

I hurried around the side of the house, already texting Tori the details of the evening with Mark, as she had insisted I do after every date.

"I'm keeping a record so there can be no confusion about whether you've met the terms of the bet," she'd said. "Each time you go out, you need to log the day, date, time, place, and the tall boy's name and height."

I hit send, feeling better than I had after the date with Tim. This time, at least, I was sure there would be a second date with the tall guy, and I hadn't made the mistake of taking him to Jim's.

On Sunday, Chloe came around and, over cups of Cinnamon Surprise which she rated "disappointingly one-noted", she did her calculus homework while I sat at the sewing machine, alternately cursing and coaxing it as I struggled with my latest effort — a pair of skinny pants with extra-long legs, in a black denim patterned with shadowy gray roses.

When they were finally finished, I tried them on, delighted with the hems which reached past my ankles.

"What do you think?" I asked, rotating on the spot.

Chloe tilted her head from side to side, evaluating. "Something's not right."

"It's the pattern on the fabric. I couldn't get the roses to line up on the seams." Not without making the skinny legs wider. There was more to this designing and sewing thing than I'd thought. "And the machine had a seizure, so that's why it's all puckered over here."

"Maybe that's it," said Chloe, shrugging. "Hey, want to come to dinner at our place on Wednesday? It's my dad's birthday, and Mom's planning a special meal. There will be *cake*."

"Tempting, but that's the night of my second date with Mark." I pulled off the jeans and examined the rucked-up hem.

"Think you'll last three dates with him?"

"Sure. He's a nice enough guy."

"Whoa! Don't get carried away by your wild enthusiasm there, Peyton."

"Sorry. He's a *very* nice guy, with excellent manners. And we can talk about things — which is more than I can say for Tim." I'd told Chloe all about that disastrous date.

"And physically?"

"We didn't touch." No kissing *Mark* on the first date. Or before. "He didn't even try."

"Nice, and not a groper. He sounds like a true gentleman and a good guy."

"He is," I said. And then said again, more firmly. "He really is."

There was an unmistakable note of mockery in Chloe's

voice when she said, "I can tell you can hardly wait until Wednesday night."

"Only three more sleeps."

Until Wednesday *morning.*

~ *10* ~

On Wednesday morning, I got to the meeting place behind the parking lot a full eight minutes before Tim did.

Our meeting did have a *Casablanca* feel to it. The smoke from the stoners and smokers skulking between the trees looked like mist, and though Tim wasn't wearing a trench coat or a hat, he did have a cigarette dangling from the corner of his mouth.

"Pleasure doing business with you," he said, when we exchanged manila envelopes.

I couldn't stop to read the report — as it was I'd have to rush to be on time for first-period French — so I ripped open the top of the envelope and pulled out the pages to scan while I strode through the straggling students hurrying toward the back entrance of the school.

Stapled to the top of the thin pile was a page of color images. I recognized a few of them from my totally non-stalkerish internet searches, but two of them were new: one of a small boy wearing a Snoopy costume, complete with floppy beagle ears — so freaking cute! — and a smiling head-and-shoulders shot of him which looked like it had been taken in the school cafeteria. It was a great shot, clear enough to show his freckles, and I examined it carefully, tracing a finger over his nose — slightly crooked at the end, I now noticed — while I walked.

Until I walked into a low-hanging tree branch, banging my forehead, hard. Cursing and blushing, I snatched up the page I'd dropped and shoved it back into the envelope. It would have to wait. I couldn't risk someone seeing, and wondering why I had a collage of Jay pictures. With my luck, the news would get back to him, and he'd for sure think I was after him. Which I most definitely was not.

In French, my plan to hurry through the assigned translation exercise in the hope of earning a few free minutes to study the report backfired. Mme Dumas, who was strolling between the rows of desks murmuring compliments and corrections over her students' work, stopped beside me and tittered, "*Oh la vache*, Peyton, what were you thinking?"

"What?"

"Jam — in the French it is not *un préservatif*. It is *la confiture*."

"It is?" French was always tripping me up like this.

"*Oui*."

"What is *un préservatif*, then?"

"It is," she said, pulling her mouth into a *moue* of regret, "a prophylactic."

I had no idea what that was either, and my face must have shown my confusion, because Mme Dumas explained, "It is a condom, Peyton. What you use so that you do *not* get in a jam. *Comprends?*"

Cue wild laughter from the class and my second embarrassing moment of the day.

"*Oui, Madame*," I muttered.

She found three more mistakes in my work, and by the time I'd made the corrections, the bell was ringing for the end of the period.

I hurried to the classroom a few doors down where Chloe and I had Health. While I waited in the hallway for her to arrive, I carefully extracted the first page of the report and began reading. It was very professional — if Tim could turn in history papers this neat and comprehensive, he'd be acing A's.

PERSONAL REPORT — JAY ANDREW YOUNG

So his initials spelled "Jay" — nicely played Mr. and Mrs. Young, nicely played.

Age: 17 years, 1 month

Birthday: July 30

Star sign: Leo

Oooh, what were Leos like? I had no idea. I'd have to research it later.

Physical appearance:

Height: 6 ft 4"

Ha! I'd been spot-on in my estimate.

Hair: brown

Eyes: green

Uh-huh. That much I could see for myself, Tim.

Weight: 190 lbs. (estimate)

Feet: size 15

Awesome! I'd bet his hands were bigger than mine, too. I'd bet—

"Hey, what are you so absorbed in?" Chloe had arrived.

"Nothing." I hurriedly thrust the report back into the envelope.

"Are you hiding secrets from *me*?" Chloe said, peering up at me suspiciously. "What's in the envelope? It's not a lab report, is it? You're not sick or something?"

"No, of course not."

"Pregnant?" she mouthed, a look of fake horror on her face.

"Funny. Completely LOLious."

"Yeah, with your lack of boy-action, I guess it would have to be a second immaculate conception."

I gave her the look that deserved.

"So what is it, then?"

Chloe made to tug the envelope out of my hand, but I held it up high where she couldn't reach it even if she jumped. There are some advantages to being a tall girl.

"Give it to me!" Chloe demanded, leaping up and down.

"For the first time, I understand the phrase 'hopping mad'," I teased her, holding it higher still.

"Pey-ton!"

"I'll tell you all about it later, okay?"

Just then, I felt a tug as the envelope was pulled from my grasp. I spun around. Tim Anderson stood there, grinning widely and dangling the swinging envelope from his fingers. Beside him stood the very last person I wanted anywhere in the remote vicinity of that report — Jay Young.

"Give it back!" I demanded.

"What, this?" Tim held out the envelope to me, but as I made to grab it, he pulled it back and held it up high. Now I was the one reaching and jumping. And discovering that tall boys also came with disadvantages.

"Tim!"

"Give it back to her," Chloe insisted. "If anyone gets to have that, it'll be me." Then, to me, she said, "Want me to kick him in the shins?"

"Hey, easy, midget," said Tim, and I had to hold Chloe back from attacking him.

Just when I thought things couldn't get worse, they did. Jay, probably trying to be helpful, snatched the envelope out of Tim's hand, and I stopped leaping. Stopped talking. Stopped breathing.

Jay peered at me, a concerned frown furrowing his brows. "You okay, Peyton?"

I couldn't feel the spreading hotness that usually accompanied my blushes, so maybe I'd gone pale — pale with shock and panic and absolute terror that he might look inside the open envelope. Or that one of the incriminating sheets might slide out.

"What happened to your head?" he said.

"What?" My thoughts were still on that report.

"Did you bump it?" He tapped his own forehead and nodded at mine.

I ran my fingers over my face and found a tender lump located square in the center of my forehead. Great. It probably looked like a massive blind pimple.

"I walked into a tree."

"Again?" said Chloe, unsympathetically.

"Can I have that back, please?" I tried to keep my voice casual as I gestured to the envelope.

As Jay made to hand it to me, Tim stretched out a hand to stall him. "Whoa, not so fast, Jay."

Freaking Tim! What an ass. Why had I ever asked him out? What had possessed me to commission a report from him?

"Don't you want to see what secrets Peyton's hiding inside this? What's so all-fired important that she doesn't want us to see?" Tim teased, flicking a finger against the envelope.

"No!" I gasped, glowering at Tim. He was such a douchebag. He was the doucheiest douchebag that ever douched.

Jay merely handed me the envelope. I immediately rammed it deep into my book bag.

"Thanks," I said, giving him a shaky smile.

"What are you still hanging around for?" Chloe said to Tim. "You already got your A in assitude."

Tim just laughed and strolled off, and with a "See you later," Jay followed.

I sagged in relief against the hall wall.

"Can you believe Tim — just snatching your stuff like that?" Chloe sounded so outraged that I felt obliged to point out that she'd been attempting the exact same thing just minutes before.

"Don't judge me by the things I did minutes ago. I've changed since then," she said in a wounded tone. "Besides, I'm your best friend, and he's nobody to you. And you know what they say?"

"I'm sure you'll tell me."

"Sisters before misters," she said as we entered the classroom and took our seats. "That is what they say, Peyton, *sisters before misters.*"

"Right."

"It's like ovaries before brovaries. It means you should share stuff with your girlfriends that you wouldn't with guys."

"Uh-huh."

The teacher was calling the class to order, but Chloe was still pleading from her seat beside me, her eyes boring like lasers into my bag.

"Like secrets and stuff. You shouldn't keep secrets from your bestie," she whined.

"Later, okay? Tonight. Wait, no, not tonight." I was going to the movies for my second date with Mark. "Tomorrow," I whispered.

Her eyes lit up with excitement. "Promise?"

"Promise."

She locked pinkie fingers with me, squeezed tight and hissed solemnly, "Breasties before testes!"

~ *11* ~

Half an hour before my date with Mark that evening, I finally set aside the report on Jay I'd been studying all afternoon. Too lazy to make my way to my mother's room, I sent her a text telling her I was going out.

Going to movies, bye.

Her response: *Who are you going with? What are you going to see?*

There she went again, coming over all concerned like a regular, normal, involved parent — which she so was not. It made me mad, so I ignored her questions and merely replied: *See you later.*

I slung my purse over my neck and across my chest, tossed the rope ladder out of the window and made my way down to the ground.

My phone chirruped.

What time will you be home? It's a school night, so please make sure you're home by 10 pm. Love, Mom.

I ignored that one, too.

Mark was already waiting at the movie theater by the time I arrived.

"Hi, Peyton, how are you?" Mark tended to speak in an unusually formal way. I wouldn't be shocked if one day he bowed and said, "Good evening, Miss Lane. I trust I find you well this eventide?"

Mark glanced briefly at my forehead but was apparently too polite to make any reference to the lump in its center. Unlike Jay. Jay who had an impressive 3.9 GPA, a soft spot for the school cafeteria's grilled chicken and Caesar salad, and who drove a two-year-old Honda Civic. Jay whose current relationship status was "involved". With Faye freaking Fenton. All five foot three of her.

"I've already bought the tickets," said Mark, holding them up proudly for me to inspect.

Batman. Another one? How many versions of the story could there be? I reminded myself that it could've been be worse. It could've been a *Fast and Furious*.

Mark was staring at my jeans — the extra-long pair I'd sewn for myself.

"Are those another of your home-sewn garments?" he asked.

"Yeah. What do you think?"

"I'm not certain."

"Right, so — popcorn? Soda?" I offered.

"Yes, please. A medium popcorn and a medium lemonade. Small isn't quite enough, and I always find that large is too much," he explained. He smiled as he said it, which made me wonder if there was a jokey proverb buried in there somewhere.

"Two medium popcorns, one medium lemonade," I told the girl behind the refreshment stand.

Mark nodded approvingly.

"And one large chocolate milk."

"You're really tall!" the girl said when she handed over my change.

I sighed and handed Mark his snacks. He sprinkled a moderate amount of salt on his popcorn, frowning at my shake-the-salt, tap-the-box, shake-the-salt routine. Then his glance returned to my jeans and, judging by his wrinkled forehead, he wasn't thinking complimentary thoughts about them, either.

"It's the pattern of the fabric," I explained as we headed inside the theater. "I couldn't get the roses to match up — that's why it looks a little messy."

"No, it doesn't look messy."

"Cool!"

"It looks strange."

I looked strange? "Nice to know," I said.

"I think the proportions are wrong," Mark explained as we took our seats. "The legs are too long."

"*My* legs are too long, Mark. That's why I made the jeans extra-length."

"What I mean is, the legs are too long for the top part. It looks lopsided. It makes you look out of proportion."

"Better and better," I muttered.

"It's like a stretch limo. Just making a car longer, without changing the size or shape of the front, only makes it look super-long. That's the first thing you notice about a stretch limo, isn't it? That it's abnormally, disproportionately long.

That's how you look tonight — like a stretch limo."

Mark leaned back in his seat, apparently satisfied with his explanation, and took a slurp of his lemonade.

I had just been told I appeared abnormal, like a disproportionately long stretch limo. And I was thrilled about it. Because I understood exactly what he meant — if I was going to look good in a dress or shirt or pants I made for myself, I'd have to design them differently. I couldn't just add extra length to hems and cuffs. That wouldn't make the garments better, it would only make them longer. They needed to be designed differently, so that the proportions would look flattering on a tall girl like me.

I would have to redo the patterns from scratch.

In the darkened cinema, my thoughts raced. I smoothed a hand over my thigh, imagining the jeans cut differently. A higher waist to balance the leg length? A pair of mom-jeans popped into my mind's eye. Ugh, no. How about a broader waistband, with a wider belt? Or turn-ups to break up the lines of the long leg? Oversized pockets, front and back, with conspicuous stitching to draw the eye up? My fingers itched for my sketchpad and pencil, so I could capture the thoughts and images that chased each other through my mind's eye.

I needed to learn more about how this stuff worked. I wondered whether the local community college offered night classes and what they would cost, and made a mental note to check their website. Of course, there was nothing stopping me from doing some self-study. My mom had stacks of fashion magazines — I'd haul those into my room and pore over the photographs, figure out how garments were supposed to look, analyze the impact of different proportions on the final effect. And surely there would be books on fashion and dress-design in the local library — libraries were free — and I'd watch Project Runway to pick up tips.

I was so lost in my imaginings that I jumped when Mark took my hand in his.

"This part is a little tense," he said.

Did he think I needed to have my hand held through the scary parts? Or maybe *he* did.

On the screen, which I'd been staring at, unseeing, for the last while, Batman was roaring around Gotham City, flames shooting from the exhaust of his Batmobile, growling vengeance at the foes pursuing him. Nothing new there.

Mark gave my hand a slow, reassuring squeeze. His hand was big and soft, and just the slightest bit damp. It made me feel nothing except a slight desire to wipe my own on my jeans. I wondered what Jay's hand would feel like and just like that, my mind snapped back to that report.

His sole extracurricular activity, according to Tim's report, was drama club. He seemed to be quite serious about drama all-round. The printout of books he had borrowed from the school library included: *The Glass Menagerie*, *A Streetcar Named Desire*, *Theater-craft* and, strangely, *Platforms, Pipelines and Petroleum: An introduction to Off-Shore Oil Drilling.*

I knew that he regularly attended Gold's Gym, an expensive place in the upscale suburb where he lived, about three miles south of our own much more modest neighborhood, but he hadn't tried out for any of the school's sports. Tim had it as "confirmed" that Jay had an Achilles tendon injury, and as "unconfirmed" that he'd played quarterback at his previous school. He did attend Friday night football games, but this might have been to watch Faye, who was on the cheerleading squad. Of course she was.

I knew a bunch of facts about Jay, but still felt like I knew nothing. Every fact I read had sparked more questions. Why had he changed schools? What was his family setup? How had he injured that tendon? Did he really like Faye — I mean *like her,* like her? And what did *his* hands feel like?

Mark was squeezing mine again. Looking up at the screen, I was startled to discover that the end credits were rolling.

"Well, I enjoyed that. Did you enjoy it?" Mark asked.

"Sure."

Outside the auditorium, Mark paused to dispose of our empty cups and cartons.

"You know, if being an accountant doesn't work out for you, you could always get a job as a cleaner," I cracked.

"No, no, I'm sure being an accountant will work out fine for me," he said, perfectly seriously.

The problem with Mark was that he was always perfectly serious. The thought came before I could stop it. *No, no, no,* I chided myself. I didn't want to have critical thoughts about Mark. I wanted to have three dates and the prom with him. I didn't want to dwell on how serious he was, how sober and earnest, how utterly lacking in any sense of humor. Mark was a good guy — way nicer than Tim. He was polite and respectful and decent and ... dull.

There was just no getting away from it. He was boring. I felt like I was dating a middle-aged man — no, a middle-aged accountant.

"May I drive you home?" he asked.

"Nah, there's no need to drive me. My house is just a few blocks away. I'll walk."

"Then I'll walk you home."

Feeling guilty because of my unkind thoughts about him, I didn't object.

We walked slowly down the street, holding hands.

"Thank you for your tip about the proportions of garments," I said, to fill the silence. "It's given me something to think about."

"I'm glad I could help. I always find that when you really think about a problem, it definitely helps to find a solution," he said. "As my dad always says: 'If at first you don't succeed, try, try again'."

I made myself smile. Then I said, "Mark, tell me something interesting about you. Surprise me, quick."

He looked taken aback. "Something interesting?"

"Yeah, what's the most interesting thing about you?"

"Hmm, I need to consider that."

He thought for a long while. Perhaps, my inner bitch suggested before I had a chance to mute her, he had to look long and hard to find something interesting.

"Well, okay. This is something rather unique about me."

Hope!

"Yeah? What is it?"

"I've made a little study of the history of accounting."

Despair.

"It started out as a paper for school, but it's become my special hobby. I have quite a collection of books, including a modern reproduction of the original *Summa de Arithmetica* by Luca Pacioli. He was the Franciscan friar and mathematician who invented the double-entry bookkeeping system used by Venetian merchants," he said, and then added, as if he thought this part would truly fascinate me, "In 1494!"

"Right. Wow." It was all the response I could muster.

I learned more than I cared to about old Pacioli and his double-entries on the way home.

When we got to my house, I said, "So, goodnight."

"Thanks for a lovely evening Peyton. I hope we can do this again sometime soon."

"Yeah, sure."

"Next time you can pick the movie. I think that people should take turns in a relationship, don't you?"

We were in a relationship?

"I guess."

Mark took a step closer, leaned forward from the waist, and planted a peck on my cheek. When he drew back, he looked pleased — as if he'd checked off another entry in a relationship bookkeeping column.

"Goodnight then, Peyton. I'll wait here until you're safely inside."

"You really don't need to wait, I'll be fine."

"That's okay, I'm not in a hurry." He seemed planted in the sidewalk.

I walked slowly down the path that led between the overgrown bushes and grass to our front door, then turned and waved from the front step, hoping he'd take the hint. But he merely waved back and continued to stand as solidly immobile as the statue of Pacioli, which — I now knew — stood outside a church in Sansepolcro, Italy.

I unlocked the front door and with a final wave, went inside. Immediately the heaviness of home closed around me. I sighed and texted Tori the details of my second date with Mark. When a peep out of the window beside the door confirmed that he was gone, I made my own way back to my bedroom, moving as quietly and carefully as a cat, so as not to alert my mother.

Just call me Cat Woman.

~ 12 ~

"Saturday night and you're not on a date. Ready to concede defeat?" Tori asked when the early evening rush at the diner had subsided and we had a moment to catch our breaths.

Steve was there, too, wiping the sticky plastic covers of the menus and looking smugly expectant.

"Perhaps you need reminding: I have already had two dates with Mark Rodriguez, the most recent of which was only three days ago. And he is a full six feet three inches tall."

Mark and his family had flown to Texas for the weekend to attend a cousin's *quinceañera*. Mark thought it was important to keep up family relationships with visits like this — not too many and not too few. He also thought routine was a good thing in a relationship, so he wanted a regular Wednesday night date. Fine by me. It wasn't like I was craving more frequent dates with him.

"I like things to be stable and predictable," he'd said. "Besides, I don't think we should rush this relationship. Not too fast, and not too slow. A weekly date should be just right."

Mark was a regular Goldilocks.

"And," I told Tori and Steve now, "our next date — our *third* date, please note — is in four days' time."

Steve's smile soured a little at this news, but Tori was quick to remind me, "Well, good for you, Big P. If date three happens, then you just need to make it to prom."

Prom was in April. That was seven months away. *Seven months* of Wednesday night dates with Mark. I figured it might be easier to earn the money with extra shifts at the diner. But then I'd have to pay *them*, plus put up with Tori and Steve's gloating. And I'd be letting Team Tall down.

"Not a problem," I said, pulling my hair over my hot ears.

I spent the next day going through piles of fashion magazines — studying designs, measuring lengths, and comparing proportions. When my mother saw me lugging a bunch of Vogue magazines upstairs to my room, she followed me to see what I was doing. Then she got all enthusiastic.

"I've got a stack of Harper's Bazaar somewhere, too, I know I have. They have great fashion spreads in there. I'll go see if I can find them," she said excitedly.

"No thanks. I don't need any more magazines. These are enough for now."

I stared pointedly at her and, with a guilt-inducing sigh, she left. I would have felt sorry for her if I didn't feel so damn irritated by her.

The magazines were old — some dated back ten years ago — and so the fashions were outdated. But while the trendy stuff changed radically from season to season, many of the spreads were of timelessly classic designs that I could study to figure out the details of what never really went out of style.

I was beginning to get some concrete ideas for what would work on a taller frame — these models were hardly short, after all — when I was distracted by a feature article on the New York School of Fashion. The school was situated in the heart of New York City's garment district, and it sounded fantastic. According to the article, they offered a two-year associate's or a four-year bachelor's degree, with classes on the basics, like fashion design, fabric styling, draping, sewing, tailoring, and pattern-making, as well as optional credits in more specialized stuff: corsetry, accessory design, and the history and future of fashion.

Did the school still exist? I fired up my old PC and checked in with Professor Google.

As I studied every page on the school's website, a longing began to blossom inside me. Is it possible not to know what you want until the moment you see it? It must be, because now I knew that what I wanted was *this*. I wanted to be *that* student sketching the laced bodice of a steampunk ball gown. I wanted to be that guy pinning the folds of a forest-green coat on a dressmaker's mannequin. I wanted to be the girl in a block print dress and kickass Moto boots pouring over the Visual History of Hemlines.

I clicked on the "Course Fees," and at once my bubble of excitement popped. So much for that dream. They may as well have been asking for a million bucks. My savings seemed pathetically small now — a drop in the ocean of what it would cost to study, and stay, in the Big Apple.

I was so disappointed, so frustrated with the sucky

circumstances of my life and finances, that I'd already clicked on the block to close the site, when I registered what my eyes had seen in the last split second.

Scholarships.

I reloaded the page and read it through carefully. Every year, the school offered one full ride, including tuition and housing, to the financially needy student whose application impressed them most. I read the requirements feverishly. In addition to submitting details of my financial circumstances, I would need to design a full fashion range including shirts, pants, dresses, skirts and scarves, and then submit sketches and a full-size completed example of each garment, along with a written motivation for the theme of the range. And I needed to send it in by mid-January.

My mind raced ahead to all the things I'd have to do. And buy — good-quality fabrics and threads, and gorgeous buttons, buckles, braid and zippers. It wouldn't come cheap. I could try to get more shifts at the diner, but that would reduce my time available to design and sew. Bottom line: I had to win that tall-boys bet, I just *had* to. Eight hundred dollars would restore the damage making the portfolio would do to my college fund. In the meantime, though, I'd start with the sketches and patterns, maybe test-sew a few samples on the cheap stuff from the reject warehouse.

I could do this. If I worked harder than I ever had at anything, and dedicated every spare minute to this project, I could do it. But I'd need help — especially with the theory part of the application. I grabbed my phone.

"I need your expert advice. Can I come over?" I asked Chloe.

"Is this about boys again?" she asked unenthusiastically.

"No, it's —"

"Or that report?"

Chloe had pumped me for all the details and given me a knowing, skeptical eye-roll when I insisted that I had no interest in Jay Young apart from avoiding him.

"*No.*"

"Is it about the auditions on Tuesday? Have you decided to try out?"

"Yes, I'll be auditioning but no, it's not about that. It's about —"

"Because you realize that if Jay is such a theater fanatic, he'll probably want to be in the play? Is that why you're auditioning?"

"No, that's not why. I'm auditioning because an extracurricular activity would look good on my college application, Chloe, not because of some *boy*." I could feel my ears getting hot. "Anyway, that's not what I need your help for."

"Then what?"

"It's about my *future*."

"Please to explain."

"I know what I want to study and where! But I need some help with the scholarship application."

"Ooh, that sounds like a three-cup conversation. Come on over right now, and I'll mix up a tea specially for you."

"Can't we have chocolate milk for a change?"

"Rosemary and peppermint, I think. Rosemary's supposed to stimulate mental focus and clarity," she explained.

"And peppermint?"

"Creativity."

Good. Because in addition to creating designs and writing applications, I'd need to bring my creativity A-game to the play auditions. *And* I'd have to think of imaginative ways of making dates with Mark more fun if our "relationship" was to last all the way through prom.

Which it now absolutely *had* to.

~ 13 ~

Even seated, Jay Young stood out head and shoulders above everyone else.

He and Faye — the top of whose head didn't even reach his shoulder — sat in the second row of seats in the school auditorium. I sat several rows back beside Chloe, who'd come along to the Tuesday auditions to support me.

Ms. Gooding, the senior drama teacher, welcomed the assembled hopefuls and then introduced our student director, Doug Escher. "I believe my students learn best if they're left to stage the production entirely by themselves. This evening, I'll be sitting in while catching up on my marking, and in future I'll pop in from time to time to check how you're coming along, but other than that, I'm handing full responsibility over to Doug."

She headed back to the far corner of the auditorium, and Doug took her place up front.

"*Romero and Juliet,*" he said, "is a modern-day adaptation of *Romeo and Juliet.*"

"*Shakespeare,* man?" Zack, a loudmouthed senior from my

homeroom class, complained loudly from directly behind me.

"I said 'modern day,' Zack. It's not written in Elizabethan English, but the basic story of feuding families and star-crossed lovers is as relevant today as it ever was."

"So, it's a love story?" asked Faye.

"Partly."

"Where's it set?" That question came from Jay.

"If you guys give me half a chance, I'll explain." Doug was getting tetchy. I'd been in productions with him before, and I knew he was gifted at tetchy. "It's set right here in Baltimore. *Modern-day* Baltimore" — this with a significant stare at Zack — "a city that is financially depressed, has high unemployment, and rising tensions between the haves and the have-nots. The Capitanis, our modern-day Capulets, are an obscenely wealthy family who live in a mansion in Roland Park."

Behind me, Zack gave an appreciative whistle. "Man, I need to marry me a Capitani. Sorry, Peyton, you know I like the girls with long legs, but I like the girls with the big bucks more."

"I'll try not to collapse under my disappointment," I murmured.

"Mr. Capitani is a mega-successful captain of industry — the CEO of a massive steel plant. And the apple of his eye is his beautiful, rather spoiled daughter, Juliet. Romero Montagna's family, on the other hand, are working-class stiffs from Washington Village —"

"Pigtown, man!" said Zack.

"— who are struggling to survive tough economic times, which get even tougher when Capitani Steel tries to lay off a third of its workers, including both of Romero's parents. Mr.

Montagna heads up the local chapter of the United Steelworkers Union, and he mobilizes the whole workforce to come out on strike in protest at the layoffs."

"Where's the romance come in?" asked Faye.

"I'm getting there," Doug snapped. "So, it's against this backdrop that Juliet, the pampered daughter of capital, meets Romero, the son of a workers' rights activist, on the beach at Rockfish Point, a tiny seaside town somewhere on the Chesapeake Bay. They fall in love, each not knowing who the other is. And then …"

"The brown stuff hits the fan," said Zack.

"It kinda sounds good, actually," Chloe whispered.

I thought so, too.

"If he's so poor, how come he can afford a holiday at the beach?" asked a petite tenth-grader with blond hair and delicate features.

"He has a summer job as a lifeguard."

"And does everyone still die in the end?" Faye again.

"Nah. We've got to fill this theater for three nights in a row" — Doug gestured to the rows and rows of chairs in the large auditorium — "and that won't happen if we have a Debbie-downer of an ending."

"Romeo and Juliet with a happy-ever-after?" Jay asked. He sounded skeptical.

"That's why I said it was an *adaptation* and not a *version*," said Doug, tetch cranked to the max. "Now, maybe we can get to the auditions? The female roles include Juliet, her mother, her maid and Rosa, Romero's love interest at the start, before he lays eyes on the ravishing Juliet. The male roles are Romero,

Mr. Capitani, Mr. Montagna, Patrice (our Paris), Tyrone (our Tybalt), Matteo (Mercutio, Romeo's best friend). Oh, and the friar — who in our adaptation is a priest. So, four parts for girls and seven for guys."

Typical.

"Why, when there are always way more girls wanting to act in school productions, do the directors always choose plays with more male parts?" I asked Chloe.

"I've got a male part for you, daddy long legs," Zack whispered to me. "Come on over and sit on my lap and I'll show you."

Chloe raised an expectant eyebrow at me. When I said nothing to put Zack in his place, she glared at me and then at him.

"Sexual harassment is unacceptable behavior, Zack. Cut it out! Besides, if Peyton sat on your lap, which will not happen in this lifetime, she'd probably crush you. You must be a foot shorter and a good twenty-five pounds lighter than her."

"Thanks for that, Chloe," I said. "Now I feel loads better."

"I'm stronger than I look, Big P," Zack said. "And you know what they say — all girls are the same height in bed." He cackled loudly at that, and only stopped when Doug, who'd been handing out copies of the audition pieces, began speaking again.

"There are three audition pieces — a dialogue between Romero and Juliet, one between Romero and Matteo, and the last between Juliet and her nurse. I mean, her maid. Choose one piece you'd like to read and prepare it. We start in ten minutes. Any questions?"

"When will we know what part we got?" Faye asked.

"I'll post the cast list on the senior notice board on Thursday morning. Anything else?"

I put up my hand — don't know why, it wasn't like Doug was a teacher. "Um, do the male parts have to be played by males?"

Doug considered for a moment, checking who had turned up to try out, and maybe registering that most of us were female.

"I guess there's no reason why we can't have a female Paris or Tybalt," he said. "But I'm thinking we need to keep Romeo male and Juliet female."

"Scared of controversy?" Chloe asked. Doug merely shrugged in answer.

"Romero and Julio, man!" Zack snickered. "Or, wait, let's get some girl-on-girl action — Ramona and Juliet!"

I scanned the three audition pieces.

"What do you think?" I asked Chloe.

"You could try for the female parts — you never know, you might get one."

"Yeah, don't hold your breath."

My audition went okay, though I felt like a giant Amazon standing next to Wren, the blond sophomore, who was tiny — not even five foot — and pretty, too. She probably looked like a fairy standing beside me. I read for the part of the maid, trying hard not to be distracted by the gestures aimed at me from the "audience". Chloe grinned and waved both hands in the air, giving me a thumbs-up with one hand, and fingers crossed with the other. Zack fondled imaginary boobs on his chest, pointed at his lap and then at me, smiling lecherously all the while. Most distracting of all was Jay, who gave me an encouraging grin just before I began and an approving nod just after.

I stayed to watch everyone's auditions and learned some very interesting things.

Firstly, Faye couldn't act her way out of a wet paper bag. If this were a first-grade concert, she'd have been given the part of a tree, or maybe a rock. No way did she belong in this production.

Wren was a shoo-in for the part of Juliet. Not only could she act well, but every pretty and petite inch of her was perfect for a lovelorn, winsome Juliet. All the boys seemed entranced by her.

Watching her smile flirtatiously as she read a romantic piece with Jay, Zack sighed deeply. "Dayum. Can't beat that level of sexy with a stick."

There was a chance that I might land the role of Mrs. Capitani, but I reckoned I was mostly in competition for the part of Juliet's maid with Liz Cruller, a tubby senior with short red hair who clearly had acting talent.

The last thing I learned was that Jay Young was the best actor I had ever seen in the flesh. Even with mere minutes of preparation time, his performance put the rest of us to shame. Doug gave Jay a standing ovation after his reading and was clearly over the moon at the prospect of finally having a superbly talented male actor to work with.

The director's big problem now, I figured, would be how to stage a production that wasn't lopsided, with one actor being blisteringly good and the rest of the cast looking like hopeless amateurs by comparison.

~ *14* ~

Mark and I had our third date on the evening after the auditions. I could hardly wait to get through it to text Tori the details — news of a third date with the same guy would surely dent her smug conviction that I was undesirable and undatable.

I suggested movies again, because I didn't think I could face hours of Mark's earnest conversation when I was on edge about the cast announcement due the next morning. When he reminded me that it was my turn to choose, I picked a romantic drama set in World War II, so I could check out the period costumes.

Unfortunately, the romantic scenes inspired Mark not only to hold my hand, but also to cuddle me, pulling my head onto his shoulder. I didn't want to hurt his feelings by pulling away too soon, but it was an uncomfortable position to maintain, and I had to stare sideways out of the corners of my eyes to take in the details of padded shoulders, box-cut suits, cinched waists and jaunty berets.

Mark insisted on walking me home again after the movie

and looked mildly concerned at the loud clicks my neck made when I cracked it, trying to get rid of the kinks.

"I'm sure I've read that it's not good to crack your neck," he said.

"Yeah, I guess I should leave the crick-cracking to professional chiropractors."

"I don't approve of alternative health practitioners. Or 'complementary' practitioners, as I believe they prefer to be called. I think it's more sensible to stick to real professionals like doctors and physiotherapists. That's what my dad advises, and I usually follow his advice."

"Right."

"I'd like you to meet my father, Peyton, and my mother. After all, we have had three dates now."

I said nothing.

"I'd like to meet your parents, too," Mark hinted, looking hopeful.

"My parents are divorced," I said quickly. "I hardly ever see my father."

"You live with your mother?"

I nodded. I did not like where this chat was headed.

"Maybe I could come in when we get to your house and meet her?"

"No."

Mark looked a little affronted. "You don't want me to meet her?"

Yes. "No, it's not that, it's just that she's ... sick." No word of a lie. "And I don't want to disturb her when she might be resting."

This appealed strongly to Mark's considerate common sense. "Of course, I fully understand. My father says when people are sick, they need peace and quiet to recover properly. Tell her I hope she gets better soon."

"Sure, okay." Anything to shut down this conversation. "Hey, did you hear the joke about the germ?"

"I don't believe so."

"Never mind, I don't want it spread all over."

No response from Mark.

"Ba-dum-tsss!" I said, hitting an imaginary drum and cymbal in the air. "That's it. That's the joke."

"Ah, I see — because germs are contagious. Is that it?"

"Yes, Mark, that's it."

"You're very amusing, Peyton." Mark laid his hands on my shoulders, gazed down seriously into my eyes, and announced, "I would like to kiss you now. Is that okay?"

Oh, dear.

"I guess."

Perhaps his kiss would spark something inside me. Perhaps it would be lively or wild or fun.

But no. It was just moist.

There was no surge of tingles, no impact on my breathing, no rushing wind in my head. It was nothing like it had been with Jay. Damn, there he was in my head again. Trying to get my head back in the present, I returned Mark's kiss. Returned it with interest. I pressed my lips firmly against his, wrapped my arms around his neck, and pushed up against his body.

Instantly, his kiss got moister — wet to the point of sloppy. And immediately, I felt just awful. Because, judging by his groans and his body's reaction, which I could clearly feel against mine, Mark seemed to be enjoying this. And I … wasn't.

He lifted his head, took a deep breath, and kissed me again. This time I did feel something, a bunch of somethings, actually — mild revulsion, an urge to push him away and run off down the path to my house, anxiety about how I was possibly going to be able to ride this out until prom, and guilt. Crushing guilt that I was just using Mark to win the wager when I already knew I had absolutely zero romantic feelings for him. Guilt that he might be falling for me in a thoroughly unsensible and immoderate way, and that it might hurt him if he found out how I truly felt.

I pulled away, gabbled, "Oh look at the time. I'd better hurry," and set off quickly in the direction of home.

"Of course," Mark said, his voice full of understanding. "You must be worried about your mother."

"Yeah." Let's go with that.

"I worry about my mother, too. She works too hard. I keep telling her she needs a better balance between work and home life, but she says her work is too important to take it easy." Mark shook his head and tutted at his mother's immoderate attitude.

"What work does she do?"

"She's a particle physicist."

"Wow!" Mrs. Rodriguez sounded way more interesting than her son.

"What does your mother do?" Mark asked.

"She works from home. She's a virtual assistant for an outdoor adventure crowd." Was anyone ever less suited to their line of work? "But your mother's job — that's impressive."

"Yes, that's true. But it's also a bit of a bummer really."

"Why do you say that?"

"She's managed to secure the position of a lifetime to work on the Large Hadron Collider."

I must've looked blank, because he continued, "You know, it's the largest machine in the world, it smashes particles together at near light-speed in the hope of finding the God Particle and understanding the nature of the universe."

"But that's amazing!"

"Yes, but it's going to take years. And that means that our whole family will be moving to Switzerland. My father says —"

"Wait, Switzerland?" I interrupted. "You're moving to *Switzerland?*"

"Yes. To Geneva, to be precise."

"When?"

"My mother takes up her position in November, but my father thinks it would be more sensible for my sister and me to finish the semester. So the rest of us will follow in December."

"But, but ... *December?*" That meant that by April, by prom to be precise, Mark would be in Ge-freaking-neva.

"Yes, there are implications for our relationship." Mark frowned and gave my upper arm a consoling squeeze.

"But what about school? Wouldn't it be better for you to finish your senior year right here?" I protested. "They probably have a completely different school curriculum in Switzerland, you'd have to start from scratch."

I'd have to start from scratch — and there were only two more names left on the tall boys list.

"I'll finish my senior year at the American International School in Geneva, so the curriculums are perfectly compatible. Though, of course, I'm expecting a period of adaption to acclimate to the different culture and, naturally, I will miss my Wednesday dates with you." Mark gave me a sad smile.

"Will you at least be coming back for the senior prom?" I asked desperately.

Mark chuckled. It was the very first time I'd heard him laugh, and I hadn't been joking.

~ *15* ~

The Tall Boys List:
1. ~~*Jay Young*~~
2. ~~*Tim Anderson*~~
3. ~~*Mark Rodriguez*~~
4. *Dylan Jones*
5. *Robert Scott*

Wednesday nights were no longer date nights with Mark.

I'd weaseled out of the relationship by suggesting that if we took it any further, it would only make the upcoming separation harder. I'd tried to do it gently, but maybe some of my relief at not having to date him anymore showed, because Mark looked hurt and asked, "But don't you want to spend our remaining time together? Don't you like me?"

I felt like a complete cow. When I'd asked him out, I hadn't stopped to consider what his feelings might be, or might become. It had been wrong to use him like that. Mark was a good guy. He deserved better.

"Of course I like you. You're a really likeable guy. It's just that I think it wouldn't be sensible or responsible to continue when we know this relationship will need to end before you leave."

"There's truth in that," Mark said, blinking away a tear. "Long-distance relationships seldom work out, my father says."

I'd given him a kiss on the cheek and slouched off, resolving that I'd give the next guy one date, and if I wasn't interested in him, I'm come clean about the bet and take it from there.

I gave myself permission to take a couple of weeks off from dating. It would seem heartless to ask another boy out when I'd only just ended "the relationship" with Mark, and besides, I had plenty of time to get a couple of dates in before prom. Also, my mind, my eyes, and other parts of me, were undeniably preoccupied with the feloniously filched number one. Because Wednesday nights were now dedicated to *Romero and Juliet*.

At our first rehearsal, on the last Wednesday in September, Doug made us sit in a circle of chairs in the center of the stage.

"Tonight, we'll just do a read-through."

Not wanting Jay to think I was putting the moves on him, I took the chair farthest away from him, realizing too late that this put me directly opposite him, where I could avoid neither feasting my eyes, nor catching his. Wren, who had of course been cast as Juliet to Jay's Romero, took the seat beside him — a move which Faye observed with narrowed eyes from the front row of the auditorium. Even seated, Wren was elf-like. Her tiny feet in their delicate pumps didn't reach the floor, and the top of her head was only as high as Jay's armpit. So now even Romeo and Juliet were breaking the Law of Tall Girls.

Zack, who'd landed the part of Matteo, claimed the seat on my right and immediately began making cracks about how much he'd always wanted to sleep with a member of the clergy. Because I'd got the part of the friar.

Of course I had.

As soon as I told Chloe, she'd warned me that I'd have to be careful not to look longingly at Jay.

"That would just be all kinds of wrong," she'd said, pulling a face.

The cast had a different reaction to me being cast as clergy. They got sidetracked on a debate as to whether the friar could be a female part.

"Peyton's not a friar in my version," Doug pointed out. "She's a priest."

This was met with a chorus of protests that there were no such thing as female priests, even in twenty-first-century Baltimore.

"Fine. She's the local community's nondenominational religious-leader-type person. Happy?"

"The local community's nondenominational religious-leader-type person — that'll fit easily in the program's cast list," I muttered.

Doug, who was handing out scripts, didn't hear, but Jay must have, because he snorted a laugh.

The read-through went well. Jay was exceptional. He'd have every female — and a fair few males — in the audience swooning by intermission. Zack surprised us all by bringing a rough energy to his reading, which galvanized the character of Matteo into life. Liz, although apparently unable to resist sending me regular gloating glances, read the part of the maid with impeccable comic timing.

Wren seemed set to play Juliet as a sweet and gentle victim of circumstances, rather than as a spoiled rich brat. She nodded and smiled prettily at Doug's encouragements to inject more petulance into the character, and carried on reading precisely as before. I caught Jay's eye after one of these charming refusals to take direction, and judging by his grin, he'd noticed it, too.

At the end of the rehearsal, Doug said, "You guys are great!"

He seemed relieved, but his pleasure faded when we tried to set a rehearsal schedule that didn't interfere with anyone's studying or SAT test dates.

"Fine!" he said eventually. "We'll meet three weeks from today, on the twenty-first of October, and we'll be rehearsing both Wednesday evenings and Saturday afternoons from then on. Anyone who can't commit to that had better quit now." Doug stared at each of us fiercely.

Zack answered for all of us. "Chillax, man, we'll be there."

"Make sure you know your words for Act One."

At the next rehearsal, however, not a single member of the cast knew their words. Not even close. That was the first thing that irritated Doug. I was the second.

He started the rehearsal by getting each of us to walk around the stage in character.

"Slowly, Liz, the maid is an old woman."

"Lovely, Wren!"

"A bit more snooty, Angela."

"Perfect, Jay, that's great!"

"Keep your hands to yourself, Zack!"

Doug immediately disliked the way I moved. He had me stand, sit and shuffle about the stage for ten minutes, growing more frustrated by the minute.

"It's just that I imagined the friar —"

"The nondenominational religious-leader-type person of unspecified gender," I corrected.

"Don't start with me, Peyton."

"Sorry."

"I imagined him — her — being a bustling sort of character, always in a flurry of movement, scurrying here and there."

"Yeah, and?"

"But when it comes to hurrying and scurrying across the stage, you just look, I don't know, wrong. I think it's just because you're too ..." He twisted his mouth in an expression of dissatisfaction.

"Tall?" I suggested.

"Yes. Sorry. You're just too tall to bustle about."

"Perhaps if I played it differently? I could be more serious and stalk about slowly. Less like a funny friar, more like a grim and sober monk." I adopted a serious, pensive expression and took a few slow strides across the stage.

Doug's expression lightened. "That just might work. Okay, you practice the monk-walk while I work with our lovers. Romero? Juliet?" he yelled.

Jay and Wren were the third thing that ratcheted Doug's mood from cranky to a state somewhere between *this-cast-is-*

going-to-be-more-difficult-than-I-thought and *what-the-hell-have-I-let-myself-in-for?*

As Doug blocked Romero and Juliet's first scene, the rest of the cast sat in the auditorium, watching. And sniggering. Because now everyone could see what had been obvious to me, even when we'd all been seated for the read-through.

"Man, Jay is ta-all!" Zack said.

"You could say that Wren is short," I replied.

"Say it any way you like — they don't fit, man."

That was because they were breaking the Law of Tall Girls. Which existed, as I regularly reminded Chloe, for good reasons.

"It *is* a bit of a mismatch," said Angela.

"Bit of a mismatch?" Zack sniggered. "Only couple that'd be more mismatched would be, like, Hagrid and Dobby, man."

Everyone laughed at that, earning a glare from Doug, who was directing proceedings from right up close to the stage.

"Would you lot keep it down? I'm trying to *direct* here," he snapped, then turned back to the couple on stage. "Wren, why are you looking up at the sky on that line? It doesn't work."

"I'm not looking at the sky, I'm looking up into Jay's eyes."

"Only time she'll be able to look directly into Romeo's eyes is when she's on the balcony and he's on the ground," Angela said.

"Will you shut up?" Doug barked in our direction, but his face appeared more worried than mad. We'd all seen the set that was being cobbled together backstage, and the balcony was low enough to make Angela's prediction a distinct possibility.

"You'll just have to cheat the sight-line," Doug told Wren. "Look at his chest and maybe take a step back from him so it's not so obvious."

"Hmm. A pair of star-crossed lovers that can't come within a yard of each other," Liz whispered. "This should end well."

"How are they going to, you know, kiss?" I asked.

"Maybe he could sit and she could stand?"

Angela shook her head. "It's not just that he's taller, it's that he's so much *bigger*. She's tiny as a fairy next to him."

"Yeah. If they got some action on, he'd crush her," Zack said.

Liz nodded. "And she looks too young."

"Juliet was only thirteen or fourteen years old in the original," Angela said.

"Yeah, but Wren's so tiny that she looks even younger than that," Liz replied.

"Bottom line, Jay looks like a man, and she looks like a little kid," Zack said. "We ain't careful, we gonna have us some *real* controversy."

We all stared at the couple on stage. Faye, sitting across the aisle from me, leaned forward in her seat and glared at Wren as Romero and Juliet snuggled in close, rotating on the spot in a romantic slow dance. They were each supposed to speak their lines over the other's shoulder every time they faced the audience, which — in theory — was a great staging idea. In practice, it just didn't work.

Wren's lines were completely muffled because her face was nestled up against Jay's sternum, and even on tiptoes she couldn't speak over his shoulder. Worse, every time Jay's back was to the audience, Wren was completely masked by his body, so that it looked like he was dancing alone. Everyone cracked up laughing again, sending Doug into a frenzy.

"Shut up! SHUT UP! It's not an effing comedy — why are you all laughing? It's not funny."

"Not funny? I am sorry to inform you, Mr. Director, but you have a serious case of the wrongs," said Zack.

"The thing is," Angela said, her voice all tactful, "they don't really fit together."

"That's often a problem when really tall guys hook up with short girls," I added, unable to resist the opportunity to educate the cast about one of the basic laws of the universe.

"So, it sometimes looks a little, well … funny," Angela finished.

Jay and Wren had stopped their revolving and stood, staring down at us.

"Any ideas?" Jay asked Doug.

"I've got an idea," said Zack. "We need to shuffle the cast a little. First off, you should make me Romero, man, I'd be a much better size for our Juliet." Zack leered at Wren and added, "I'd be the *perfect* size for you, babe. I'm getting a tent in my pants at the thought of it."

"Would someone just get this boy a leg to hump already?" Liz said, smacking the back of Zack's head.

"So, if you're Romero, where does that leave me?" Jay asked.

"You can be Mr. Capi, and then Peyton can be Mrs. Capi — you and the Big P are a good height match, so you won't look funny as a couple."

Well, yes, my feelings exactly. So exactly that I could feel my cheeks going pink. I studiously avoided looking at Jay.

"What about me then?" asked Angela.

"You can be the nurse," said Zack, on a casting roll now,

"and Liz can be the holy woman. There you are — sorted!"

"Zack, you're making me crazy," said Doug.

"You've gotta admit, recasting would make it look better, man."

"Maybe it would *look* better, but …"

I knew what Doug was thinking. Either he had to put the best actors into the lead roles, but risk the audience rolling in the aisles at the physical mismatch and awkward staging, or — having finally found a high-school boy who could bring energy, poignancy and freaking epic acting skills to the role of Romeo — he'd have to waste him on a bit part.

"I'll discuss it with Ms. Gooding," Doug said. "See what she thinks."

Faye didn't look enthusiastic about anyone playing next to Jay, as either his star-crossed lover or his wife. I figured she'd have preferred the play staged in real Elizabethan style, with boys playing the parts of girls. As soon as rehearsal ended, she latched back onto Jay.

"Let's go. Now."

She grabbed his arm and steered him down the aisle, no doubt wishing they were in a church rather than a theater, all the while whispering urgently into his ear. He pulled away from her when they reached the exit, and shoved the door open much harder than was necessary.

I may have been deluded by wishful thinking, but it looked a lot like they were fighting.

~ 16 ~

The Tall Boys List:
1. ~~*Jay Young*~~
2. ~~*Tim Anderson*~~
3. ~~*Mark Rodriguez*~~
4. *Dylan Jones*
5. *Robert Scott*

*L*ife's for learning — that's what Chloe says.

What I learned that Saturday morning doing my mother's and my laundry at the Wishy-Washy down the street from our house, was that the cheap fabric of my newly sewn garments didn't stand up too well to the rigors of machine-washing.

"You should've used cold water. And a handful of salt to set the color," the woman who worked in the laundromat said.

"Right, thanks." For the super helpful tip given half an hour too late.

The black dye on my rose-print jeans had run, so that the pattern was now merely an indistinguishable series of gray smudges, and my blue cotton top had shrunk so much that I doubted even Wren would be able to fit into it.

"I'll remember that for next time," I said, not looking at the woman. She had a tuft of hair on her throat that always drew my eye, and I didn't want to make her uncomfortable by staring.

She, however, had no such reservations. Every time I came to do laundry, she stared at me as if I was a giraffe in a rabbit hutch, and commented on my height.

"Are your parents tall?" she asked that day.

"Sure."

"Are you a model?"

"No." I was never flattered by the question — people leapt to the idea only because of my height.

I bent over double to shove the wet laundry into the dryer. While the clothes tumbled about inside, probably shrinking even more, I *eeny-meeny-miny-moe'd* over the two names remaining on the Tall Boys list. I should probably have chanted a spell or sacrificed a baby goat — anything to improve my dating luck. *Catch a tiger by the toe.* My finger landed on Dylan Jones.

Dylan was a skinny, slouchy junior who always looked so surly that I gave myself permission to ask him out over the phone, rather than in person. I got his number from information, crossed my fingers and dialed. Then hung up as it started to ring. I cursed myself and called again.

"Yeah?" The voice on the other end radiated surl.

"Dylan?"

"Yeah."

"This is Peyton Lane."

"Who?"

"Peyton Lane? I'm a senior at Longford High?"

"Yeah?"

"I wanted to know if you'd like to go out sometime."

"What?" Could this guy even string two words together?

"Like on a date. You, me, maybe a movie?" A movie would be better than any setup where we'd need to talk. Dylan was no chatty-Cathy. "A date."

"Hah." It wasn't a laugh. More like a sneery, surly exhalation of breath.

"Well?" Now I was doing the one-worders. Perhaps it was contagious.

"Huh?"

"Would you. Come out. On a date. With me?"

"Yeah?" Was he agreeing, or was he just falling back on his default-setting utterance?

"Yeah? You'll come?"

There was a rustling sound down the line, then, "Who is this?" The words — *three* of them in one go — as well as the female voice were a clue that Dylan had been relieved of the need to make more conversation.

"Who is *this*?" I countered.

"I'm the person who wants to know why you're talking to Dylan."

"Date," I heard Dylan mutter in the background.

"She's asking you out on a date?" Then loudly, right into the phone, "You're asking him out on a *date*?"

"Yeah."

"And who exactly are you?" There was a tone of real aggression in her voice now.

"Um, Sully." The toy's name was the first that popped into my mind.

"Well, Sally, I regret to inform you that Dylan is well and truly taken."

"Taken?"

"Yes, taken. By me. We are, in fact, dating. So back the hell off, bitch!"

Strike three. I drew a line through Dylan's name on the list.

It was too soon to panic — there were still five months before prom. But there was only one name left on that list of rare specimens.

⁓

At the start of that afternoon's rehearsal, Doug clapped his hands to get our attention and said, "Listen up, I've got something important to tell you. I've discussed it with Ms. Gooding" — he nodded in the direction of the drama teacher, who, tonight, again sat in the back corner of the auditorium — "and after lots of thinking and agonizing, I've decided to recast the play."

"Yes!" Zack pumped his fist in the air. "Just call me Romero. Hey, Wren, I think we need to get to know each other a whole lot better to amp up our onstage-chemistry. Are you free tonight?"

"Not so fast, Zack. You're still playing Matteo," Doug said.

Zack's face crumpled in disappointment. "But —"

"You're too good in the part. No one else could do it as well as you."

"When you put it like that … I mean, I *am* good." He glanced around for confirmation.

"You're awesome, Zack. The very best," said Liz, deadpan.

"So, what roles *have* been changed?" Jay asked.

"You'll be glad to know, I'm sure we'll *all* be glad to know, that you're still Romero, Jay."

Jay blew out a breath, grinned and said, "Cool. Thanks."

"It was the girls' parts I had to shuffle." Doug cleared his throat nervously and then said very quickly, "So Wren will play the maid, Liz will play the friar-person, and Peyton's Juliet."

"Come again?" I could not have heard right. "What was that?"

"Yeah," said Wren, looking grumpy. "Run that by us again."

"You're the maid, Liz is the nondenominational religious-leader-ty —"

"And who's Juliet?"

"Peyton," said Doug, with an expression that looked like a wince.

"Me? *I'm* Juliet? You want me to play a girl part? You want me to play the freaking lead? Opposite Jay?"

I glanced across at Jay and found he was already watching me, nodding slowly and smiling slightly, as if he thought this might not be the most absurd idea ever suggested in the history of theater.

"Yes. You can act well, I know that from past years. I mean, I've never actually seen you play a part written for a woman," he qualified, "but I'm sure you can do it. And, of course, there's the all-important physical match. You're the perfect height to play opposite Jay."

"Huh." For once in my life — for perhaps the very *first* time in my life — my height had landed me something good.

Emotions tumbled around inside of me, like the tangled clothes in the dryer this morning. I was proud to be trusted with a great role for once, thrilled at the challenge of such a fantastic part, excited to play an honest-to-God woman for a change. But I was also terrified. Could I pull it off? Judging from the skeptical looks being directed my way, most of the cast had some serious doubts about my ability — even Doug didn't seem entirely convinced.

"I wanted to play Juliet," Wren told Doug, blinking tears away and pouting prettily.

"You're an awesome actor, Wren. But you're in tenth grade, and you've got another two years to play great lead roles. Jay's a senior, so it's his last chance. And I'm sorry, but the two of you look plain wrong playing next to each other. But," Doug said, "I've added some extra lines for you, and I have some great ideas about how you can play her in an amazing new way."

Wren sniffed, but looked mollified. "Okay," she said. "I guess."

"Liz, you okay with playing the friar-type person?"

Liz shrugged. "I get to poison the popular boy — what's not to like?"

"Jay, you okay with the changes?" Doug asked.

"Sure, yeah. Let's do this, Peyton!"

My stomach flipped over as I realized what playing opposite Jay would mean. Hours spent rehearsing together, murmuring romantic lines to each other, gazing into his eyes and having him stare longingly back. Kissing!

I felt my body stiffen with rising panic. I, the girl infatuated with Jay, was going to play the part of a heroine head over heels in love with Romero, but not let Jay, the boy dating Faye, realize how I felt about him in real life. I'd be acting offstage as much as I was onstage. How the heck was I going to manage it?

My panic must have shown on my face, because Doug said encouragingly, "You can do it, Peyton. You can. And Jay will help you. We'll do whatever it takes — extra rehearsals with just the two of you, trust-building exercises, private sessions for body work."

Zack sniggered. I stared at Jay and swallowed hard. He chuckled.

"Right, let's begin all over again with a first read-through, this time with everyone in their new roles," said Doug.

Once again, we arranged a circle of chairs on the stage, but this time I sat down next to Jay, instead of on the other side of the circle.

"You okay, Tiger Eyes?" Jay said softly when I perched on the seat beside him. "You look a little freaked out."

"I'm okay," I croaked.

Trying to avoid looking at him, I stared instead at his left hand, which lay relaxed on his thigh. It was a big hand, bigger than mine — I was sure of it. His fingers were long and his nails short, and the skin on the back of his hand had a sprinkling of freckles like the ones on his nose.

"Peyton?"

I turned to look into those olive-green eyes. Felt my stomach flip again. How was I going to do this without melting into a puddle every time he looked at me? How was I going to hide my feelings to avoid humiliating myself and embarrassing him?

"You don't have to worry. I promise I don't bite."

He didn't need to bite. Just his smile was enough to unbalance and befuddle me.

~ 17 ~

I was stuffing my backpack with everything I'd need for the day — a jacket, my dog-eared and annotated *Romero and Juliet* script, my almost-empty wallet — when my mother knocked at my bedroom door.

"Oh, are you going out?" she asked when I let her in.

"I'm helping Chloe with her Halloween stall at the farmers' market this morning, and then I've got rehearsal this afternoon, and work tonight."

"Are you okay for lifts?"

"Yes." What would she do if I said no?

"It's such a pity you have to work on Halloween."

"Yup."

"I suppose you'd rather be at home, working on your sewing projects?" She moved over to my sewing machine and picked up a couple of the pieces from the old patterns to examine more closely. "You're very clever to be able to make head or tail out of these."

Making an effort to do it gently, I took the pattern pieces out of her hands and slid them back into their correct envelopes, before they could get lost. I wished my mother would stay away from my stuff, or even better, from my room. These mother-daughter chats were all kinds of awkward and uncomfortable. We had nothing to say to each other. Or, rather, she had a never-ending stream of nothings to say, and I had so much to say that I didn't dare say anything, in case everything came pouring out.

"But then you always had clever fingers — even as a little girl you loved making clothes." She paged through my sketchbook, smiling at the places where, instead of fabric, I'd cut patterned candy wrappers, fall leaves and old gift-wrap into the shapes of garments for my sketched models.

"I did?"

"Yes, don't you remember? You were just a tiny little thing, and you used to make clothes for your dolls and toys. You'd make dresses for your Teddy and Barbie out of dishcloths. And hats out of paper and tissues and such. Dressing them up was your favorite game, and even back then you had a real flair for it."

"Did I sew the clothes?" I asked, interested in spite of myself.

"I think it was more scotch-tape and rubber bands than sewing, but I could check, if you like? I've got all your old arts and crafts safely stored in the basement." Her face lit up at the idea of unearthing the old treasures. "And, of course, I still have Teddy." Her smile faded.

"Have you eaten breakfast?" I asked.

"I had two Snickers bars, does that count?"

"Snickers? For breakfast?"

"I opened the package of Halloween candy I bought for tonight, and I just couldn't resist."

"You know chocolate makes your asthma worse. You've got to take better care of yourself."

"Are *you* nagging *me* about nutrition?" she asked, smiling wryly. "Just who's the mother around here?"

Good question.

"Anyway, having sampled it, I can confirm that it's great candy, not cheap knockoffs. The trick-or-treaters are going to love them. And I got an excellent last-minute deal for a bulk package."

I knew she was only trying to make conversation, but I had neither the time to hear about how she planned to feed other peoples' children, nor the patience to hear about her online shopping expeditions.

When I made no response, she asked, "Did you hear what I said about the bargain I got on the candy?"

"What do you want — a medal for spending more money we don't have?"

"You're so hard on me, Peyton," she said, eyes brimming with tears.

I wished she'd get mad at me, instead of sad. I suspected I needled her precisely to provoke her temper, but if so, the effort was futile. She never got mad, never shouted at me, or confiscated my phone, or grounded me. She just let me hurt her and then looked at me with wounded, liquid eyes. Which only annoyed me even more. I wanted to grab her by the shoulders and shake her until her teeth rattled, shout, "Wake up!" I wanted to shock her or scare her, or infuriate her back into life. But whatever I did only seemed to make things worse.

I had to get away for good before I damaged both of us beyond fixing.

"What did I ever do to make you so angry?" she asked. She made no move to wipe away the tear trickling down her cheek.

"It's more what you *didn't* do."

"What do you mean?" She seemed truly puzzled. Was she really that clueless, so wrapped up in herself?

"Mom, I don't even know where to begin."

Luckily, I didn't have to, because just then a distinctive three-beat honk sounded from outside. Saved by the horn.

"That's Chloe, I've got to go."

As I swung over the windowsill, I caught a last glimpse of my mother standing in the center of my perfectly neat room, still clutching the sketchbook. She looked forlorn and something more — lonely, perhaps. I felt a pang of guilt, or perhaps compassion.

"I'm sorry. I didn't mean to make you miserable," I said. "Save some chocolate for me, and we'll have a midnight feast when I get home from work, okay?"

She gave me a smile so pathetically grateful, I immediately felt even more guilty. And irritated. I was at least as bad a daughter as she was a mother. We made quite the dysfunctional pair, her and me.

The farmers' market was cute — wooden stalls, straw bales, carved pumpkins, orange bunting, and wandering minstrels playing flutes and tambourines. Small children, their faces painted to resemble skeletons, witches and kittens, raced up and down the aisles, and excited dogs burrowed into the raked piles of fall leaves.

Chloe's stall was a perfect picture of stomach-turning Halloween treats: witches' fingers made from green-frosted sponge cake, with slivered almond nails; slippery jello worms; chocolate spiders; brownie graves pierced with white chocolate RIP tombstones, and red-velvet cake pops decorated to resemble bloodied eyeballs.

"Where did you find the time to make all these?" I asked when I saw the full range displayed on the skeleton-print tablecloth. I knew Chloe's school workload was at least as heavy as my own.

"My mom made most of these."

Must be nice.

"But I sprinkled the shredded coconut on the spiders' legs," Chloe added proudly.

"Good job — they're almost too revolting too eat." Almost. I'd already gobbled one that had lost a few legs in transport. "And you can tell your mother they're delicious."

A little kid dressed as a bandaged mummy came over to inspect the goods. "How much are they?" he asked, with a nose-clearing snort.

"A dollar each." Chloe tapped the sign which showed the price.

"A *dollar*?" he whined.

"But I'll do a special price, just for you — three for two dollars."

"Three for two?" Another phlegmy sniff.

"Just for you," Chloe confirmed, "because you're special."

"Well, I don't know." The kid leaned over the spiders, and I expected at any moment to see mucus drip onto their hairy legs.

"You strike a hard bargain, sir," Chloe said. The kid grinned at that and nodded so vigorously that a bandage on his head began unraveling. "Tell you what, if you buy two, I'll throw in one for free!"

"For free?"

"Yes."

"I'll take two spiders and one grave," the kid said.

"You got it, sir!"

When he walked off, already happily dismembering the spider, I laughed. "You're a natural-born seller."

Chloe had said she was selling the Halloween treats to add to her college fund, but it was clear from her smiles and glowing face that she was also doing it for the sheer fun and challenge of the to-and-fro selling game. Through the course of the morning, I saw her make several just-for-you deals and special offers, and wondered how many online sites were suckering my mother with similar lures.

"The trick is to package the pitch just right for each customer. You want them to think they got a real bargain, but you still want to make a healthy profit for yourself," Chloe said, after getting a harassed-looking father to buy a dozen brownie graves for ten dollars.

"As ways of making money go, this standing around in the sunshine and sampling the wares sure beats waitressing at the diner. Especially since Tori and Steve are still on my case."

Every time we drew the same shifts, they hassled me about my lack of progress on the dating scene. I was still determined to win the bet. Apart from the minor issue of winning — or losing — eight hundred dollars, there was the fact that, with every long fiber of my tall being, I did *not* want them to be proved right. Because that would be me being proved right, too. Deep down, I didn't think guys liked Amazons either.

"Though, to be honest, I'm so busy between school, work and rehearsals that I don't know when I'd find the time to date anyway. I'll wait until January before I put the moves on Robert Scott. That'll give me three months to wangle three dates out of him, and maybe my luck will be better next year."

"It's a pity I don't know of a love potion tea that we could slip into *someone's*" — here Chloe gave a loud cough that sounded a lot like the word *Jay* — "water bottle, so that he'd fall for you."

"He's still seeing Faye," I said, staring glumly down at the eyeballs. They stared back, reminding me of her — how she sat front and center at every rehearsal, watching Jay's every move and giving me filthy looks.

"Rehearsals must be majorly awkies."

"You have no idea."

"Want to talk about it?"

"What I want to do is check out some of the other stalls. You okay on your own for a while?"

"Run free, little one!"

~ *18* ~

I meandered through the market, admiring a display of hand-wrought pewter jewelry and another of blown-glass baubles shimmering with iridescent colors in the October sunlight, and tasting the delicious samples set out at the food stalls. It was a treat, for a change, to taste something that hadn't been cooked in a microwave. A girl could get real tired of TV dinners.

But the stall that held my attention was one called *Past Times*, which stocked vintage clothing — some old military uniforms, a fifties-style flared skirt in pink taffeta, a double-breasted box-jacket with brass buttons, and even a white, tasseled flapper dress from the 1920's. All the garments were gorgeous. The colors, textures and lines of the fabric invited my hands to touch.

Though I couldn't afford even one of the satin gloves, I couldn't resist trying on a full-length coat of finest scarlet wool, with large black buttons and a snug waist. The saleslady raved, popped a matching red beret on my head, and insisted I admire myself in her full-length mirror.

Full-length, my eye. The mirror reflected only as high as my chin. To see the beret, I had to bend my knees, which ruined the effect of the coat.

"When I am queen of the world," I informed Chloe back at her stall, "all mirrors will need to be fixed at least a foot higher on walls, and freestanding full-length mirrors will need to be placed a minimum of one and a half feet off the ground. This measure will ensure that tall girls can see their whole reflection in one go."

"I think that would discriminate against shorties," said Chloe. "They'd have to stand on stools to see the whole of themselves."

"It would serve them right," I muttered, thinking of all the violators of The Law. "But okay, I shall decree instead that all full-length mirrors will need to be at least 6ft in length."

"And what about big girls?" asked Chloe, holding her arms away from her sides. "They can't see all of themselves in mirrors either, and I don't hear them complaining."

I narrowed my eyes at her. "Are you *trying* to annoy me, or is it just coming naturally?"

"This might be a good time for me to go get us some tea," said Chloe.

She hurried off and was soon back with two steaming cups. "Cinnamon spiced pumpkin tea for me."

"Sounds gross," I said.

"And calming chamomile for you. I think we can both agree that you could use it," she said, handing me the cup.

"Did you see that stall with the vintage clothing? Wasn't it beautiful?"

She wrinkled her nose. "Old and moldy doesn't do it for me."

"I *love* all those old-timey styles. I've been thinking that for my fashion range, I might pick a retro theme. Choose an era from the past and then reinvent modern items in that style — an old-meets-new kind of thing. What d'you think?"

I'd been watching old movies on TV and researching on the net, thinking about how to adapt the fashions for modern tastes.

"Well, it's good that you like vintage styles, because you're going to be working on the project for the next couple of months."

"I can hear a 'but' coming."

"*Bu-ut*, I'm not sure it's original enough to stand out. Every few years some designer changes up old-fashioned designs instead of coming up with something new. You don't think maybe it's been done to death already?"

"Hmm." It was something to think about.

Just then, Chloe's mother and little brother walked up to our stall. Ben leapt into my arms and demanded to climb onto my shoulders. "You're so high, Peyton, it will be like being on top of a tower."

"Benjamin!" said Mrs. DiCaprio, clearly embarrassed.

But Ben was unabashed. "I want to see the whole world! This is my favorite thing."

It was one of my favorite things, too. I loved to wrestle with Chloe's brother and to sneak in quick hugs when I could. I loved his wiry body, his cheeky smile, the little-boy smell of him.

"Hi, Mrs. D," I said.

"Hello, girls, how are you? Hungry yet? I brought you some lobster rolls."

"Mrs. D, there's a place in heaven for angels like you," I said, biting into the warm, buttery, salty goodness.

Mrs. DiCaprio smiled fondly at me as I polished it off in a few more bites, then tapped Ben on the knee. "Come on, time to head home. Daddy's waiting to take you to soccer practice."

"Yeah, scram, kiddo," Chloe said.

"Aww." Ben slid reluctantly down my back.

"High five?" I said.

Instead of slapping the hand I held up for him, he placed his own hand against it. Comparing the sizes of our body parts was another of Ben's favorite things.

"I think you're a giant, Peyton," he said.

"Maybe, you're just a gnome. Or a little goblin!"

He laughed loudly at that and marched off beside his mother chanting, "Fee Fi Fo Fum!"

"Argh!" Chloe made a noise of disgust. "Sorry about that. Little brothers are just the worst, most annoying nuisances that ever …" Her voice trailed off, and she cast me a look full of concern. "Oh, Peyton, I'm sorry. That was so thoughtless of me."

"Don't worry about it."

"When I know what it's done to you, and your family …" She still looked mortified.

"I said, don't worry about it."

"Am I forgiven?" Chloe asked.

I gave her a hug, holding on tight until the lump in my

throat eased, then changed the subject. "So, are you still going to Greg Baker's party tonight?"

"Sure. My mom bought me a zombie costume, so I'm all set to join the walking dead. Do you still have to work tonight?"

"Yeah."

"Bummer," Chloe said.

Not really. I was pretty sure Jay would be at his cousin's party, and I did not feel like watching him and the felon circling the dance floor, or worse, making out in a dark corner.

"Jim wants us all to wear Halloween costumes tonight to add to the vibe, so I'll have to put together an outfit after rehearsal."

"There's a stall selling costumes in that far corner."

"Thanks, but I don't feel like spending money on a once-off outfit, especially not one for work."

"I'll buy it for you," said Chloe impulsively. "They're not expensive."

"No, it's cool. Thanks anyway." I had to hold the line against her buying me stuff. Her family might not have the financial woes mine did, but I didn't want to be anybody's charity case. "I'm thinking I'll just go as a witch. When I get home from rehearsal, I'll sew a cloak out of some black trash bags and make a pointy witch's hat — ha, I'll finally have a hat that fits me!"

"A trash-bag witch? That won't get you much in the way of tips. I thought you wanted to make money. You should wear a sexy outfit — go as Wonder Woman, or a nurse in high heels and fishnet tights."

"I think you're describing a hooker, not a health-worker."

"Whatever. Wear a short skirt to show off those long legs, and put the ladies on display, too," she ordered, nodding at my chest.

By the time we started packing up the stall — a bit early, so Chloe could drive me to rehearsal on time — we hadn't yet sold all the stock.

"Here." Chloe crammed the leftover treats into a cardboard cake box and gave it to me. "Snacks for the cast."

"Excellent! I'll be popular for once."

"What — they don't like you?"

"No, it's not that. But I can tell they thought Wren was a better Juliet. They're not convinced I can play the part well enough."

"Do *you* think you can?" Chloe asked, eyeing me shrewdly as she folded the tablecloth.

"Yeah, I think I could."

"So, what's stopping you?"

What was stopping me? Only the fear that if I let go, if I released myself fully into the part of a girl infatuated with a guy she couldn't have — myself, basically — I wouldn't be able to reel it back in. Everyone would see, and know how I really felt about Jay. *He'd* know. And he'd pity me.

I didn't think I could stand that, so I kept on holding in and holding back.

~ *19* ~

That afternoon's rehearsal went about as well as usual — in other words, not very well at all.

Doug grew more concerned with every week we inched closer to December eighteenth. It was supposed to be our first books-down practice, but most of the cast-members were hiding their script pages in pockets and under sweaters, sneaking quick looks when they thought Doug wasn't looking. No one, not even Jay, was anywhere close to being word-perfect.

"You know what makes me grateful about this production?" Doug snarled halfway through the afternoon.

"Our talent?" Zack said.

"No, Zack. Not the talent. There are members of this cast who would seriously need to brush up on their talent for me to be grateful."

I studiously avoided meeting anyone's eyes.

"No," Doug continued, running his hand through his hair so furiously that I worried he'd yank out a chunk of it by the roots, "what I am grateful for is that we're not doing the play in the original Shakespearean English, because it seems hard enough for this cast to memorize their lines in *normal* effing English!"

"Sorry," a couple of us muttered.

"Or to inject the smallest amount of energy or passion into your dry, lifeless performances!"

All six foot something of me shriveled, because I was sure he was talking about me. My performance *was* corpselike, I could feel it.

We all apologized and promised Doug that we'd learn our words and try our hardest to bring our characters to vivid, passionate life. But that was a promise I broke a mere half-hour later, when Jay and I had to rehearse the scene where we kissed each other for the first time. Or rather, when Jay got to kiss me — because I just stood there, still as my dressmaker's dummy.

On the inside of me, though, it was a zoo. My heart leapt about like a mischievous tiger cub, my stomach was home to a tumult of butterflies, and my mind bleated pleas not to let anyone see the effect Jay was having on me.

He was only giving me a peck on the lips each time — nothing to freak out about. But because it was *Jay*, because he pressed his warm lips against mine so softly and tenderly, and seemed to pull back so reluctantly; because he stared down into my eyes with such intensity as he said his lines of love, I *did* freak out. Not a crazy, screaming, eye-rolling, limb-flailing, whackadoodle freak-out, but a silent, stiff, holding myself tight, pressing my lips together, and keeping all my crazy tightly buttoned up kind of freak-out.

Jay's passion was just acting. Between scenes, he was

completely laid back — no more or less friendly to me than he was to any other member of the cast. So I knew these kisses were just a performance, but still, they felt real, and I was distracted in the lines leading up to them, and flustered afterwards.

It did not help that we had an audience — the rest of the cast, plus Faye in the auditorium. And Zack, who watched avidly from the wings.

Doug grew increasingly frustrated with each of my half-hearted smooch attempts, and eventually yelled, "Peyton! What is the matter with you? You're all over the place today — what is your actual problem? Why are you so awkward and distracted?"

"I *am* distracted, Doug. Sorry. It's just ..." I hesitated, trying to think up a possible excuse, because no way could I tell him the real reason. "It's just that we're running late."

"Because we keep having to repeat this scene!"

"Yeah, I know it's my fault, sorry." I pulled an apologetic face at Jay, who was looking as chill as ever. "But I'm really worried I'll be late for work tonight. I cannot afford to lose my job, Doug, and I'm scared my boss will fire me if I'm late again." That was a total lie. Jimmy would never fire me for being late. Jimmy would never fire me, period. I doubted he'd ever fired anyone in his life. "And," I continued, ignoring my hot ears and laying on anxiety thick enough for anyone to be dead impressed by my performance if only they knew I was acting, "I've still got to go home and make a Halloween-themed costume to wear to work, and I'm running out of time."

"Fine, let's just finish this scene with you and Jay, and then you can go, and we'll work on a scene without you," said Doug.

Damn. I'd been hoping he would call this love scene quits and let me escape, but no such luck.

"Here." Doug fished in his pocket and brought out a set of keys, singling one out for me to see. "This is the key to the backstage wardrobe room where all the costumes from old productions are stored. I'll let you raid it for something to wear tonight."

"Really?" I asked, delighted.

"On one condition, Peyton: that you put some of your heart and soul into this scene, okay?"

"Okay."

My voice didn't sound very confident, but I was determined to force myself to relax and pretend well enough for one run-through of the kissing bit. Sometimes, as Chloe likes saying, the only way out is through.

"Now, once more, what's your motivation for this scene?" Doug demanded.

My motivation? I needed to escape — my nerves couldn't take much more of this.

"Love," I said.

"Yes! And I want to *see* that love. Throw yourself into your performance — especially the kiss. Make it convincing, or the deal's off."

I must have appeared worried, because Jay gave me a reassuring smile and said, "Don't worry, it's not a real kiss."

"It isn't?" said Doug.

I was surprised, too. I'd been dreading that kiss — well,

both dreading and longing for it — precisely because I'd thought it *would* be the real thing.

"No, we'll do it the way professional stage actors do it."

"Which is how?" Doug asked.

"Yeah, how?" I wanted to know.

"Open mouth, no tongue," Jay said.

"No tongue?" Zack said from his spot in the nearest wings. He sounded both outraged and disappointed.

"No tongue?" I said, massively relieved. I'd be able to keep my head in that case, surely?

"No tongue," Jay confirmed. "We just move our mouths together, trying not to block each other's faces from the audience, or mash our noses. It's pretty cold-blooded, technique-y stuff. In fact, we should probably block it out. How about I go this way first," he tilted his head one way, "count to three, then the other way. And maybe kiss the side of your mouth before and your lip after, each for a count of two. Okay?"

"I guess."

If it wasn't real, if it was "cold-blooded" choreography rather than passionate tongue-wrestling, then I didn't have to worry.

"I'll put my arms around your waist, like so" — he demonstrated — "and you should probably put yours around my neck, okay?"

"Sure. That's fine, I can do that."

I could. Trying to remember the sequence of moves and all the counting would keep me grounded.

"To be honest, I don't care whether or not you use tongue,

just make it look like the real thing, I beg you," said Doug.

He marched off, Zack hid behind a wing curtain, and Jay and I were left alone on the stage.

"Right, so from the part where Romero says, 'I want you, I need you'," Doug instructed from the first row.

And, just like that, Jay switched on. His green eyes turned golden-hot and heavy-lidded, his mouth twisted into a sexy half-smile and his hand reached to take mine, caressing my knuckles with his thumb.

"I want you. I *need* you, Juliet," he said, pulling me closer.

I gazed up into his eyes and, just like that, I was falling.

Jay dipped his head and kissed the corner of my mouth, once, twice. That was the last counting I got done, because when the actual kiss started, all capacity to think, let alone count, evaporated. He pressed his lips against mine, harder than before, and they were firm and warm. Then he turned his head so his open mouth slanted across mine, and his lips moved. Slowly. And it was just like kissing.

The roaring started in my head again. I couldn't catch my breath, and it was all I could do not to kiss him back — properly. The talk of technique and choreography had lulled me into a false sense of security, because the caresses were still real, and the kiss was anything but cold-blooded.

It felt like we were making out. Naked. And in public.

~ 20 ~

As the rest of the cast watched Juliet kiss Romero, I melted into Jay. My body softened, and the edges of me blurred as I molded against him. My hands inched up his back, moved over the top of his shoulders and tunneled into his hair, tugging his head down. In just another second it would be a real kiss, because I couldn't seem to stop myself.

But then Jay pulled back.

"Much better!" someone called from very far away.

I took a deep, ragged breath. My eyes were still locked on Jay's. He stared down at me with a quizzical expression, like he was perplexed about something. He was probably just waiting for my next line of dialogue, but I was so dazed, I'd forgotten what to say. Forgotten how to speak, probably.

"Well, that was a lot better," said Doug from downstage.

Jay was apparently as cool as ever, ready to receive direction. I was totally flustered. And blushing too — I could feel it. I tried to focus all my attention on Doug, who still didn't look satisfied.

"But, Peyton," Doug continued, "if you can't act and remember your lines at the same time, then we have ourselves a real situation, now don't we?"

"Yeah," said Zack, who'd inched out of the wings and was standing close by. "We do."

"For God's sake, will you stop answering my questions! They're rhetorical — do you even know what that means?"

"Not really, man."

Doug, turning his back on Zack as if to blot out the sight of a village idiot, said, "That's why you — all of you — need to be word perfect, so the words come automatically, and you can just inhabit your characters. That's when you forget about trying to remember them."

Down in the auditorium, Liz gave a loud snort. "Well, that makes perfect sense."

"Books down next rehearsal!" Doug bellowed.

"Um, may I be excused now?" I asked.

"I suppose," said Doug, and he handed me the set of keys.

I scurried backstage, unlocked the door to the wardrobe room, stepped inside and sat down on an old trunk to calm down. This had to stop — I couldn't lose my head, and more of my heart, every time Jay touched me. I needed to find a way to lock up the soft, sappy, needy part of me and stay in control.

I rubbed a hand over my face and scanned the dusty treasure trove of costumes surrounding me. None of them looked particularly Halloween-y. The longest rail was crammed with heavy Victorian dresses and tattered urchin street wear from a production of *David Copperfield* a few years back. I was interested in the gowns from the point of view of my fashion-school project, but I didn't have time to study the bustles and puffed sleeves because now I truly was running late for work. I'd have to hustle if I wanted to catch the five-thirty bus.

I had a quick look through a rail hung with faux animal skins — costumes from an adaptation of *Clan of the Cave Bear* both Doug and I had acted in two years ago — but had no desire to spend the night waitressing in a loincloth or leopard-print wrap.

At the far end of the room was a rail hung with the costumes from last year's farce, in which I'd played the butler. I felt a moment's nostalgia when I laid eyes on my old costume. I missed that role now. There had been no emotion to express, no need to hold back or open up, no discombobulating kissing scenes. Doug's directions to me had amounted to: keep a poker face, no matter what's happening onstage. Easiest role ever. And not only had the butler *not* done it, but he'd been killed off at the end of the first act, so I'd only had to attend half the rehearsals and could spend the last two acts of performances chilling backstage.

I took the butler's suit off the rail and held it up against me. It smelled of mothballs, but it would fit. And, frankly, how many outfits in this room *would* fit me, especially the girls' costumes? But Chloe had been right — wearing a man's suit would hardly rake in the tips. And I could just imagine what Tori would say. "Ah, Peyton, finally you're dressing the part. Hey, you look kinda hot, want to go on a date?"

I jammed the suit back between a maid's outfit and a petite-sized evening gown and frantically hunted through the garments, sending up a cloud of dust which set me sneezing.

My hands stilled. A maid's outfit! Weren't French maids supposed to be one of the hottest of skanky Halloween ensembles?

I pulled it out. It consisted of a short black dress with a laced bodice, thigh-high black stockings with a garter belt, a frilly white apron and lacy headpiece, and a teeny pink feather-duster. Hmm. Caitlyn had worn this in last year's production and she was tall — not as tall as me, of course, but it just might fit. Only one way to find out.

A couple of minutes later, I was dressed and bending at the knees to see my reflection in the mirror. It was tight. Very tight. The top was made for someone a good size (or two) smaller than me, but here's the thing — I have good boobs. I mean, really good. They're the only part of my body I truly like, apart from my ears — tiny, pixie ears stolen from some elfin baby and reassigned to big old me at birth. They're even slightly pointed.

But my boobs are first-class — round, firm and perky. And in that super-tight dress, they bulged out of the low-cut décolletage. The skirt was way too short, and the garter belt and stockings peeped out from under it in a way that they hadn't for Caitlyn, but the resulting spectacle was kind of … hot. I was all long legs and round curves.

The costume begged for black high heels, but there were no shoes in the room and, even if there were, I'd bet my whole college fund that not one of the ladies' pairs would fit my boat-sized feet. I'd just have to wear my flat black ankle boots. They looked odd with the sexy ensemble, but I could almost hear Chloe saying, "Girl, I don't reckon anyone will be looking at your feet!"

Screw it, I'd do it! I bundled my jeans and sweatshirt into my knapsack and left the wardrobe room, locking the door behind me. I couldn't sneak out unseen via the back exit because I needed to return the keys to Doug. Just my luck, Jay and Zack were still rehearsing their scene, with Doug beside them giving notes, and so I had to cross the stage to get to the auditorium under their full view.

Zack was speaking, but his words petered out to silence when I appeared. "Is that you, Big P?" he asked, gaping.

"In the flesh."

I handed Doug the keys. He gave his head a little shake, as if to clear it.

"Why the hell didn't I cast you as the maid last year?" he said. "You were wasted as the butler."

I shook the feather duster dismissively at him, releasing a puff of dust. Another sneezing fit seized me, and my boobs came dangerously close to bursting free from their laced restraints. Jay's eyes — which had been fixed on my chest — boggled, and he muttered something that sounded a lot like "Holy shit!"

I crossed the stage and headed off down the aisle to the exit at the back of the auditorium, walking as fast as I could without breaking into a run, because I feared that might cause a serious wardrobe malfunction. As I passed them, Wren and Angela pulled their heads together to whisper something which I was sure, from the direction of their gazes, was about me, and not in a good way.

I ran the two blocks to the bus stop, but as I turned the corner for the home-straight, I saw the bus pulling away. I ran down the sidewalk, yelling and waving both arms above my head like a maniac, but the bus disappeared down the road.

Crap! That bus was always late. Always.

The honk of a horn made me jump. "Hey baby, cute ass! Wanna come clean my house?" a truck driver yelled at me as he cruised by.

Ignoring him, I spun around and walked back to the bus shelter. A middle-aged man puffing on a cigarette outside a corner convenience store smirked at me as I walked by.

"Smile, honey. Your frown is ruining the show."

I gritted my teeth and kept walking. When I got to the bus stop, I checked the timetable pinned on the side of the shelter. The next bus would only be in half an hour. I'd be late for work for sure, and in the meantime I'd have to stand here in my skimpy outfit, in the chilly breeze, suffering catcalls and come-ons from Neanderthals.

A car pulled to a stop in front of the shelter, and I was just gearing up to tell the driver where he could shove his sexism, when I saw who it was — the rhyming couplet. Jay, with Faye in the passenger seat beside him.

"I thought you had to hurry to work?" he asked.

"I missed my bus."

"Jump in, we'll give you a ride."

Faye's glance shot daggers.

"No, it's okay, really, the next bus should be along soon."

"Don't be silly, it's on our way."

"No, it's not," corrected Faye.

I was tempted to accept just to piss her off.

"Well, it's not far *out* of our way," said Jay. "Plus, I wouldn't want you to be late and lose your job."

Trapped by my own lie, I accepted. Faye sat up front, and I folded myself into the middle of the tiny rear of the car, all arms and long, stockinged legs and pushed-up boobs. Rearranging my limbs, trying to find a more comfortable way of perching, I caught Jay's glance in the rearview mirror, and he grinned back. Faye scowled and pursed her lips into a dog's bottom of disapproval.

"Don't you have a car?" she said.

Why, yes, of course. I just prefer not to use it because I have a secret fetish for public transport.

"No," I said.

I tugged my skirt down, trying to cover more of my legs, but it was no good, the full length of my thighs, with their garter belt and stocking tops, was exposed. I could swear that more than once, Jay's glance flicked back and to the side to take in the spectacle.

A soon as we pulled up outside Jumping Jim's, I thanked Jay and scrambled out of the car. Jim himself met me at the door. He seemed a bit surprised at my outfit, but kindly told me I looked fine, and serenaded me with an Elvis song which informed me that while I looked, walked and talked like an angel, I was really the devil in disguise.

~ 21 ~

I was good at keeping secrets. I had to be. I'd learned how to hide things, how to prevent anybody finding out the truth. And I'd had loads of practice concealing what I felt, at hiding the real me. Turns out this was a good thing, because I was still disguising how I felt about the boy playing Romero to my Juliet.

And how I felt, was that I liked him. *Really* liked him. Spending so much time with him, I'd discovered that he was a genuinely good guy, so much more than his awesome eyes and heart-stopping height. But my infatuation was a dangerous business. For one thing, it would be dead humiliating if he or the cast detected I had the serious hots for him. For another, he liked Faye.

She still attended every rehearsal — although she'd been looking increasingly sulky, and she no longer applauded at the end of every one of Jay's scenes. To be fair, she just didn't applaud at the end of his and my scenes, and that may have been because I was screwing them up.

Between our scenes, I forced myself to hang out with other

cast members, rather than allowing myself to gravitate toward Jay as I wanted to. I worked furiously not to blush or let my face light up when he came over to chat with me. As I spoke Juliet's lines of love and longing, I kept a tight rein on the deepest parts of me — the parts that wanted to stare dreamily up into his eyes and touch his arm, his hip, his jaw. That wanted to ask him a thousand questions about himself. And every time we rehearsed a kissing scene, I busted a gut holding myself back.

I was so focused on this performance of forced casualness, so careful not to put too much of me into my acting, that I still wasn't putting *enough* of me into it. I knew this was a problem, knew it before I overheard Doug discussing it with Jay during a break in one of our Wednesday night rehearsals.

"She's holding back," said Doug.

"Give her some time," Jay replied. "It'll come right."

"I hope so. I mean, she's passable, not awful. But honestly not great."

My stomach sank. I'd be the weak link in this production, not because I couldn't play Juliet well enough, but because I couldn't play just-not-that-into-you to save my ass. I didn't much want to hear more critique of my performance, yet I stood still in the darkness of the wings alongside them, eavesdropping.

"Do you think maybe she's uncomfortable getting into the part — getting into you — with Faye looking on?"

"Could be."

Yeah, let's go with that.

"Do you think maybe you could speak to her — Faye, I

mean. Ask her to stay away from rehearsals?"

Jay must have appeared skeptical at the chances of that request succeeding, because Doug added quickly, "Or even just sit, like, more toward the back of the auditorium?"

"Sure, I'll ask her."

"Cool. I think that'll help Peyton's performance. Maybe. Hopefully. I mean, I'm not frantic about it — you're good enough to carry the both of you," Doug continued, "but I guess I was just hoping for more … spark, more energy sizzling between our star-crossed lovers. She was pretty good that time you two did the first kiss, and I hoped she was loosening up, but she's stiff as a board again."

"She's anxious."

So much for hiding my feelings from Jay.

"She needs to learn to trust me before she opens up, I think," he added.

"Yeah, maybe that's it. But do what you can to loosen her up and get some *feeling* out of her tonight, okay?"

"Sure."

That evening, I noticed the extra effort Jay put into our scenes. He stared even more deeply into my eyes; he took my hand and kissed my knuckles in one scene, and tucked a curl behind my ear in another, and traced a finger across my cheek in the part where we danced. And even though I knew this was just an act to get me loosened up and lovelorn — as per Doug's instructions — it still had a dizzying effect on me.

Because Jay was that good an actor. Too good.

So good that I might have imagined — from the intense heat of his gaze, and how tenderly his hands caressed my bare arms, and the way his lips seemed to linger on mine in the kiss — that he was totally into me. But I knew better. It was just a performance.

Still, it *felt* real. So the harder Jay tried to get me to loosen up, the greater was the danger that I might slip up and reveal my true feelings, so the tighter I clamped down on myself, and the more lifeless my performance became. The goose bumps on my arms where he had stroked me were the only part of my performance that was spontaneous that night.

Zack kept trying to give me tips on how to kiss Jay better — "Hold him close, and grab his butt — do you want to practice on me?" but not everybody was as unhappy as Doug with our lack of visible chemistry. Faye seemed mollified, and Wren seemed delighted. Judging by the told-you-I-could-do-it-better expression she regularly wore, she hadn't given up hope of reclaiming the role from me.

Rehearsal ended with Doug setting up the first private session for Jay and me, for the trust and body exercises.

"I've got cheer practice on Thursdays. We'll need to make it another time," Faye complained once Jay and I had agreed on a time for the following afternoon.

Oh, crap. I was going to have to build trust and be close to Jay's delicious height and man muscles in front of his girlfriend? She'd find me out for sure.

"I don't think —" Jay began, but Doug said baldly, "You weren't invited."

Yeah, suck it, Faye.

"What do you mean, I'm not invited?" she snapped.

"I want the two of them" — Doug gestured to Jay and me

— "to work alone together. To build a sense of connection and intimacy, I want them to look like — to *be* like — they're lovers."

Faye's eyes narrowed to slits, and her mouth did that dog's bottom pucker again. "We'll talk about this later, Jay," she said, before spinning on her heel and stalking out of the auditorium.

"Do you need to go after her?" Doug asked.

"Nah." Jay waved a hand. "Let her go."

Yeah, just let her go.

"Okay. Do I need to explain what you two need to do?" Doug asked Jay.

"No, we've done plenty of those sorts of exercises in drama class; I'll choose some of the better ones."

"Great, then I'll expect a huge improvement at Saturday's rehearsal. Peyton, I've got two words for you: trust, and relax, dammit!"

At school the next day, we got our midterm reports, and I was relieved that I'd done okay. But still, I was anything but relaxed when I arrived at the trust-building session that afternoon. Jay was already waiting for me, seated on the edge of the stage in the deserted auditorium, doing breathing exercises. And he was alone.

"Hiya," I said. "No Faye tonight?"

"Nope. No Faye any night." He gave a rueful smile. "We've called it quits."

Yesss! Elation at his newly single status — and his reinstatement on the list of tall boys, I realized happily — fizzed through my veins. I wanted to laugh and pump the air with my fist. But since I was a better actor than anyone had yet been able to see, I merely pulled a sympathetic face and said, "Sorry, that must be tough."

"It's been coming for a while."

"Sure you're up for us tonight?"

"What d'you— Oh, right. Yeah, of course, I'll be fine."

And in truth, he hardly seemed heartbroken. "So, trust exercises first, you reckon, or bodywork?" he asked.

"Trust," I said, suddenly nervous again.

Jay stuck a hand into his backpack and pulled out a long, black silk scarf, running its length through his slender fingers.

"Do you always keep a scarf in your bag?"

"Oh, yeah, definitely. I like to be prepared," he said with a sexy smile. "You never know when you'll need to blindfold a girl."

I swallowed.

"Or" — he gave me a wink — "tie her up."

Heat flooded my cheeks.

"Um," I said, my eyes on that length of black silk. He was wrapping the ends around his hands as if he might be getting ready to throttle me with it.

"Kidding! It's my mom's, I just borrowed it for tonight. But there is going to be blindfolding tonight. Ready to start?" Jay held up the scarf in question.

"You first."

"See, no trust. Zero trust. We need to fix that." He wrapped the scarf twice around his head, covering his eyes, and tied it at the back. "Right, now I can't see anything. I'm entirely in your hands."

He reached out blindly for my arm but brushed his hand against my breast instead.

"Sorry! Sorry," he said, while I thanked God that he couldn't see my face had turned nipple-pink again. "I need your arm."

I took his right hand and placed it on my left forearm. It felt pleasantly heavy, like a promise of strength. He slid his grasp down to rest on top of my hand, then linked his fingers through mine. His hand was warm — and dry (sorry, Mark). And indisputably bigger than mine. I sighed in pleasure.

Jay turned his face toward mine. "What?"

"Nothing," I said hurriedly. "What do we do now?"

"You lead me all around this place. Don't make it too easy — it's supposed to be like an obstacle course. I've got to trust you not to walk me off the end of the stage, and to tell me when we're going upstairs, or when I need to duck — that sort of thing. Okay?"

"Sure."

This, I could do — no problem. This was easier than the acting because I had an excuse to hold his hand, and I could study his features to my heart's content — which I did now, staring at his lovely lips.

"Whenever you're ready."

"Right, okay. We're going to turn to your left and walk about ten paces. No, make that six — your legs are *long*. And over here are steps going down, five of them … Careful. And … last one. Good job!"

He smiled at the praise. His lips were full and a deep rusty pink, with a perfectly etched cupid's bow. They were pretty enough to be a woman's lips, but on his face with its square jaw, shaded with a hint of stubble at this time of the day, and slightly crooked nose, it saved the strong angles from being almost too masculine.

I led him up toward the lighting box, enjoying the feel of his hand on mine and growing almost cocky at the ease of the exercise.

Then Jay said, "Right. Now it's your turn."

He wrapped the soft scarf twice around my eyes and then gently tugged it tight behind my head.

"All in the dark?"

I hesitated a moment, debating whether to go with the truth or a self-protective lie. If I looked down while keeping my head level, I could still see a thin sliver of the floor. It made me feel safer and less helpless, but also like a cheat.

"I can still see a bit," I confessed.

Jay adjusted the silky fabric until I nodded that I was now completely blind. I was aware of the complete silence, apart from Jay's breathing beside me, and the fast beat of my heart in my chest. I felt exposed and vulnerable, and the realization that I'd have to depend on him entirely to keep me safe was unsettling.

"I don't like this," I said, sounding almost panicky. "I'd rather not do it."

The hand that I lifted to yank off the blindfold was caught in his and laid on top of his forearm.

"Peyton, do you trust me, even just a little?" he said, and I thought I heard an edge of intensity in his tone.

"Um …"

Truth was, I didn't trust anyone. In my life, I'd perfected the skill of *self*-reliance. If you didn't need people, you weren't as vulnerable. If you were totally independent, you couldn't get hurt as deeply.

"*Can* you trust me, Peyton?"

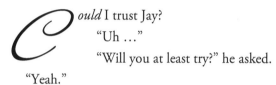

~ 22 ~

ould I trust Jay?

"Uh ..."

"Will you at least try?" he asked.

"Yeah."

"Good." His voice sounded like he was smiling. "I promise I'll take care of you. I won't let you get hurt. You can rely on me."

Those words, and the sincere way in which he said them, brought a catch to my throat, and a prickle of tears to my eyes. They were words I'd never heard before, not spoken to me.

I nodded an acknowledgment, but on the inside I was slapping my face, because I needed to get a grip. Jay was talking about the exercise, not a freaking lifelong commitment to my health and happiness.

He spun me around on the spot a couple of times, so that I lost all sense of direction, and then we started moving. Strangely, it was way easier than I'd expected. I realized that I *did* trust him. It was me I had the problem with. Me I didn't trust to take care of myself, to protect me from being hurt by the world, to lead me in the right direction, to see and avoid the obstacles which tripped me up and laid me flat.

Beside me, Jay's deep voice and his strong, steady arm guided me as I wove between curtained wings, climbed up ladders and down stairs, and turned on taps and drank water (without chipping a tooth) in the backstage dressing rooms.

Eventually, we stopped, and he let go my hand.

"Hold on," he said.

Then his hands were at my waist, and I — all six feet and one-and-three-quarter inch of me — was being lifted into the air and deposited gently on my butt, on the edge of the stage. No one in my life had ever lifted me up without groaning and complaining. Well, maybe when I was a baby, but it was hard to remember myself as anything other than massive. Easier to imagine I'd been born a giant, that maybe I'd put my father's back out when he lifted me from my cradle, and tested my mother's biceps when she hauled me out of the bath.

Now I felt light as thistledown, as petite as Wren, as feminine as any girl on the planet, and I only just restrained myself from pathetically thanking him for the novel sensation.

There was a tug of the blindfold, and then I was blinking at the light. Jay hopped up onto the stage to sit beside me, clearly pleased at the success of our first exercise.

"No bangs or bruises?" he asked, grinning.

When he smiled like that, the softness of his mouth flattened out, and he was all male. I stared at his lips, dreaming of sinking into his arms, of having him hug me tighter than anyone ever had while repeating what he'd said about taking care of me. And gently kissing the top of my head as I nestled against his chest. It was a superb fantasy.

"Peyton?" He was asking me something.

"Huh?"

"Are you okay?" He was staring down — *down* — at me, with a concerned expression.

"Sure." I pried my gaze away from his and made myself stare instead at my feet, where the blue canvas of my sneakers was separating from the white rubber of the toe. "What's next?"

"Next, you fall into my arms."

"*What?*"

Had I given myself away, somehow? I could feel the shock and horror on my face, and it must have looked ludicrous because he threw back his head and laughed.

"It's just an exercise. Here." He stood up, held out a hand and then effortlessly pulled me to my feet. "Like this." He turned me around so that I stood with my back to him, and then said, "Take a couple of steps away from me. Just a little further. And one more, that's it — stop there."

I stood in the center of the stage, staring into the wings, feeling uneasy. "Now what?"

"Now you just fall backward, into my arms."

"I just do what, now?" I spun around to peer disbelievingly at him.

"You fall backward, as if you were fainting, and I'll catch you."

"No. I'll be too heavy for you."

Some things were certain, like the effect of gravity on apples, the magnetic attraction online sales exerted on my mother, and the inability of anyone to catch my deadweight if I fell.

"No, you won't. Not even close," he said, sounding like I'd

insulted him. "Here, fold your arms like this." He stepped over to me and crossed my arms over my chest.

"I feel like a corpse."

Which is what I would be when I toppled backward and hit the deck of the stage like a felled tree in a forest. The floor would tremble, the flats stacked against the back wall of the stage would tip over, stage lights would shake loose from their rigging above, and Jay would realize my size, finally catch on that I was more giant redwood than thistledown.

"Peyton," he said, and his voice was deep and warm beside my ear, "do you still not trust me?"

"No!" Desperate times called for honest measures. "No, I don't, okay?"

"I promise I'll catch you. I will not let you fall."

My eyes were stinging again.

"Promise?" I asked.

He grasped my hand and placed the palm over his chest, covering it with his own. "I promise," he said. "Hand on heart."

"Okay," I whispered, "I'll try."

"Can't ask for more than that." He took a few steps backward and indicated with his fingers that I should turn around. "Cross your heart," he said.

"And hope to die," I whispered, folding my arms across my chest and digging my fingers into the soft flesh between my shoulders and neck.

"Now just fall backward," he said.

So I did.

It took everything I had to shift my balance those few inches — all my scarce trust, every meager grain of faith in the power of others to support me and keep me safe. But I did it. I fell back. And he caught me, hands under my arms, holding up my back. And — extra credit to the big guy — he didn't even grunt in exertion, or complain afterwards about pulled muscles or dislocated vertebrae.

"You didn't let me fall," I marveled.

"I promised you I wouldn't. Ready to try again?"

I thought about that. On the one hand, I now trusted him a bit more — a leeeeetle bit more. On the other …

"What if you've exhausted your muscles?"

"Peyton," he said, one side of his mouth quirking up, "please don't be ridiculous. Do I look exhausted?"

He looked strong and fit, and anything but feeble. I turned around, crossed my arms and fell backward. He caught me. And this time I laughed at the sheer joy of the rare experience.

"There you go," he said, smiling. "That's how you do it."

I toppled into his arms three more times and then insisted that I take my turn catching him. He apparently had no trust issues, or doubts about my ability to catch him. Without a second's hesitation, he spun around and collapsed back into my arms. I managed to keep his head from banging onto the stage floor when he fell, but frankly, it was an effort. A major effort. If it had been Zack, I wouldn't have had a problem, but Jay was tall. And heavy.

"Umph," I grunted the first time.

The second time I toppled backward, and he landed on top of me.

"Are you okay?" I asked, sitting up and bending over his head to inspect him for injuries, aware that I'd failed in keeping him upright, though I had at least cushioned his fall.

"You know," said Jay, lying on his back with his head in my lap. "This is surprisingly comfortable."

It was. I could smell his faintly spicy scent, and was close enough to count his freckles. Jay sighed and seemed in no hurry to move. My hand lifted of its own volition and moved to his head. My fingers were already just touching his hair, ready to run my fingers through it, when I caught myself and snatched them back.

"Peyton?"

"Yeah?"

"Do you like acting?"

"Yeah."

"Why?"

"Why?"

"Yeah, why."

"I dunno," I said, and waited.

This was a tactic I often used when people asked me difficult or awkward questions. Most people couldn't stand a silence and rushed in to answer their own questions, letting me off the hook. But Jay wasn't most people. He held the silence patiently, and the question hung in the air, gathering weight, until I spoke.

"I guess maybe because I sometimes enjoy not being myself," I finally said. "When I get into a part, I feel what it's like to be someone else."

"You don't like being yourself? You don't like who you are?" A small frown furrowed the space between Jay's eyebrows.

"Well, it's more that the character in a play is clear on who she is. She knows what she has to say and do, and where and how to move. Her lines and moves are written for her. In real life, I often don't have a clue how I'm supposed to be. And I don't get rehearsals."

His head, still lying in my lap, nodded his understanding.

"I guess I also like to disappear for a while."

"Disappearing while you're onstage in front of a watching audience?" He was smiling again. I loved that smile.

"Yeah. When I'm in character, I can be both seen and invisible. Crazy, right? But I don't mind having all those eyes on me while I'm acting, because then I'm another person. They're watching the character, not me, see? That's easier than walking down a crowded hallway with everyone staring at me like I'm some kind of mutant."

"Yeah, I've noticed people gawking at you. But that kind of comes with the territory, don't you think, of —"

I was already sighing, getting ready to respond with, *Of course, but I don't have to like it, do I?* when he finished his sentence.

"— beauty."

"Huh?" I said, completely thrown by his last word.

"When you have tiger's eyes and a rocking body, people are going to stare, Peyton, that's just how it is."

I laughed so hard I bounced his head right out my lap.

He sat up, and asked, "What's so funny?"

"You are! They're not staring at my eyes, Jay, or at my *beauty*." I sketched quotation marks around the word. "They're gaping at my freakish height!"

He tucked back his chin in surprise and gave me a bemused look. "Do you really think that?"

"I've lived in this super-sized skin for a long time, and trust me, I know how people feel about it."

"I think," said Jay, tapping a forefinger against his lower lip, "I think it's more about how *you* feel about it."

I could feel the confusion on my face.

"I think you don't feel comfortable in your own skin. It's *you* who's super-aware of your height, not others. You're self-conscious, that's what it is."

"Look, I might be self-conscious, but —"

"Might be?" he teased.

"Okay, I am self-conscious, but other people *do* notice my height. They're always calling me a giant or an Amazon, and asking me for weather reports from the stratosphere."

"Really?" he said, momentarily distracted. "They don't do that to me."

"It's different for guys," I retorted, irked. "You may have heard of this thing called the double standard? Guys are supposed to be tall. Height is a masculine trait, so very tall girls are seen as freakish or unfeminine, whereas guys who are tall are just seen as hot." Dang, that last word just slipped out.

"So ... I'm hot?"

"You're missing the point," I said quickly. "They're clocking my height, not my eyes, or whatever."

"Okay, so they may *notice* that you're taller than most girls, but do you really think they *care?* Or even think about it again? You're the one that's constantly aware of it."

Could there be some truth in that?

"Besides," he said, getting to his feet, dusting off the pants of his jeans and holding out a hand to help me up. "You know what Dr. Phil says …"

"I'm listening," I said, not letting go of his hand.

In a perfect Texan accent, he drawled, "You would care a lot less about what people think of you, if you knew how seldom they did."

~ 23 ~

The Tall Boys List:
1. Jay Young
2. ~~Tim Anderson~~
3. ~~Mark Rodriguez~~
4. ~~Dylan Jones~~
5. Robert Scott

Jay Young was back on the Tall Boys List.

Now that he was free of Faye, I could ask him out on a date, but I was reluctant to do so. It felt too soon to move in for the kill, like I was some dating vulture who had been watching and waiting all this time, ready to pounce the moment his relationship with her flatlined.

Chloe disagreed with me on this. "Do it now, before someone else snaps him up," she'd said, when I told her that he and Faye were officially over.

"I'm scared."

"Of what — rejection?"

Always. But also, "I'm scared of screwing up this production.

If a date with Jay goes badly, having to act opposite him afterward would be awful. And it won't be fair on the rest of the cast if it messes up the show. Everyone's put so much time and effort into it already."

Also, a date with Jay would matter in a way it hadn't with Tim, Dylan or Mark. If I asked Jay out, and he said no, I'd care about that. If he said yes, I'd get my hopes up — and not for winning the bet. If we dated and it went belly-up, that would upset me. No, I'd just have to hang tight until after the production was over before I made a move.

By the third week of November, with exactly one month until our production, we'd all more or less memorized our lines — Jay and me more (him because he was a pro, and me because I still feared Wren snatching the role back for me if I didn't deliver), and Zack less. So, we were all feeling a bit more confident.

Until Doug threw us a curveball.

Romero and Juliet, he explained, was not only going modern, it was going multimedia. Giant flat screens mounted on either side of the stage would show close-ups of our faces, or panoramic shots of scene settings like sunset beaches, wild raves, and Juliet's bedroom. Popular songs would blast out from surround-sound speakers located throughout the auditorium. And there would be a hashtag (#RomeroandJuliet4eva) so audience members could live-tweet and Instagram the performance.

"It'll be part movie, part theater, all red-hot razzmatazz!" Doug did full-on star-fingers as he said this.

"Great," said Liz sourly. "My pimples will be displayed on a giant screen for the whole school to see."

"We'll be very selective about what we project," said Doug. "But we seriously need to work on timing, so you don't wind up trying to say lines over the music."

Jay didn't look enthusiastic at the addition of the multimedia. "It's going to be pretty distracting — to the audience and to us. You don't reckon it'll interfere with our performances?"

"You guys are so negative! It's going to be great," Doug said firmly. "It'll be something different, so it'll get a buzz going and help sell tickets to the kind of audience who normally wouldn't come to a performance of *Romeo and Juliet*. You want full houses, don't you?"

I did, though when I thought about my performance, I still had concerns. Scratch that. I had major doubts and the sort of dark terrors that sent me into cold sweats. But even I could tell that the scenes between Jay and me were going a lot better after our joint exercises. I still wasn't giving it my all, but at least I knew him better now. And I trusted him enough to loosen up and let more emotion into my acting.

Wren's Juliet had been sweet, gentle, innocent. My Juliet was more edgy and tense. I hadn't planned it that way — I guess my natural nervous reserve just bled into the way I moved and said my dialogue — but I thought it worked better for the modernized play. In this millennium, if a girl was nothing but nice, kind and inoffensive, she'd be boring at best and a complete sap at worst.

Jay reacted to my way of playing Juliet as a tough and prickly rich girl by accommodating his own performance, becoming more bold and challenging, and less smoothly tender in his own characterization. He also began letting his stubble grow — telling the complaining teachers that he needed it for the role — so he looked rougher and tougher. And hotter.

After our first rehearsal with accompanying audiovisuals, we felt lost and clueless, but Doug surprised us by not only *not* freaking out ("It's your first time with the multimedia, I've got to expect some hiccups,") but by taking us out for burgers at Jumping Jim's to thank us for trying.

I got a lift to the diner with Zack. I wasn't entirely sure how that happened — I would have preferred to catch a ride with Jay, or with anyone else, really — but Zack somehow got all the girls into his fast and noisy muscle car.

"Listen to that engine, ladies," he said, revving at the traffic lights. "That's the sound of power and adrenaline. That's the mating call of a real man."

It didn't seem to be a mating call that appealed to any of the females in the car, who reacted with eye rolls, snorts and giggles. At least the journey was short, and for a change, I got to ride shotgun.

Inside the diner, we joined up a few tables so that the cast and crew could all sit together. Somehow, I wound up sitting next to Jay. I was hyper-aware of his thigh pressing up against mine and the odd brush of his elbow against my arm. As luck would have it — my luck, other people didn't seem to struggle like this — Tori was on duty and working our table.

When she delivered our meals, she sidled up beside me and whispered furiously, "I see you sitting there next to your tall boy, Big P, but this doesn't count as a date even if you are making out under that table."

"Shh!" I hissed.

"It's a group outing — let's both be clear on that."

"Fine!" Now get lost.

"What was that about?" Jay leaned over to ask, his gaze on Tori's departing form.

"Nothing."

No way was I going to tell him about the wager — it was just too embarrassing. Sure, he'd been a good sport about the kiss that first night, but I'd be mortified if he discovered that I couldn't get a guy to go out with me for three paltry dates. And if he felt sorry for me and volunteered to help me out again? It would be a pity date, just like Tori had said.

It was also kind of shameful. What had I been thinking, agreeing to date boys to get money? Once the production was over, I'd come clean about the bet and ask Jay out. But not before.

~ 24 ~

*J*ay's house was in a different universe, on a planet called Happy Families.

He lived in an enormous two-story colonial-style house, with a neat front yard and flower boxes below the windows. His mother — slim and elegantly dressed, with a shiny bob of brown hair — smiled as she welcomed me inside and led me to the living room.

My eyes took in all the gorgeous details: luxurious Persian carpets resting on the gleaming expanse of polished wood floors; framed black-and-white photographs and original paintings on the walls; tiny, tasteful collections of interesting *objets d'art* displayed on side tables; thick, luxurious drapes in light colors; fresh flowers in vases — yellow lilies in the hall and white roses in the center of a low table set between dark leather couches in the living room. Everywhere, there was a sense of space.

It felt like I'd stepped into a full-color spread from Beautiful Homes.

The cast members, most of whom had arrived before me,

were the only messy elements in the lounge. They sprawled on the couches and armchairs, tossed their coats and scarves on a club chair, and spoke in voices somehow too loud for this beautiful room. To me, it seemed created for quiet, refined pursuits — some meditation, perhaps, or listening to soft classical music while reading one of the books neatly stacked on the tall shelves against the far wall. But now it was filled with the noisy troupe of actors displaced from the school auditorium by a high-school debate competition.

"Grab a seat," Jay said.

Zack moved to the middle of a couch, patted the spaces on either side of him in invitation, saying to Jay and me, "Tall thing one. And tall thing two."

I met Jay's raised eyebrow and suppressed a giggle as I opted instead for the floor, leaning up against a soft leather ottoman. Jay took a seat in an armchair opposite me, and Zack pouted in disappointment.

Doug clapped his hands twice — always his signal for us to shut up. "So, we won't be able to rehearse with movements, obviously, or the audiovisuals. But we can't afford to lose any rehearsal time. Opening night is December eighteenth, which is only three short weeks away, people!" He stared around at us severely. "I thought that tonight we should talk about our characters, maybe give each other ideas about what might be motivating them in different scenes. I'll give you my thoughts on where you can deepen emotion." His eyes strayed to me when he said this, and I dropped my gaze and tugged at my socks (men's), trying to cover the ankle gap between the hem of my jeans and my sneakers.

"But first we'll do a couple of speed run-throughs," Doug added. "It's a fabulous way to cement your memory of your lines. I still think some of you are thinking so hard about your words that you're not fully *inhabiting* your characters."

Certain that he was talking about me again, I kept my eyes down, this time staring at my arms, at the five or six inches of bare forearm between my shirt cuffs and my wrists. A familiar irritation gripped me. This was supposed to be a long-sleeved shirt, but long-sleeved shirts always ended just past the elbow on me, unless I bought a man's shirt. Honestly, did no one in the world make clothes for tall girls? How hard could it be for a store to carry a tall girls range — clothes that fit in the waist but had longer sleeves and legs, shoes and socks long enough for our feet, dresses with lower hems? Someone ought to design *that*.

A thrill of something — anticipation? Excitement? Exhilaration? — rippled over my scalp. Energy surged through me. Finally, I had it — the perfect theme for my fashion school project. The somebody who ought to design a range of clothing for tall girls was *me*. Why had I never thought of it before? I'd make beautiful garments, ones that flattered the long limbs and lines of tall girls, ones that showed we did have waists and boobs, dresses that weren't indecently short, tops that didn't resemble circus tents, necklines that were generous enough to slip easily over our large heads, gloves that didn't cut off circulation, bathing suits long enough in the body that they didn't threaten to slice you up the crotch, fitted T-shirts that didn't constrict your breathing, and an elegant evening dress that would make any tall girl feel like a princess for a night.

"Peyton, *Peyton?*" Someone was calling my name.

While I'd been lost in my glorious super-sized visions, Mrs. Young had brought in trays of refreshments and was now asking me what I'd like. I blinked — half to clear the image of a slinky black velvet dress with plunging backline, and half because I was dazed by the splendor of the offerings. Fresh coffee in a French press, mugs of hot chocolate topped with teeny marshmallows, homemade snickerdoodles, and apple pie.

I took a slice of the apple pie with a dollop of whipped cream on the side, and a mug of hot chocolate.

"Thank you so much," I said. "This is wonderful!"

"Why thank you, dear," Mrs. Young said, looking faintly bemused at my obvious enthusiasm.

A quick glance at the others told me no one else was raving. Did they also regularly get feasts like this in their homes? Amazing.

Although I was desperate to start sketching my ideas for the new range, I forced myself to concentrate on the discussions and read-throughs. I think some of my inner excitement must have shown in my expression or filtered into my voice, because Doug complimented me on my "almost manic energy". At least, I think it was a compliment.

We were into the second run-through when the door burst open with a bang, and a tall, dark-haired man stuck his head inside. There was enough of a resemblance for me to realize that this must be Jay's father.

"Well, hellooo, troubadours! How goes the *rehearsal?*" he said loudly.

I snuck a quick glance at Jay, just in time to see an

unreadable expression flit across his features before they settled back into their usually relaxed expression.

"It's going great, sir," said Doug.

"Yeah, especially with the cookies," added Zack, who'd eaten three-quarters of them by himself.

"Good to hear, good to hear!" said Mr. Young with hearty enthusiasm. "Well, you kids have fun with your play-acting, now. And shout if you need anything."

After that, we moved into the character analysis that Doug had promised. Jay, who was always serious about acting, seemed even more intense than usual when speculating about Romero's motivations and his sources of anger and antagonism, while Zack kept saying things like, "I'd like to motivate you, Candypants," and Liz speculated about whether her nondenominational religious-leader-type person of unspecified gender might be bi and therefore "both equally attracted to, and jealous of, Romero *and* Juliet."

We were close to calling it quits for the day when I slipped out of the room, in desperate need of a toilet.

"Can I help you, dear?" Mrs. Young was passing by with a tray, presumably on her way to collect our dirty cups and plates.

"I was looking for the bathroom?"

"The one down here's occupied, but if you go upstairs and turn right, you'll find another at the end of the landing."

When I'd finished in the bathroom (fluffy towels, a rose-shaped bar of soap, fragranced hand lotion, and clear marble counter), I walked slowly back down the landing, hoping to get a glimpse of the upstairs rooms. Surely one of them had to be Jay's. The first door was ajar and, after a quick look around to check I was unobserved, I pushed it open with my toe and stuck my head in for a quick peek. It was a neat room with a black-and-white color scheme, a couple of books on shelves dominated by a music system and an enormous CD collection, and a painting on the main wall of a stormy ocean scene.

Was this Jay's room? Somehow, it didn't seem to fit him. He must have a brother — older, probably. A younger kid's room would be more messy, have some toys and school books lying around. This space had the empty feel of a visitor's room.

The door of the next room along the landing was wide open, and I knew at a glance that it was Jay's. The walls were filled with framed posters of famous stage productions — *Les Mis*, *The Glass Menagerie* and *Othello*. The window was framed by red velvet drapes, held open by roped tie-backs — a theatrical look which seemed to suggest the world outside was merely a stage. The bed was extra long. I'd bet *his* feet didn't hang off the edge of his bed.

There was a pile of books on the bedside table and another on the desk, and Jay's black leather jacket hung over the chair. The room wasn't messy, but it was lived-in. I was tempted to slip inside, to scrutinize every aspect. I wanted to check the titles of the books he was reading and see what type of music he liked. Hell, I was tempted to fling myself on his bed, bury my face into his pillow and inhale his scent, but an outburst of laughter coming from below brought me to my senses.

I scampered away from Jay's bedroom and was halfway down the stairs when the front door opened and a young woman stepped inside. She was tall — though not as tall as me — with a rangy build and short, spiky hair.

She spotted me at once and gave me a big, confident smile. "Hi, who are you?"

"I'm one of the cast members, from Jay's play? We're rehearsing here today."

"Ah," she said, nodding. "Can you —"

Just then, Jay came out of the living room. When he saw the new arrival, his face lit up with joy.

"Hey, it's so good to see you!" he said, flinging his arms wide and hugging her tight.

Oh. Like that.

~ 25 ~

"Have you met Peyton?" Jay said.

"Hey, Peyton," the new girl said.

"Peyton, this is my sister, Jack."

"You have a sister? Called Jack?" I said, equal parts relieved and puzzled.

"Her real name is Jacqueline," said Mrs. Young, walking into the hallway and embracing her daughter before stepping back to examine her face. "Look at you — you're so sunburned!"

Jack pulled a face. "Mo-om."

"She's never answered to Jacqueline," Jay told me.

"Would you?" challenged his sister.

"I'm a boy," Jay said.

"Just because a person is female doesn't mean they should get names that are so … ornamental," countered Jack, but she grinned as she said it, and I had the sense they were running through a familiar old argument.

"I tried calling her Jackie and even Jaycee, but no luck there either," said Mrs. Young.

"Jackie is a name for a dog. And Jaycee — what am I, Jesus Christ? My name is Jack."

"Pleased to meet you, Jack," I said. And I was — she seemed amazing.

"Hey Peyton, can you help me with my bags?"

I saw then that she had dropped two huge duffel bags just outside the front door.

"Sure." I grabbed one and slung it over my shoulder.

"Here, I'll help you with that," said Jay, offering to take the bag I was carrying.

I would gladly have let him take it — that bag was *heavy* — but Jack smacked his hand away and said, "She's female, not handicapped. Besides, this one looks strong!" She winked at her brother, grabbed my hand and half-dragged me up the stairs with her.

I glanced backward over my shoulder. Smiling, Jay shrugged and gave me a look that clearly said, "I know. She's crazy, right?"

Jack's room was the black-and-white one.

"Home sweet home," she said, flopping onto her bed and sighing with pleasure. "I know it seems a little impersonal, but I hate clutter. I like things neat and tidy."

"I like neat and tidy, too," I admitted.

"You're not a pink and frilly type of girl, are you?" I was already shaking my head when she continued, "I couldn't handle it if Jay dated pink and frilly."

"Oh, we're not dating. I'm just on the cast."

"You sure?" She cast me a doubting look.

"Yeah, I think I'd have noticed."

Jack laughed. "What play are you doing?"

"It's an updated version of *Romeo and Juliet*."

"Let me guess, Jay's Romeo?"

"Of course."

"And you are …?"

"Juliet," I said, hastening to add, "but only because I'm tall. They swapped me out for the short, pretty girl who can act because the height difference between her and Jay was making everyone laugh. Your brother's really tall." I was horrified to hear myself sigh on the last two words.

A knowing look came into her eyes, but she merely nodded and said, "I wouldn't sweat it. Just trust him and go with the flow. He'll make you look like Oscar material. Nobody's as good as he is when it comes to acting, and there's nothing he wouldn't do to get the perfect performance."

She sat up, hooked the strap of the nearest bag with her foot, and pulled it toward her. "Better start sorting the laundry for Mom."

"Have you been away on vacation?"

"I wish. No, I'm just back from a month-long stint offshore. I'm a trainee driller on an oil rig."

"An oil rig?" I couldn't keep the surprise out my voice. "Oh, so that's why he had that book."

"What book? Who?"

"Nothing, never mind." I waved my hand as if to erase the words from the air. "That's such a cool job!" I was impressed. I'd rather work on an oil rig than be a kindergarten teacher, or an accountant (sorry, Mark) or, say, a butt-doctor. Though I would still rather be a fashion designer. But not, definitely not, of pink and frilly clothes.

"Yeah, it is cool. Don't get me wrong, it's freaking hard work. Brutal in fact. But it's exciting, mostly outdoors, the pay is fantastic, and" — here she gave me a broad wink — "the men are many, manly and hot. And that's hottt with three T's, that rhyme with *please* and *tease* and Oh *Jeez*!" She writhed and gasped as she said the last words.

Over my giggles and Jack's chortles, I heard the unmistakable sounds of the rest of the cast departing.

"Sorry, I've got to run. I need to hitch a ride home with one of them," I said. "It was great meeting you."

"Yeah, likewise. You" — she pointed a finger like a cocked gun at me — "can come again. And I don't say that to all Jay's girls."

All? How many were there?

"I'm not his girl," I explained again, feeling I ought to set the record straight.

"Not yet, maybe. But I'm thinking playing Juliet against Jay's Romeo should give you plenty of opportunities to change that, eh? Am I right? I'm right, aren't I?"

"Uh, gotta go," I said and rushed out of the room.

I hurried down the stairs, but the hall was empty except for Jay. The others had already left.

"Is your mother or father coming to get you?" he said.

"My dad lives in Blue Crab Bay. They're divorced."

"Oh. I'm sorry."

"Don't be — it's not your fault."

"So, your mom's coming?"

I was thinking about how to imply that she was without actually lying when Jack called from upstairs, "She was going to get a lift from one of the others, and now she's stranded, Jay. Peyton desperately needs a ride."

Was it my imagination, or had she laid special emphasis on the last word? I glanced up to see her grinning wickedly down at me from the landing.

"No problem," Jay said, grabbing his keys from a carved wooden bowl on the table beside the front door. "Ready to go?"

I grabbed my coat and bag, tracked down Mrs. Young to thank her, and waved goodbye to Jack, who dangled over the upstairs bannister, calling dramatically, "Farewell, sweet Juliet! Parting is such sweet sorrow."

Outside, the night was cold and crisp, with stars glittering in the endless darkness above, but we were soon enveloped in a bubble of warmth from the heaters inside the car. I gave Jay my address, and we headed out, neither of us speaking for a few minutes.

"Your sister's great," I said eventually.

He grinned. "My mother says I'm the actor onstage, but Jack's the real character off it."

"You get on well, though?"

"Oh yeah, we're very close, though these days she's not at home that much. She works offshore in four-week bursts, alternating with two weeks' leave."

"An oil-rigger, yeah, she told me."

"Do you have any brothers or sisters?"

"I ... no. No, I don't." I didn't know how to explain things, where to begin, how to answer his question without getting into all the rest of it. "It's just Mom and me living in ye olde Lane Mansion. Take a left at the lights, and then right at the next street."

We turned a corner, passing the old Frozen Fun ice rink.

"My dad used to take Jack and me ice-skating when we were young," Jay said. "I think he was hoping I'd become a speed-skater, and Jack would get into figure-skating."

"Somehow, I can't imagine her in a tutu."

Jay gave a bark of laughter. "Right? Or me in one of those Lycra onesies. Do you skate?"

"I did when I was little. Right back there at the Frozen Fun."

"Hey, we should go sometime. Might be fun?"

He wanted to spend time with me? Oh, yes please.

"I'm not very good," I warned. "I wasn't good even back then, and that was many, many years ago."

"What are you, sixty? You'll be fine. I reckon it's like riding a bicycle, it'll come back to you."

"Are you an expert or something?"

Just my luck he'd be a skilled, graceful skater, and I'd be the huge, clumsy lump beside him.

"Last time I went, I could go forwards and stop. If you're expecting more than that, you'll be seriously disappointed."

"Okay, then, in that case, yes," I said, and heard myself adding, "I'd love to go."

"Cool, Saturday after rehearsal?"

"Sure."

"It's a date then," he said.

Was it, though? Did he mean we were going as a couple on a date, or had he just been confirming the date and time?

By 7.15 pm on Saturday, I still wasn't sure. By 7.16 pm, I had my answer.

~ 26 ~

The last time I'd visited the Frozen Fun ice rink must have been when I was about seven or eight, before Mom's condition really got its claws into her, but it still looked pretty much how I remembered it. The barriers around the ice were still the same battered blue plastic walls with dented steel kickplates running around the bottom. The old raked rows of bright-orange, molded-plastic chairs circled the rink, though more of them now had butt-pinching cracks in the seats and eye-boggling graffiti scrawled onto their backs. The chilly air was laced with a familiar mixture of sweat, mildew and teenage desperation — a single whiff transported me back a decade in a second.

The skate rental desk hadn't changed either. You still had to hand over your shoes while standing on the puddled rubberized floor in your socks, and declare your shoe size before being issued with the plastic rental boots — stylish black for boys, hideous purple for girls. And I was willing to bet, maybe not eight hundred but ten bucks at least, that the shoe-exchange procedure hadn't changed at all.

"Next." The guy behind the counter had a thin blond ponytail, a wispy soul patch, and a bored expression.

Jay waved me ahead of him with a polite "Ladies, first."

"Why don't you go first?" I suggested, not wishing him to witness the conversation I knew was about to occur. "Then you can go ahead and change in the meantime. They sometimes have, er, delays with the girls' boots."

"That's okay, I can wait."

"Next!" said Soul Patch.

There was no help for it. I walked up to the counter and handed over my sneakers. Jay stood directly behind me.

"Size?"

"Thirteen," I whispered, then remembered something else from the past. These skates pinched like the devil's own imps. I'd always had to take a half-size bigger than usual. "Wait, make that thirteen and a half."

"Wa's that?" Soul Patch cupped a hand behind his ear.

If Jay was going to reject me when he discovered I was Bigfoot's size-matched mate, I might as well know it sooner rather than later.

"Thirteen and a half," I said, staring the clerk straight in the eye. "But —"

"*Thirteen and a half?*" he exclaimed, loud enough for everyone in the greater Baltimore metropolitan area to hear.

Ah yes, this was following the usual pattern. The next thing he would say was …

"I don't even think they make boots that big, man."

"They do," I said, painfully aware of the heat rising up my neck. "But only in men's b—"

"Jethro, Jethro!" the guy called over his shoulder down the aisles of shelves. "What's the biggest boot we have for girls?"

"Ten," came an answering shout.

"You can give me —"

"We don't have boots that big, man," Soul Patch said, shaking his head and looking at me with an expression somewhere between disbelief and alarm. Maybe he was scared I'd deck him. Or kick him with my giant feet.

"Dayum," he said, looking me up and down and seeming to register my size for the first time. "You're really tall, you know that?"

God give me patience, I thought. *If you give me strength I will only punch him in the face.*

"I'll take a size twelve," I said. "In black."

"Those are boys' boots."

"Last I heard, we don't have sex-specific feet."

He stared back at me blankly.

"Do you keep your junk in your socks?" I demanded angrily.

Soul Patch went pale. "How did you know, man? Are you a narc, like an undercover cop? Are you even a lady?"

"What?" Now I was the one confused.

Jay stepped to stand beside me. "Get the *lady* a pair of size twelve black skates." His voice was low and threatening — nothing like his usual laid-back tones — and the words were spoken in a perfect Russian accent. He sounded like a Soviet mobster.

Soul Patch's eyes widened. "Um, Jethro," he called, his voice cracking into a higher octave. "Can I give black boots to a lady?"

Jay leaned forward, his face twisted into a thin-lipped snarl. "Do it. And do it now," he said, in a deep, rough voice which evoked echoes of snow and blood and vodka.

"Yes, sir, right away." Soul Patch scampered off with my sneakers and was back in less than a minute with a new-looking pair of black skates. "And for you, Mr. ... Sir?"

"Size fifteen," Jay growled.

Yes! Dylan's report had been accurate — Jay's feet were bigger than mine. Another fantasy ticked off on my bucket list of experiences to have with a tall boy.

"Thanks," I said as we walked off with our skates.

"Yeah, you should thank me."

Taken aback, I shot him a quick glance.

"It's not everyone who gets a free performance of Vladimir, the Russian bodyguard."

"Oh, were you a bodyguard? I had you pegged as a gangster."

"I am wounded, deeply." The rasping voice and strong accent were back. It was kind of sexy. "Did I not bring tubular protection to guard for your body?" He patted the pockets of his jacket.

"You brought ... protection?"

I couldn't help where my mind went. And it went there. Jay, bringing protection, for me. *Tubular* protection.

Jay stuck his hand into a pocket and whipped out ... a pair of black socks, patterned with white *Phantom Of The Opera* masks.

"Okay. That was not what I was expecting to see."

"Just what were you expecting, Peyton?"

The blush was back in an instant. "Did you really bring those for me?"

"Of course, these boots can be brutal on tender feet. Wearing two pairs of socks helps protect against blisters."

I didn't know what touched me more — that he had stood up for me at the counter, that he seemed unfazed by the size of my flippers, or that he'd brought socks to protect my feet, like they were tender, sensitive little things. But the combination of kindnesses made me want to kiss him. If we'd been rehearsing the love scene at that moment, I could've infused it with sweet, gentle schmexiness, no problem.

I sat on the bench, pulled Jay's socks over my own and wrestled my feet into the skates. They were ugly — even bigger, clunkier and heavier than I remembered — and I would be the only girl on the ice wearing boys' skates, wearing my freak on my feet.

Jay sat down beside me and pulled off the socks he was wearing. He said something about wanting the dry pair against his skin, but I wasn't paying much attention. I was fixated by the sight of his bare feet. They were enormous, clearly both longer and broader than my own, but they were also beautiful, with long toes and high arches. And the tops were freckled, just like his hands. I stared at those feet until they disappeared into his socks, mentally checking off yet another bucket list item.

Then a thought struck me. "Won't skating be hard on your Achilles tendon?"

"My Achilles?"

"Yeah, don't you have an injury there?"

"How do you know about that?"

I cursed myself. I almost never said what I was thinking, I'd perfected the art of biting back comebacks and thinking carefully before I spoke or answered questions, but with Jay, I couldn't seem to prevent myself blurting out the first thing that popped into my head. I didn't want to lie to him, so I went with an edited version of the truth.

"I think I heard it from Tim Anderson." It was the truth, but not the whole truth — maybe that's why it didn't come out sounding as casually offhand as I'd intended.

"Right," said Jay.

"So it'll be okay? Your ankle, I mean?"

"I'm sure it'll be just fine — let's go!"

~ *27* ~

he ice seemed way more slippery than I remembered. In less than a minute, I was on my butt in the middle of a puddle. Jay tried to pull me to my feet, but a second later, he was beside me in the wet, both of us laughing. He got to his knees, dragged himself up by clinging to the side wall, and then hauled me up beside him with a combination of brute strength and total determination.

He hung onto my hand, even once I was up and (more or less) steady on my blades, and after that we just kept holding hands. I wasn't sure if this was just to support me, or if we were holding hands because it was a date.

Jay, I was relieved to see, was not a more skilled skater than me, but there was a grace and confidence to his movements that I lacked. He trusted his body, expected it to do what he told it.

My mind went back to the exquisite torture of that night of trust exercises with him, and the things he'd said about me being self-conscious and not comfortable in my own skin. Unlike me, Jay *was* at ease inside his skin. He wasn't at war with his body. He wasn't constantly trying to minimize or disguise it. Jay was at home in himself.

How the heck could I get myself to that place?

Carefully, and very slowly at first, we made our way around the rink, being lapped by kids a third of our age who could do amazing things at terrifying speeds on their tiny skates. We got better as the old muscle-memory kicked in, but there was still a whole lot of bumping, tripping, falling down, pulling up, and hanging on to each other. I laughed so hard that I soon forgot to feel anxious — either about my body, or about being in contact with his.

But as Jay rescued me from another fall, a rogue thought snuck into my mind. Had he invited me skating because he wanted to spend time hanging out with me, or was this just another trust-building exercise aimed at getting me to deliver a better version of Juliet? After all, his own sister had said there was nothing he wouldn't do to get the perfect performance.

I was still considering this when the last song of the session — a slow romantic number which made me hyper-aware of how I was out of breath, hot (and probably red-cheeked), and wet all over — came to an end, and we cleared the ice along with all the other skaters.

Jay and I bought a couple of milkshakes from the concession stand, and then slumped into a pair of the orange seats to rest while the Zamboni machine wove its way across the rutted ice, leaving cleaned and resurfaced trails in its wake.

I puffed hair out of my eyes and checked the time. It was 7.13 pm — I'd have to head home soon, else my mother would start worrying and texting. But first, I wanted to clarify something.

"Jay?"

"Yeah?"

He'd taken off his boots and was rubbing the toes of one foot. How good would it feel to have him massage *my* feet just like that?

"Can I just ask ... Us, here tonight, skating," I said, haltingly. "Is this another exercise for the play, or is this, like, a date?"

Jay stopped kneading his feet and met my gaze directly. "Do you want it to be a date?"

Uh-oh. I'd wanted him to call it, but he'd passed the buck to me. While my brain scrambled for a way to make him speak first, my mouth opened again.

"Yes," I heard myself saying. "I think I do."

"Me, too. So, it's a date, then," Jay said, with a long, slow smile that filled me with something light and lovely. Hope, maybe.

The music cranked up again. The Zamboni was leaving the ice at one end, and skaters poured onto the rink at the other, while Taylor Swift warned her latest crush that he looked like her next mistake.

"I just don't want this" — Jay waved a finger between the two of us — "to impact badly on the production if ... things don't work out."

"Yeah, I understand that. It wouldn't be fair on the others, on Doug."

Over our heads, Taylor pondered the odds of love lasting forever, or going down in flames.

"Let's agree now that whatever we do, whatever happens,

we'll keep it professional on stage, yeah?" Jay said. "For the sake of the production."

For the sake of the production.

"Okay, sure. Agreed." I nodded and held out my baby finger in a crook. "Pinkie promise."

He grinned at that but linked his finger with mine. I cut the connection with my other hand, and out of habit of doing this with Chloe, who knew how to answer, said, "Bogart."

"Bacall," Jay said immediately.

Amazing. He was perfect.

"You want to skate some more?" he asked.

"Nah, I think I'm done. Unless you want to?"

He shook his head — maybe his Achilles was playing up — and helped me tug off my skates. We reclaimed our shoes from a now eager-to-please Soul Patch and headed back to the car.

"So, you like old movies?" Jay said, then added in a perfect impersonation of Humphrey Bogart, "I think this is the beginning of a beautiful friendship."

I smiled. "I love them. Do you?"

"I like all movies. I want to be an actor."

"Like, professionally, when you leave school?"

"Uh-huh." He opened the passenger door for me and, once he was inside the car, continued, "I've applied to the Julliard School of Performing Arts in New York."

Wow, even I'd heard of that. "You'll get in for sure. I've never seen anyone act like you can."

Were *his* cheeks reddening a little now? It made a nice change.

"That's why I transferred to Longford High," he explained

as we pulled out of the lot. "Ms. Gooding is an amazing drama teacher — she trained at Julliard too, many years ago. I'm hoping she'll be able to knock me into shape for the audition."

"You have to audition to get in?"

"Yeah, and they say it's hectic. You've got to prepare a song — don't ask me why, I don't want to be a singer — plus four monologues. Two classical and two modern."

"Let me guess — one of your modern pieces will be from *A Streetcar Named Desire*?"

"How did you know that?" Jay said, shooting me a startled glance.

Oops, I'd done it again — speaking before thinking. I'd guessed it because the play had been on the list of items Jay had borrowed from the school library in Tim's report, but I could hardly tell him that.

"I want to go to school in New York, too," I said quickly.

"Yeah? NYU?"

"No, the New York School of Fashion. It has a kind of audition process, too — you have to design and sew a range of clothes and submit them, along with a paper, and be assessed to see if you qualify," I said, then added hesitantly, "The top submission wins a full-ride scholarship."

"You're aiming for that?"

"It's the only way I'll be able to go. We can't afford the tuition, and no way would we qualify for a loan."

Jay nodded but didn't say anything glib about being sure everything would work out for the best, which I appreciated. Because things often didn't. Sometimes, things turned out spectacularly bad.

"So, that's why you're sometimes trimmed with thread." Jay's comment broke into my thoughts.

"Huh?"

"When you come to rehearsals, you sometimes have bits of fluff and thread on your clothes or your hair. And these fingers" — he lightly stroked the tips of the first two fingers on my right hand, sending a tingle up my arm — "are often stained with black. From sketching?"

I nodded. "I spend every spare moment sketching designs and practicing my sewing. And now that I've changed the entire theme of the range, I have to start all over again."

"What's your new theme?" Jay asked, as we turned into my street.

"Tall girls." It came out sounding like a question, like I was asking for permission.

"Tall girls?"

"It's just, I struggle — and I mean, *really* struggle — to find clothes that fit properly and that look good. You saw tonight, with the shoes. If you're tall and female, it's nearly impossible to find stylish clothes in your size. I figure other tall girls must have the same problem. And since we can't buy them, it seemed like a good idea to design and make some."

It sounded lame as I explained it. I bet the other applicants had way cooler themes — urban decay, or dystopian diva, or eclectic elegance.

"I think it's an epic idea. Good luck with your submission. Wouldn't it be great if you and I both got into New York schools for next year?"

I smiled my agreement. We'd arrived at my house — time

for the usual duck and dive. When Jay had dropped me off after last Saturday's rehearsal, I'd urged him to stay in the car, and he had — waiting until I was inside the house before driving off. But now, to my dismay, he insisted on walking me right to my front door.

"Really, it's not necessary," I protested.

"Yeah, it is."

"You didn't feel the need last time you brought me home," I said, walking as slowly as possible.

"That wasn't a date. When it's a date, a gentleman escorts a lady to the door."

There was no shaking gentleman Jay. He even had his hand at my elbow, which I would have enjoyed hugely in other circumstances. When we got to the front step, he gazed down at me expectantly. Were we going to kiss? Was he waiting for me to make the first move?

"So …" I popped my lips uncertainly. "Thanks, I had a great time."

"I could use a cup of coffee," said Jay. "Are you going to invite me in?"

"No!" I blurted out.

Jay looked taken aback, maybe even offended. I hurried to make my usual excuses.

"I mean, I would, but I can't. It's just that my mom's sick." That was true, she was. "And I don't want to disturb her if she's resting."

I racked my brains for a ruse to get him away from the door.

"Sorry to hear that. What's the matter with her?" He sounded genuinely concerned.

I made a show of patting my pockets and checking the side compartment of my bag.

"I can't find my keys. I think they must have fallen out in the car," I said, switching into helpless female mode and giving him my best wide-eyed look of appeal.

Like the good guy he was, Jay volunteered to go check. I waited until he was at the car, head stuck inside the open passenger door, before whipping my keys out of their usual compartment in my bag and holding them up.

"Found them!" I called cheerfully. "Goodnight, see you soon." Then I quickly unlocked the door and slipped inside.

I pulled aside an inch of curtain at the window beside the front door and peered out. Jay was still standing there, frowning at the spot where I'd disappeared.

"Go!" I whispered in the dark of the front room. "Go back to your perfect home and family, just *go*."

And after a few more moments, he did.

~ *28* ~

On Sunday, I sat on the floor in my room with my phone in my hand, thumb hovering over the keypad. After another moment's hesitation, my thumb moved away from the *send* button and hit *delete* instead.

It's no good, I can't do it :/ I texted Chloe.

Do what?

Send the details of the date with Jay to Tori for her pathetic little log.

Why not?

Yeah, why not?

Scruples?

Scruples? LOL!! :D

How to explain this when I didn't fully understand it myself? Sending Tori the details would feel like a betrayal, as if I'd just gone out with him for the bet, when I totally would have done it anyway. In a heartbeat.

Another message came in from Chloe.

> *You'll have to get over your 'scruples' if you want to win the bet and get that money. Unless you plan to date another tall boy at the same time as Jay? And I'm guessing you've got some scruples about THAT? These dates with Jay need to count toward your total.*

> *It would feel like I'm using him.*

> *Hate to break it to you, kiddo, but you used them all.*

Ouch, that stung. But Chloe was right.

> *And he was on your target list from the beginning.*

> *But that was before I knew him. Now it just seems wrong.*

> *Your call. Gotta go, mom's calling for lunch.*

The growling of my stomach told me it was time for my lunch, too. I opened my small refrigerator, grabbed a ready meal — "French *coq au vin* with buttered spring vegetables" — and shoved it in the microwave to heat up. The cardboard sleeve showed a mouth-watering photograph of chicken stew and baby veggies, but the plastic tray I pulled out three minutes later contained chewy chunks of beige meat in a bland sauce, with mushy gray lumps on the side. I ate less than half and dumped the rest in my trashcan. Once I'd washed and put away my plate and fork, I turned my attention to my fashion range.

I'd completed a series of large pencil sketches — a foot and a half high by a foot wide each —and wanted to get an idea of what they would look like once made up, to figure out what sorts of colors and patterns would work best for which designs.

Surely, somewhere in this godforsaken house, there must be some fabric I could experiment with? Hadn't I once seen Mom's old sewing basket in the attic? Searching up there would be a dusty job, with no guarantee that it would even contain any suitable fabric. It might be easier just to find some old clothes and cut them up. There would be lots of those because my mother never let me throw away my outgrown or worn out clothes.

"Waste not, want not. I'll sort through them and donate what we can't use to Goodwill," she always said.

I groaned as I got up off the floor. Last night's skating had left me sore and stiff in places where I never even knew I had muscles, and all the tumbles onto the hard ice had left my knees and elbows spectacularly bruised. Still, thanks to the extra pair of Jay's socks, now hand-laundered and hanging over the back of my chair to dry, my feet were wonderfully free of blisters. I smiled — not my usual reaction to thinking about my feet.

I searched every likely place in the house but didn't find any handy stashes of stylish fabric. I did find a bundle of old dishcloths, but terry cloth or super-absorbent waffle-weave wouldn't give me an idea of how the garments would look with proper fabric. The only old clothes I could find were a bunch of Dad's, stuffed into a huge Rubbermaid storage container. Why had Mom never given them back to him? Nothing about the brown corduroy jacket, moth-eaten underpants, and old T-shirts inspired me.

After an hour or more of hunting, I was ready to give up. I considered asking my mother — she always swore she knew where everything was stored — but I was afraid she'd get all enthusiastic about the project, and I wouldn't be able to shake her off for the rest of the day. Guilt pricked at me. I knew she was lonely, and I felt sorry for her. But she also felt so sorry for herself, and that irritated me so much when she did nothing to make her life better, that it invariably drove me to being nasty. Nope, better if we kept to our separate zones as much as possible.

On my way back to my bedroom, I spotted four massive wallpaper sample books tucked behind the big bookcase in the hall. Wallpaper — that might just work as a temporary fabric substitute. I dragged the heavy books out and lugged them up to my room, blowing off dust as I walked.

The sample books were filled with an amazing range of colors and styles. Some of the patterns were smooth and matte, others had a sheen, or were embellished with metallic stripes or raised patterns of velvet flocking. I wouldn't want any of these on my walls, but they'd be perfect for the sample pictures I had in mind. Best of all, the designs were grouped in coordinated ranges — each with four or five matching prints. I could use the basic pattern for the main parts of the garments and the coordinating patterns to accentuate details like linings, sashes, and contrasting collars, cuffs and turn-ups. They were perfect. Well, as perfect as a material could be without actually being a fabric.

I cut out shirts, trousers and coats and stuck them onto my sketches then added the contrasting trim. It worked well — the wallpaper was stiff and substantial, so it didn't tear like the candy wrappers had, and I could press it into folds and pleats to give a three-dimensional effect. I was busy sticking a cream paper patterned with black *fleur-de-lis* onto my drawing of a dress with an A-line skirt when my mother knocked at the door.

Go away. "Yeah?"

She came in, nibbling on a bag of jelly beans. "Would you like some?"

"No, thanks."

Did this dress need a pop of color — perhaps a scarlet sash, or silver edging on the hemline — or was the design bold enough to stand up to the starkness of color?

"What is that? What are you *doing?*"

I stared up in surprise. Mom sounded, and appeared, genuinely upset.

"I'm using these sample pieces of wallpaper in my designs."

"But why?"

"Because there is no fabric in this house — or if there is, I can't find it."

I'd told my mother about my plans to apply to fashion school. She'd seemed about as interested in them as in anything else in the outside world that didn't involve shopping.

"But you're cutting them up! Destroying them!" Mom picked up the wallpaper book closest to her and hugged it protectively against her chest, spilling jelly beans across my floor.

"Chill, okay? This is important to me. I want to be accepted into that school, and I want to win a scholarship. I can't practice on expensive fabrics, so I'm using these."

"But I kept these specially!"

Did my mother have tears in her eyes?

She snatched at the book I was using. I grabbed it and pulled it back. We were having a tug-of-war over scrap paper. This was insane — one of the craziest things ever to happen in a house full to the brim with crazy.

"I don't want you tearing those up, Peyton, stop it."

Yup, she was crying again.

"Why not, Mom, were you planning on doing some redecorating? You want to start papering the walls, now?" I said, my voice heavy with sarcasm.

"Well, yes — one day."

Ah yes, *one day*. I knew one day well.

Mom gestured to the sample books. "That's why I got those in the first place."

I tapped the sticker on the top right-hand corner of the book I was holding. It showed the year the range was released. "You got these in 2006 — I think we can safely say one day never arrived."

I tore out another piece of wallpaper, and when my mother looked like she might make a grab for the book, I slammed it closed, put it on top of the others, and sat on the pile.

She patted her pockets, found her asthma pump and took a puff. "You have no right! Those are mine. You should have asked permission before tearing them up."

"No point — you would have said no."

"That's because I don't like you interfering with my stuff!"

"Golly gee, I would never have guessed. You should have said."

The loud clatter of a stone against my window made us both jump.

"That's Chloe," I said, getting up to open the window and toss down the ladder. When my mother made no move to go, I gave her an expectant look. "Are you staying for tea?"

"I can see you don't want me here," my mother said.

No, I didn't want *me* here. I wanted me far away — preferably in New York, with Jay somewhere nearby.

Still clasping the one wallpaper book she'd been able to rescue, my mother turned and walked out while Chloe clambered in the window and I scrabbled about on the floor, picking up the jelly beans. It was like a staged production of a farce, with the players knowing all their exits and entrances.

"Here, an experiment and a peace-offering," said Chloe, handing me a small paper bag and a Krispy Kreme box.

I groaned in pleasure at the donuts (chocolate-glazed — my favorite), but sniffed suspiciously at the contents of the bag.

"Lemon verbena on a green-tea base, with just a hint of ginger. It's my own mix."

"What's that supposed to do — spark my creativity, ramp up my sexiness, or ease my anxieties?"

"It's supposed to be a mild sedative. And should you be suffering from flatulence, it'll help with that too." She grinned at the look I gave her, took the packet and began her usual tea-brewing ritual in the corner of my room.

"What's the peace offering for?" I asked, taking a giant bite of glazed donut deliciousness.

"Mom says we're doing Thanksgiving over at the grandparents' this year. Something about 'maximizing the time we have left together'. I think she's worried they'll shuffle off to the great rocking chair in the sky one of these days."

Thanksgiving was that coming Thursday. Some years I spent the day at home with my mother, but the best holidays were the ones I spent with Chloe's — great food, a happy family gathered around the table, and time to play football with Ben in their back yard.

"Not a problem," I told Chloe. "My mother will be glad I'm home for the holiday. But do me a favor, mix me up a special Thanksgiving herb tea. Use whatever will make me more patient —"

"Lavender."

"— and grateful."

"Hmm. Red clover — which, incidentally, will also boost your fertility."

"Nice to know."

"But I feel bad, leaving you here for Thanksgiving. Are you sure you'll be okay?" she said, handing me a cup of her special brew.

"You know, you really should create your own range of teas. Teas to wake you up, or put you to sleep, or rev your engine. I'm sure there'll be some project in business school you could use it for."

"Will you call me if you're not?" she said, frowning. "I'll make my parents bring me straight home."

"Sure I will. Now come see my fabulous new designs."

I spent the rest of the afternoon drinking tea with Chloe while reading her college application essay, working on my designs, getting an update on Ben's latest mischief-making (he'd painted their cat orange), and, of course, dissecting every last detail of the date with Jay, and what exactly his text message this morning meant.

Morning, Tiger Eyes. I enjoyed our icy night. See you tomorrow. J.

"Let's just say that, if these words were herbs," Chloe concluded, "they would be patchouli, with a sprig of fennel."

~ 29 ~

On Monday morning, I was returning my French books to my locker when I felt the disturbance in the Force that always signaled Jay entering my planetary field. Sure enough, when I looked up, there he was, walking down the hallway and looking straight at me. Smiling.

It was hard to believe this was happening to me, but if this was just a hallucination, I was glad to be on the wrong side of sane.

My happiness was replaced by anxiety when I saw Tim Anderson walking beside him. Just how much could I rely on Tim maintaining professional confidentiality if he became best buddies with Jay? He was a spy — one who could easily turn double agent.

"Hey, these belong to you," I said, handing Jay his socks.

His fingers brushed against mine when he took them. I chose to believe the contact was deliberate.

Tim watched the exchange with great interest. "So, Jay left his socks at your place? Things are moving fast." He nodded and gave me a knowing look.

"It's not what you're thinking," I said quickly. I didn't want him spreading rumors about Jay and me.

"For your information," Jay told Tim, "I've never set foot in her house."

"Hey, man. House, car, motel — I don't judge."

I shot Tim a filthy look, while Jay ignored the comment and turned his gaze on me.

"Would you like to come around to our place for Thanksgiving dinner?" he asked. "Jack is still on shore leave, so the whole family will be together, and my mom says she'd love to have you over."

"Huh. Meeting the family — sounds serious." Tim gave me a broad wink and another I-knew-you-wanted-to-know-about-him-so-you-could-hook-up-with-him smirk.

"I'd love to. But I should probably do Thanksgiving with my mother."

"Oh, your mom's invited, too."

"She won't be able to come. She's sick."

"Still? What's the matter?"

Was I imagining it, or did Tim's ears prick at this exchange?

"It's …" What — complicated? Unfathomable? Incomprehensible? "It's a chronic condition."

"Sorry. That must be tough for you," Jay said. "How about if you come have the big turkey lunch at our place, and I'll get you home in time for dinner with your mom? We'll send a plate so she doesn't have to cook."

"Cool. Tell your mom I say thanks."

With another quick grin, Jay left for his next class. But there was no shaking Tim, who walked beside me all the way to our History class.

"So," Tim said, "Mom's got a chronic illness, has she?"

My stomach churned at the strange emphasis I thought I detected in his tone. I wondered just how much he knew about *me*. Tim Anderson would make a very successful blackmailer, because he seemed to have, or be collecting, the lowdown on everyone's private life.

I now felt horribly guilty about commissioning the report on Jay. I shouldn't have done it. If I'd wanted to know more about him — and let's face it, I had — then I should have come by the information honestly, by getting to know him. I shouldn't have paid someone to ferret out the details of his life. How would I feel if someone commissioned a snoop on me and Tim found out all *my* private stuff?

If things developed between Jay and me, I'd have to come clean about the report. I was hiding too many secrets — about the spying, the bet, things at home — and it was getting to me. I was starting to realize that growing close to someone meant trusting them enough to open up. And it terrified me.

On Thursday, I presented myself at the Young house at eleven-thirty precisely. Mrs. Young opened the door and ushered me inside, calling upstairs for Jay. When I'd visited for the read-through, I'd thought this house was perfect, but now — redolent with the mouthwatering aromas of cinnamon, fresh bread and roasting turkey — it was perfection on steroids.

Jay came bounding down the stairs in skinny black jeans, a plaid shirt over a white T, and his *Phantom* socks.

"Hey," he said, giving me a hug.

"Hey."

We were at an awkward stage of our relationship — if I could even call it that. We had, after all, only had one date. We'd "kissed" and embraced and confessed our love a hundred times on stage, but not done more than hold hands in real life. I wanted more contact. Right then I wanted to kiss his cheek, touch his full lips, feel the growing beard on his jaw — but I kept myself in check.

Mr. Young joined us, held out his hand to shake mine, and said, "I'm Jay's father, Jeffrey. You must be Peyton?"

"Pleased to meet you, sir," I said.

"Hey, you," plus a solid punch on my upper arm, was Jack's welcome.

"*Jacqueline*, ladies don't punch," said Mr. Young.

"Good thing I'm not a lady, then, *Joffrey*," Jack said.

"Lady or not, your mom needs some help in the kitchen."

Jack drew an outraged breath and began, "And why is it just me that —"

"You can both help," Mrs. Young said, looking from Jack to Jay.

"I'd like to help, too," I said.

"Thank you, honey. The kitchen's this way. Would you prefer to make the pastry, or mix the pie filling?"

Pastry? Pie filling? She may as well have asked me to prove $E=mc^2$.

"Um, is there something easier I could do? I'm not too handy in the kitchen."

"And why should you be?" Jack defended me. "Just because you're female doesn't mean you should know how to cook."

"Give it a rest, Jack," said Jay.

"Fine. Dibs on making the potatoes." Jack grabbed a potato-masher from a kitchen drawer and began bashing down on the contents of a large pot on the stovetop.

"How about topping and tailing these?" Mrs. Young suggested, passing me a mound of green beans on a chopping board.

"Sure," I said, staring down at the beans, and feeling like a fool.

Topping and tailing sounded like something Fred Astaire and Ginger Rogers would do. Or possibly wear.

"Like this," Jay said softly. He took a sharp knife and chopped off the stalky top and pointy bottom of a bean. Oh, top and tail, got it.

While I trimmed the green beans, intent on not cutting off the tip of one of my clumsy fingers — that kitchen knife was psycho-sharp — Jay pressed pastry into a pie dish, and Mrs. Young stuck golden-yellow and orange flowers into a low floral arrangement with a giant sunflower at its center. The moment she left to place it on the table, Jack sidled up to Jay and handed him a piece of paper with some kind of grid printed on it.

"Let the games commence!" she said.

"I think we should backdate it by twenty minutes, because I've already got two," said Jay tapping two of the blocks on the grid. I peered around his shoulder — a novelty for me, usually I was peering over shoulders — and saw that there were phrases written in the blocks of the grid. Jay was indicating the two which read: *Dad calls J Jacqueline,* and *J says, "Just because she's female doesn't mean ... "*

"No backdating, no way," said Jack firmly. Then she asked me, "Do you want to play? I can get a new one printed off in a minute, if you'd like."

"Play what?"

"Family bingo," Jack and Jay said together.

"What's family bingo?" I was starting to think I didn't understand anything in this house.

"It's like normal bingo," Jay explained, "except you fill the blocks with the things that always happen or get said at family gatherings. Then you put a check in the blocks when that thing happens, and the first to get a line of five has to take the other one out to lunch."

"You've never played?" said Jack, sounding amazed.

"We don't really have family gatherings," I said lamely.

Just then, Jay's parents came into the kitchen, and the bingo sheets disappeared faster than brownies at a full-cast rehearsal. Mrs. Young set about checking whether the turkey was done ("Another forty minutes should do it,") and Mr. Young poured himself a glass of wine ("It's one o'clock somewhere in the world!"), at which both Jay and Jack surreptitiously checked their bingo sheets.

"Are you going to change before lunch, Jack?" Mrs. Young asked, eyeing the work jeans and old sweatshirt her daughter was wearing with disapproval. Mrs. Young herself was wearing a pretty mauve dress with matching kitten-heeled shoes.

"No," said Jack, energetically whipping butter into the potatoes.

When all the food was cooked, transferred to blue-and-white patterned serving plates, and laid out along the center of the table, we took our seats — Mr. Young at the head, Mrs. Young at the end closest to the kitchen, Jay and I together on one side, with Jack opposite us, on her father's right.

Mrs. Young said a simple grace and wished us, "*Bon appetit.*"

Mr. Young said, "Past the lips and over the gums, look out stomach — here it comes!" and poured himself more wine.

~ 30 ~

I eyed the Youngs' beautiful lunch table uneasily. It was set with a bewildering collection of china, silverware and condiments in fancy containers. Which of the confusing collection of forks, knives and spoons arranged around my plate was I supposed to use to eat my spicy crab salad starter? I glanced sideways to check which utensils Jay picked, and then followed suit. I'd copy him for the rest of the meal.

The main course was succulent turkey and gravy with creamed potatoes, warm hush puppies (with whipped butter served in a tiny silver dish), green beans and baby carrots. Jack took a double helping of potato, as though to compensate for Mrs. Young who, with a comment about watching her waistline, had none. We all agreed the spread was feastworthy and paid Jay's mom so many compliments, she turned pink with pleasure.

Mr. Young made a show of sharpening the carving knife on a steel rod with ridges down the side, and then handed the knife and a long-pronged fork to Jay, saying, "It's about time I passed the carving tradition down to my son."

"I thought you were supposed to hand over the family rituals to your firstborn?" complained Jack.

"Be my guest," said Jay, handing her the carving knife and fork. "Just make sure I get dark meat."

Mr. Young frowned and then redirected his attention to opening another bottle of wine, red this time.

"Don't butcher it so, Jack," said Mrs. Young as her daughter plonked a roughly hewn chunk of bird down onto Jay's plate. "And you really should serve our guest first."

"Sorry, Peyton. Do you want white or dark meat?" asked Jack, her hands poised over the huge, crispy-skinned bird.

"Anything is fine." I wasn't fussy. It was treat enough to have this delicious home-cooked meal.

Jack's face broke into an evil grin, and she chopped off the obscenely big turkey butt bit and dumped it onto my plate.

Okay, then. Hoping my revulsion didn't show on my face, I mumbled a polite, "Thanks."

Jack and Jay burst out laughing. Soon I had a few roughly sawn slices of breast on my plate, and the disgusting bit was back on the serving plate, hidden under a mound of parsley. When Jack had served everyone, she took her seat but peered at something under the table and grinned again. Her hands disappeared for a few seconds, and I guessed that pranking someone with the turkey butt-flap was something of a Young tradition.

We were on to our dessert, a rich pumpkin pie with a crispy sugar top, when the conversation turned to sport.

Mr. Young clapped his hands together and announced, "The

Ravens are playing the Rams this afternoon. Who's going to watch the game with me?" He directed an expectant look at Jay, but it was Jack's face which lit up at the mention of football.

"I'm in. We have *got* to beat the Rams, or my life back on the rig is going to be harder than a bridegroom's baloney pony on his wedding night."

I choked on a sip of water, Mrs. Young tilted her head and frowned in puzzlement, but Mr. Young thumped his hand down on the table and yelled, "Jacqueline Young!"

Jay grinned and ticked off an item on his family bingo sheet. Jack thumped my back until I stopped coughing, explaining that her boss was from St. Louis and would love an excuse to give her a tough time.

"Why would he want to do that?" asked Mrs. Young.

"He doesn't believe women belong on oil rigs."

"Neither do I," muttered Mr. Young, earning himself a scowl from his daughter. "You watching the game, too, Jay?"

Jay turned to me and asked, "Would you like to watch the game? There's a Fellini film festival running all day on the classic channel if you'd prefer. We could watch it on my TV upstairs."

"It's Thanksgiving!" protested Mr. Young. "And the all-American way to spend Thanksgiving is eating turkey and watching football, not watching some frog film."

"Italian," Jay said, his mouth tight with some emotion I couldn't easily read. Anger? Embarrassment?

"Whichever, it still has subtitles. And it's still not a sport."

"Not everyone likes sports, Dad. I was just offering our guest a choice."

"Well, let's give her a choice then. Peyton, would you rather watch the game or some old *Italian* movie?"

"Um," I said, playing for time, because there was no good answer to that question. I might not know about pastry-making or family bingo, but I know about arguments. And I didn't want to be in the middle of one in Jay's house.

"Let them do what they want, Dad. I'll watch the game with you," said Jack eagerly.

But Mr. Young appeared not to hear her. He tossed his napkin onto the table and spoke directly to me.

"What do you think of that, Peyton? I have a daughter who likes football so much she tried to join the boys' team at high school, who can beat her brother at arm-wrestling" — Jack mouthed the words *true story* at me — "and who can work a rig with the best oilmen out there, but won't be seen dead in a dress and doesn't know the meaning of the word 'ladylike.'"

"Damn straight!" Jack said proudly, while beside me, Jay surreptitiously checked off another two blocks on his bingo sheet under the table.

"And ..." Mr. Young paused to sip his wine, noticed that his glass was empty, and reached for the bottle.

"Dear, how about some apple juice instead?" Mrs. Young said softly.

"*Aaanndd*" — Mr. Young poured himself another full glass — "I have a six-foot-four bruiser of a son, built like a fullback, with hands made for catching a ball and shoulders wide enough to power through any defensive formation. But what does he want to be? An actor!"

Jack's hands slipped under the table again.

"He wants to prance about on the stage — he won't even *try* to play sports."

"A, I don't prance," said Jay, sounding angry now. "And B, it's not true that I didn't try sports. I gave both football and baseball a shot in junior high, and I was hopeless at both. Besides, I work out at the gym, and I run."

"That's exercise — not sport," said Mr. Young, waving a dismissive hand in the air. "It's not a sport unless it's a competition, unless there's a winner and a loser!"

So, Tim's report was inaccurate on at least one "confirmed fact." Jay hadn't played football at his last school. I wondered if he even had an Achilles tendon injury, or whether that was just the excuse he used to get people off his back about trying out for sports.

It didn't seem like there was any getting his father off his back though. Lunch at the Young house had been delicious and fun, but it had also made me anxious and a little sad. The family that had appeared so happy and content had turned out to have its own set of tensions and conflicts.

I'd always felt like my excuse for a family was freakishly bad, but maybe no family was perfect. Even though Jay's parents were married, and they all lived together in this beautiful house, there were deep strains running through their relationships like riptides below a seemingly calm sea. Jay had his own pressures to deal with.

Maybe everybody did.

It was almost three o'clock by the time we'd cleared away the lunch remains and helped Mrs. Young with the dishes, so when Jay's father asked again whether I wanted to watch the game or a film, I tactfully declined both.

"It's getting late. I really should be getting back to my mother."

"I'll give you a ride," said Jay.

"You kids be sure to put on your coats and hats, now. It's freezing outside, and I don't want anyone catching their death of pneumonia," said Mrs. Young.

Jack punched Jay in the shoulder and smirked. "Bingo!"

~ *31* ~

The first Saturday in December was extraordinary for many reasons.

First, we had our rehearsal in the morning, because Liz was going to be a bridesmaid at her sister's wedding that afternoon. Second, it was our first full technical rehearsal (always a shambles). Plus, we had to squeeze costume fittings in between our scenes. Ms. Gooding popped in briefly to see how we were progressing but, as usual, said nothing. It seemed like she really believed in the "sink or swim" method of letting students mount their own productions.

Doug looked maniacally stressed — nothing unusual there — and kept reminding us, "We are less than two weeks from opening night, people!"

Our technical director, a senior boy called Sanjay, marked where we had to stand for our camera close-ups by sticking crosses of different colored tape on the stage floor, and made notes of exactly when to fade the music in or out so as not to drown out our lines. Then he worked his magic on the sound, lights and video feed from the control board in the lighting box located at the back of the auditorium.

It was seriously awful seeing my face on the big screens mounted at an angle on either side of the stage. I could see every freckle and blemish, and the mole on my temple had never seemed so freakish. Jay seemed a little thrown at first, too, but soon he was experimenting with body angles and facial expressions, checking the effect on the screens — a total pro in search of performance perfection.

Because the play was set in modern-day Baltimore, we'd all just sourced what we needed for our costumes from our own wardrobes or borrowed from friends. Even Liz, our gender-neutral, nondenominational religious leader, was merely dressed in black pants with a white shirt and an enormous crucifix.

I had three costume changes, and our wardrobe mistress (Doug's mother) had me try them on and parade around the stage in each so she and Doug could approve them. They all passed inspection, except the outfit I needed to wear for the last scene of the play — denim shorts and a top which I'd made by cutting the sleeves off an old pink T-shirt, and which I was supposed to wear with a cute sun hat. The only hat I'd been able to find was an old one of my mother's and, of course, it was too small for my head.

"We can fix the hat easily. I'll cut a slit into the base and disguise the gap with a broad ribbon," Doug's mother said. "But the top is more of a problem. See how the armholes gape? She'll be showing her bra unless she keeps her arms by her side for the whole scene."

"I've got an idea," I said, running back to the dressing room.

That morning, for extra warmth, I'd worn a spaghetti-strap tank top under my sweatshirt. It was one of those with the built-in bra section, and it would work just fine to eliminate the possibility of side-boob exposure. Plus, the extra layer would be welcome — the theater was cold.

Five minutes later I was back on stage, where the director and his mother were now checking Jay's outfit — khaki shorts and a white T under a blue button-down shirt which Jay wore open.

"That covers things up nicely," Doug's mother said, nodding approval at my outfit.

"Can I see it without the overshirt?" Doug asked.

So much for staying warm. I pulled off the sleeveless pink shirt and turned around in a circle wearing just the black tank top, rubbing my hands up and down my arms.

"It looks nicer with the pop of pink," Jay said.

"Yeah, okay, wear both," Doug agreed. "Might as well keep that outfit on — we need to rehearse the final scene now."

The last scene of the play was the passionate kiss of our happily-ever-after ending, set on a beach with a sunset lighting effect projected on a plain backdrop at the back of the stage. We made our fiery declarations of everlasting love, then Jay had to remove my sun hat and lay his beach towel out on a massive "rock" in the center of the stage. The play ended with me perched on top of the rock, with Jay kissing me passionately while around us the light gradually faded from crimson through fifty shades of coral, to a final pinky purple on the back screen, and the two of us outlined in dark silhouette up front.

The big "rock" was constructed from chicken wire folded

around a wooden crate, covered with glue-hardened canvas painted brown to resemble a rocky outcrop, complete with a trail of fake green seaweed at its base. I lived in fear of it collapsing under my weight. In the second run-through that night, it made a cracking noise and gave way a little under my butt, but when I yelped in surprise, Doug yelled, "Keep going! It'll hold up, I promise."

What refused to hold up was my tank top — the spaghetti straps kept slipping off my shoulders to hang down my upper arms. I made a mental note to sew them to my shirt's shoulder straps.

When I pulled back from Jay to give the smile I had to give him before our final clinch, both shoulder straps fell down. Staying in character, Jay merely smiled, reached out and lifted the straps back onto my shoulders, slowly trailing his fingers up my arms as he did so — flustering me entirely before leaning in for the final kiss.

I had prepared myself, over the course of all the rehearsals, for the touches we'd blocked and practiced, but every time Jay went off-script and improvised these sorts of tender caresses, it threw me entirely, because it seemed to bounce us out of Romero and Juliet's scripted stage relationship, and into Jay and Peyton's budding one.

Since Thanksgiving, Jay and I had exchanged daily good morning and good night texts, sat together at lunch, and had two more dates. I'd dragged him to the weird and wonderful Museum of Visionary Art, and he'd taken me to see Macbeth at the Roundhouse. The couple sitting in the row behind us groaned as we sat down and didn't bother to lower their voices as they complained about how they couldn't see a thing because of the two giants sitting in front of them.

"Should we offer to trade seats with them?" I asked Jay softly.

"Then we'd just block the view for the couple behind them, and we'd keep moving backward until we were in the back row and *we* couldn't see a thing."

"I feel guilty."

I tried to slide down in my seat, but with my knees already jammed up against the seat in front of me, there wasn't anywhere to go.

"Life is tough for all of us. You don't have to play small for the benefit of others," Jay said.

I got a kick out of watching him watching the play. He leaned forward as though to catch the lines before the rest of us, his eyes bright with excitement and his lips moving silently on some lines. Occasionally the hand holding mine twitched at a particularly intense moment.

"Wasn't that brilliant?" he asked afterwards, beaming his megawatt smile.

"The best," I agreed.

Only one of us was talking about the play.

As usual, Jay dropped me at home. That night I didn't want to play games to keep him from the door, so I just said, "Please, stay here. I'll let myself in."

He tilted his head, studying me quizzically, and just when I thought he was going to demand an explanation for why I never invited him in, he leaned over the stick shift, kissed me softly on the lips and said, "Goodnight, Tiger Eyes."

It was just a peck, but it was real, not scripted, and I treasured it.

The kiss in the climax scene of the play, however, was one that I both loved and hated. Although the final kiss in the play was not "real", it was still intimate. I wanted to kiss Jay, but not with these fake kisses. I felt like a fool pressing my lips and twisting my face, while my butt perched uncomfortably on the slowly sinking surface of the rock. Zack and Wren, watching the scene projected in unforgiving close-up onto the screens, were reduced to helpless giggles, but Doug, judging by his deep frown, only found further fault with my technique.

I was relieved when the rehearsal ended at twelve-thirty. Leaving Doug to nail down the production details with the technical and backstage crew, I changed out of my costume and left with Jay and the rest of the cast.

"I vote we all go out for lunch," said Zack. "How about Jumping Jim's?"

"Again?" Wren said.

"Peyton can get us her staff discount."

"I'm in," said Liz.

"Me too," said Angela.

"Yeah?" Jay asked me.

"Um …"

I did not want to go to Jim's, no sir, no ma'am. Tori worked every Saturday, and I'd had enough of her prying eyes and sarcastic comments. So far, I hadn't reported any of my three dates with Jay to Tori. I felt a powerful urge to protect what was developing between Jay and me from the ugliness of the bet.

"I was hoping to take you to lunch, and spend the afternoon with just you," I told him softly.

"We're out," Jay told the others, grinning broadly.

"Are you two a thing now?" Wren said, wrinkling her nose.

I glanced at Jay. "Yeah?" I asked.

"Yeah."

"Aww, man. I thought I was in with a chance there," Zack complained.

"In your dreams," muttered Jay, and he linked his arm through mine and drew me off to his car.

~ 32 ~

We spent the rest of the afternoon and evening together — another extraordinary aspect of that day.

As we drove to the Inner Harbor district, we got to talking about movies. I knew more about classic old films, while Jay was the expert on actors. As a souped-up red Camaro sped past us and shot through a just-red traffic light ahead, Jay declared a movie quiz.

"Best movie car-chase sequence of all time?" he asked.

"You go first," I said, playing for time, trying to remember *any* car chase at all.

"Okay then, I'd have to say *Drive*."

"And that would be …"

"The one with Ryan Gosling playing a getaway driver. The opening sequence was so clever — no crashes, no mad music, just those close-ups of him thinking and scheming. Your turn."

I'd thought of one. "*The Bourne Identity*."

"The red mini racing through the streets of Paris? That was a classic, too. Let's call it a tie — one hundred points each."

"This is a competition?"

"Hey, you heard my father on the critical importance of competition," he said with a wry grin.

"He's on your case about playing sports a lot?"

"He doesn't understand me. Or Jack either. He just wanted a girly-girl and a boy's boy and instead he got … us."

We left the car in a parkade and headed toward the waterfront, strolling through the throngs of tourists and Christmas shoppers.

"And your dad's not happy about your studying drama next year?" I asked.

"He hates it. He says the chances of me succeeding are next to zero, and I should study something as a 'backup'. He thinks I should do programming or accounting."

"No!" I said it so fiercely that Jay quirked a brow at me.

"You feel strongly about that, do you?"

"Yes." The thought of this awesomely gifted person burying his brilliance under a boring bushel of debits and credits was too dreadful to think about. (Sorry, Mark.) "Anyway, you'll make it big time — no two ways about that."

"You've seen the future?" he asked, grinning.

"I have. Spoiler alert: you win the Oscar for best actor in 2021."

Admiring the rich, burnt-orange coat of a woman walking ahead of us, I promptly decided to include a garment in that precise color in my fashion range. Perhaps a button-down shirt, with extra-large cuffs and pointed collar.

"Do you get on with *your* father?" Jay asked.

"We're not close — I hardly see him. My folks divorced

when I was six years old, and we've just seen less and less of each other with every year that goes by."

"Why did they —"

"I'm getting cold. This okay for lunch?" I indicated a nearby seafood restaurant.

"Sure."

The hostess who showed us to a table with a view over the harbor gave me an astounded look and exclaimed, "Why, you sure are tall! How tall are you?" And without waiting for an answer, added, "You know, you should wear flats, honey, the heels on those boots just make you even taller."

Stand on something and say that to my face, lady.

I gave Jay a what-did-I-tell you look and took my seat, fitting my legs between his under the table. Soon we were sharing a bucket of succulent shellfish, and back to talking about the movies.

Jay fished a massive crab leg from out of the bucket and cracked it open with the tiny mallet that had come with the silverware.

"Okay, here's a quiz question for you," I said. "Best onscreen murder?"

Jay narrowed his eyes in thought while he sucked at the leg and pulled the tender white meat out between his teeth. I stared at his buttery lips, aware of a tautening in the pit of my belly.

"I bet we're thinking the same scene," he said.

"Huh?"

What had we been talking about?

"Psycho," he said.

Oh yeah. Murder.

"The shower scene?" I checked.

"No contest."

"The original Hitchcock, though. Not that awful remake."

"Of course!"

We chatted easily as we made our way through the spicy shrimp and steamed clams. He told me that his first-round Julliard audition would be at the end of January next year, with final callbacks if he got through (which I knew he would) in March. I learned that Jack was in love with one of the guys on her oil rig, and that their mother had been a champion ballroom dancer when she was young.

Jay didn't learn too much about me, which was intentional on my part. After all, what wasn't a secret wasn't very interesting. He asked how my portfolio was coming on, and I told me, "Great," while realizing that this lunch had probably cost me the equivalent of fabric for several of my garments.

I didn't regret a single clam.

After a long lunch with several refills of coffee, we strolled around the harbor. It was a chilly day. The heavy gray clouds had crowded out the sun, and already the light was beginning to dim. I was glad I'd worn my parka (men's department, Bargain Box Outlet Store) and, whatever the restaurant hostess thought of their heels, my boots. Jay looked warm — and dead sexy — in his black turtleneck sweater and leather jacket, but when he saw me rubbing my cold ears, he insisted on buying us a couple of warm beanies — black for him and ruby red for me. "To match your lips," he said.

We passed two panhandlers, wrestling drunkenly for possession of a bottle of cheap wine. They hung onto each other, moving in unsteady circles like a four-legged crab, too tanked to do much harm.

"Best movie fight scene?" Jay demanded.

"If we're counting gunfights, then *Butch Cassidy and the Sundance Kid*. Definitely."

"Butch who and the sun what?"

"How can you not have seen it?" I was appalled. "The gunfight at the end — it's a classic!"

"*Fight Club* is a classic," he countered.

I shuddered. "Okay, I'll see your Fight Club and raise you some serious magic: Voldemort versus Dumbledore in *Order of the Phoenix*."

"There were some pretty cool special effects," Jay conceded. "But I'll call you. *The Matrix* — Neo versus Agent Smith."

"I can live with that," I said, earning myself one of his glorious smiles.

They did something to me, those smiles. They cracked open my heart and filled me with sunshine and color and warmth.

"Hey, how about a trip across the bay?" Jay suggested

Ten minutes later, we were sitting on the benched seats of the harbor water taxi, along with a crowd of other travelers — tourists and locals headed home after a long day. The skipper maneuvered the boat away from the mooring and headed out into the bay. Bands of colored light trembled on the rippling surface of the water, reflected from the waterside bars, clubs and crab joints, which were fully lit up in the gathering gloom of the evening.

It was freezing cold out on the water, and when Jay pulled me close, I snuggled gratefully up against his warmth, resting my head on his shoulder and my cheek in the crook of his neck. He smelled of nothing but himself.

"This is special," I said, surprised to hear myself speak my thoughts out loud.

"Hmmm?"

"Nothing."

This beautiful moment wouldn't — couldn't — last. I hugged the happiness tight inside me, so I'd still have the memory when the magic ended. Life had taught me that it always did.

The boat docked at Harbor Point and most of the tourists disembarked, probably headed for the restaurants in Little Italy.

"What are you thinking?" I asked when we were moving again, this time headed past Pier Five toward the massive aquarium with its triangular glass roof and its World War II submarine tethered to the jetty outside.

"Best onscreen romantic couples."

Oooh, he'd been thinking about romantic couples?

"Okay, how about Scarlett O'Hara and Rhett Butler in *Gone with the Wind*, or Heathcliff and Catherine from *Wuthering Heights* — any version," I said.

"Hmm, so you like crazy-intense, kinda scary love?"

"Is there any other kind? Your turn," I said, then quickly added, "No, wait. I've changed my mind. The best onscreen couple ever — Humphrey Bogart and Ingrid Bergman as Rick and Ilsa in *Casablanca*."

"You sure like your movies old."

"That's because they knew how to make clever, stylish movies back then. And they knew about romance, too." At his skeptical look I said, "Fine, *you* name a great romantic couple from recent movies that can stack up against Scarlett and Rhett, or Rick and Ilsa."

"Define recent."

"This century."

"Bella and Edward," he said, laughing, and when I pulled back to give him a look, added, "Or are you team Jacob?"

"Be serious."

"Yeah, you're right, romance is serious business."

"Well? I'm waiting for your modern classics," I challenged him.

"Katniss and Peeta? Tris and Four? Schmidt and whatshisname, the Channing Tatum character, in *22 Jump Street*?"

"Bromances don't count. Do you give up? Do you agree that the best movies are the old ones?"

"I've got it!" Jay said, snapping his fingers.

"Oh yeah?"

He made the sound of a drumroll.

"Anytime now," I said.

"Shrek and Fiona."

"I'll admit, they are a pretty good couple," I said grudgingly.

"What do you mean, 'Pretty good'? They're awesome, and I won. Hallelujah, hallelujah," he sang the movie's theme tune.

"Eh, not so fast. If we're allowed to submit lovers who aren't real —"

"Peyton!" Jay stopped singing abruptly, gaped at me as if shocked to the core, placed a hand over his heart and said in a voice that throbbed with emotion, "Just because they're animated doesn't mean they're not real."

"My bad. Forgive me."

"It's not me you should apologize to," he said with an injured sniff.

His face was pulled into taut, sad lines, and he wiped away what I could've sworn was a real tear. Had I really upset him?

"Jay?"

"Gotcha!" He threw his head back and then doubled over in that full-body laugh that I adored.

I punched him, none too gently, on the upper arm. "You really had me going there!"

He was still chuckling when the water taxi drew up at the final stop. It was only when we climbed out from under the boat's canopy and onto the dock that we realized it had started drizzling. We set off for the parkade at a brisk walk.

"Who were you going to suggest? For the couple?" Jay asked.

"Belle and the Beast from *Beauty and The Beast*."

"To avoid being beaten up again," said Jay, rubbing his arm as if it still hurt, "I'll declare it a tie."

At that moment, the icy rain picked up and began to pelt down. We glanced at each other and then, by unspoken mutual agreement, set off at a run toward the nearest bus shelter, about fifty yards down the street.

And it was there, under the arced protection of its roof, that the most special, extraordinary thing of the day happened.

~ 33 ~

The rain hammered on the roof of the bus shelter. Standing in our small dry spot, surrounded by a deluge of water and noise, we might have been alone in the world — a boy and a girl with rain-spotted clothes and wet hair, and a sudden charged intensity in the space between them.

Jay pulled me close and tucked my icy hands inside the warmth of his jacket. He gazed down into my eyes, his own golden-green gaze so intense, I felt my cheeks growing warm.

Eventually, he spoke. "Best movie kiss?"

I had to clear my throat to find my voice.

"Hmm … That steamy scene with Deborah Kerr and Burt Lancaster rolling around on the beach in *From Here To Eternity?*"

"Is this another movie from prehistoric times?"

"Smartass." I snorted. "What's got your vote?"

"The one between Tris and Four in *Divergent,* where they were both angry and totally hot for each other. Definitely a winner. Unless you've got another contender?"

"I do!" I'd just remembered my favorite kiss scene ever. "The *Spiderman* one. The original with Toby Maguire, not that recent rubbish."

"Remind me?"

"It's raining, and Spidey and Mary Jane are in this dark alley where he's just rescued her from a bunch of rapey thugs, which is dead-romantic right there — the rescuing, I mean, not the thugs."

Jay gave a small laugh.

"And then he hangs upside down against the wall —"

"I remember now! Her dress was kinda see-through. And wet. *Hot.*"

"And then slowly, slowly she peels his mask down just enough to expose his lips, so he's just all mystique and mouth. And then she leans over and softly kisses him, with her hands on the sides of his face. Oh!" I sighed deeply. Just remembering it made me swoony. "It's hands down the best. Ever."

Jay cocked his head, giving me an enigmatic look for a long moment. Then he went around to the side of the bus shelter, climbed onto the trashcan and pulled himself up onto the roof.

Laughing, I stepped out and turned to look up at him. "What are you *doing*?" I asked, blinking in the rain.

Jay rolled up the neck of his black turtleneck sweater and tugged his beanie down over his eyes, then lay down on his back on the top of the shelter and dangled over the edge, inching backward until his covered face was level with mine.

I gasped in delight.

Fingers trembling, I took the edges of the neck of his sweater and slowly, slowly peeled it back until just his lips were exposed. I leaned over and took his bottom lip between mine and sucked it gently, then nibbled his top lip. Jay groaned, and the tautness in my belly melted into a heavy ache. I covered his mouth with my own and then, finally, we were kissing.

It was all kinds of wonderful. Soft and gentle at first, then harder, wilder. Fevered. The wind was back, stealing my breath, roaring through my head and filling my body with whirling, rushing currents of *now* and *here*. And my heart was expanding — wider, lighter, higher in my chest, so that I felt like a balloon ready to lift off and float up into the night sky, and it was only Jay's lips that kept me connected to the earth.

When we came up for air, he yanked off his beanie, flipped backward off the shelter roof, and stood before me, his green eyes heavy-lidded. Then we kissed right side up — deeper, fiercer, longer. I let my hands do what they'd been craving for months, to run up the hard bulges of his arms, to push my fingers through his hair, to scrub my knuckles along his jawline and press my fingertips to the curved lines at the sides of his eyes.

His hands were on me, too — the one in the small of my back pulled me tight into him, then moved lower, pressing my ass against his hips, so that I could feel the hardness of him. He pressed a line of small kisses along my throat, while his other hand moved up along my spine and tangled in my hair, then moved lower to cup the swell of my breasts. And I couldn't breathe, couldn't think, couldn't hold back the moan of pleasure. I —

A horn sounded behind me, harsh and loud. I yelped and leapt apart from Jay. The bus had arrived and was waiting with its door open. I guess it had already been there for a while, because several grinning faces were pressed up against the wet windows, watching us. A few were even cheering or clapping, but the driver looked unamused.

"You two plan to get on the bus before one of you gets knocked up?" he called, and cursed when Jay waved him on.

We were alone again, but the wild magic of the moment was broken. We couldn't carry on making out on the street, and it was probably time to get home. Plus, the rain which had cut us off from the rest of the world had stopped.

But the moment was also not broken, because although there was an easing of the expectant tension between us now that the first real kiss had happened, there was also an exquisite increase in whatever it was that connected us. It was there in our hands when they effortlessly found each other as we ran down the wet streets splashing through puddles. It was there in the laughter we shared when we were inside Jay's car, and in the look we gave each other when we pulled up at my house, before we kissed again.

Even once I was back home, in my bed and on the verge of falling asleep, I still felt connected to him by that indefinable link. And I knew, just knew, that wherever he was, grabbing a snack in that neat kitchen perhaps, or dozing off under the posters of *Les Mis* and *Othello*, he was thinking of me, too.

~ *34* ~

*H*oly hell.

I stared down at my computer screen, battling to believe what I'd just read.

It was late Wednesday afternoon, two days before the opening night of *Romero and Juliet*, and I'd been busy finalizing the theory part of my fashion-school application, hoping to incorporate Chloe's suggestions and get it finished before I left for the dress rehearsal, when a distracting ping told me I had a new email.

It was from my father, and pretty much as soon as I began reading, my jaw hit the floor.

> *Dear Peyton,*
>
> *Exciting news! Lucy and I are going to have a baby! We've known for a while, but didn't want to share until the first trimester was safely under the belt, because we've had several disappointments before now.*

They had? First I'd heard of it. I wondered what had gone wrong.

Pickle (that's what we call him) —

Him. Oh jeez, they were having a son. This was going to be super hard for my mother. I checked the *To* field on the email and saw that it had been sent to me only. Had he sent a separate note to her, or would it be my job to break the happy news?

— is due in mid-June.

I'm afraid that a new baby will mean lots of extra expenses, so I won't be able to continue giving you and your mother financial top-ups. We're going to have to stick to the financial agreement from now on. I'm sorry, Peyton, I know a bit of what things must be like for you, but I can't keep bailing your mother out.

Great. More good news.

Anyway, we're so excited and really hope you are, too, and that we can make a plan for you to spend more time with us, so your kid brother really gets to know you.

I was going to be a sister. I was going to have a baby brother. A rush of images and sensations flashed through me — toes like tiny pink pebbles with impossibly small nails, the gurgling sound of a baby's laugh, golden-brown eyes like my own — sparking a flood of emotions. Joy, longing, melancholy. Fear.

What if it happened again?

I started typing my reply: *Damn, Dad, do you really think you should be risking this? Does Lucy know what could happen? Have you thought about what this will do to Mom? And should you be taking on a whole new kid at this stage of your life anyway? You're 49, not 29. You'll be close to 70 by the time this kid goes to college — are you up for that? Maybe you should have gone with the standard midlife-crisis Porsche rather than the permanent responsibility of creating a whole new life. Too late, now, I guess.*

No, no, no. Couldn't say that. I held a finger down on the backspace key until all the doubting, unkind words had been deleted, and started over.

> *Dear Dad and Lucy,*
> *Congratulations!! That's awesome news! I hope th —*

My screen went black. My desk lamp was out, too. I got up, flicked the main light switch on and off. Nothing. Had my mother been using her toaster again — the ancient one that tripped the lights — or was the whole neighborhood out? I peeped out of the window and saw the neighbors' windows were shining brightly in the dark of the early winter's evening. Just us then.

I sighed. I was on my way to the electric box when a thought struck me. I grabbed my phone and called the utilities company. A bored-sounding operator checked our account and informed me that we had been cut off due to non-payment of our bill.

"We did send repeated notices and a final warning, hun. I'm sorry. You'll need to settle the full amount plus the reconnection fee before we can hook you up again. You have yourself some happy holidays now!"

Yeah, that's likely. It was the middle of winter, a week to go until Christmas, and we had no electricity. I was so angry, I wanted to kick something. I wanted to kick my mother. I'd reminded her to pay the bill a bunch of times, and she'd promised me she would. Obviously, she'd spent the money on something else. Some irre-freaking-sistible online bargain for more stuff we didn't need and wouldn't use.

I stormed to her bedroom, tripping in the hallway and banging my elbow hard on a bookshelf in my attempt to stop myself from going sprawling. Eyes watering from the pain in my funny bone and from my growing fury, I pushed my mom's door open without knocking. It banged into some obstruction on the other side and bounced back at me, slamming into the toes of my right foot. Ow! I didn't know whether to clutch my elbow or my toes.

"Mom!" I yelled, sticking my head around the door.

She sat on her bed in the small puddle of light cast by a candle perched on a stack of books on her bedside table. Real safe, Mom. Her face was glistening wet with tears. Clearly, she'd received a babymail from Dad, too.

"You didn't pay the power bill."

"Did you get Dad's news?" she asked, her face twisted with pain.

"They've cut off our power because you didn't pay the bill. Why didn't you pay it?"

"They're having a little boy. I can't bear it, Peyton. They're going to have a little baby boy. Why is this happening to me?"

"It isn't."

"Nobody thinks — nobody cares! — what this will do to me. How will I cope?" She covered her face with her hands and sobbed silently.

Inside me, fury warred with compassion. And won.

"I don't know, Mom. I'm too busy worrying how we'll cope with no heat and no lights."

"My life is so unfair, so hard."

"Mom, hey Mom!" I clicked my fingers at her, trying to snap her out of her misery-trance. "The more urgent problem here is that we. Have. No. Power! You have to pay the full bill, plus a reconnection fee. Look at this total!"

I shoved the impossibly large figure under her nose.

She shook her head feebly. "I can't."

In other houses, in other families, it was the kids who whined, "I can't" and the mothers who retorted, "There's no such word as 'can't'." In this house, my mother said it all the time. She ought to have a T-shirt: *I can't — so don't bother asking* or perhaps: *There is too such a word as 'can't' — I should know.*

"Why not?"

I don't know why I bothered to ask — I already knew the answer. But perhaps we were both so well-practiced in our little relationship dance that the steps of the recurring arguments just came automatically.

"I don't have it."

"You mean you spent it."

"Perhaps your father …"

"He can't give us any more money. He said so in the email to me, so I'm pretty sure he told you, too. No more money means no more spending, Mom. No more!"

I glared at her, waiting for some kind of response, but she just hugged her knees against her chest and said again, "A baby boy."

I swore viciously and retreated to my room, now crying myself. I always leaked when I was angry. I swore again when I saw the time — I was running late for the dress rehearsal. Using my phone and praying my dwindling data and battery life would last, I logged onto the banking site, transferred the bulk of my college savings into the fat coffers of the utility company, and then called them back — being put on hold for even longer this time — to request an urgent reconnection.

While I was on hold, my phone buzzed three times — Doug and Jay texting to find out where the heck I was.

Now over half an hour late, I grabbed the bag with my costumes and props, tossed it out of the window, scuttled down the ladder and set off at a sprint. Jay had had a private drama lesson with Ms. Gooding directly before rehearsal, so I'd told him I would catch the bus, but I had missed the last one.

I'd have to run all the way to school through the freezing darkness, my bruised toes protesting on every other step.

~ 35 ~

"You're an hour late! Where the hell have you been?" was Doug's greeting.

"I was worried. Are you okay?" was Jay's.

"Man, your face is red as an angry bird and sweaty as a smackhead in a drug store," was Zack's contribution. "Plus, you puffing and panting like a lizard on a hot rock. You been up to something naughty?"

"Poor thing, you look all upset," said Wren. "Is the pressure of playing the lead getting to you? Do you want me to step in for you? I know all Juliet's lines and movements. I would hate for you to overextend yourself."

"Call my girl an eclipse 'cos she's throwing so much shade," said Zack, winking at Wren.

"Sorry! I'm sorry," I gasped. "Family emergency."

"Is your mom okay?" Jay asked.

Define okay.

"Need to get changed," I said and limped to the backstage dressing rooms.

I was back onstage, ready for the start of scene one, less than ten minutes later.

"Finally," said Wren.

I took my place, breathed deeply a few times and tried to get into character, but I was flustered and upset. I felt bad for making the entire cast wait on me, and I was still furious with my mother. My chest burned, my toes hurt, and there was an ache of tears behind my eyes. Who's feeling sorry for herself now, Peyton?

The face I turned to Jay in our first Romero-Juliet interaction was not the bright, expectant face of a happy girl laying eyes on the soon-to-be love of her life. My face was pinched tight with emotion, I could feel it. When I spoke my lines, my voice was constricted with anger and frustration, and my movements felt jerky and stiff, rather than fluid and natural.

Jay tried his best, but he couldn't carry the scene by himself. My anger turned back on myself. Why couldn't I just set the personal stuff aside and immerse myself in my character like everyone else did? I was hopeless. I didn't need to hear the muttered oaths and derisive snorts from the others to know that I was single-handedly ruining the production.

At the end of Act I, Doug marched up to where Jay and I stood in the wings — Jay murmuring consoling words, and me fighting back tears of humiliation — and yelled at me, "What the hell is the matter with you tonight, Peyton?"

"I'm sorry. I know my performance is a bit off."

"A bit *off?* It's effing craptastic!"

"I know, I'm sorry. I just had a really bad day and I can't —"
That word again.

"It's called 'acting,' Peyton. It's called 'acting' because you

stop being yourself and pretend to be someone else. Just act!"
Doug snarled. "Get it together already."

I heard muffled laughter coming from the wing beside us.
Wren, taking delight in my misery?

Pushing furious fingers through his already-wild hair, Doug
stalked off downstage then spun around. "And, FYI, the stage
kisses look ridiculous on the big screens, patently fake. Do real
kisses from now on," he ordered, then marched off.

I wanted to crawl into a corner and bawl my eyes out. I
wanted someone to follow me, hug me, tell me everything
would be okay, and take care of me. What I did not want was
to kiss Jay — for real — on a stage, in front of an audience,
with every minute detail projected onto enormous screens for
everyone to scrutinize.

By the time the scene with the big kiss came, I'd forgotten
my lines twice and skipped a chunk of dialogue in the scene
with Angela, cutting out five of her precious lines and earning
myself a suspicious look. Plus, the straps of my bra top (which
I hadn't yet secured) kept slipping down my arms.

Worse, about twenty seconds before my scheduled
passionate and "real" kiss with Romero, I realized that what
with being so upset and distracted, I'd forgotten to brush my
teeth before the scene — a habit I'd followed religiously until
now. And I'd had an Italian pasta TV dinner for lunch, no
doubt loaded with garlic. Could this day get any worse?

Yes. Oh, yes, indeedy.

Trying to breathe through my nose and keep my mouth
closed until the last second, I placed my palm flat against Jay's
and said my line.

What I was *supposed* to say was, "Let our lips do what our hands already are."

What actually came out of my semi-closed mouth was, "Let our lips do our hands already."

A frown briefly creased Jay's brows. Was he annoyed? Worried I was ruining the play? Wondering what he'd ever seen in me and thinking how best to let me down gently?

As though to drain any remaining smidgeon of romance or chemistry, my neck cracked audibly as I tilted my head back to receive Jay's kiss. He would probably have corpsed with laughter if he wasn't afraid that would tip Doug over the edge. Scratch that. Maybe Jay didn't find any of this funny. Like not funny at all. Maybe he was considering asking Doug if Wren could play Juliet after all.

The kiss was Bad. Bad with a capital B that rhymes with D that stands for dreadful, dire, disastrous.

I felt myself tensing, and Jay's murmured "Just relax," didn't help.

I heard whispering and sniggering in the wings, and a loud groan of frustration coming from out front. The tears which had been threatening all afternoon welled and spilled over, and my nose started to run. There was no dizzy excitement in my head this time, no rushing wind. Involuntarily, I pulled back. Jay tightened his grip, and it was only his hold on me that kept me from wrenching myself away and bolting home.

When the last words had been spoken and that freaking endless sunset had finally faded, there was still no escape. Doug gathered the whole cast and crew together for a colossal shit-fit. He could only thank God that Ms. Gooding hadn't been here to witness the fiasco, or she'd probably pull the plug on the whole production. The lights were still not focused right, the music was too loud, Angela was too slow in coming in with her lines, and Liz's footsteps were as loud as a rhinoceros's. Wren wasn't audible at the back of the auditorium — didn't anyone know how to project their voice properly, for God's sake? Even Jay didn't escape the wrath of Doug. Where was his violent rage in the scene where he fought and killed Tyrone? And how, in the name of all that was holy, was it possible that Zack *still* didn't know his lines?

But Doug's worst anger and his harshest criticism was saved for last. For me.

"And as for you, Peyton, that was pathetic! Underwhelming to the nth degree. You had no life tonight, no emotion, no chemistry with Jay, no passion in your performance at all."

Every brutal word hammered me further into my hole of humiliation in the ground.

"Wooden! You were like a wooden plank."

Wren nodded self-righteously at this, a gloating grin on her stupid pixie face.

"Stiff and expressionless as a broom!" Doug continued.

"Hey, now," said Jay in a warning tone. He held up a hand as though to stay the flood of insults, but I said, "It's okay, he's right."

"Damn straight, I'm right. We haven't come this far, worked so hard for so long, for you to tank at the last minute. Can you get it together by opening night, or should I swap Wren in right now?"

Wren perked up at this. Her eyes glittered with excitement.

It was enough to put a tiny bit of backbone back into me.

"Yes, I'll get it together, okay? I'll be perfect and passionate, I promise."

"You'd better. And you" — Doug turned his glare on Jay — "I don't know what's going on here, or what's wrong with her, but for the love of God, fix it."

Then he stalked off backstage, where a loud crash suggested he'd punched or kicked his anger into something breakable.

Zack gave a low whistle. "Man, Doug shouldn't bottle up his feelings like that. He should say what he really feels."

His comment broke the tension, and everyone burst into subdued laughter. Everyone but me.

"I'm sorry, guys," I said to my feet. "I'll get it together, promise."

"Of course you will," said Jay. "Anyway, a bad dress rehearsal means a great opening. It'll be alright on the night."

I hurried to the girls' dressing room and hid in the toilet stall until I was certain everyone had left, but when I finally emerged — puffy eyed and drained from a crying jag — Jay was still waiting for me.

"Listen," he said, pulling me into his arms and holding me close, "we all have days like this. It's not the end of the world." He kissed the top of my head and then my forehead. "Come on, I'll give you a ride home. There's something I want to ask you."

I eyed him warily, running through the possibilities in my head.

Jay said nothing until we were both in his car under a light in the school lot, with the engine running and the heater at full blast, the icy night surrounding us. He made no move to back out of the space. He just ran a hand down over his face, took a deep breath and then turned to face me, more serious than I'd ever known him to be.

Oh, dear. I braced myself for the worst, but what he said still came as a shock.

"Peyton, what's the secret you're hiding?"

~ 36 ~

I swallowed hard.

"What's my secret?" I repeated.

"Yes, what's your very worst secret? The one you keep locked up tight in the deepest part of yourself," Jay said.

I just stared at him, lips pinched tight together.

"C'mon, Peyton, everyone has a deep, dark secret. And I *know* you're hiding something big from me."

"What … What makes you think that?"

"It's obvious. You hardly talk about yourself, you've never invited me into your house — hell, you won't even let me see you inside the door. You're all zipped up and folded in on yourself like you're determined to stop something slipping out. What is it?"

I hadn't fooled him. Not at all. I was an idiot to have thought I could. Here was someone who studied body language and facial expressions, who read what *wasn't* said in between the words that were. Of course he'd noticed I was cagey and evasive.

"What's the one thing that you wish no one knew, that

you'd do anything to keep to yourself? What's the skeleton in your closet that makes you cringe with shame and embarrassment?" His voice was soft and kind, but his words were terrifying, and his intense gaze probed mine, as though trying to read my secrets in my eyes. "Tell me that now."

"Why?" I asked, my voice sounding hoarse. My throat was tight, closing around the secrets that threatened to rise up and spill out at this invitation to let go and release, to trust someone enough to share. "Why do you want to know?"

"I want to know everything about you," he said simply.

"But why now? Why tonight?"

"I think that if you share your awfully awful with me, then you'll have nothing to fear. When you realize that I won't freak out or disappear on you —"

"You will." My voice was a rough whisper in the darkness of the car.

"When you see that I *don't*," said Jay, taking both my hands in his, "then, finally, you'll be able to trust me fully and be completely open with me. There'll be a connection between us — more than that, there'll be a deep *bond*, and that will come through in the performance. The audience will see it."

"So you just want this for the sake of the performance."

"I never said that. I want us to be closer, and we can't do that with secrets between us. I want to know you, and I want you to know you can trust me. Don't *you* want that for us?"

I stared out the windshield. It was starting to snow. Light flakes, fragile as faith, drifted down through the darkness to dissolve on the hood of the car.

My resistance was weakening. All along I'd known I'd have

to let Jay in on my secret sometime for us to have a shot at a real relationship. I just hadn't been ready to tell him yet.

"But if sharing something important about yourself also happens to help your performance," he said, "don't you want that, too?"

I did. I wanted to turn in a great performance, for the sake of Doug and the whole cast and all the work they'd put in. For the sake of Jay, who had to act across from me in so many scenes. And for me. I wanted to be good for me.

Plus, there were other reasons why I was tempted to open up. I was so tired of keeping secrets, of hiding the truth, of keeping friends and foes and even family at arm's length, of avoiding, covering up, and making excuses. Of deceiving.

It was exhausting, and terrified as I was of his reaction, I longed to share the load.

"Screw it," I said. "I'll do it."

"You'll tell me?" He sounded half-surprised.

"No." I shook my head. "I'll show you."

I heard him blow out a long breath of air.

"Tomorrow, after school, you, Jay Young, may have the great privilege of bringing me home and escorting me all the way up to my room. And" — I tapped the side of my nose, like a gangster in an old movie — "I'll spill the beans. All will be revealed."

I was aiming for a light, joking tone, but on the last phrase, my voice was thick with dread.

In December, the light begins to thin and dim early. By four-thirty the next afternoon, the sun was close to setting, and I was cold, inside and out.

By this time the following day, I'd be backstage, putting on my makeup, getting into costume and character, ready — if Jay's experiment worked — to give it my all. But now, as Jay's car pulled up, I was sitting on the front step of our house, hugging my knees and wondering if I was about to make the worst mistake of my life.

I watched him walk slowly up the path between the overgrown shrubs and weeds of the front yard. Chloe was right — he was slightly bowlegged. A cowboy without a horse arriving for high noon at the Lane corral.

Jay smiled as he reached me, and held out his hand. If only he could pull me out of my life as simply as he tugged me to my feet.

"Ready?" he asked.

"No."

"Changed your mind?"

"No." Our breaths made white puffs in the chilly air. "Let's do this. Walk this way."

I led him around the side of the house.

"I thought you were going to take me inside."

"I am. This," I said, when we reached the bottom of the hanging rope ladder, "is *my* entrance."

He cocked his head, clearly puzzled. "Why do you have a ladder to your room? And what the heck is *that*?"

I followed his gaze upward, to where the dark shadow of a human form was silhouetted against my bedroom window, and snorted. It did look a little creepy.

"Afraid?" I challenged.

"That depends. Is this the Bates Motel, and is that the stuffed body of your mother?"

"Only one way to find out." I swung onto the lowest rung and began climbing up. "Follow me. If you dare."

He waited until I'd reached the top, opened the window and climbed inside, before following, which was probably wise — I didn't know if the ladder could carry the weight of two giants simultaneously.

"Ta-dah!" I sang when he stepped over the sill into my room.

He grinned at the dressmaker's mannequin beside the window and patted it on the shoulder, before taking in the details of my space — the neatly made bed, the small television set in the corner, the desk with the sewing machine and sketchbook, my shelf of ordered books, the bare walls, and the absence of any knickknacks or mess.

"Well?" I asked.

"It's very … neat and tidy."

"My mom calls it sterile, but I find it soothing."

He picked up my sketchbook and flipped through the designs. "Are these for your college application?"

"Yeah. I still need to do them full-size and in fabric."

"They're really good. I'm impressed."

He stuck his head into my small *en suite* bathroom, but there was nothing much to see there either — no collection of foam bath or scent bottles on display, no muddle of cosmetics on the counter, no damp towels or underwear heaped the floor. Everything was hung up or packed away.

He walked over to the corner I used as my kitchenette, trailed a hand over the microwave and toaster, then opened the small fridge and peered inside.

"You're a fan of *Chef in a Jiffy*, I see." He inspected the neat rows on my shelf of foods — no more than two of every item, each with their labels facing forwards. "And also of instant noodles, Cup-a-Soup, and Cheerios."

"I'm not one to boast, but I can make a damn fine bowl of cereal."

"Can I ask why you have a mini-kitchen in your bedroom?"

"I need to eat."

"And you can't eat in your house's kitchen because …"

This was it, the moment of truth. The scene called for some dramatic music as a backing soundtrack, but all I got was my heart thudding unpleasantly and a voice in the back of my head urging me to run, escape, shut this show-and-tell down right now.

Instead, I took a deep breath and said, "Come see for yourself."

I unlocked and opened my door, stepped outside my zone of tranquility, and switched on the hallway light. Jay followed but immediately pulled up short, as if reeling from a blow.

In psych class, we'd learned about this phenomenon called *habituation,* which explained how you became used to things over time, stopped seeing them after a while, hardly noticed gradual, incremental changes. Even the insanely abnormal became utterly ordinary, if you lived with it long enough. And I had been living with this for a very long time.

Now I followed Jay's shocked gaze, seeing it afresh, as though through his eyes. And it was horrible.

The untamed jungle of stuff started in the hallway. Towers of stacked storage boxes grew up one wall, reaching almost to the ceiling, while an undergrowth of newspapers and magazines drooped in untidy piles against the walls, here and there slipping into a groundcover of decaying paper.

Teeming inside a bookshelf with a glass-paneled front, like plants inside a tropical terrarium, were old photo albums, rulers from a geometry set, an assortment of kitchen gadgets still in their original packaging, several years' worth of old planners, an old-timey soda syphon, and a chipped green vase. A purple piggy bank, stacks of paper plates and bulging manila folders, and a broken-stringed guitar sprouted from the top of the bookshelf.

"Home sweet home," I said.

I snuck a quick look at Jay's face. It was blank with shock, his eyes unreadable in the dim light, his mouth gaping.

"This way. Careful where you step." I indicated the mere five inches of relative openness that snaked a path through the chaos of clutter.

"Huh?" Jay refocused his eyes on me. There was a crease between his eyes now, as though he was struggling to reconcile the me he knew with these surroundings.

I sighed. "Have you seen enough? Do you want to go back? Do you want to go home?"

"No. Show me everything," he said. Then, in a firmer voice, added, "Lead on, Macduff."

"Right," I said. "Follow me, Macbeth."

Jay sucked in an appalled breath, along with a lungful of dust, and coughed for a few moments before gasping, "Never say the name of the Scottish play! Don't you know it's bad luck?"

I gave him a wry smile. "I don't think luck gets much worse

than this." I gestured to the surroundings.

"Don't tempt fate, Peyton, I'm not kidding!"

"You're superstitious?" I asked, glancing over my shoulder as I moved slowly down the hall, kicking aside a knotted tangle of bamboo tubes that had once been a wind-chime.

Jay followed behind, moving cautiously. "I'm an actor — of course I'm superstitious."

He was taking it well. He hadn't fainted, sworn, judged or bolted. He was a keeper all right. Then again, maybe it was too soon to call. He hadn't seen the worst of it yet.

An old television set, with rounded screen and bulging rear, blocked our path. A tangle of computer cables and old phone chargers trailed over its top, like vines growing over a boulder.

"Here," Jay said, lending me a steadying hand as I climbed over the obstacle.

I battled to find a clear spot to put down my foot. A huge laundry basket, filled with my old shoes, had tipped over, regurgitating slippers, tennis shoes and boots across the carpet. I picked up a small sandal to fling it out of the way and saw that it was a size seven. Had my feet ever been that small?

"Right." I paused outside the next door along the hall. "This here is ground zero. Ready to go in?"

~ *37* ~

I pushed open the door, flicked on the light, and stepped inside. Jay followed and stood beside me in the tiny clearing just beyond the door as he took in the scene.

The walls were glimpses of a faded sky blue, just visible behind the forest of stuff. A mobile wilted from the light fixture — Winnie the Pooh, Eeyore, Roo, and Tigger trapped in a lattice of cobwebs. The cot was a thicket of stuffed toys, with Solly Monster perched on top.

Shelves teemed with tributes to babyhood — porcelain statuettes of chubby cherubs; a bronzed baby shoe; small books made of board and cloth; a wall calendar with fading photographs of babies curled up in mother-of-pearl shells and pea pods and the hearts of sunflowers; tiny crystal ornaments — rocking horses, teddy bears and train locomotives — their faceted surfaces now dulled by time and dust; hand-knitted booties; a jumble of bibs, and, imprinted in green paint on a piece of white board, an impossibly tiny pair of footprints.

"Look, Peyton, Ethan's got such teeny, tiny feet!"

A giant teddy bear sat on a rocking chair. Draped across its arms was an old-fashioned christening gown, with yellowing lace collar and cuffs. That was the chair where Mom had sat when she fed Ethan. I'd longed to climb up into her lap and be rocked to sleep, but I was the big sister — the one sent to fetch bottles of formula and medicine.

"No, Peyton, you're not a baby. You're a big girl now. You're Mommy's little helper."

Beside the chair was the changing dresser where Ethan had lain, cycling his thin legs in the air whenever we changed his diaper.

"Look at him go! He'll be a champion cyclist one day."

Now its surface was a shrine — a white votive candle, never lit, surrounded by a mass of framed photographs of Ethan as a baby. There was one of him in the incubator at the hospital, lying on a lamb's wool blanket and connected to a matrix of tubes and machines, and another of him in my mother's arms on discharge day. There were several of him at home — in his high chair being fed applesauce by Dad, an action shot of him kicking over a tower of blocks on the blue carpeted floor of this very room, and one of him propped beside me on the couch in the living room.

"You must be very gentle with him, princess.. He's not strong like you are."

We were surrounded by things my baby brother had never used, *would* never use — a red tricycle, a blackboard and chalks, tubs of playdough, wax crayons, Lego blocks, and dozens of books — all the things that had once been mine and which should have been handed down to him, but which had wound up in this mausoleum of a nursery instead.

I turned to check Jay's reaction and was disconcerted to find him staring intently at me, rather than at this display of melancholy nostalgia and frozen grief. I could see the questions in his eyes.

"This was my baby brother's room. His name was Ethan."

I stepped over a mound of mothering magazines, snagged the incubator photograph, blew the dust off, and handed it to Jay.

"He had a congenital heart defect — tricuspid atresia with co-occurring ventricular septal defect. Basically, a hole in the heart."

Jay stared down sadly at the picture.

"He'd already had one surgery and was due to have another when he caught pneumonia, and just never recovered."

"How old was he?"

"When he died? Nine months."

"How old were you?"

"Four."

"Oh, Peyton. I am so sorry."

Jay pulled me against him and hugged me tight. I wished he could hold me so tight that all my broken pieces would click back together.

I spoke against his shoulder. "It was a long time ago."

So long ago that I treasured the few memories of Ethan that still remained. The baby toe on his left foot that crossed over the one beside it. The sweet smell that sweated out his scalp whenever Mom fed him pureed peaches. Even the bluish lips.

"I don't know that you *ever* get over something like this," Jay said.

I sighed and pulled back. "Well, my mother sure didn't. She kept Ethan's stuff. All of it — even the disposable diapers and the bottles of baby food. That's how it began."

She'd kept the last clothes he'd worn in a Ziplock bag and never washed them.

"I can still smell his scent on them."

"She was smashed flat with grief and depression," I said. "I guess when she couldn't save him, she hung onto the next best thing — his stuff."

"I lost my son. I won't lose anything else."

"Then she started buying more stuff — baby things, at first, but gradually just anything that caught her fancy. She became obsessed with her possessions, with shopping. At the time, I didn't understand what was happening. I was just a little kid excited by all the new purchases, you know? Now I think she was trying to fill up the hole inside her."

"Does she still buy so much?"

"Oh, hell yeah. She shops online like her life depends on it, even though we *really* can't afford it, even though she doesn't — *can't* — use what she buys. It's an addiction — it helps her zone out and go numb. When she's staring at a screen, the blinkers are on and she doesn't see the rest of it, doesn't have to acknowledge what's happened to her life."

"Or to yours," said Jay, returning Ethan's photograph to its spot.

"Next, she quit throwing *anything* away. The clutter just spread through the house. Like a slow-flowing river." Like a disease. "It reached a point where she just didn't care anymore."

"And your father?" Jay asked.

I squashed a deflated soccer ball beneath my foot. "They struggled on for a couple of years — trying to make it work. But there was just too much grief and guilt between them."

"If only I'd ..."

"You should never have ..."

"But I didn't know he ..."

"What if you'd ..."

"Dad spent less and less time at home — I guess initially to avoid my mother, to avoid dealing with Ethan's death. But I suspect that he also started having an affair back then. One day he packed his bags and moved out. Pretty much said, 'Have to go,' and went."

"So you lost him, too," said Jay, staring deeply into my eyes. "You lost your baby brother, your mother to her depression and her belongings, and then your father left."

I shrugged. I hadn't thought of it that way before — as a triple blow of loss.

"As soon as the divorce came through, he married Lucy. And yesterday" — I kicked the ball aside — "we got the news that they're having a baby. A son."

"Holy shit, Peyton."

"Yeah." I cleared my throat. "Anyway, after Dad left, my mother just stopped going out. I mean, not overnight, but gradually less and less. I don't think she's set foot outside this house in five years."

"God!"

"Yeah, she's a hoarder and a shut-in, I know," I said, feeling defensive.

"What must it have been like for *you*?"

"You need to be brave for your mother, princess. Come on, smile – there's my girl!"

"Oh, you know," I said breezily, squeezing the words through my tight throat.

"No, I don't. Tell me."

My eyes were stinging. I turned away from his penetrating gaze and left the room. Back in the jam-packed confusion of the hallway, I picked up my load of shame. Ethan's room, awful as it was, was just about comprehensible. The rest of the house was simply a humiliating, filthy disgrace.

Jay sneezed several times, and I asked, "Still up for the grand tour of the whole mansion?"

"Yes. But I also still want to know what it was like for you."

Jay was nothing if not persistent. Still, wasn't that supposed to be the aim of this exercise — to open up to him? To trust?

"It was difficult," I said, as we headed toward the landing, picking our way between teetering towers of bulk packs of toilet paper. "And it got worse over time. I don't just mean the mess, though obviously that escalated. I mean my experience of it. I grew up with this all around me, so it was my normal, you know? And my mother messed with my head by minimizing it, and saying it was just a bit untidy, and acting like everything was just fine."

"Look, dear, I bought you these new dresses – aren't they pretty?"

"Before I pack away all my lovely things, why don't we play a game of hide-and-seek?"

"We'd play games amongst the piles of crap, have treasure hunts. It was fun. So, for the longest time, I didn't realize how stuffed up it really was." I gave a little laugh. "Literally."

~ *38* ~

*J*ay and I paused on the landing at the top of the stairs and, like a pair of pioneers surveying an unexplored wilderness, contemplated the haphazard landslide of junk that clogged the way down.

Clothes, fraying blankets, and old towels swathed the bannisters like climbing creepers weighing down a trellis. Draped on top were a bunch of tacky plastic party banners — one of my mother's "irresistible" online purchases. They'd probably been printed somewhere they didn't speak much English — *Happy Birday! Congratulation! Mazel Tov on your Bar Mitsah!* — but she insisted on keeping them for a party she was planning.

A party. In this dump.

"You think she would have tossed these two, at least." I smiled grimly, pointing to a pair of grimy banners which read: *Is a boy!* and *Happy Anniversary!* "But this place is a black hole. No matter ever escapes."

"When did you realize that it wasn't normal?" Jay asked.

I thought about that for a while, kicking at a rolled-up carpet lying on the top stair.

"I think it must have been in fourth or fifth grade, when I went to a birthday party at Bree Rogerson's house. It was my first sleepover at a friend's who wasn't Chloe."

"Does Chloe know?"

"About this? Yeah. But she's the only one. And now you." I puffed out a breath. "You've no idea how hard this is for me — to let someone else into the secret."

He nodded slowly, and I was suddenly aware how still he'd been holding his body. He was guarding his facial expressions and keeping his voice neutral. He *looked* relaxed, but he was an actor. I could sense that he was anything but at ease. If he surrendered to his instincts, he'd probably run screaming from this madhouse and spend the rest of the day scrubbing himself clean in a hot shower.

Too late to turn back now, Jay, for either of us.

"Chloe and I have been best friends since kindergarten," I explained as we made our way down the stairs, hanging onto each other for balance as we stepped over and around the junk. "We kind of grew up in each other's houses, so she knew. But somehow I never compared the way she lived to the way we did. That was just how Chloe's house was. I guess I thought everyone's house was different and unique. Careful here, these are sharp and rusty."

I edged around a brace of rebar rods. Why we had steel reinforcing bars inside our house, let alone on our staircase, was anybody's guess.

"But the penny dropped at Bree's house that night, because her house was just like Chloe's: clean, neat and tidy. And her mother was" — I struggled to find the right word — "I don't know, *put together*. A bit like your mom. Hair combed, face made up, bright smiles as she handed out the hotdogs and buttered popcorn and reminded us to brush our teeth before we went to bed. And then I saw the pattern: it wasn't that Chloe's house was different from mine, it was that my house was different from everyone else's. *We* were the abnormal ones, the freaks."

"Freaks?"

I pushed aside a broken fax machine spewing a trail of paper and took another step down.

"I was already looking kind of freakish — I was at least a foot taller than the other girls in my grade — and my mom was undeniably acting freakish. And there were things I just couldn't say or do."

"Such as?"

"Apart from Chloe, I couldn't have any friends over — not even for a playdate, let alone a sleepover."

"No, Peyton, I'm afraid not. They wouldn't … understand."

"Which meant that I couldn't accept their invitations either, because I wouldn't be able to return the favor. And it's hard to keep friends when you never hang out together, so I just stopped making friends. I never had a party or a movie night, and when I had to do group projects for school, I never offered to have the kids come to my house. I got a reputation for being snooty and unfriendly. At first, they called me a stuck-up cow, then 'the snooty girooffy'."

"The what?"

"The snooty girooffy. You know, like giraffe — because I was so tall?"

"Oh. Hilarious," Jay said, unamused.

"I made up all kinds of excuses to keep the kids from trying to come inside — we had a vicious dog, our house was being renovated or fumigated, my mother was too sick."

"I believe I've heard that one."

"It's the one I used most often. Still do. Because it's not a total lie, you know? And I hated all the lies I had to tell, but I knew without anyone telling me that I *had* to keep the secret. I was scared that if anyone found out, we'd lose the house, and I'd die of embarrassment and humiliation. To be honest, I still worry about those things."

We both ducked to worm our way under a pair of crutches wedged across the bannisters.

"If someone reported us, Social Services would come nosing around, and they'd haul my lunatic of a mother off to the nuthouse, and me to a scary orphanage."

"This story is breaking my heart," Jay said. He sounded like he meant it.

"Well, this tour of our house is more likely to break your lungs," I said. We were several steps from the bottom of the stairs, and Jay had started sneezing again. "Here, you should put this on."

I handed him one of the two facemasks I'd stuffed into my pocket earlier.

"You're kidding, right?"

I shook my head. "It's real bad down there. Worse than upstairs."

"*Worse?*"

"Worse," I confirmed. "It just keeps getting worse."

"Keep going," he said, and clarified, "With the story."

"But it's so boring."

"I want to hear it," he insisted.

"Fine. Don't say I didn't warn you."

I dusted my hands on my jeans as we stepped off the last stair and flicked the switch for the sconces. Amazingly, two of the lights still worked.

"You were talking about the excuses," Jay prompted, seemingly more interested in me than the cluttered chaos of the hall.

"Okay, well, when my mother stopped leaving the house, I had to come up with all sorts of reasons as to why she couldn't attend parent-teacher conferences, class mom get-togethers, or mother-and-daughter breakfasts. I'd forge an acceptance reply, then on the day of the event send an apology text or email in her name, saying she was sick, away on an unexpected business trip, had a family emergency in New York, had fallen down the stairs and broken her ankle. Oh my God, all those lies!"

I'd collected deceit and excuses like my mother had hoarded crap.

"No wonder you're so good at keeping secrets and hiding your real self."

"I got skillz, yo!" Time for some humor — this was getting too intense for me.

Jay gave me a sad smile and tucked a stray curl of my hair behind my ear. "And at deflecting."

"Deflecting?"

"Yeah, deflecting. Warding off questions and closeness. Steering clear of intimacy. It's like" — he ran fingers through his hair, clearly searching for the right words — "It's like your shields are up so hard and so tight that people just ricochet off you."

"Now that's just crazy talk." I grabbed a broken umbrella with faded red fabric hanging forlornly off its jutting spikes, and slashed aside a snare of spiderwebs. "Look at us, just like Tarzan and Jane, hacking our way through the vines. It's a jungle down here."

"You're doing it right now," he accused.

Guilty as charged.

I felt my fake smile subside into bleak lines, and my shoulders slump in defeat. "The *family* room," I sighed, tossing aside the umbrella.

The room was filled four feet high with stuff that held the unfulfilled promise of normal family life: an ancient Christmas tree still decorated with tinsel and baubles; racks of VHS tapes in disintegrating cardboard sleeves; a garden of mummified potted plants on the mantelpiece; dingy sun-faded drapes hanging off their rails; a bicycle wheel jammed between toppled lamp stands. And things never used: a sagging stack of old board games that I didn't remember us ever playing; a bundled value-pack of cleaning equipment — broom, mop, feather duster — still sealed in plastic; and boxes of Ikea furniture, never opened or assembled.

Our house was full of could'ves, would'ves, should'ves.

Jay turned his back on the accumulated crazy of the living room and fixed his attention on me.

"I think you and your mom are similar in many ways," he said.

"*What?*"

I did not want to be like my mom, not at all. Not in any way. It was one of the reasons I kept my own space so immaculate. The horror movie that regularly played itself out in my nightmares was that I allowed myself to buy one nonessential item, to hang up a picture or keep a book after I'd read it, and the weeds of mess multiplied until my space was overrun. And I was trapped.

"I'm like my mom?" I said. "You mean, more than us both being freaks?"

"You're not a freak, you're a goddess," Jay said, flicking my chin with a finger.

He thought I was a *goddess*. I tucked that word deep inside my heart, where it would stay shiny-clean and beautiful.

"And your mom's … ill."

"Well, you know what they say about magazine hoarders? They have a lot of issues."

He rolled his eyes at me. "I'm no shrink, but it seems to me that both you and your mother keep people at bay. She uses clutter. No one can come around with the house like this, right? And she never interacts with people in the outside world because she's stuck inside — what's it called, that condition?"

"Agoraphobia."

"Right. And *you* keep the world at arm's length with your secrets and advanced skills in avoidance. I've seen how you hide behind your humor. I think you even hide behind your height."

"Huh?" How was that even possible? "I think my height makes me the opposite of invisible, Jay."

"Well *I* think that maybe you secretly like that it's all people see of you. It's like, I don't know, maybe you'd rather they focused on your height than probed a little deeper."

Clever boy.

"My point is," he continued, "I reckon you and your mother are both protecting yourselves against the same thing."

"The Clean House crew? The men in white coats?"

He didn't smile. He frowned and puffed a breath out through his lips. "Rejection, I think. And abandonment."

Wow. That felt like a punch in the guts.

"Hey, I could be wrong — I'm not a psychologist — but I figure you're terrified of loving and losing again. And if you never get close to anyone, you don't have to risk the pain of losing them, like you did with Ethan and your father."

There were tears rolling down my cheeks now. I made to wipe them away, but my hands were dirty, and my shirt was covered in dust and cobwebs. Jay stepped close, lifted his sweatshirt and wiped my face with the inside of it.

"Thank you, Dr. Freud," I said, twisting my mouth into something I hoped resembled a grin.

This time, he allowed me to deflect the emotion.

"You promised me a tour of the entire mansion, and I won't feel I've had the full experience unless I see the kitchen," he said.

"Fine. Hope you've got a strong stomach."

~ *39* ~

*M*oving carefully in the dim light, Jay and I maneuvered our way through the maze of old furniture and piles of newspaper; past a broken ironing board; and around clothes and handbags mushrooming from broken-zipped suitcases, and headed toward what remained of the kitchen.

We were hit by the smell of damp and mildew as we reached the guest bathroom. Inside, the basin overflowed with old deodorant cans, empty shampoo bottles, rusted disposable razors, and half-used bars of soap, while the floor and bath were buried under a mountain of old books infested with a thriving silverfish colony.

"The library," I announced.

Jay gave a low whistle.

"Not to worry, though. My mother says these won't be here for long."

"I'm just storing them here temporarily. Some of those are first editions, you know. That means they're valuable."

Jay eyed the heaps of crumbling paper, detached covers and

mold-speckled spines. "How long have they already been here?"

"Oh, just six or seven years."

Slipping and sliding on the compost of magazines underfoot, we covered the last few feet to the kitchen, squeezing through a narrow section of hallway where a mattress topped with old bedding slumped vertically against the wall. A brace of dusty pillows fell onto my head as I walked by, sending us both into coughing fits.

"Time to put on our masks," I said, pulling my own up.

We couldn't see much except shadows in the gloom beyond the open kitchen door. But we could smell it.

The acrid stink of rot and mold and decomposition enveloped us like a cloud of poison gas. It was rank — so pungent it was almost solid. It caught in my throat, turned my stomach and made my eyes water. Beside me, Jay had the back of his hand pressed against his masked mouth, holding back a gag.

Oh yeah, worse.

"The light switch is somewhere here," I said, reaching around the doorway.

As soon as the light flicked on, Jay cursed. *Finally*, I thought, *now I'll see the depth of his revulsion.* Then I saw that he wasn't reacting to the contents of the room. His worried gaze was fixed on the exposed wires and dangling metal plate of the light switch.

"Damn, Peyton, those wires are live — you could have shocked yourself!"

"I'm okay."

I was anything but. We were surrounded by a swamp of

garbage bags — black ones stuffed with trash, and transparent ones filled with empty water bottles and soda cans.

"I need to clean and sort them before I take them to the recycling depot. Stop nagging me, Peyton, I'll get to it one day."

Jay glanced up at the sagging ceiling, with its water damage stain shaped like a giant, brown moth, and then down at the floor covered by a three-foot-deep mulch of debris and decay — scraps of waste and garbage that had never made it out to the trash: old pizza boxes; cheese and cracker trays with moldy crusts of food; an open, half-eaten jar of peanut-butter; empty cookie boxes and nested egg cartons; half-petrified apples with sunken, wrinkled cheeks; the remains of a birthday cake topped with a macabre frosting of blue-green fuzz. A rust-colored garden hose twisted its way under and around the silt of waste, and every surface was dotted with tiny black droppings.

"This whole place is a death trap — one spark and it would go up in flames," Jay said.

"Would that be such a bad thing — if it burned to the ground?"

"Don't joke," he replied, though I'd been entirely serious. "It's not safe for you to live here. You could be burned to a crisp, or buried alive."

Buried alive? Been there, done that, got all the moth-eaten T-shirts lying somewhere here to prove it.

He wasn't wrong about the fire hazard, though. There was paper everywhere — shoeboxes overflowing with bills, letters, invoices, tax documents and appliance warranties, haphazardly filed alongside store catalogues, flyers, junk mail and cash register receipts.

Jay clambered over a rusting laundry rack and lifted the top picture off a stack of my elementary school art cluttering a nearby counter. He grinned down at it before handing it to me.

It was a macaroni-framed picture entitled, "My family, by Peyton Lane, 2nd grade." Beside a red-roofed house with the obligatory border of flowers and yellow sun overhead stood a stick-figure family — all happy faces and splay-fingered hands — and a whiskered cat. Mom and Dad held hands, and I held a smiling blue bundle in my arms, even though by the time I'd drawn this, Dad had already left, and Ethan had been dead for a couple of years. And we'd never had a cat, thank God, or its desiccated corpse would probably be resting six feet under the crap in this room.

I tossed the picture on the kitchen table, which was already piled high with dirty dishes, empty spice bottles, two computer keyboards, a knot of wire coat hangers snarled around a juicing machine, and an ornamental birdcage. We'd never had a pet bird, either.

I caught Jay eyeing the refrigerator and quickly said, "Look, I don't know about you, but I need to get outside and take some deep breaths of clean air. Have a quick look around, just so you can honestly say you earned your Medal of Honor for acts of valor above and beyond the call of duty, and then let's get out of here."

I hated to think what putrefied remains might be entombed inside the refrigerator — it hadn't worked for years.

But Jay stayed where he was, rotating slowly on the spot like a man in a trance, staring at a broken-doored cupboard stuffed with bloated cans of long-expired foods, and a four-tiered shelf with peeling laminate that hung drunkenly off one wall, at the chipped tiles, peeling wallpaper, rotting linoleum, an overturned typist's chair with a missing wheel. Everywhere things were broken, unrepaired, unused, expired and incomplete.

Neglected.

"It's like the epicenter of an earthquake," he said.

He was onto something there. My mother's hoarding was like a decade-long natural disaster — a slow-motion flood with no hope of rescue from emergency services.

The stove top and sinks were choked with dirty dishes, encrusted pots, mugs, used Styrofoam cups and paper plates, and trails of black ants. Overhead, flies buzzed lazily, and I didn't need to look closer to know that there would be maggots feasting on the decaying food. I lifted my head at a sudden rustle to the side of me, just in time to see a scuttling blur of black disappear behind a tarnished coffeepot. It was either a small rat or a very large roach.

I shuddered. "I'm sorry. There are no words for this."

It was beyond words, beyond comprehension.

"I can understand why she wants to hang onto your brother's stuff, but why doesn't she chuck out the garbage?" Jay asked.

"She can't. She feels compelled to make the perfect decision about what to keep and what to toss. And because there is no perfect decision, she gets anxious and keeps everything, just to be safe."

"Well, if *she* can't make decisions or take action, why don't you?"

"You think I haven't tried? You think I haven't tried

everything? I've asked, encouraged, offered to help, negotiated, begged, shouted, shamed, sulked, begged her to see a shrink, and threatened to report her. Nothing works. She ignores or dismisses what I say."

"Can't *you* just throw out the junk?"

"If I toss anything out, or even just move it, she goes into a complete meltdown. Then she's down and out for days, blaming me for making her feel out of control. Like *this* is being in control!" I swept an arm across a countertop, sending a stacked set of never-used Tupperwares flying.

"So, nothing works?" Jay said gently.

I shook my head. "It's taken years, but I've finally realized that she *can't*. I mean, she doesn't *want* to — I know that — but she also just can't. She can't make decisions, can't prioritize. She has asthma, but she can't toss dust traps and mildewed books. She can't distinguish between the value of a working computer and a dead one, between a pair of pearl earrings and a pair of broken shoes, a painting and a cracked flowerpot. Everything is valuable. She once told me that this stuff, all these things, are her 'friends'. I mean, what do you even say to that?"

"What *did* you say?"

"I told her she loved her stuff more than she loved me."

Jay winced.

"You're just selfish, Peyton. You value empty space over my peace of mind and happiness. You don't understand what it's like to be me."

She'd been right about that last one, at least.

~ *40* ~

*J*ay and I retreated into the hallway, where I kicked the pillows ahead of me as we passed the mattress.

"I used to feel guilty that I couldn't save her from this, couldn't help her get better. But I've given up. I just live as separately and differently as I can. I'm out of ideas, and I've got nowhere else to go."

I could hear the despair in my voice. Veering dangerously close to self-pity, Peyton.

"I did once try to go to a Hoarders Anonymous meeting, but I couldn't get in – the house was packed."

Jay ignored my feeble joke. "Does your father know how bad it is?"

"I don't think so. He hasn't been here for years. And I don't exactly give him updates."

"Why not?"

"He doesn't want to know. If he did, he'd have to face up to things, own some responsibility, take action. And Dad's also gifted at avoidance. *Denial before dealing* – that could be the Lane family motto."

I held my breath as we passed the guest bathroom.

"But living with him would have to be better than this, surely?"

"Maybe. But I'd have to change schools and move to Blue Crab Bay. I'd miss Chloe." And now you, too. "And if I left, I don't think my mom would cope. She's not good at taking care of herself."

"But you've applied to college in New York. She'll be alone then?"

I sighed. "It's a real problem. I mean, I want to *go*. I'm desperate to leave this disgusting dump. And I deserve to, you know?"

"Hell, Peyton, you don't have to convince me."

"If I'm going to have my own life, I need to get out of here. But that means leaving her alone. And so … I worry."

We emerged back into the hall, and I saw that my mother was standing on the lowest step. Had she overheard us talking, heard me saying I planned to abandon her?

"Oh, hello," she said, with a nervous laugh. "You've got company."

"This is Jay, from school. Jay, this is my mother."

"Pleased to meet you, Mrs. Lane."

My mother gave a tight smile and smoothed her hair with a hand that wasn't completely steady. She was clearly flustered by Jay's presence.

"I hope you forgive my little mess. I haven't got around to tidying in a while, so things are a bit disorganized."

I gave Jay a what-did-I-tell-you-about-denial look. My mother let her gaze skim over the scene, eyes slightly unfocused — all the better not to see reality.

"One of my resolutions for the year will definitely be to sort and organize my treasured collections." She pulled a green plastic toy out of her sweatpants pocket and added it to the other Happy Meal toys heaped on the half-moon hall table below the cloudy hall mirror. "Though I don't know where I'll find a spot to display them. It's a bit full down here. I'm thinking of renting a storage unit because I truly do need more space. But in January, I'm definitely going to get everything shipshape and squeaky clean." Again, the tight little laugh. "*I'd be unstoppable if I could just get going* — I have a coffee mug that says that."

"Watch this," I whispered to Jay.

I picked up the broken red umbrella and held it up in my mom's line of vision.

"Perhaps we can start with this," I suggested.

"Start what?"

"The sorting and cleaning and ship-shaping. Let's start by tossing this."

The puzzlement on her features was instantly replaced by an expression of alarm.

"I can't just *throw things away!*" she said, in a tone she might use to exclaim, "I can't just *drown puppies!*"

"It's broken," I pointed out.

"There's still lots of use left in it. All it needs is a few drops of superglue. I've got some tubes packed away somewhere … somewhere here." She gazed around her as if there was a snowball's chance in hell of finding anything in the mishmash of madness surrounding us. "I'll fix it later." She tugged the umbrella out of my grip and carefully balanced it on a towel-covered section of bannister. "It's not rubbish, Peyton. It still has value. You can't just cast aside things when they're a little old or damaged."

Was she still talking about the umbrella?

"Sure, okay. Then how about tossing this?" I said, bending over to retrieve an old newspaper from a collapsing pile.

"No, I couldn't do that," said my mother.

"Why not? It's from" — I checked the date printed near the rat-nibbled corner — "four years ago. It's old news."

"But there might be something important in there." She made to take it from me, but I pulled it out of her reach.

"Like what?" I challenged.

"Well, I don't know — I haven't had a chance to read it yet, have I? But it might contain restaurant reviews, or perhaps some delicious recipes. Or even some good coupons."

"We don't go to restaurants. We don't cook. The coupons will have expired."

"There may be news that's important, or information supplements that you could use for a school project."

"All the information and news I'll ever need is online, where I can find it in seconds. We don't need to store it in our house."

She frowned at me. "Now that might be short-sighted, dear. I read somewhere that people who kept physical copies of newspapers from 9/11 made a fortune selling them on eBay."

"It's okay," said Jay, softly. "Let her keep it."

But I pressed on, reading the headline out loud. "'Governor plans to cut state budget.' It must've been a slow news day. I can't think this issue is too valuable."

"We might need it one day."

Ah, *one day*, my old friend. I wondered when I would hear from you again.

"My things are important to me, Peyton, you know that." She was starting to sound panicky. "Besides, they're not in your way."

I shot Jay another significant look.

"I think I'll just toss it for you," I said, rolling up the paper and tucking it under my arm, like I planned to take it with me when I left.

"Peyton, I've asked you not to do that! Don't mess with my stuff! I'll get to it, okay? Just give me some time," she said, her voice high with emotion. Tears filled her eyes, and her hands patted her pockets in search of her asthma pump. She was on the verge of hysteria. "Just stop! I like it the way it is."

"Enough," Jay murmured beside me. "I get it."

I held the newspaper out to my mother. She snatched it quickly, as though she feared I might change my mind about letting her keep it, and laid it back on top of its pile.

"I need to get home now, Mrs. Lane. Thank you for having me. It was very nice meeting you." Jay spoke in a gentle voice, like a horse-whisperer soothing a skittish mare.

My mother said her goodbyes distractedly, and before Jay and I had even turned to leave, she was checking and restacking the newspapers, crouched down in the waste of times past and a life unlived.

~ *41* ~

$\mathcal{I}$ was worried — afraid that after the Lane house show-and-tell, Jay would think less of me, despite his reassurances last night. When we'd stepped out of the dusty despair of the house and into the crisp winter air, he'd told me that no, he didn't think I was dirty or disgusting, and that yes, he still wanted to keep dating me, and that no, of course he wouldn't tell anyone my secret. Then he'd hugged me tight for long minutes and kissed me goodnight.

I'd gone to bed, confused and disoriented, like the solid ground beneath my feet had shifted, propelling me into a whole new territory. I'd done the unthinkable, shared my secret, shown someone I cared deeply about the full horror of the way I lived, let him in on the crazy that ruled my mother's life, which might even flow through my veins.

And, seemingly, nothing had happened. My life had proceeded this day very much as on any other Friday. Nothing was different, and yet everything was.

I felt lighter, freer, more hopeful. I'd thought I'd been keeping the secret, but now I realized that the secret had been keeping me. Holding me back, trapping me in mistrust and isolation.

Yesterday had deepened my feelings for Jay. He must have been shocked and appalled at what he'd seen and learned about my life, but he'd handled it — calmly, tactfully and compassionately. What's more, he hadn't run around the school or social media airing my dirty laundry. And he'd been right — I did trust him more now that I had nothing left to hide, or at least not much. I still needed to tell him about the wager, but compared to yesterday's grand reveal, the wager was a minor thing, just a silly joke.

Even so, the snatched moments with Jay between classes and at lunch had felt a little awkward, and that had been enough to jack up my fears. By the time I arrived at the theater that evening, two hours before curtain-up on our opening night performance, I was a tightly spun bundle of nerves. I needed reassurance that Jay and I were still good, but I resisted the urge to call him out of the boys' dressing room. And kept resisting while I applied my makeup, sewed the spaghetti straps of my bra tank top to my top's shoulder straps, and hummed, hissed and tongue-twisted my way through vocal warm-ups.

When even the deep inhalations and slow exhalations of my breathing exercises didn't calm me down, however, I cornered him in a quiet spot in the wings.

"And now? Do you want to get into character by practicing our kissing scenes?" He asked when I grabbed his upper arms and rotated him until his face was in the light, and I could see his eyes.

"No."

"No?" The disappointed expression on his face was adorable, but I was not going to be swayed from my mission. I was, as Shakespeare had put it, "bent to know, by the worst means the worst."

The words were from Macbeth, so I didn't say them out loud in case breaking the superstition might actually bring bad luck. I didn't need any of that tonight.

"After last night, I need to know where your head's at." And your heart. "And please be honest, Jay."

"You want the truth?"

Oh, God, probably not. His expression was so earnest that the news couldn't be good. I swallowed hard and made myself say, "Yes."

"Okay, then. The truth is that last night has changed how I feel about you."

I knew it. I *knew* it. So why, if I'd just proved myself right, did I feel so terrible? My heart sank. I dropped my eyes, stared hard at a stray button lying on the floorboards of the stage, trying to force back the tears gathering behind my eyes.

"Right," I whispered hoarsely. "I see."

"I don't think you do," Jay said. He cupped my face in his hands and gently tilted it up to look me full in the eye. "I respect you more," he said, at the same moment as I said, "I'll understand if you —"

I blinked. "Wait ... what?"

"I mean I already knew that you were beautiful, sexy, funny and talented."

He had?

"But now I know that you're also strong and brave and

resilient. And amazingly resourceful — finding a way to live your life your way, despite your circumstances, in the face of them! Plus, you're there for your mom —"

"I am not." I shook my head in denial. "I am mean and resentful. I am only ever unkind to her. I'm a grade-A bitch."

"Your mother's condition robbed you of your childhood, yet you've busted a gut to keep the family secret. You've mothered your mom and protected your dad from the truth so he could be free. That kind of self-sacrifice comes from love, Peyton. And a kind heart."

The ground was rippling beneath me again. It was as though someone had recognized parts of me I hadn't known existed. In that moment, I felt real, whole — less a collection of fragments and more solidly myself. The warm glow of love for him deep in my core blazed white hot, pulsed through my body, and radiated from my eyes as I stared into the golden-green depths of his.

I wanted this to be just us, to be private, but other members of the cast were moving onto the stage, and I could hear Doug issuing last-minute instructions nearby.

So I stood on my toes, pressed my cheek against his, and breathed into his ear, "I love you."

I felt his cheek curve into a smile against my own, and then he pulled his face back to touch his lips to mine, where they moved in four silent but unmistakable words.

"I love you, too."

"Places, please!" the stage manager shouted beside us, making us jump, and laugh, and spin away to our separate sides of the stage.

I waited for my old fears to nibble away at his words, for the familiar voice of doubt to shake my belief in him, but instead, I felt a deep sense of calm spreading out from the center of me, filling me with joy and confidence. With hope.

Not even Wren's snide "Sure you're up to it tonight, Big P?" could dent my exhilaration and self-assurance.

"Peyton," Doug pleaded just before the curtain went up, "give it your all tonight, okay? I beg you, please give it *all* of you."

And I so did.

I *became* Juliet. I felt intoxicated with excitement and happiness. I felt just like a giddy, light-hearted young girl at a ball, dancing and flirting. For the first time, I felt just like Juliet.

There were still undercurrents of the old caution and reticence, but only in my interactions with Mom and Pop Capulet and the others, which was just how it should be. When I was playing against Jay, however, when Juliet was with Romero, it was easy — effortless — to be fully present and completely open, to show my true emotions, to trust him without reservation.

I was a girl in love. My face glowed and my voice thrummed with the emotion of it. My body was relaxed in Jay's arms, my hands were comfortable in reaching out to touch him. The connection between us crackled with chemistry. I'd thought I'd seen the best of Jay's talent, but tonight — with me giving him more, giving him everything, plus the energy flowing from the audience — he soared. And for the first time, he wasn't acting *around* me, lifting my performance with the magic of his. Instead we acted together, played off each other's energy, elevated each other's performance.

We *were* the star-crossed young lovers, blissfully unaware of the tragedy that threatened.

I was so immersed in my character that when we got to the passionate kiss in the last scene, I lost myself completely in the moment. I forgot that I was on a stage, with images of me projected on enormous screens; lost all awareness of the audience. I was so in the moment that I was oblivious to everything except this amazing, crazy-sexy guy who seemed wild about me, too.

The remaining barriers of clothing between us frustrated me. My hands itched to touch his skin, and without my consciously willing it, they peeled off his button-down overshirt and flung it aside, leaving him in the tight white T. A split second of surprise flickered across Jay's features, but when I ran my hands up the muscled length of his arms, he shivered with pleasure. His eyes grew heavy-lidded, and those beautiful lips twisted into a sexy grin.

"All right," his expression seemed to say. "You want me? You've got me. Let's do this!"

He lowered himself slowly back onto the flat top of the fake rock, pulling me right along with him. When I lay almost on top of him, he turned his head to nibble on one of my earlobes, while the hand that the audience could see wrapped around my back to pull me tighter against him. The hand they couldn't see roamed slowly down my side and came to rest on the side of my ass. Goosebumps rippled over my skin, and my nipples were pebbles against his chest.

My body pulsed with need, my head swirled, and my heart lifted. I only came back to a vague sense of reality when the curtain dropped, and the roar of applause penetrated my fog of desire.

Still a little dazed when the curtain rose again, I grinned sheepishly at Jay as we stepped forward to take our bow. The applause swelled, punctuated by cheers and whistles, and soon the whole audience was on their feet. When the curtain finally came down, the whole cast hopped about excitedly on the stage in a wild round-robin of high-fives, back-slaps, hugs and compliments.

Ms. Gooding looked seriously pleased and more than a little relieved. "You have vindicated my faith in you — congratulations! Jay and Peyton, you were magnificent tonight!"

Wren seemed a little reluctant in her praise of my performance, but the rest were clearly impressed.

Liz punched me hard in the arm and sounded sincere when she said, "That was fantastic!"

Doug was ecstatic. "You were *all* fantastic. Magnificent! Jay — you were awesome, and your timing in that duel was perfect! Zack, you had them in stitches, and Peyton, you had them in tears. I *knew* you could do it — I never doubted you for a moment. The chemistry! Talk about sizzling hot! And that stunt you pulled with Jay's shirt — inspired! Do it again tomorrow night."

Zack gave me a giant grin. "Yeah, Big P. You and Jay getting all hot and heavy, and half-naked — I was getting bonerfied just watching from the wings. Now if you revealed just a little more skin, I'd be living my best dreams."

"Your wet dreams, you mean," Angela said, and everyone — except Doug, who was looking suddenly thoughtful — cracked up laughing.

Apparently unoffended, Zack said, "Let's go grab a burger

at Jim's. I'm too buzzed to go to bed, man. Unless one of the lovely ladies wants to volunteer to help take off the edge?" He cupped his nut purse to emphasize his meaning.

When we all finally began to make our way back to the dressing rooms, Doug said, "Jay, hang on a sec. I've got a couple of ideas for tomorrow night."

A throng of supporters was waiting to congratulate us when, still high with excitement, we tumbled out of the stage door fifteen minutes later. Chloe whooped and jumped up and down while she hugged me, assuring me it was the best performance I'd ever given. Her mother showered me in praise, and Ben insisted on climbing onto my shoulders, telling anyone who would listen that I was his pet giant.

I waved shyly at Mr. and Mrs. Young and wished Jack was there to see her prediction come true. A bunch of clearly infatuated girls wanted to congratulate Jay, and Greg Baker slapped Jay's back, pronounced his performance "freaking awesome!" and loudly bragged that Jay was his cousin.

Delighted by the size of the group that descended on the diner, Jim programmed an all-Elvis playlist on the jukebox and gave us a free round of drinks. We clinked our glasses together and toasted the cast, the crew and Doug.

"We love you, man!" said Zack, slopping his strawberry milkshake as he knocked his glass against Doug's.

"Yeah, you were magnificent! We knew you could do it. We never doubted you for a moment," I said, grinning.

"Are you mocking me?" Doug said.

I winked back, but my smile faded when Tim Anderson stopped by our table.

"Hey, how did the show go tonight?" he asked Jay.

"Great!"

"Cool — I've got my ticket for tomorrow. I need to see how this" — he gestured to Jay and me — "turns out."

"Yeah, see you later," I said, curbing the impulse to manhandle him out of the diner.

The next two hours were spent laughing, teasing, and happily conducting a post-mortem on the play. It was a great way to end the night.

Tori was on duty, and although she wasn't serving our tables, she could hardly miss noticing that Jay and I were now most definitely a couple — we couldn't keep our eyes, or hands, off each other. Every time she passed our table, I smiled up at her, and she scowled down at me.

When the crowd started to break up and head home, I saw her talking to Tim near the door. Was she confirming the status of my relationship with Jay? Wondering why I hadn't logged my dates with him? Tori's back was to us, but she must have said something that surprised or amused Tim, because his eyebrows shot up and he glanced my way for a second. Then Tori looked back over her shoulder at me, and I didn't like the sly smile that curved her lips, not one bit. I sat up straight, unsure what to do, but at that moment, Jay pulled me onto his lap — just as if I was no bigger or heavier than the average girl — and covered my lips with his own. And nothing else seemed to matter much after that.

~ 42 ~

Saturday night was to be our second and last performance. After the success of the opening night, I was feeling so confident that not even Faye could dent my enthusiasm.

She popped backstage before the performance, allegedly to give the cast her best wishes. I saw her give Jay a lingering hug — still hoping for a felonious reconciliation? — and then she breezed up to me.

"I hear you weren't completely terrible last night, Peyton."

"Er, thanks."

"And that you were all over Jay."

I had nothing to say to that. This was maximally awkward.

"Good luck for tonight, then. Good, good luck!"

"You're supposed to say, 'break a leg'," I pointed out. "It's bad luck to wish an actor good luck."

"I know," she said, smiling sweetly. "See you later."

Doug gathered us together for a final pep talk. "It's a full house tonight. Everybody's heard how amazing the show is and wants to see it. We've even added extra rows of seats at the back.

296

Give it your all again, people! Jay, you remember the notes I gave you last night? Wren, you can come in quicker on your lines, and crank up the comedy a notch. Peyton, change nothing."

Ha! It was a rare day when Wren got direction and I didn't.

"Make it happen, people!"

The first half of the play went great — at least as well as the night before. The audience oo'd, ah'd and laughed at the right spots; no one forgot their lines, and the video and audio feeds were in perfect sync with our performances. The only hiccup came when Tim Anderson stumbled in, fifteen minutes after we'd started, and flopped into a chair in the middle of the front row. He applauded enthusiastically between scenes, yelled an encouraging "Stick the pig!" in Jay's fight scene, and wolf-whistled during the balcony speech. He was obviously drunk or high. Probably both.

During the intermission, the stage manager came to the dressing room, where I was busy changing for the second half, and told me that Tim was at the backstage door, demanding to speak to Jay and me.

"You've only got ten minutes, so make it quick," she warned me. "And tell Tim to shut up in the second half. Better still, tell him to go home and sleep it off."

I quickly yanked on my shorts and combination sleeveless-top-tank-bra top, checked my makeup in the brightly lit mirror, and hurried out, catching up with Jay just as he got to the stage door.

Tim was there, swaying slightly and grinning broadly.

"Ah, man! Ah, man!" he said. He blinked his bloodshot eyes

a few times — to clear the double vision? — and reached out to place a steadying hand on the wall beside him.

"I wanned to congratulate the lovers. You guys are awesome. Awesome! I'm so glad you got it together. I gotta wish you to … for …" He paused for a moment, clearly trying to figure out what he was supposed to wish us, before ditching that train of thought. "And I'm so proud, dude, dudess."

"Proud?" said Jay.

"I was the matchmaker, wass'n I? The cupid!"

Uh-oh. My heart gave an unpleasant jolt and my stomach went cold. I needed to shut this down.

"We should go, Jay. We don't want to be late for curtain-up."

"Thanks for the congrats, Tim. Though I think it was Greg who introduced us. I remember the occasion very well." Jay smiled warmly down at me.

"But I gave her your name, man, on the list." Tim slumped against the wall and hiccupped loudly.

"What list?" Jay asked.

"Nothing. He's talking nonsense," I said, tugging at Jay's arm. "Come on, let's go. That's the warning bell for the audience."

"The lis' of tall boys, man."

Oh, crap.

"What?" Jay said.

"Five minutes!" the stage manager called.

"She wanned the names of all boys six foot three at school. And taller. Was only five. Or six." Tim rubbed his temple, as though thinking hard. "No, is was five. Def'n'ly! And you're on it." He grinned at Jay.

Jay was not smiling. "What list?" he asked me.

"I ... I can explain," I said.

Maybe. But where to begin? How to make this sound anything other than awful?

"*I* can 'splain," Tim said. "Big P asked for a lis' of all the tall boys at school, so I gave it to her. A freebie."

"Why?" Jay asked me.

"It was nothing. Just, like, a silly joke," I said, trying to pull Jay away from Tim, as the stage manager gave us the four-minute warning. "We really need to go, Jay."

"S'wasn't a joke!" Tim said indignantly. "Was a bet!"

Shit. My heart was thudding, and my mouth was dry as ash. This was like witnessing a slow-motion car crash.

Jay turned and took a step closer to Tim. "A bet?" he repeated.

"That girl at the diner, the butch one, she told me everything, man. She bet Big P eight hundred dollars that she couldn't do it."

"Do what?"

But Tim had slid down the wall, patting his pockets, and mumbling incoherently.

"Do what?" Jay asked me this time. His voice was low and edged with something dangerous. "Is he talking about that bet when you kissed me, the first time we met?"

"Please, Jay, I'll explain later."

"Naah!" Tim waved a dismissive hand in the air. "Was a bet about prom."

"Three minutes. Places, please," the stage manager called.

"What was the bet, Peyton?"

Oh, God. I'd fully intended to tell Jay. I'd wanted there to be no secrets between us. But I'd planned to do it at the right moment, when I could explain, and make it sound like the stupid nonsense it had been.

I puffed out a breath and forced myself to meet Jay's eyes. "Tori bet me that I couldn't get a tall guy to take me out on three dates plus the prom."

Jay pulled back, a series of expressions chasing each other across his face — shock, hurt, anger.

"*That's* why you asked me out?"

"I didn't ask you out, you asked me out!"

"But would you have come if you didn't stand to make money out of it? Were you just using me to win money — or, should I say, *more* money? Because I'd already won you four hundred bucks with the kiss." His voice was cold and flat.

"Please Jay, it wasn't like that!" I said, desperate to make him understand. "This had nothing to do with you. When I took the bet and got the list, you were still hooked up with Faye."

"Two minutes!"

"But when we broke up, you made your move," Jay accused.

"That's not true!" Was it? "And it's not fair! You —"

"She moved in for the kill, dude," Tim cackled, lurching to his feet, triumphantly clutching a fifth of vodka.

"Will you shut the hell up!" I snapped at him.

"You didn't wan' me to shuddup when you ordered the report. You wanned me to spill the beans then," Tim said sullenly, taking a long pull on his bottle.

"What the hell, Peyton? What's this report he's talking about?"

"I can explain. Please, Jay, we've got to go. I'll explain everything afterwards."

"*I* can 'splain. Me," said Tim, thumping his chest with his thumb. "She could'n afford to pay so we bartered *services,* but don' tell anyone — is a secret. Naughty, naughty!" Tim dissolved in giggles.

Jay gave me a stunned look.

"I didn't! It wasn't like that!" I laid a hand on Jay's arm, but he shrugged it off.

"Time!" the stage manager yelled at us. "Get onto the stage now!"

"Got her all the deets on you, dude," Tim said. "Your classes, your car, your library record, your injuries."

"Was any of it real, Peyton?" Jay said, staring down at me as if I was a stranger. "Do you even like acting, or was that just a way to get close to the tall guy on your list?"

"No, of course not. Jay, please, it was never like that — not with you. I got the report because I wanted to know where you were so I could steer clear of you! That's all. I thought you thought I was stalking you."

"And *were* you stalking me? All those times we just bumped into each other?"

"No! Honestly."

Jay's mouth twisted into a bitter imitation of a smile at that word.

"I was trying to *avoid* you, Jay."

"That's was she *said* — 'avoid'. But it was for the bet. Cos that's why she dated me, too, see? That black-lips chick at the diner told me everything las' night." Tim gave me an accusing

301

look and added, "S'not cool, man. I thought you were thirsty for me."

"You dated Tim?" Jay asked. "When?"

"Once! You dated Faye umpteen times. I had one date with Tim before you and I —"

"Did you date *him* just for the bet?"

"I— Yes. Okay? Yes. You know why I needed the money." My eyes were brimming with tears.

Jay scrubbed the back of a hand over his mouth, as though wiping away the taste of something bad.

The stage manager marched up to us and hissed through clenched teeth, "You guys are late! Move!"

"But all this time she really had her eye on *you*." Tim tapped Jay on the shoulder with the hand holding the bottle, splashing him with vodka. "You! Jay Young: tall and hot. Is two birds an' a one stone. An' a one stoned." Tim giggled again.

At that point, the stage manager lost all patience. She grabbed Jay and me by our arms, yanked us away from Tim, and didn't let go until we were standing in the darkness behind the stage curtains. I could hear the hushed rustling of the audience beyond, and from the wings, the whispered mutterings of the stage manager to Sanjay up in the lighting box.

Beside me, Jay took a deep breath and blew it out in a long, controlled breath before speaking. "You'll need to scratch my name off that list. Move onto the next tall guy."

And all I could hear, as the curtain rose, was the sound of my relationship with Jay collapsing into rubble around me.

~ *43* ~

My acting, in the second half, was absolute crap. It was a freezing night, and whether because of that or because of the icy fear growing inside me, I felt cold and shivery. And I was completely distracted. I felt guilty at what I'd done, angry that I hadn't had a chance to explain, and scared that I wouldn't get one. I could only hope that the audience mistook my distress for teenage angst.

Jay didn't let his emotions get in the way of his performance — of course he didn't — but in his scenes with me, I was close enough to see what he was really feeling. His deep voice sounded as loving as always, but when he held my hand, it was too tight. When we embraced, the hug was hard and brief, with distance between our hips. Our kisses were fleeting and felt soulless. There were no extra, lingering caresses. A muscle in his jaw pulsed, and though no one else probably picked it up, I could tell he was simmering with rage. When he grabbed the weapon for the duel, his knuckles bunched white, and he looked ready to run Tyrone clean through. Whereas the night before, the audience had picked up on our sexual chemistry and responded to that, tonight they were swept up by Jay's mad energy. There were fewer laughs and more gasps.

For the video close-ups, he angled his body away from the camera so that the cold contempt in his eyes wouldn't be projected. Instead the lenses found me, and a quick glance at the screens told me I looked like a dumb, frightened rabbit. Maybe the audience would think I was a naïve girl scared of my lover's next moves. Well, I *was* scared. But of what Jay would do in anger, not in love.

Our scenes raced by at breakneck speed. Jay spoke his lines quickly, almost overlapping mine, as if he couldn't wait to be finished with this charade. There was no time to talk in the wings, no moment to ask if we could meet after the play to talk things through. Before I knew it, Jay and I were alone onstage for our final scene – the sunset kiss.

At first, we just went through the motions with our hands and our lips. It was faster and rougher than the night before. And unsettling, especially when it began to transform into something else. Something wild and fierce. Something dangerous.

It was like we were striking each other with our caresses, attacking with our kisses. He pulled my bottom lip into his mouth and sucked on it, hard. That wind started up again in my head, a howling hurricane accompaniment to the violent storm between us. It was electrifying. And terrifying.

I pulled back from Jay to suck in a breath and to try to make out the expression in his eyes, but a movement in the wings behind him caught my eye. It was Doug. He was bare-chested and frantically waving his shirt in the air.

Damn. I'd forgotten about pulling off Jay's shirt. Looking up into his eyes now, I was almost too scared to do it. Because the heat in his eyes was not warmth or passion, but fury.

Right, then.

I leaned in, peeled off his shirt, flung it aside, and pressed the scripted three kisses to his neck. When I pulled back, I met his gaze again — he was still furious. I hesitated uncertainly for a few seconds, before returning to the rehearsed moves. Forcing a smile onto my lips, I held my hands out to Jay. This was the cue for him to pull me down on top of himself, so we could writhe passionately on the rock as the rosy sunset light faded out and the curtain fell.

Instead, Jay glanced over my shoulder for a fraction of a second, and then, face set and eyes still icy, he reached out, grabbed the bottom of my pink top, ripped it off and flung it behind him into the wings.

Leaving me completely topless.

There was a collective gasp from the audience. For a moment that lasted a hellish eternity, I sat bare-breasted, open-mouthed and paralyzed with shock, my boobs displayed in close-up, hugely magnified, erect-nippled detail on the big screens.

A piercing whistle from the audience broke the trance. As I pressed my hands over my chest, I was buffeted by a wave of yells, stomping feet, laughs, cheers, and furious shouts from outraged parents. The stage went pitch-black, the curtain fell, and an uproar of confusion surrounded me.

Son of a bitch! I couldn't believe what Jay had done. I'd known he'd been angry, but to strip me in front of the audience? That was insane. And crazy-malicious.

In a panic, I patted the stage floor, searching in the darkness for a towel or Jay's top. Where the hell had it landed? Someone stood on my finger, and I cursed.

"Can we have some effing light back here!" I heard the stage manager yelling.

In a moment, the stage was bathed in light, and I was on display again — topless on my hands and knees — albeit only for the cast's eyes. I folded my arms across my chest.

"I have died and gone to heaven," I heard Zack say.

Looking up, I saw him watching me, clutching Jay's T-shirt to his chest. He stood out of striking range, but that could be remedied.

I leapt to my feet. I'd start with him, beat him to a pulp, and then move onto Jay.

Wren stepped between us. "Here," she said, handing me one of the beach towels.

At this unexpected kindness, tears filled my eyes. I wrapped the towel around myself quickly, gave Jay the filthiest look I could summon and was just starting to say, "How could you?" when the freaking curtain rose.

The younger members of the audience were on their feet, applauding wildly, but the laughs, catcalls and whistles told me the appreciation was for my wardrobe malfunction, rather than for my performance. I could see the fuming faces of incensed parents, too — there would be hell to pay for this.

Last night, Jay and I had held hands during the curtain call. Last night, we'd taken several bows together. But now I clutched the towel around my torso and bowed stiffly only once. Jay, too, took just a single bow before dashing off backstage. He either couldn't wait to get away from me or didn't want to face me. Either way suited me just fine. I never wanted to see him again.

Never wanted to see *anyone* ever again.

My face was burning hot, my vision blurred with tears, and I could feel my body starting to tremble. Liz and Wren held me tight, supporting me in another bow.

"Please keep them busy for a few minutes," I begged them in an urgent whisper.

Then I wrenched myself free and fled into the wings. In the dressing room, I pulled on my sweatshirt and coat, shoved my hair up into my red beanie, pulled that down low, and grabbed my bag. As I ran out of the back entrance, I could still hear the raucous audience — Wren and Liz must be milking the applause to buy me time for my non-scripted exit. I knew a moment's deep gratitude for their sisterly solidarity.

I flew down the back stairs, tripped over an obstacle on the path, and went sprawling on the rough cement. Wiping my scraped palms on my jeans, I scrambled to my feet and swung my bag back over my shoulder. In the dim light, I could just make out the crumpled, snoring form of Tim on the ground. I had only a moment — already I could hear the scraping of chairs and the rumble of the audience starting to leave the auditorium — but a moment was all I needed. I gave Tim a savage kick on first one shin and then the other, and as he groaned and blinked up blearily, I bawled, "Thanks for *nothing*, asshole!"

Then I turned and ran. Ran away from Tim, and the cast, and the smirking people who were starting to trickle out of the hall. Away from Jay and what we'd had. Away from his cruel betrayal and my humiliation.

I ran out of the school gate and down the dark road, and kept running, crying through the night.

~ 44 ~

I was still crying over an hour later as I lay in my bed, replaying the night's events in my mind. Occasionally, a shockwave of denial would temporarily halt the sobbing — how could he have done that? How could I have been so mistaken in believing he was a good guy? Had tonight even happened, or had it merely been a horrible nightmare? Please let it have been just a nightmare. But then the feelings of rage and humiliation would resurface, and my bitter tears would resume. I felt hurt and stupid. More, I felt *violated*.

A clink at the window interrupted my obsessive thoughts. Chloe? Maybe she'd decided that our constant messaging wasn't enough, and she'd come over to give me a hug. I needed a hug. I'd never felt so alone.

I opened the window and stuck my head outside, squinting in the darkness at the figure below.

"You!"

Where were flaming arrows, vats of boiling water or burning-hot pitch when you needed them? I grabbed the first object my hands touched to hurl down as a missile — the dressmaker's dummy — wrestling it through the open window and launching it out at Jay.

He leapt aside, and the dummy landed headfirst in the dirt.

"Dammit, Peyton!" he bellowed. "Are you trying to kill me?"

"Yes!" I hissed furiously. "And shut up, or you'll wake my mother."

"We need to talk about what happened. Can I come up?" His loud stage whisper carried up easily to me.

"No."

"Let me explain!"

I glanced around for something else to throw at him. "What can you possibly say that can explain, let alone justify, what you did?" I whispered furiously.

"It was an accident!"

"An *accident*?" I cried, forgetting to keep my voice down. "Dropping a vase is an accident. Walking into a tree is an accident. Baring your girlfriend's boobs in front of the assembled school? That's intentional cruelty!"

"Peyton. I'm so sorry. I never meant that to happen."

"Didn't you? You were pretty pissed off at me. So you decided on some spur-of-the-moment payback?"

"No! Doug told me to do it."

That pulled me up short.

"*Doug?*"

"After last night's performance, he gave me notes. You'd pulled off my shirt last night, and Doug thought it was a great move. He told me I should do it to you tonight."

Could this be true? I remembered Doug telling Jay to stay back for notes the night before.

"But I swear I didn't mean to embarrass you. I knew you wore that black tank top under your pink shirt — I saw it at the costume fittings, remember? And every time the straps slipped off your shoulders? I honest to God did not intend to yank them both off, but I must've grabbed your bra together with your top."

I slumped against the windowsill as realization struck.

"No, you didn't," I said flatly. "I sewed the straps of my tank top to my overshirt so that it would stop slipping. So when you grabbed the top, the whole lot came off. There was no way you could've known."

"Oh. Well, that explains it, I guess."

It had been an accident, a misunderstanding and miscommunication worthy of Romeo and freaking Juliet.

"Please would you explain to Principal Perez, about the top?"

"What?" I asked, pulled out of my musings about other tragic lovers. "Why?"

"*Why?* Because this has turned into a major shitstorm, Peyton. Parents are complaining, it's blown up online — my God, you should see the things I'm being accused of on Facebook! Perez hauled Doug and me into his office straight after the performance. He was looking for you, too, so expect a call. He grilled us for half an hour straight about what exactly happened. He's scheduled a meeting tomorrow with Ms. Gooding and our parents, and he's talking about reporting this to the police. He says they may want to open a case of sexual assault!"

Jeez.

"I'll explain, I'll tell him it was an accident, explain how it happened. Don't worry, I'll tell him it wasn't your fault."

"I really am sorry this happened, Peyton."

I could feel my anger leaking away, like air from a punctured balloon, and I wasn't ready to let go of it yet — it was the only thing holding me up.

"You didn't think to at least warn me – that you'd be yanking off my top?" I asked.

"Did you, with me?"

"No, you're right." I sighed deeply. "I shouldn't have done that either. I didn't plan to. I just … I just got carried away in the moment."

"Yeah. Anyway, I *was* going to warn you to expect it, but then Tim happened."

"Yeah, Tim happened."

Jay crossed his arms and stared down at his feet for long moments while silence, icy as the winter wind, stretched on, widening the gap between us.

I needed to explain that I was truly sorry — about the bet and the list, for not coming clean to him, for him being dragged into this mess tonight. I opened my mouth to apologize, but I'd hesitated too long.

"Fine. See you around," Jay said coldly. He turned on his heel and left. I sat on the sill watching him disappear into the darkness.

Wherefore art thou, Romeo?

~ *45* ~

"**O**h, hello, Chloe. I didn't know you were visiting," my mother said when I unlocked my bedroom door for her.

"Hey, Mrs. Lane. Yeah, I'm here to bring Peyton some tea and sympathy — she's not feeling too good this morning."

I cast Chloe a warning glance. I had no desire to share the story of last night's fiasco with my mother.

"What's the matter, dear?" my mother asked, staring at my puffy eyes and red nose with concern.

"I think I'm coming down with a cold," I said. Then, realizing that I would need to do better than that if I was going to play hooky for the last three days of the semester, I added, "Actually, I think it's the flu. I'm feeling awful."

Honestly, I was.

I'd call in sick for my next few shifts at work, too. The diner was a favorite hangout for the kids at school, and once Tori and Steve got to hear about Saturday night, I'd never hear the end of it. I'd be leaving Jim short-handed, but it wouldn't be for long — he always shut up shop between Christmas Eve and January the fifth.

"I'm sure I've got some flu medicine stored somewhere," my mother said.

"Don't worry about it." Any flu remedy she could lay her hands on would no doubt be long past its expiration date. Besides, there wasn't any medicine to treat what really ailed me. "Was there something you wanted?" I asked her.

"I just wanted to know how last night's performance went."

"Fine."

"It was spectacular!" Chloe said, grinning enthusiastically. "Everyone's talking about how stunning Peyton was. She really bared herself, and showed them her all. It was amazing exposure for her" — Chloe caught my threatening look and finished — "talents."

"Goodness! I wish I'd seen that."

"You could've," I said, even though I was glad she hadn't. "There was nothing stopping you."

My mother gave me a wounded look and left without another word.

I locked the door behind her and took another sip of Chloe's tea. It was a special blend of whatever herbs and flowers were supposed to treat a broken heart, deep regret, lingering anger, fatal humiliation, and a strong determination never to step outside my bedroom again. Ever.

"So, are you going to join us for Christmas next week?" Chloe asked.

She'd been trying to distract me from my gloomy preoccupation with the horror of last night ever since she'd arrived, and helped me to lug the mannequin back into my room. It stood in the corner now, its dented, muddy head a silent reminder of everything that was wrong with my life.

"What do you say? There'll be turkey and all the trimmings."

I was very tempted to spend Christmas with the DiCaprios, but the thought of my mother sitting alone in her bedroom, watching reruns of *It's a Wonderful Life* over a heat 'n eat meal, added a dollop of guilt to my festering emotions. I swallowed the remainder of my tea — maybe Chloe's potion could ease guilt, too.

"Thanks, but I'd better spend it with my mother."

That way at least there would be two of us sitting in her bedroom watching reruns while eating TV meals. Probably under the plastic banner that said *Merry Xmas and Good Year too!*

"Hey, what with all the drama, I forgot to tell you my good news." Chloe's face lit up with excitement. "Guess what?"

"What?"

"I got accepted to Johns Hopkins!"

I screamed and hugged her tight. "That's so awesome! Oh, Chloe, congrats — I'm so happy for you, and so proud!"

"Yeah, I'm totes excited. Though I'll miss you if you go to fashion school in New York. How are those plans going?"

"Not bad. I'll have to apply for admission by the third of January, and my scholarship application and portfolio needs to be submitted two weeks after that. I've finished the designs." I pointed at the pile of sketches with their wallpaper garments. "I've been saving to buy good quality fabric — I can't risk the cheap stuff for the submission — and I'm going to spend winter break making the full-size patterns."

"Sounds good. It'll help keep your mind off the Grand Reveal."

I groaned. "Don't mention it!"

"Oops." Chloe gave me an apologetic grin. "But now that I did, I think we should deal with the elephant in the room." She poured me another cup of tea and said, "Sooo, about last night … Everybody's talking about it, texting about it, posting about it on Facebook."

"And by 'it', you mean …?"

"Boobgate."

I flung myself onto my bed.

"And by everybody," Chloe continued, "I mean all the sweet peoples at Longford High. Except Jay. There hasn't been anything from him since his Facebook post last night explaining how it was an accident."

I hadn't heard anything from him since our conversation last night either, and I wasn't expecting to. We either had too much to say to each other, or nothing at all. He clearly thought what I'd done was a deal-breaker, and I was still hurting at being dumped. In addition to making up my fashion range, I'd be spending my winter break licking my wounds and sewing up my torn heart.

"I saw *your* posts, of course." Chloe patted my arm in approval. "That was the right thing to do."

After Jay's comment about Facebook last night, I'd gone online to check the damage. It was horrible. People were calling him a sexual predator who should be expelled from the school or worse, and slut-shaming *me* for being a skank who'd flashed the world. I half expected the greater Longford community to rock up at our houses with pitchforks and burning torches.

I'd written a post explaining that it was an accident, giving the technical details of precisely how it had happened, and asking everyone to stop dog-piling on Jay, since it wasn't his fault in any way. I'd posted it on his Facebook page as well as my own, plus on Twitter, Instagram, Snapchat, Tumblr and every WhatsApp group I belonged to. Then, keen to get away from the ugly abyss of social media, I'd switched off my computer and deleted the apps off my phone.

"Have you seen or heard anything about ... my home situation?" I said.

I was almost too scared to ask.

"Not a peep."

I breathed a sigh of relief.

"But Brooke posted a cartoon caricature of you on Instagram."

I punched a pillow and growled, "When I'm queen of the world, I'll ban social media."

"She got close to seven hundred likes, too," said Chloe, clearly impressed.

"Can I just die now?"

"It's like you're a meme or something."

"I get the picture!" I yelled, throwing the pillow at her. "You know what else I'll be doing this winter break? Sewing a stuffed doll with Tori's black lips and hair and sticking pins into it!" I'd make a Tim pincushion, too.

"Yeah, she screwed you over, alright."

"And for a bet! To save herself a few dollars, she's caused me terminal humiliation."

"Look, you're having your fifteen minutes of fame. In a day or two, a gorilla will win America's Got Talent, or a Kardashian's ass will explode or something, and everyone will move on and forget about your boobs."

If only I could believe that.

"And here's something to help you cheer up."

"Oh yeah, what's that?"

"It's amazing, incredible really. I've spent the whole morning online and in message groups, and I haven't seen a single picture — by which I mean an actual photograph — of your girls. Not anywhere."

"Really?" This *was* good news.

"Truly. I reckon a teacher confiscated the video footage from Sanjay before he could copy it or send it out into the world. So, everyone may be *talking* about it, but they're not *looking* at it. And no pervs will be drooling — or, you know … over pics of your ladies."

I groaned again. "I don't know how I'll face everybody." Whenever I thought about school, about the comments and wisecracks I'd have to endure, I wanted to throw up. "I'll die of embarrassment."

"I don't think that's an actual cause of death," said Chloe.

At that moment, her phone rang. She answered, looked surprised and handed it to me. "It's your father. He wants to speak to you."

"Dad?"

"Why aren't you answering your phone?" he demanded. "I've been trying to get hold of you all morning."

I'd switched it off last night and disabled voicemail, wanting only to hide in my hole.

"The landline just rings, and your mother's number gives a

message that her service is inactive."

Probably due to nonpayment. As for the landline, that had been disconnected years ago.

"Sorry, Dad, my phone was off."

"What's all this business about some boy stripping you stark naked in front of the whole school?"

Holy cow. Bad news travelled fast *and* far.

"I wasn't naked, it was just my top that came off. And it was an accident."

I explained the whole story to him, but he didn't sound mollified when next he spoke.

"Well, it's got the school in an uproar. I've had a call from Principal Perez this morning. He said he couldn't get hold of your mother."

"I'm planning to explain everything to him. I'll go in tomorrow afternoon." *Late* tomorrow afternoon, hopefully after most of the kids had left for the day.

"We've already scheduled an urgent meeting for this afternoon at three-thirty. I'll collect you on the way, and then we can go in together and sort this out."

"You're driving through? Today? To meet with my school principal?" I asked, seriously amazed.

"Peyton, you're my *daughter*. Of course I'm coming. This is serious. I want to help you deal with it in any way I can."

Wow.

"Are you alright?" he asked gently.

No. "Sure, just a bit embarrassed."

"If you like, we can get you some counseling?"

"No, I'm fine, really."

"Well, think about it. And if you'd like to get out of town and come stay with Lucy and me for a while, just say the word. We'd love to have you."

"Okayyy."

"But I'll see you this afternoon. Maybe we could go out for a meal after the meeting, chat about this business, and catch up generally?"

"Sure, that would be …" Unusual? Unprecedented? "Nice."

This was not my father's usual behavior, but maybe having another baby was bringing out his long-dormant paternal streak. I wasn't sure, but I thought I kind of liked it.

"See you at three-fifteen sharp."

"I'll be waiting. And, Dad? Thanks."

"No problem, princess."

"What did he say?" Chloe asked when I handed her back her phone. "You look sort of … stunned."

"My father is being —" there was no other word for it "— *supportive.*"

"Good for him. And about time, too," she said.

After we'd washed and put away our teacups, Chloe drew me back to the subject of school.

"So, when are you going back?"

"Not this semester. Maybe not ever."

"You have to go back. You don't have a choice about that. But you do have a choice about how you do it."

I picked at a nail, but stayed silent, curious to hear what she had to say.

"You can go in victim-mode, if you like — head down and tail between your long legs, acting as if you've got something to be ashamed about."

"I do!" I interrupted.

"No, you don't. You didn't do anything wrong. Well" — she paused as if reconsidering this statement — "not anything to do with the wardrobe malfunction, anyway. But if you act as *if* you did, the bullies and bitches will move in for the kill."

"Yeah." I could imagine that scenario all too clearly.

"Or," Chloe said slowly, "you can go like a queen."

"Come again?"

"Stand tall, hold your head up high, be proud. Of course some jerks will make fun of you — that's inevitable. Jokers gotta joke, haters got hate."

"Are you going to tell me to shake it off?"

"Hey, Swifty was onto something with that. No one can make you feel embarrassed without your cooperation. So you've got to have a sense of humor about this, or pretend you do. Laugh along with the jokes, smile at the envy."

My eyebrows shot up. "*Envy?*"

"You, my friend, have great breasts. And now everyone knows it."

That made me smile.

"The way I figure it, there's nowhere to go but up. It doesn't get more embarrassing than this, right?" Chloe said.

I sniffed and nodded glumly, still feeling sorry for myself.

"Stop hiding in your own life!" Chloe was growing annoyed. "For all your slouching, you've never been invisible. News flash: you're over six foot. And now that everyone's seen you topless, you may as well let them see the rest of you — the real you. And give them hell! Stop letting their jibes get to you, whether they're about Boobgate or your height. Give as good as you get. It's time to stand up, Peyton. It's time to practice for the day when you're queen of the world."

~ 46 ~

*C*hloe was right. It had taken me most of winter break to fully accept it, but by the first day of the new semester, I was ready to face the music and laugh. Scratch that, I wasn't ready. Nowhere close. But I was determined.

Taking no chances that I'd make a run for it, Chloe fetched me from my house on that Monday morning and frog-marched me through the freezing air to the corner where we caught the school bus, maintaining a steady barrage of encouraging pep talk all the way.

"Repeat after me: I can do this!" she said.

"I can do this," I said, although the queasy mass of nerves in the region of my stomach said otherwise.

"Chin up, shoulders back, chest out." She poked the various parts of my anatomy. "And game face on!"

I tried, but when I saw the big yellow bus of vulgar insults and rude laughter lumbering up the road toward us, I nearly bolted.

"I don't think I can do this, Chloe," I whimpered, white-knuckling my coffee travel mug.

"Don't be ridiculous, Lane! You're an actor, aren't you? This is just another role. Fake it till you make it."

"But I don't know the lines. I don't know what to say," I wailed.

"Then pretend it's like that whatchamacallit — where you make it up as you go along — impromptu?"

"Improv?"

"That's the one. You don't have to know the lines, you just have to get into character, and the character will improvise the lines for you," Chloe said as the bus stopped in front of us.

If I didn't have to be me, then maybe I *could* do this.

"Just be someone cool and sassy, like Rebel Wilson, or Ellen DeGeneres."

"You're a genius!" I said to Chloe's back as she climbed onto the bus.

She gave me a quick grin and said, "Ready, and action!"

I straightened my shoulders and stood tall, took a calming breath, and followed.

About a second later, it began — cheers and jeers, catcalls and wolf-whistles from the boys; sniggers, snide comments and judgy looks from the girls. I had no idea how to respond.

But Ellen did.

I smiled widely, winked broadly and swept into a deep, dramatic bow, even giving a flourishing twirl of my hand out front. Then I pulled up straight and held my coffee mug to my chest like a winning actress clutching her Oscar, and said loudly, "I'd like to say a special thank you to my director and my wardrobe mistress, without whom none of this would have been possible. Thank you all!"

The bus driver told me to quit fooling around and take a seat, but most everyone else laughed and clapped.

Chloe gave me an approving nod and mouthed, "Boom!"

As we walked down the aisle to our usual spot, a spotty-faced senior called Dave made boob-fondling gestures in the air and said loudly, "I enjoyed your lady-display at the play, Big P."

"Glad to hear it, Little D," said my inner Ellen, "because that's as close as you're ever going to get to my ladies."

"Smack down!" The girl sitting beside him snickered.

We took our seats — Chloe at the window and me on the aisle as usual — and I was amazed to see that most of the kids of the bus were already returning their attention to their phones and friends.

Not Brooke, though. She called to me from two rows back, "Hey Peyton, hang onto your shirt there. We don't need to see you letting it all hang out again."

I turned in my seat so that I could look her in the eye and said, "Why not?"

"Yeah, why not?" said Will — the freshman we'd met on the first day of school, who was sitting directly behind us. "I mean, *I'd* like to see it all hang out."

Brooke seemed stumped for a moment, then said, "Because it's gross, that's why."

"Ayyy," said a guy on the opposite side of the aisle, "you couldn't call those puppies gross, Brooke. I thought they were mighty fine."

Brooke ignored this. "I mean, like, who wants to see *that?*"

Will and all the guys nearby — plus one keen-looking girl — stuck their hands into the air. The boy sitting next to

Brooke, presumably her boyfriend, also tried to lift his hand, but she grabbed it and forced it down.

"Oh, shut up, all of you," snapped Brooke.

"Sounds like you just want to keep the competition covered up," I said, with a nod at Brooke's chest, on display in a tight knitted top with a low neck. "I think you got yourself some boob envy there, Brooke."

"As if!" she bit out, but I was pleased to see her turning red.

I turned back around in my chair and directed a so-how-am-I-doing glance at Chloe.

"Like a boss!" she said, grinning widely.

There was no more boob-banter on the bus until we pulled up outside Longford High, but no sooner were we all walking toward the school entrance than Brooke's boyfriend, presumably at her urging, made a point of coming up to me.

"How's the weather up there above the clouds, Big Bird? It looked like you found it a bit chilly the last time I saw all of you," he said, staring meaningfully at my chest.

I stared down my nose at him and replied sweetly, "It's lovely up here. How is it down in the Shire, Bilbo?"

Chloe cackled loudly at that. "Girl, you're on fire!"

A bunch of people were waiting to give me a go inside the school, but my inner Ellen was on a roll.

When a junior I'd never met rudely yelled at me to "Show us your tits, Juliet!" I called back loudly, "Only if you show us yours first."

This came across much meaner than I'd intended — the junior was an obese kid who had man-boobs double the size of mine.

"I've created a monster," Chloe said, giving me a shocked look.

"Hey, if he can't take it, then he shouldn't dish it out," I said defiantly, even though I felt bad.

"Eh-oh." Chloe nodded in the direction of the small crowd grouped around my locker. Judging by the shoving and sniggering, something offensive was waiting for me.

Sure enough, when I got closer, I saw that someone had stuck a caricatured sketch of me, with full, naked breasts and saluting nipples, onto my locker door. The picture was titled "Pert Peyton's Pointy Puppies."

The smirking crowd watched to see how I'd react. Part of me — the mortified part —wanted nothing more than to rip the picture off the locker, crumple it up, and ram it down someone's throat — preferably Zack's since he was standing right up front and making a ridiculous show of ogling the image. But I was prepared for this.

Chloe and I had discussed the possible forms of taunts I was likely to encounter, and we'd both agreed that it was a dead cert someone would stick a bare-boobed sketch of me up somewhere at school — though we'd predicted a notice board or stairwell wall. And we'd brainstormed how best I should respond.

So now I was able to smile slyly, remove a red Sharpie from my bag and lean in to make some additions of my own to the sketch. When I stepped back, the picture-Peyton sported stars and tassels on her nipples, and in a speech bubble, she declared, "If you've got it, flaunt it!"

Everyone gathered around burst into laughter, but it seemed more good-natured than mocking.

Zack nodded admiringly at me. "You impressing me, girl. No shame, no fear! Respect."

"No shame, no fear," was overstating it, but I did feel proud. Before my public humiliation, any comments about my appearance, especially about my height, had upset me and made me blush, but now I either laughed along with them, ignored them, or gave snappy comebacks. Frankly, I was amazed at how well the strategy was working. And I was astonished to realize I was enjoying myself. It was fun — no, more than that, it was exhilarating — to fight back.

Why had I never tried it before?

~ 47 ~

There were fewer and fewer comments and wisecracks as the day wore on. It didn't escape my notice, however, that two individuals were paying neither my chest nor the rest of me any attention.

Tim had caught my fierce look in history class and then studiously avoided me for the rest of the day. He even scuttled out of my way when he saw me walking in his direction in the hallway. I was sad to see that he wasn't limping or wearing casts on his legs.

"I obviously didn't kick him hard enough," I told Chloe.

And Jay stayed away from me too. We had only one massively awkward encounter when we both turned up at our lockers at the same time. My foolish heart, forgetting it had been torn in two and was now dead and beyond repair, fluttered into exaggerated life, just as it always had in his presence.

"Peyton," he said. His voice was perfectly polite, but his look was flat and hard.

"Jay."

"Thanks for sorting it out with Perez and Ms. Gooding," Jay said.

"Of course."

Ellen's cockiness evaporated, and all my hurt, angry bitterness — plus a wave of guilt — resurfaced. I stared hard at one of his freckles until the tears that had been threatening receded. I had my pride. I would keep the sadness and loneliness out of my voice, and I wouldn't beg. This wasn't the first time I'd been ditched, or left behind — hell, I'd coped with *that* all my life. The strange and unbelievable part of Jay was not that he'd dumped me, it was that he'd ever wanted me in the first place.

When he caught sight of the sketch on the door, Jay seemed momentarily disconcerted. Then with another quick glance at me, he turned and left. I saw so little of him after that that I wondered if *he'd* commissioned a report on *me* from Tim — strictly for avoidance purposes.

In English and Psychology, we both gave each other the cold shoulder, though it wouldn't be true to say we ignored each other. You have to be hyper-aware of someone to not so much as glance in their direction, to be sure you're never the one handing out papers on their side of the classroom, not to let your eyes stray in their direction or your face light up when you catch sight of them, and to time your exits and entrances from a room so that you're never near each other.

Jay and I both played our parts with cool, indifferent perfection.

It helped that at least part of my mind was worried about the wager. Although it was only the first day back, prom suddenly didn't seem so far off. There was only one name left on my tall boys list, and I needed to get cracking immediately if I was going to win the bet. And I *was* going to win that damn bet.

For one thing, I was determined to stick it to Tori. For another, I could *not* afford to lose any money. Plus I'd need the eight hundred dollar win to replenish my college fund which was already seriously dented by the utilities bill, and would be more so after the shopping trip I had planned for the next day after school. I'd made a long list of all the things I'd need to buy — fifteen different kinds of fabric with matching thread, plus hat-elastic, suspenders, bias binding, and all kinds of fastenings and decorative details. It was going to cost a small fortune.

As soon as the last bell rang, I hurried out of math class and headed for the steps outside the entrance. Chloe joined me a couple of minutes later, and together we scanned the throng leaving the building, looking for Robert Scott.

"That's him!" I knew what he looked like because he played varsity football. No doubt he'd be another boring sports jock, but beggars, I reminded myself, couldn't be choosers.

"Hey, Robert? Robert, over here." I beckoned him over to a quieter spot.

"He's kinda cute," said Chloe.

His face wasn't a patch on the sharp-lined and hard-angled attractiveness of Jay's, but yeah, he was cute. And young — he was a junior, and looked even younger than that. I felt a bit cougarish.

"I'd make a play for him myself only, you know, I'd have a

permanent crick in my neck," said Chloe, tilting her head at an increasingly acute angle as he approached us, a frown of puzzlement between his baby blues.

"Um, hi." A split second later, recognition hit. "Hey, I know you. You're the girl who —"

"Yeah, I'm her. Look, I wanted to ask you — do you want to go out sometime?"

"You and me?" He seemed surprised, but then they all did when I asked them out. It was like they'd never thought of me as being a girl. "Like on a date?"

"Exactly that."

"Um, okaayyy. Like, when?"

"What are you doing tonight?"

"Tonight?" he squeaked. Oh dear, his voice hadn't finished breaking yet. I was definitely feeling my age.

"Yeah, are you doing anything tonight?"

"Chemistry homework?"

"Fine," I said. "Do you know Jumping Jim's Diner? I'll meet you there at six o'clock."

"Okay, yeah, sure."

"Is this your new dating approach — ambush and manhandle?" Chloe asked when we left Robert and headed for the bus.

"I've got eight hundred bucks riding on him," I said firmly. "I can't afford to accept no for an answer."

That night, I arrived at the diner ten minutes early and immediately regretted it. Steve and Tori, both of whom were on duty, scurried over to where I was hanging up my coat and immediately began hassling me.

"You," I interrupted Tori, "are mean. And you're a poor sport, and a cheat! But you won't win this bet."

"We'll see," Tori said, smugly. "So, are you going to quit your job here and apply at Hooters?"

Steve snickered. "Nah, she wouldn't qualify. I hear they have a maximum height restriction to keep out the giants."

I stepped right up close so that I towered over him, gave him a cold-eyed smile and retorted, "I'm sorry, I don't speak Dwarvish. What are you trying to say, little person?"

Even Tori laughed at that.

"I want a quiet table," I said, heading over to one of the booths.

"Why? Is this another *date*?" Tori asked.

"Yes. Robert Scott, six-three. Date one."

"I'll log it on my date list. By the way, what happened to Jay Young?"

"He was never on your list," I reminded her, then waved at Robert who had just come in.

"Cool shirt," he said when we sat down in one of the booths.

I was wearing a T-shirt that Chloe had given me for Christmas. It was bright red with bold black printing on the front.

Yes, I am tall.
6'¾". Yes, really.
No, I don't play basketball.
No, I'm not a model.
The weather's great up here.
I'm so glad we had this conversation.

"Yeah. So, shall we order some drinks?"

I had a sense of déjà vu because of the other guys I'd been here with, but I'd learned my lesson and was determined that this time would be different.

As soon as Robert had his Coke and I had my chocolate shake, I said, "Look, I want to be completely up front with you. This is a date. I mean it's definitely a date, but …"

"Yeah?" He sounded wary.

"Full disclosure: I'm only doing it for a bet, not because I'm wildly infatuated with you or anything."

Amazingly, he looked relieved. Had I scared him so much earlier with my strong-arm tactics?

"A bet?"

I nodded toward where Tori and Steve stood observing us, and explained the terms of the wager.

"I just don't want there to be any misunderstandings or hurt feelings," I ended. "I mean, no offense or anything, but I don't expect to fall in love with you."

I didn't want to fall in love with anyone ever again.

Robert gave a deep sigh and smiled. "You don't know how happy that makes me feel."

"Thanks," I said, sarcastically.

"No, no — I don't mean it like that. I'm sure you're a great person and all. And you're pretty, and obviously your" — he circled his hands over his chest area — "are a real hit. But *I'm* not attracted to *you*, either."

"That should make things easier, I guess. Though why would *you* want to date someone you're not into?"

"I think we can come to a mutually beneficial

arrangement." A cunning look had come over his face.

"I can't afford to pay you," I said at once.

"I'm not talking about money." He sounded offended. "I'll be your boyfriend for three dates and the prom, and you'll be my cover. It'll be a win-win."

"Back up there — I'll be your what?"

Robert leaned across the table and whispered, "Can you keep a secret?"

~ 48 ~

"Rob," I said, "I think it's fair to say I could keep secrets for the Olympic team."

"Because no one can find out, Peyton. No one!"

"I promise." I crossed my heart.

He still appeared wary. "Prove it."

"How?"

"Tell me a secret of yours. A big one."

"No way!" was my first reaction.

"It's only fair. That way we'll each have something on the other. Mutually assured destruction."

Could I do it?

"You go first," I said.

"*You* go first," he said.

Which was harder — trusting another person, or going through my life hiding my secrets, being isolated by them?

"Together," I said, before I could think better of it. "On the count on three. One, two —"

"I'm gay!" he said, just as I said, "My mother's a hoarder!"

"Your mother's a whore?" he said, shocked.

"A *hoarder*," I enunciated. "She collects crap."

"Oh. I've seen them on TV. Jeez."

"So, you're gay?"

"I'm not so much the black sheep of my family as the rainbow-colored one. My parents are not the open, accepting sort. If my father found out, he'd disown me. And the guys on the football team would so not be cool with it. I don't need my life to be any harder than it is, Peyton. Can you understand that?"

"I really can, more than you know."

"I'm staying comfortably in the closet."

I laughed, shook my head. Rob didn't belong in his family either. He was hiding a massive secret, too. Just like me, he wasn't comfortable in his skin. Were we all like this? Did we all feel like freaks?

"And *nobody* knows?" I asked. "Apart from me, now."

"Someone knows. One guy."

"I hope for your sake it's not Tim."

"Why?" he said, looking nervous.

"Never tell him anything you don't want made public, trust me on this one," I said and added bitterly, "He'd blab on what happens in fight club."

He nodded. "Do we have a deal then? We'll do our three dates and the prom — my folks will be happy, suspicions will be put to rest, and you'll win the wager."

"Done!" I shook his hand. This had turned out better than I could have hoped. My dates were set, and I wouldn't have to lie or pretend. A sudden worry popped into my head.

"And you'll definitely be here for prom? You won't be in Switzerland or anything?"

"Why would I be in Switzerland?"

"The God particle," I said darkly.

"You're a little kooky, you know that? But I like it. At least these dates won't be completely boring."

I wasn't listening. The money was in the bag — or as good as — and I was already dreaming of fashion school.

I ran all the way home, elated. New York, here I come!

I emptied the mailbox on my way in and scrambled up my ladder, feeling better than I had in the longest time. I was already planning my shopping agenda for the next day — Debois Textiles first, for the luscious black velvet I'd spotted in their racks, and then Buttons and Bling for most of the accessorizing details, including a pair of vintage-style brass-studded epaulettes.

I sorted through the mail, dropped the junk directly into the trash can, and set aside a letter to forward to Dad — ten years on, we still got some of his mail here. A postcard from the blood bank reminded me that it was time to part with another pint. I entered the date into my phone's calendar and tossed the card, thinking of the bloodred satin I wanted for my formal jacket's inner lining.

The last letter, in a buff-colored envelope, bore the Maryland state seal in the top corner. As soon as I saw that, even before I noticed the pink overdue stamp in the opposite corner, my stomach turned, and dread — as cold and heavy as a rain-soaked cloak — settled on me. This couldn't be good.

I tore open the letter with shaking hands, and my panicked

gaze skimmed over the printed pages inside. *Refuse area, county property tax, state property tax, water qual protect* — most of it was unintelligible, but three phrases printed in bold were clear enough, even for me: *total amount due, late payment penalty,* and *due by date.*

A scream of unrestrained fury and anguish ripped from the core of me. And another.

A minute later, my mother was banging on my door.

"Peyton! Peyton, are you all right?"

I unlocked the door and flung it open.

She was white-faced with shock. "What's the matter?"

"You!" I snarled. "You're what's the matter!"

I shoved the property taxes bill at her and stepped back, seriously scared I would hit her if I stayed too close.

She stared down at the bill. "Oh dear," she whispered.

"Another bill you didn't pay. There's a late-payment penalty due on this one, too."

She pinched her lips together.

"And I'm betting the reason you didn't pay is because you maxed out your credit cards on Black Friday. That's about right, isn't it?" I accused. "I'll have to withdraw all the money out of my college savings — money that I've worked years for — to pay this. Because if I don't, we'll lose the house. And then what, huh? Then what?"

"Peyton, I'm sure we can make another plan to pay it somehow," she said. Her fingers folded the bill into a tiny square, as if by making it physically smaller, she could ignore its significance more easily. "Don't make a mountain out of a molehill."

I swore viciously. "This is *not* a molehill. It *is* a mountain! A mountain of debt. A mountain of stuff."

I grabbed her by the shoulders and shook her, hard, as if I could shake the illness and the idiocy out of her. The bill fell to the floor — a tiny white square big enough to obliterate my dreams.

"Let go of me," my mother gasped, wrenching herself out of my grasp.

"If only I could. But I'm stuck with you, stuck *to* you. New York! Who was I kidding?"

We were both crying now. I strode across my room and flung myself on my bed. "The two of us are trapped together in the middle of this refuse dump, and I'll never get out, never get away, never be able to live my own life. We're both buried here — this place is a tomb and I'm like the guardian of the dead."

"I am not dead."

"You're not alive!"

"And you're not my guardian, I'm yours," she said. She was beginning to look angry — something I hadn't seen in a while. "In case you hadn't noticed, I'm the mother here."

"Don't make me laugh. I wanted a mother. I needed a mother. But instead I got a house full of crap."

"Peyton, I love you — you must know that. I love you more than anything."

"More than your possessions? More than your grief?" I challenged, but my white-hot anger was fading now, extinguished by a rising wave of despair. I sighed. What was the point of hurting her? It wouldn't change anything. In a resigned voice, I said, "Maybe you do. Maybe I just can't see it because of the wall of stuff between us."

"I'm truly, deeply sorry."

My mother was actually acknowledging some responsibility?

She walked over to the pile of designs with their wallpaper garments on my desk. "I so much wanted you to follow your passion."

"Yeah, well, that's not going to happen now. There'll be about fifty-seven cents left in my account once I pay that bill. And without money to buy fabric, I can't make up my sample portfolio. And without *that*, there's no hope of a scholarship. So, no college for me, not this year. But hey, there's always 'one day', isn't there?"

Mom pulled a tissue out of her sleeve and dabbed at her eyes. My irritation began rising again. I didn't have any energy left to feel sympathy for her sadness. I was too full of my own.

"Please just go," I said.

She moved to the door, giving my designs one last look.

"Wait!" I said.

The look of hope in her eyes as she spun around nearly killed me. There's no hope, Mom, don't you get it?

"Take these." I shoved my stack of giant fashion designs into her arms. "Chuck them on a pile somewhere. I think I saw a few inches of open space in the basement."

~ 49 ~

I hadn't gone fetal when Jay and I ended — I wasn't the sort of girl to curl up and die — but I'd been miserable. I was still sad. And angry, though I wasn't sure who I was madder at — Jay for stripping me publicly, albeit accidentally, and dumping me, or myself for keeping the secrets I should have trusted him with. We'd had something so good and, between us, we'd blown it.

I missed him. I missed his funny impersonations, our discussions on movies and acting, our good morning and good night texts, and sharing the best and worst parts of my day with him after school. And I really missed how I'd felt when I was with him: beautiful, normal-sized, precious.

I buried myself in schoolwork to keep from wallowing in self-pity. School was school, same as it ever was. Or rather, the same as it had been before Jay and I had gotten together.

Tim apologized to me for spilling the beans. "I'm sorry man, I was just so buzzed," he said as we left history class on the second Monday in January.

"You were more than buzzed."

"Okay, okay, so I was shit-faced."

"That's no excuse. You screwed things up for me. I'm still pissed at you."

"I said I was sorry, what more do you want, dude?"

"You know, Tim, if you used your brain more and recreational substances less, I reckon you could start a very profitable private-eye business when you leave school."

Tim looked impressed at the suggestion for just a moment, then he gave me a mournful-puppy look and asked, "So do you forgive me?"

"Whatever."

He grinned. "When do I get the second history paper?"

"Um, try never."

"What? You owe me, P."

I muttered a curse under my breath. This guy was a piece of work.

"What's that you said?" he asked.

"Two words. One finger," I replied, with a matching gesture.

The Boobgate furor finally died down when our principal failed to return to school on the first of February. Rumors buzzed through the school — he'd been arrested for embezzling school funds, he'd run away to Las Vegas with his mistress, he'd been killed in a drive-by shooting — and the formal announcement that he'd retired for health reasons was generally believed to be a cover-up.

"People don't care about the real story, not when it's boring or uncomfortable. They want dirt, not truth," said Chloe sagely.

I felt sorry for Principal Perez, but I was selfishly glad to no longer be the center of attention at Longford High.

Valentine's Day was tough. A day's exposure to other people's romantic bliss only reinforced how much I missed Jay. Zack spent half of our math class showing me all the Valentines cards he'd received and hitting on all the girls in class, including me. Brooke's boyfriend filled the hallway near my locker with a gazillion helium-filled red balloons which resisted my irritated attempts to swat them away.

"Stop being such a love-Grinch," Chloe said, gazing upwards at the bobbing mass of red. "I think it's romantic."

Easy for her say — she wasn't suffering from a bad bout of cynicism brought on by crushed dreams of love. Also, she was too short to have the dangling ribbons tickle her face. I took a compass out of my pencil case and stabbed an explosive path through the balloons to my locker. The bangs made a few people duck, and Brooke yelled at me, but I thought I saw a smile flit across Jay's face as the balloons showered pink confetti on everyone beneath.

I was still brushing the odd mocking speck of confetti from my coat when I walked up the path to our house that afternoon and saw something beside the front door — presumably my mother's latest online purchase.

Strangely, things had been a bit better between my mother and me in the month that followed our massive fight. Chloe said this was because I'd gotten everything off my chest. I thought it might be because I'd given up any hope of things improving. I'd surrendered to the undeniable truth that I couldn't change her. Without hope, there was no disappointment, and without disappointment, there was a lot less hostility and resentment.

I might have been imagining it, but I thought she'd changed, too. She'd stopped playing the pity card, was keeping her hair clean and brushed, and it had been a good few weeks since I'd come home from school to find an online delivery waiting on the front step.

Which was why what was waiting beside the front door today was a surprise. Except that it wasn't a purchase. It was a big black trash bag, and it was full. Hardly daring to hope, I unfastened the ties and peered inside. It was stuffed with newspapers, some of the rotten trash from the kitchen, and the broken red umbrella. Wow.

I hauled the bag to the sidewalk for the next day's trash collection and was about to head around to my side of the house when my curiosity got the better of me. I unlocked and opened the front door and took a quick peek. A narrow pathway, mostly free of junk, stretched between the front door and the bottom of the stairs.

Holy cow. My mother had actually cleared a few yards through the clutter. Stunned, I immediately put a lid on my rising excitement. We'd been here before. Every few years, my mother resolved to "get organized" and made a start on tackling the mess. But she only ever started. She never followed through.

No hope means no disappointment, I reminded myself as I took my usual route to my room.

I'd given up hope of going to fashion school that year, but I was determined to try again the following year. Jim had baulked when I'd asked him to take me on full-time for the summer — "You need to go to college, Peyton" — but he'd eventually come around. I was a good worker, and he liked me better than Steve or Tori.

Those two asshats hit new heights of obnoxiousness as February ended. I took this to mean that they were getting seriously worried about losing the bet, because my requisite three dates with Rob were locked, loaded and logged. We'd agreed not to bother with any more dates with the exception of prom. He was a nice enough guy, but we didn't have much in common.

When I'd tried telling him about my plans to study fashion design on our last date, he'd informed me, "Just because I'm gay doesn't mean I'm interested in fashion, you know."

When he'd tried to tell me all about the football team's latest tactics and triumphs, I'd come back with, "Just because I'm tall doesn't mean I'm interested in sports, you know."

I had learned a few things about him, though. He was addicted to onion rings; he planned to study Information Science and invent the "app of the decade" so he could retire rich by the age of twenty-five; and he was madly in love with a guy whose name he refused to mention. I'd tried to winkle the information out of him during our last date.

"Is he at Longford High?"

"Yes."

"Do I know him?"

"Yes."

"Is he a senior?"

"Not saying."

"Has he come out?"

Rob laughed hysterically at that. "No way! He's so deep in the closet he's almost in Narnia. That's why I can't tell you his name, see. It's not my secret to tell."

Fair enough. "Is he tall or short?"

"He's hot! More than that I'm not telling you. Identifying details must be concealed to protect the innocent."

"Does he-who-must-not-be-named know you like him?"

"He does. And he likes me, too, though he's scared to let it show."

"Well, I think it's a damn shame that two people who really like each other can't just be together," I said, sighing heavily.

"You don't understand. How could you? You know nothing about prejudice, about how people judge what they don't understand, how hard they can make your life just because you're different to them."

How to respond to that? Where to even begin?

I let it slide and instead asked, "So are we still confirmed for prom? I need to start making my dress."

"We are confirmed," he said. "I've never seen my dad so excited. And my mother has already ordered my tux and the" — he circled his fingers around his wrist — "that flower thingy."

"The corsage?"

"Yeah, that. We are *so* going to look the part of the dating couple."

I spent spring break making up my prom dress. Chloe loved my design for the evening gown in my fashion collection, and for my birthday, she'd given me several yards of the most beautiful lush black velvet fabric.

"That dress needs to be made and to be worn. Make it for yourself, for prom," she'd said.

"You think so?" I'd been planning something a bit less revealing, a bit more conventional.

"I know so. The new Peyton is done hiding in boring clothes. Besides, you've designed it for a tall girl — you'll look sensational!"

I wanted to look elegant from top to toe in that dress, so I trawled the web for stores that sold high heels in my size, finally finding an outlet called *Trading Places* that appeared to stock a huge collection of ladies' footwear in large sizes.

The premises were in a shady part of town, but it would totally be worth the two bus rides and ten-block walk if I found the perfect pair of shoes. It was only once I was inside the store, staring at the manager behind the counter — a beautiful woman with impeccable makeup, false eyelashes, and an Adam's apple — that I understood what kind of a store it was.

She gave me a long, evaluating stare, taking in my long, plain hair and my unmade-up face, lingering a moment on my large hands, raising a plucked and penciled eyebrow at my too-short jeans, before finally frowning at my ugly running shoes.

"I'm Loretta," she said.

"I'm Peyton."

"Peyton, honey, you may be wearing a man's shirt and shoes, but you aren't a cross-dresser."

"Not by choice, no."

"You're one of *them*." She tutted sympathetically.

"One of whom?"

"One of the girls with big feet, am I right?"

I nodded. In amongst the brightly colored feather boas and sequined evening gowns, I felt like the dullest of ugly ducklings.

"We get them in here from time to time, looking for pretty shoes. Come this way and we'll find you a magnificent pair."

I followed her to the racks of shoes at the rear of the store. My eyes immediately locked on a pair of stilettos in black suede with a discreet line of crystals running down the spine of the heels.

"These. They're beautiful," I whispered in awe.

"What size?"

It was the question I always dreaded.

"Do you have them in a thirteen?"

"Sugar, we stock them up to a size fifteen."

The shoes were perfect, marginally wider than usual, so they didn't even pinch. I stood tall, admiring myself in the mirror, feeling like a million bucks. I could take prisoners, break hearts, conquer the world in these shoes.

"Cinderella is proof that the right pair of shoes can transform a girl's life," Loretta drawled, smiling at my obvious delight.

"When I am queen of the world," I told her, "I'm going to pass a law that *all* shoe stores have to stock up to a size fifteen."

"Don't go putting me out of business, your highness."

While Loretta rang up the shoes, I ran around like a kid in a candy store, trying on hats that fit and gloves that slid easily onto my hands with cuffs that covered my wrists.

"Sure you won't take those?"

"I can't afford them today. But I'll be back," I promised.

I was halfway out of the door when I paused. "Hey, Loretta? All the clothes here are" — I searched for a way to say it politely — "pretty bling."

"My ladies like a little sparkle."

"Did you ever think of stocking clothes that are less glamorous? Just normal, pretty, stylish clothes, you know, that tall women could wear to work or the market?"

"Honey, they don't make those clothes — not in the sizes my clientele would need. I'd think a big girl like you would know that already."

"Loretta," I said, stepping back inside and letting the door close behind me, "have I got a business proposition for you."

~ 50 ~

Three weeks before prom, Chloe and Greg started dating.

"No! No squeeing," Chloe told me. "It's not *lurrrvvve* or anything. He's a nice guy, and I like him. I'm having a bit of fun. And at least now we both have a date for the big night."

Two weeks before prom, Chloe announced, "He's a *very* nice guy, and I *really* like him. I'm having *serious* fun."

"Permission to squee?" I asked.

"Granted."

"I'm so happy for you!" I squealed, and hugged her until she called time.

One and a half weeks before prom, Chloe called and told me to come over to her house. "I've got news, and it's serious."

Her face, when she answered the door, was worried. "In the kitchen. I've already put the kettle on to boil, and I've made up a special brew: chamomile, lavender and lemon balm today, because they're good for shock."

Uh-oh.

While Chloe poured boiling water into a large glass teapot and stirred in her concoction of dried leaves and flowers, I sat on a stool at the central island. The DiCaprios' kitchen was warm and sunny. And spotlessly clean.

"So what's up?" I asked. "Is it Greg?"

She nodded.

"Oh, Chloe, I'm so sorry!"

"No, not that." She flapped a hand at me. "It's something he told me today."

"He's gay?" I guessed.

Greg was Rob's crush, had to be. They'd planned a double-date with Chloe and me, so they could hook up behind the bushes at prom.

"No, he's not gay!" Chloe eyed me as though I was crazy. "What made you think that?"

"I …" I hadn't broken my promise to Rob and wouldn't now. "I dunno."

"He's not gay," she repeated firmly. And then, with a naughty smile, added, "Trust me, I'd know."

"Tell me!" I demanded. "Besties and breasties and ovaries, remember?"

"Later. Right now, I want to tell you what he said about his cousin."

"Jay?" My mouth was suddenly dry. "Tell me."

"I think we might need borage flowers, too." Chloe sprinkled a small handful of dried blue petals into the tea and stirred again.

"What's the borage for?" I asked.

"Courage." She poured me a cup of the infusion.

"Exactly what are you about to tell me?"

"So, Greg and I got to chatting about Jay today ..."

"And?"

"And he said Jay was seriously cut up when you two split up. Said he was really depressed and bitter — 'unplayable', he said."

Interesting. "And?"

"And I told him that you were pretty much the same."

"*And*?" This was all fascinating, and I was gratified to hear that Jay had suffered, too, but it was hardly the sort of news that would make me feel shocked, or in need of borage-courage.

"And then I told him how hard Boobgate was for you. I laid it on thick, hoping it would get back to Jay and make him feel bad."

"Good."

"But then Greg said you were lucky."

"*Lucky*?"

"He said it could have been much worse, that photos and videos of you could've been all over the school, all over the net, if ..." Infuriatingly, Chloe paused and took a big sip of her tea.

"If *what*?"

"If Jay hadn't stormed into the lighting box as soon as the curtain fell, wiped Sanjay's video recording, checked his phone, confiscated all memory devices, and threatened him with a slow and painful death if a single image ever emerged."

I gaped at Chloe in shock.

"It was Jay who saved you, Peyton. Jay — not a teacher."

So that's where he'd run off to straight after our curtain call. He hadn't been desperate to escape me, he'd been in a mad rush to *protect* me. Even though he'd been so angry with me about the bet and the report, he'd still wanted to save me as much pain and humiliation as he could. Almost as if he still cared for me.

My face must have revealed my train of thoughts, because Chloe nodded knowingly and said, "Eh-yup, just what I was thinking."

"I'm going to need more borage flowers," I said.

When Jay arrived at school the next morning, he looked surprised to see me waiting at his locker.

"Hi," I said. "Have you got a minute? I'd like to talk."

"Now?" he said, checking his watch. It was ten minutes before the first bell.

"Yeah." I wanted to get this over with. "It won't take long."

"Okay."

"There's a sort-of private spot outside Grundy's lab, can we go there?"

He walked beside me to the alcove where the reeled fire hose hung on the wall.

"I wanted to thank you," I said. His expression said *oh yeah?* Or maybe, *could've fooled me.* I hurried on. "Yesterday, I heard from Chloe, who heard from Greg, that you were the one who stopped the pictures of … of me from getting out. I didn't know it was you — I just assumed it was a teacher — else I would have said something. But I know now, so thank you. I'm very grateful."

Jay said nothing, merely studied me intently. I'd forgotten how green his eyes were.

"And I'm sorry about the rest of it too," I said quickly. "I should have told you about the bet, and that damned report. I wanted to, I *planned* to, but I was ashamed and scared, so I procrastinated. And then it was too late."

He merely nodded. What did that mean? Was I forgiven?

"And I also just want to set the record straight about the trade with Tim. I gave him a history paper, not ... not anything else." I could feel my cheeks flaming and my throat constricting. "So, that's all, I guess. See you around."

I'd already begun walking away when he called me back.

"I'm sorry too. I know it's been rough for you with all the flack you got."

I risked looking up at him and giving him a small smile. "In a funny way, it was kind of liberating. Very little embarrasses me these days."

"So, you're seeing Robert Scott now?" he asked, his fingers fiddling with the nozzle on the fire hose.

My smile vanished. I made a movement — half-nod, half-shrug.

"Good. He's tall enough for you to win the bet, yeah?"

"Jay, that's *not* why I dated you. You have to believe me."

"I was on your list of tall boys."

"Yeah, you were. But that was before I got to know you. And then you asked me out and we clicked, and it wasn't about the bet. I didn't even log our dates with Tori, like I was supposed to. You can check with her."

"When I found out, I figured it was all just a setup." He bent the wire around the end of the hose, twisting it over and around into a tight knot. "That you were just stringing it — us

— out until prom, so you could get the money. That you'd researched me so you'd know what would appeal to me."

"No. Jay. *No.*"

"I thought —" His voice choked on the words. He paused, took a deep breath and tried again. "I thought that what you said and did with me, how we were together — that it was all an act."

The only thing that *wasn't* an act was how I felt about you, how I was when I was with you. Could I say that? No. Not without bursting into tears.

"None of that was an act," I managed.

"We're both fools," he said, pinning me with an unfathomable look.

"Yeah."

The bell rang.

"We'd better go," I said.

He walked beside me for a minute then asked, "So are you going to the prom with him?"

"What?" I said, startled out of my what-if's and if-only's.

"Robert Scott. Are you going to the prom with him?"

"Yeah." My voice betrayed my lack of enthusiasm.

"Pity," he said, with a quick look sideways at me. "I still don't have a date."

I stopped in my tracks, staring at him. How could this be happening? How unlucky could one person possibly be? I wanted to tell Jay that I wasn't dating Robert — not really, that we had an arrangement of convenience, that neither of us was even attracted to the other. That I still had feelings for him, Jay. But I couldn't explain fully without betraying Rob's trust. And he'd gone public at home and school about me being his prom date — what kind of a bitch would I be to drop him now?

"I'm sorry. I told Rob I'd go with him, I can't …"

"Hey, it's cool, no worries." Jay seemed completely unconcerned.

I, on the other hand, was miserable, and I was sure it showed. This was the worst luck, the worst possible timing. Here I was again, protecting someone else's secret at the expense of my own happiness. Was doing the kind thing always guaranteed to leave me trapped and miserable? Would I never get to do what I wanted?

"You okay?" Jay asked me when we started walking again.

"Look, I'm sure you won't have a problem getting a date, but do me a favor, will you? Please don't break The Law of Tall Girls. Again."

"The law of who?"

"Don't take a short girl, okay? Just don't," I said, then I turned down a side hall and headed for Mme Dumas' classroom, wondering what the French was for FML.

~ *51* ~

Three days before prom, I set the last stitch in my prom dress and immediately tried it on.

It was awesome — far and away the best thing I had designed and sewed so far. It was floor-length, made entirely of tightly-fitting black velvet, with a skirt that flared out, mermaid-style, from just above my knees. The front had a modest, rounded neckline, but the rear neckline was deeply scooped, leaving my back bare almost to the base of my spine. The dress was sleeveless, but from each shoulder, three glittering strands of black and clear crystals draped in loops over my upper arms, their curving arcs reminding me of the smile lines at the corners of Jay's eyes.

It fit perfectly, more perfectly than any item of clothing I'd ever worn. With the high heels on, the hem just brushed the floor. Even without makeup or my hair done, I looked undeniably sensational. Beautiful, even.

My mother knocked on my bedroom door. "Peyton, you've got mail!"

Huh?

I unlocked and opened for her, wanting to find out how she

could possibly be in possession of mail for me, and she stepped in, holding up a narrow envelope.

"Oh, Peyton, is that your prom dress? You look beautiful — you *are* beautiful!" She beamed at me, made me rotate on the spot so that she could admire me from every angle. "You look like a princess!"

"Not a princess," I said. "A queen."

I looked, and felt, like the queen of the world.

"Very regal, indeed. But every queen needs some crown jewels. You need a little classy sparkle to set that off, and I've got the very thing. Wait right there, I'll be back in a minute."

She dashed out of the room, stuffing the envelope into her pocket. The envelope! I'd been so busy bathing in her praise that I'd momentarily forgotten about the letter.

"Wait, Mom, where'd you get that letter?" *How'd* you get that letter? Surely she hadn't actually left the house to walk to the mailbox?

I was about to follow her into the hall when my phone rang, and grabbing it, I saw Rob's name highlighted on the screen.

"Hey!" I said. "At this very moment, I'm wearing my prom dress, and I feel the need to warn you that I look so brilliant you might need to wear shades on Saturday night."

There was no answer, not even a laugh. And that was strange because I'd discovered over our three dates that Rob, unlike Mark, *did* have a sense of humor.

"Rob?"

"Look, Peyton. I don't know how to break this to you gently, so I'm just going to tell you straight. I'm sorry, but I can't take you to the prom."

"What? It sounded like you said you can't take me to the prom?"

"Yeah. I'm really, *really* sorry to do this to you."

"Why are you doing it then?" My voice sounded high and unsteady.

"Because I've decided I'm coming out. I mean, I'm coming out as gay at the prom."

"So? Can't we still go together?"

"The guy I like, the one I told you about, he's also coming out. We've decided to do it together, by going as a couple."

"Oh."

"And I know the prom was important to you, because of the bet and stuff, but to you it's just a dance, just money. For me, it's my *life*, you know?"

"Yeah."

"And I promise I'll pay you back every cent of the money for the bet. Only problem is it might take me a while, because even if my father doesn't cut my throat, he's sure to cut my allowance."

"Right."

I wanted this conversation to be over. I wanted to yank off my dress, kick it into a corner and curl up somewhere dark with a bucket of my one true, unfailing love — chocolate.

"I'm so excited. I've been living a lie, and I'm sick and tired of it. I'm finally ready to be me!"

"Good for you. Okay, so bye."

"Hey, Peyton? You're okay? I mean, you're not going to go all *Carrie* on me now, are you?"

"Huh?"

"Like throw pig's blood on me and then set the place on fire?"

Tempting, tempting.

"I'm fine, really. See you around."

I ended the call and burst into tears. I wouldn't be wearing this dress on Saturday. I wouldn't be going to the prom, or winning a bunch of money. I'd be working double shifts until kingdom come to earn the money to pay a triumphant Tori and Steve. The thought of their reaction made me cry even harder. I could just imagine what Steve would say when I declared defeat: "Let me get this straight — the guy you've been dating would rather take another *guy* to the prom rather than go with you? Way to go, Big P!"

I snatched a tissue from the box beside my bed and wiped my eyes furiously.

Screw Steve and Tori. And screw Rob and the love of his life, too. And screw Tim — especially him — and Mark, and his father, and God's particle over in Switzerland. Screw them all! They weren't worth my tears. I was not going to spend tonight crying over my disappointments. I was going to eat several bars of chocolate while binge-watching the last season of the Great British Sewing Bee.

"Found them!" my mother said when she returned. "These were your grandmother's. They're antique and made of marcasite." She clipped a pair of drop earrings onto my lobes, slid a large ring onto my pinkie finger, and stood back to admire the effect. "Perfect! Here, see for yourself."

I studied myself in the mirror, turning my head from side to side so that the earrings swung and glinted in the light.

"You're right, Mom." Had I ever said those words to her? "They would have been perfect. Only problem is, I'm not going to the prom anymore." I pulled off the earrings and ring and handed them back to her. "My date just dumped me."

"He did not!"

"He did."

I told her about Rob's decision. She considered this for a few moments then said, "You know, dear, I think you could still take the most stunningly attractive and wonderful date to the dance."

"No, I can't — he's taken."

Wren and Faye had each made a point of coming to tell me that Jay was taking Jessica Summers to the prom. I estimated her height at five-eight, so at least they weren't breaking the Law of Tall Girls.

"I wasn't talking about a boy, Peyton," my mother said, her voice very gentle.

"What the heck are you talking about then? A girl?"

"No, I'm talking about you. *Yourself.* Why would you miss out on your high school prom just because you don't have a date on your arm? You don't need a boy to complete you. Take yourself, and you'll be the person with the most magnificent date there."

"You mean, go alone? I could never." How embarrassing would that be? Might as well carve a giant L in my forehead as go alone to the prom.

"Yes, you could. You're enough, Peyton — on your own, you're enough."

This was amazing — my mother was actually giving me

motherly advice. I examined at her, taking in every detail, and noticed that she was looking different. Better. She wore jeans and a clean sweater rather than her usual uniform of stained sweatshirt and track pants. Her hair was clean and tied back in a neat ponytail, and her face seemed less pinched and more alive.

"Mom, are you okay?"

"Do you know, I think I'm more okay than I've been in the longest time."

"And you collected the mail from our mailbox? You left the house?"

"I've been checking the mailbox every day this week," she said, clearly proud of her achievement.

"Why?"

"I've been expecting an important letter, and today" — she pulled the envelope from her pocket and held it out to me — "it finally arrived."

I ignored the letter. "Mom, that's fantastic. Well done — I know it must have been difficult."

"It wasn't too bad, not compared to going out to the post office back in January. Now *that* was difficult."

"You went out to the post office? *You* did? Why?"

"I had an important package to post. Now if you read this, we'll both know what's going on."

She held out the letter again, and this time I took it. For a horrible moment, I thought the logo on the front was the Maryland state seal, but it wasn't. It was the logo of the New York Fashion School.

"Mom?"

"Open it! I can't take the suspense a moment longer."

I ripped open the envelope and pulled out the letter. My gaze danced over the impossible phrases.

"We are pleased to offer you a place in our first-year fashion design program ... unorthodox and irregular submission but very impressed with the design and underlying concept and market potential of your collection ... shows exceptional aptitude ... delighted to inform you that you are one of two recipients of a full scholarship covering tuition and housing ... continued subject to satisfactory academic and practical achievement ... look forward to meeting you and mentoring you in the journey of exploring and developing your remarkable talent ..."

I screamed.

"What? What does it say?"

I screamed again and gave my mother the letter, and then we were both yelling and crying and hugging each other and leaping about my room.

"How did this happen?" I asked her when we both finally stopped squealing and blubbering.

"I filled out the application form on your behalf, and then I sent it off with your drawings and those designs you made up in wallpaper, together with a covering letter explaining our dreadful financial situation and my mental health condition. I begged them to consider your application even though your designs hadn't been made in fabric. And they did!"

"You did that, for me?" When I thought of the cruel things I'd said to her in that fight, how I'd flung the designs at her, I felt ashamed.

"Of course. You're my daughter — I'd do anything for you, don't you know that?"

At that, reality kicked in. I slumped onto my bed and said, "This is awesome and I'm really grateful for what you did, Mom. And I'm so proud of you! Honestly, I don't know what makes me happier — this letter or the fact that you've left the house." And the fact that you've finally acknowledged that you have a mental condition.

"I sense a 'but' coming," she said, parking herself on the end of my bed.

"But how can I go off to New York and leave you here alone?"

"Peyton, that blow-up we had, the things you said —"

"I'm sorry, they were horrible."

"They were honest. Harsh, yes, but maybe that was what I needed for the truth to penetrate." She fiddled with the earrings, clasping them together and then separating them again. "It was humiliating to realize that I'd failed at the only thing that ever really mattered to me."

I watched her, puzzled.

"Being a mother," she said simply. "I thought being a good mother meant never letting go of your kids. But it means the opposite, doesn't it? Loving them enough to let them move on and be where they need to be. I'm going to be a good mother now, if it kills me!" She smiled as she heard her words. "And it won't, you know, it might just be the saving of me."

"But how will you cope?"

"I've made an appointment to see a psychologist who specializes in anxiety and hoarding disorders, and she'll help me through this. She even does house visits. And if she says I need medication, then I'll take it. I'll do whatever I need to so you don't have to forfeit your dreams. Over my dead body will you be stuck in limbo in this house, as I've been. And when you finish your degree, I plan on being there in New York for your graduation ceremony."

Then we were hugging and crying again. And for the first time in forever, I had a mother, and Mom had a daughter. It felt like something — perhaps the grief over Ethan, and the fear of being unloved or abandoned — was ending. And it felt like something else, something stronger and more vital, was beginning. Why should we, my mother and I, fear loss and loneliness? We'd had so much of it that if it was going to flatten us, it would've done so by now. But we were still here, still standing, still fighting. Perhaps even hoping.

Maybe that's what coming to terms with grief was. It wasn't that one day you suddenly got over it and felt better, back to the way you'd felt before. It was that you learned to live *around* it, that you struggled on living through it, that you grew yourself beyond it, until one day your life and your love were bigger than your pain and emptiness. You never got back to normal, but you could, if you were brave, get to somewhere good.

It was time for both of us to let go of the fear that kept us small. It was time to start living.

We held onto each other in silence for a while. When Mom finally got up to go, she left Gran's jewellery on my bedside table — "Just in case you change your mind about going to the prom" — and closed the door behind her.

And this time, I didn't lock it.

~ *52* ~

I hitched a ride to the prom with Chloe and Greg.

Chloe looked both sweet and sexy in a ruby-red sheath dress which flattered her milk-white skin and her curves. She'd been delighted to hear I was coming, and we exchanged extravagant compliments about each other's dresses and up-styles on the way to the dance, but I noticed that Greg was less than thrilled at my presence.

"Don't worry, I won't be third-wheeling you guys all night," I reassured him. "I'll be out of your way just as soon as we get there."

After that, Greg was all smiles, and even came around to the car door to open it for me when we arrived at the hotel where the prom was being held. I could have used a hand under my elbow for support as we walked from the parking lot to the entrance — I was still none too steady in my heels, especially on the uneven paving.

Loud music, heavy on the bass, was pumping out the doors, and couples were milling about at the entrance. Standing on top of a line of raised platforms along the path were colorfully dressed performers — fire-eaters, jugglers, clowns and acrobats.

"It's a circus theme!" Chloe said.

"You two go ahead. I'll catch up with you later," I told her.

"Don't be silly. Come in with us. *He* may be a hottie," she murmured, with a tilt of her head to Greg, "and it's probably going to be an awesome summer, but you're my bestie. You're forever."

I don't know what I did to deserve Chloe, but I'm keeping her.

"He's so proud to have you on his arm — let him have his happy moment. I'll catch up with you later, promise. Besides, I'm determined to march in there alone. I need to do this thing, for me."

"I'm so proud of *you*," she said, then disappeared inside with Greg.

I spent a few minutes in the cool evening air, watching a rail-thin man with a pronounced Adam's apple swallow a sword. A young woman dressed as a jester danced between the couples, entertaining them with magic tricks.

"Choose one," she said, holding a fan of cards out to me, facedown.

My fingers hovered over two which protruded just the slightest bit beyond the edge of the others, then I chose one and turned it over.

The queen of diamonds. I grinned — it seemed like a good omen.

"That's a great trick!" I said.

"I haven't done it yet."

"You have more magic than you know. Can I keep this?"

"I guess."

She bent over backward, literally, grabbed her ankles and rolled down the path like a human pretzel to a couple who were just climbing out of a stretch limo — Tim and Wren, flagrantly flouting the Law of Tall Girls.

I sighed. Queen or no queen, I reckoned I'd have to give up the idea of ever enforcing that rule. Probably a good thing, too, else we'd wind up with one race of giants and another of littlies.

I grinned at the two of them, but maybe Tim thought I was baring my teeth because he leapt back when he saw me, bumping into a clown who was juggling lit sparklers. They walked off, Wren batting away the fizzing firework that had landed on his lapel, Tim patting his pockets, no doubt in search of a nerve-settling slug of something alcoholic.

"Have fun, you two," I called after them.

It was time. I took a deep breath, stepped up to the entrance — which was draped with striped canvas like an old-time circus tent — and handed my ticket to the man wearing a black T-shirt that read, "I'm the muscle." His neck was thick and his muscles undoubtedly steroidally enhanced, but he was short, and I towered over him.

"You're really tall for a girl," he said.

"I never knew that. Thank you for bringing it to my attention," I said, sweet as strychnine.

"Do you play basketball?"

"No. Do you play miniature golf?"

"Why do you wear heels if you're so tall already?"

I snatched my ticket back and snapped, "To make people like you feel uncomfortable. Now I think you should look me straight in the belly button and apologize."

"Locked, chained and effing owned, man!" a familiar voice behind me said.

Laughing, I spun around to fist-bump Zack. He looked smarter than I'd ever seen him — clean-shaven, with his hair styled back and a single stud in one ear. He wore a neon-yellow bowtie and cumberbund, and hanging onto his arm — wearing matching accessories — was …

"Rob!" I could feel my mouth hanging open as I stared from one to the other of them.

"It was you!" I accused Zack. "All this time you were … you and he!" I pointed to Rob. They both laughed at my reaction. "Why in the name of all that's holy, if this is who you are, did you pester me nonstop? Why did you act like a sex-starved perv with all the *girls*?"

"I didn't want anyone to know until I was ready, man," said Zack. He had the grace to look a little shamefaced.

"I think the official term for it is 'overcompensation'," said Rob.

"But, but …" My brain was still struggling to catch up. "You said you got excited every time you watched Jay's and my make-out scene!"

"Well, I did, but not at you, Peyton. I mean, no offense, man, but Jay …"

"Yeah, but Jay."

Zack and I both sighed.

"Standing right here and listening! Can you guys quit drooling?" Rob said.

"Can you step aside, people," Muscles said. "You're blocking the entrance."

We shuffled to the side just as a round ball of frothy pink layers ran up to me.

"Hey, Peyton, Zack."

It took me a moment to recognize Liz. She was wearing the widest dress of layered satin and lace I'd ever seen outside of a *Gone With The Wind* screening and had balanced a tiara at a jaunty angle on her short red hair. She was unapologetically dazzling and was clearly already having the time of her life.

"You look magnificent!" I told her.

"You look pretty awesome, too, Stretch. So, Zack, this is you, huh? Gotta say you had me fooled. Rob, I hope you know what you're letting yourself in for. And here's Jay — this is like a cast reunion. Hey Romero, you clean up nicely!"

He did. I was so used to seeing Jay looking heart-stoppingly handsome in old jeans, T's, and his leather jacket, that I'd have bet good money against him being able to look even better in formal wear. Another bet I'd have lost.

He wore a simple black tux with a black bowtie. No piercings, no flower at his buttonhole, no color except for the deep green of his eyes. I may have staggered a little at the impact of his beauty.

"Hey, Liz, hi, Zack. Ah, so that's how it is?" He nodded at Zack. "I should've guessed — methinks he doth protest too much and all that. Hi, Peyton."

"Hi," I said, my voice too high.

"So, if Rob's with Zack, then who're you here with?"

"Me. I came alone."

"Wow."

The look Jay gave me was bright with ... could it possibly

be admiration? And he was giving me his slow and sexy smile. I grinned back at him for a long moment before I realized his date was saying something. It sounded like, "So that's how it is, then."

I forced myself to look away from Jay's green gaze. "Hey, Jessica."

"Yeah."

Jessica was rocking a goth look — black hair spiked high, heavy eye makeup and maroon lips. She wore pants. They were beautifully tailored trousers in shimmering satin, and she wore them with an almost transparent white lace shirt that spilled over in a froth of lace at the collar and cuffs. But still, she was most definitely not wearing a dress. She looked dramatic and distinctive, and her flat, two-toned brogues looked infinitely more comfortable than my dagger heels.

"That's a fantastic outfit!" I said, and I meant it.

"You like?" she asked, turning on the spot.

"I do."

I glanced around at the group of us, each of us wearing what we wanted, each of us different. We all looked freaking amazing.

"Time to go in, yeah?" Jay said.

~ 53 ~

We all marched through the door, passing under an arched sign of twisted neon letters that read *Circ du Longford* — seemed like I was going to be the tall lady at the circus after all. Or maybe I always had been. It seemed to me that in one way or another, we were all freaks and oddballs. Maybe high school was the circus, and the students were all just performers.

A photographer dressed in the striped pants and top hat of a ringmaster had set up his equipment inside the foyer and was busy taking pictures of Wren and Tim as our group streamed inside.

"Either you're going to have to sit down," he said to Tim, indicating a nearby chair, "or she's going to have to stand on a box, because I can't fit you both in the frame."

When they'd finished taking the shot (with Tim seated and Wren on his lap), the photographer called for the next couple.

"Don't go yet, Wren. Angela and Doug have just arrived — let's have a cast picture," Liz suggested.

We arranged ourselves in a tight group. Zack squeezed in

between Wren's silver lamé and Liz's pink layers of lace, looking like the mischievous tag-along of an elf and a fairy godmother. Doug stood beside Angela on Wren's other side, and Jay and I stood at the back. When the photographer complained about our heights, Jay bent slightly at the knees, and I took off my shoes, but Angela snapped at him to make it head and shoulders.

Just as the photographer told us to say, "High school blows cheese!" Brooke came inside, all pretty, blond perfection.

"Oh, look, it's the freak-show shot," she said snidely.

As though in a perfectly timed answer, Lady Gaga began thumping out from the dancehall.

"Baby, we were born this way!" Zack yelled at Brooke.

"Only some of you were smiling," the photographer complained.

"It's time to let our freak flag fly," Doug directed. "On my count — ready? And action!"

As one, we yelled and punched the air. Liz was holding her tiara, Zack his corsage, while I waved one of my cross-dresser shoes. We all sang along to the song, laughing, pulling faces, and posing in every weird way we could imagine, while Brooke frowned disapprovingly at us, tapping her small foot impatiently as she waited for her shot in front of the lens.

There was a moment in the flash-lit madness when a realization hit me with the force of a minor explosion. We freaks were the ones that belonged. Not the Brookes of this world with their average shapes and heights, clear skin, straight hair, and blandly attractive faces. *They* were in the minority.

The rest of us, the majority of us, all felt like misfits in some way. Each of us was unique, different in some way that made us strange or unacceptable to those who wanted us to conform to their definition of "normal."

Jay and his sister confused and disappointed their father, who thought sons should play sports and daughters should wear dresses. Zack was an aberration in a family who thought straight was the only way to date. My mother was different, and I was bizarre to anyone who thought "feminine" should come in small packages. Wren was too short, Liz too tubby, Mark was too serious, and Tim not serious enough. Doug was too arty for a boy, Chloe not interested enough in fashion for a girl, and Loretta defied anyone's classifications of masculine and feminine. My father was a fifty-something father-to-be, and Jim — well, Jim loved Elvis. Enough said.

None of us was normal. But "normal," as I'd learned in math, was just a statistical concept, an averaged smoothing out of all diverse and interesting permutations to some hypothetical midpoint so generalized it was unlikely to surprise or offend. Or to delight.

Normal was nice. Normal was bland. Normal was damned boring. Our differences, our own brand of crazy, were what made each of us special and unique and fascinating.

For the first time in my life, I knew I fit right in. Right here, right at this moment, with this crazy mixed bag of kids, I *belonged*.

The photographer interrupted my epiphany. "I'm not taking any more group shots," he insisted. "You need to pair up for the couples shots. Those are the ones your parents pay for, kids."

I stepped away from the group, smiling with a joy that came from a certainty located deep inside me. Because — finally — I got it. I didn't *want* to be five foot five of normal. I didn't want regular-sized feet. I didn't want to be predictable or typical or average. I wanted to be exceptional. Hell, I already was exceptional. It was time to own it.

When my turn came, I stood straight and tall in front of the camera, lifted my chin and announced, "I have no partner," before the photographer could even ask.

"Can you sit or take off your heels?" he asked.

"No. I want a full-length shot of me in this dress, same as everyone else gets."

"You're not *like* everyone else."

"Nobody is."

Clearly irritated, he moved his tripod and made adjustments to his camera. "You're making my life harder, kid," he grumbled. "I'm not happy."

"Oh really, which one *are* you then — Dopey, Sneezy, Grumpy, Bashful, Sleepy or Doc?" I asked, cracking up Jay and Jessica, who were waiting next in line.

After I'd had my photo taken, I sailed into the ballroom and began dancing. I didn't stop all night. I danced with Zack and Rob. I danced with Liz. I danced with jesters and jokers and even, briefly, with Tim, who moved his feet so quickly, I couldn't step on his toes. I danced with Chloe, then with Chloe and Rob, and then in a massive throng, all of us jumping in time to the music until the sprung floor was bouncing, and I was sure we'd crash right through it to the world waiting beneath and beyond.

Light-headed, gasping and hot, I snuck outside for a few minutes and took a moment to send a selfie and a text.

Hey Mom, Having so much fun :D Really glad I came. Wish you could see the awesome collective craziness! Love you.

The reply came instantly.

Love you, too. I'm so proud — of the both of us!

When I went back inside, a slower song was playing.

"Can I have this dance?" It was Jay, leaning against the doorway. Waiting for me?

"Won't Jessica mind?"

"I think she's planning on running away with the D.J."

I glanced over to the music table. Sure enough, Jessica and the D.J. were all over each other.

"For old times' sake?" Jay held out his arms in invitation, and I slipped right into them.

He pulled me close, moved his hands around my waist and rested their warmth against the bare skin of my back. I threaded my arms around his neck, rested my head against his shoulder and held on tight as we swayed to the music — a new version of an old song about fast cars, and feeling like you belonged, like you could be someone. You and me both, lady. I belonged in myself, and I belonged in Jay's arms, too.

I wondered if there was a chance for us to get together again, now that there were no secrets holding us apart. For new times' sake. For the sake of the new me, who finally felt confident enough to trust her whole self in a relationship with this amazing guy.

Chloe and Greg rotated past us. His eyes were closed in apparent bliss, but she noticed Jay's and my clinch and gave me an encouraging thumbs-up before moving on.

When Jay pulled back slightly to look down at me, I almost whimpered at the loss of contact.

"Guess what?" he asked.

You still like me? You've guessed that I still like you, and none of the rest matters?

"I give up," I said.

"I got into Julliard." He said it softly but proudly, his eyes gleaming more gold than green in the dim light.

"Of course you did," I said, seizing the excuse to hug him, to plant a congratulatory kiss on the cheek of my golden boy. "I should probably get your autograph now, before you're too famous to remember me. Though it's entirely possible that I'll win my first Oscar before you do."

He frowned down at me in bemusement.

"For costume design," I said.

"You got in? At the fashion school in New York?" He grinned widely, and I only just resisted touching the smile lines fanned out at the corners of his eyes.

"I got a full ride," I said.

"So, we'll both be in New York at the same time?"

"Yeah, but it's a big city," I warned.

"True. But I'm a big guy and you're a tall girl — we stand out in a crowd. I'll find you. And if we don't screw things up again, maybe we could be big and tall together."

"Mind if I interrupt?" Jessica said. I pulled back guiltily, but Jay held on to my hand.

"Look, is it okay if I ditch you?" she said to Jay. "My ex wants to get back together again." She jerked her head back toward the D.J.

"I can understand that," said Jay, his eyes on me.

"Somehow, I didn't think you two would mind," she said, with a knowing look. She waved a couple of fingers and left.

"I've been dumped at the prom," Jay said in a tone of mock-hurt.

"You should've come alone," I teased. "It's harder to get dumped by yourself."

"I should've come with you." He was serious now.

I swallowed, gazing back at him. The beautiful song had ended, and some awful uhnts-uhnts house music was playing. In the middle of the noise and movement, Jay and I stood as still as statues. What were we waiting for? Hadn't we wasted enough time already?

"Do you think … do we have to wait for New York?" I asked him. I had to yell it over the music. "Or could we start now?"

Breathless, kind of shocked by what I'd just said, I stared hard at Jay's lips. They mouthed one word, slowly, exaggeratedly.

"Now."

He pulled me tight up against his full, glorious height and — in front of everyone, with no bet and no secrets and no holding back, and on no one's cue but our own — we kissed.

At once, the wind was back. And it was the same, but it was also different. This time it came at least as much from inside me as it came from Jay. It was a hurricane of energy that raced through my heart and blew through my head, gusting away the cobwebs of my old hang-ups, my self-imposed limits, and childish fears.

It roared inside me, this new wind, like an unstoppable

force blowing a new life into me. Blowing *me* into a new life. I knew it would carry me all the way to New York and beyond, that it would drive me up against Jay and meld me with him, that it would propel us through the passion of our love, and the adventures of theater and fashion.

And I knew that it would carry me further still — to a place beyond heartbreak or loneliness, to a place unfettered by failure or triumph. I knew that it would blow me all the way into myself and spin me around in its vortex, until I fit comfortably snug inside my own skin. Home at last.

~ 54 ~

A bliss-filled hour later, Jay and I noticed that our friends were starting to leave.

"After-party at Jim's?" I asked him.

"Hey, it wouldn't be prom without Elvis," Jay said.

I found Chloe, and we fetched our bags from Greg's car then joined the line in the girls' restrooms to change into our after-party outfits. I slipped into my wide-skirted, fifties-style dress — another homemade creation which fit me perfectly — and kicked off the stilettoes with a deep sigh of relief. Never had I been so glad to put on my roomy, flat men's high-top sneakers. It had been fabulous to be glamorous, but when it came to shoes, I realized, nothing beat comfort.

On the way to Jim's, Jay kept looking over at me and smiling, and we both talked nonstop about everything that had happened since Christmas. Plus some things from before.

When we pulled up in the lot outside the diner, I said, "Before we go any further, are we agreed we'll do it differently this time? More talking, more honesty and understanding?"

"Yeah." He shook my hand, sealing the deal. "And no Tim, or Mark, or anyone else?"

I nodded. "And no Faye, or anyone else." We shook again.

"More movies — some of them from this century — and less ice-skating."

"Uh-huh. Less family drama, and more kisses." I blushed as I said it, but I still said it. New confident me.

"Absolutely. In fact, more making out all round." This time, when we shook hands, he didn't let mine go. He played with my fingers, sending tingles up my arms and sparking a warm pulse at the core of me.

"And definitely no secrets!" I insisted, my voice breathy.

"Oh dear," Jay said.

My heart dropped. What now? "You have a secret you haven't told me?"

"A terrible one I share with my mother."

Jay's face was one hundred percent serious. But that meant nothing. He could still be pulling my leg. Couldn't he? Please, please let it not be something awful, please let nothing ruin this moment, our new beginning.

"Do you both have a third nipple, or webbed toes?"

"Worse than that, according to my father. He hates it."

"Tell me now!" I demanded.

"Come on," he said, opening the car door. "I'll show you."

Inside, Jay headed straight for Jim. After a brief chat, a beaming Jim strutted over to the jukebox, while Jay grabbed my waist, kissed the worried crease between my eyes, and tugged me onto the section of floor where the tables and chairs had been cleared away to create a small dance floor.

The music started its distinctive guitar strums, Jay pulled me close, and we started dancing. As Elvis urged us everybody to rock the jailhouse, Jay whirled me around like a lightweight rag doll with my skirts spinning out at my sides. He swung me over his back and between his legs, twirled me in an arc around his torso, scooped me up in his arms, tossed me high and caught me low, while I gasped wide-eyed, and tried not to fall or get tangled in his legs.

"You can ballroom dance!" I accused when the music thrummed to a stop and everyone in the diner stood and applauded our performance.

Tori, who stood beside the stand of condiment bottles, clutching a ketchup-stained wiping cloth, stared sourly at Jay and me. She didn't applaud. She'd cheer up when she discovered I hadn't gone to the prom with Rob, but though she'd won eight hundred bucks, I felt like I'd won something more than the bet. Something priceless. I wished Steve could've been there to see us, too, but you can't have everything — not even when you're queen of the world.

Besides, having Jay was more than enough. He'd helped me tick off every item on my bucket list of experiences to make me feel adorably cute. Except one.

"Hey, Jay? I need you to do something for me."

"What's that?"

"Scoop me."

"*Scoop* you?" He made a gesture like spooning ice-cream.

"I want to be scooped!" I lifted my arms, dug them under an imaginary person and hoisted them up, to demonstrate what I meant.

"Your wish is my command."

As though I weighed no more than your average girl, he scooped me up in his arms, carried me easily over to the table where Chloe and Greg sat, cheering us on, and sat down, holding me on his lap.

"Was that good for you?" he asked, laughing.

I kissed the smiley crinkles at the corners of his eyes. "It was perfect!"

Bucket list complete, I could let go of the need to feel like anything other than who I really was. And who I was, was gloriously tall. End of story.

I was high on love and laughter, and feeling magnanimous to everyone. When I was crowned, I decided, I'd ditch the Law of Tall Girls. Let people date whoever they liked — the world would be a better place with more love and more variety.

It didn't matter who you dated, or how you looked. What mattered was how you felt.

And I felt on top of the world, like the queen of all of me.

~ *The end* ~

Dear Reader,

I hope you enjoyed Peyton and Jay's story!

If you loved this book, I'd really appreciate it if you'd leave a review, no matter how short, on your favorite online site. Every review is valuable in helping other readers discover the book.

Would you like to be notified of my new releases and special offers? My newsletter goes out once or twice a month and is a great way to get book recommendations, a behind-the-scenes peek at my writing and publishing processes, as well as advance notice of giveaways and free review copies. I won't clutter your inbox or spam you, and I will never share your email address with anyone. Pinkie promise! You can join my VIP Readers' group at my website: www.joannemacgregor.com.

I'd love to hear from you! Come say hi on Facebook or Twitter, or reach out to me via my website and I'll do my best to get back to you.

– Joanne Macgregor

Acknowledgements

My thanks to my editor, Chase Night, and to my fabulous beta-readers, Edyth Bulbring, Nicola Long and Emily Macgregor for their invaluable feedback. I deeply appreciate each one of you!

Other young adult books
by Joanne Macgregor

Hushed

What would you give up for love? When 18-year-old Romy Morgan saves Hollywood superstar Logan Rush from drowning, she's offered a job as his personal assistant. But the movie set is a world of illusion, where appearances don't match reality, and when she discovers a dreadful secret with the power to destroy Logan, Romy must choose between love and revenge. *Hushed* is a funny and heart-warming, modern romance inspired by the classic tale of *The Little Mermaid*.

Scarred

Life leaves you scarred. Love can make you beautiful … She's scarred, he's angry, and life keeps bringing them together. *Scarred* is an intense, beautiful romance with a twist of dark humor.

Recoil (The Recoil Trilogy, Book 1)

When a skilled gamer gets recruited as a sniper in the war against a terrorist-produced pandemic, she discovers there's more than one enemy and more than one war. The Game is real, and love is in the crosshairs.

The Recoil Trilogy is also available in a great-value boxed set.

Refuse (The Recoil Trilogy, Book 2)

Everyone wants Jinxy, except the one she loves. In a near-future USA decimated by an incurable plague and tightly controlled by a repressive government, teenagers with special skills are recruited and trained to fight in the war against terror. Now a rebellion is brewing.

Rebel (The Recoil Trilogy, Book 3)

Can you win a war without losing yourself? Sixteen-year-old online gamer Jinxy James has been trained as an expert sniper in the war against a terrorist-spread plague which has decimated the USA. Now she's a wanted fugitive, on the run with a rebel splinter group, risking everything to save and protect her loved ones.

Made in the USA
Middletown, DE
01 October 2020

20955699R00234